"How many other female friends do you kiss?"

〜

Brandon gave her a small laughing smile as if she should know the answer. Then he stole another kiss. "There's just you."

His straightforward reply loosened the knot in her stomach, but something else lingered in its stead. She realized at once that it was guilt.

Remember George? her conscience prodded.

"And when you call on me, you'll be assisting with my book," she added, almost as if she were trying to give herself permission, the way she did when she allowed herself to have a second slice of cake on Sundays. "Therefore, I'll simply explain the situation to *G*—or rather—to the person whose name I cannot say. I'm sure he'll understand."

Lord Hullworth chuckled. "Tell the truth, Ellie. Isn't this *George* just someone you made up in order to incite my interest?"

"Whyever would you think that?" Yet, as she asked the question, she realized her fingers were threaded in his hair while her body was molded against his. Somewhere, pressed between them, were the blurred lines of their burgeoning friendship.

The Wrong Marquess

The Mating Habits of Scoundrels

Vivienne Lorret

AVONBOOKS

An Imprint of HarperCollinsPublishers

THE WRONG MARQUESS. Copyright © 2021 by Vivienne Lorret. All rights reserved. Printed in the United States of America. No part of this book may be used or reproduced in any manner whatsoever without written permission except in the case of brief quotations embodied in critical articles and reviews. For information, address HarperCollins Publishers, 195 Broadway, New York, NY 10007.

First Avon Books mass market printing: July 2021

Print Edition ISBN: 978-0-06-297662-8
Digital Edition ISBN: 978-0-06-297663-5

Cover design by Amy Halperin
Cover illustration by Judy York
Cover image © jumabufu/iStock/Getty Images

Avon, Avon & logo, and Avon Books & logo are registered trademarks of HarperCollins Publishers in the United States of America and other countries.

HarperCollins is a registered trademark of HarperCollins Publishers in the United States of America and other countries.

FIRST EDITION

21 22 23 24 25   QGM   10 9 8 7 6 5 4 3 2 1

To Nicole and Stefanie,
thank you for making this possible.

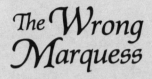

The Wrong Marquess

Prologue

England, 1810

Huddled beneath the barren branches of a hollow gray elm, Elodie Parrish stared down at the dirt staining her hand. She'd never been allowed to be dirty before. But, this time, her aunts had insisted.

"Go on, Elodie, dear," Aunt Maeve had said a short while ago, a single silver tear sliding down her careworn cheek and onto her black woolen shawl. "Take a handful and drop it in. No one will make a fuss, I promise."

Aunt Myrtle gave an encouraging nod, her black crepe dress rustling as she'd knelt down, and her eyes had looked like cornflowers floating in a puddle. "It'll make you feel better to help him along his new journey."

Even though she was nearly full-grown at seven years old, Elodie didn't understand why it was so important to give Papa back to the earth, or why she had to take part in it. She didn't want him buried underground at all. He couldn't breathe there. She wanted him back in his bed and propped on a mountain of pillows. Wanted him to pat the coverlet, calling her near to tell her stories in his quiet, raspy voice.

Their neighbors and a few of the villagers—the ones who'd followed the procession of the black horses with feathered hats that pulled the velvet-draped coffin inside the glass carriage—had all looked at Elodie with expectation. She'd known they were waiting for her to do this one terrible thing before they could all go into the house and eat the funeral feast the cook was preparing. Though how anyone could eat at a time like this, she would never understand.

But she'd done as she was told. She'd promised Papa that she'd mind her aunts while he was away.

Now, no matter how many times she wiped and scrubbed her palm against the itchy black dress the maid had buttoned her into, the filth remained. There were muddy tracks buried in the tiny creases and crevices of her flesh. They looked like rivers on one of Papa's maps. And the grit beneath her fingernails tasted like raw potatoes.

They'd put a ring on her finger, too. It was engraved on the underside with the words *beloved father, gone but not forgotten*. On the top it had a picture of clouds and Heaven's archway with a bubble of glass over the top. The circle, rimmed in gold, reminded her of the sovereigns they'd put over Papa's sleeping eyes. The aunts had told her it was to pay the ferryman so that he would have a peaceful crossing.

But if he needed so much help leaving, then why couldn't he have just stayed instead? And how could he breathe inside that box? After all, sometimes he went a long while without breathing. He'd always start back up again, after a few hunching coughs into his red-spotted handkerchief. How did they know that he wouldn't do the same this time?

The thought haunted her as she stared at the mound of glistening black dirt beside her father's grave.

A damp April breeze wafted up from the gaping hole, the smell bitter and brackish. It reminded her of the bloated worms that littered the garden path after a heavy rain, and of the black birds that would swoop down to gobble them up.

She hated that smell.

She tried to hold her breath. But it was no use. The scent of death was already inside her, deep in her lungs. Somehow, she knew it would always be there.

"What's all this carrying on about? You're acting like

someone's died or something," a boy said as he stole inside the open gate of her family's graveyard.

Seeing that it was the dreadful neighbor, she quickly swiped at her cheeks.

George was the bane of her existence. He was forever teasing her about wearing dresses and not being able to climb trees without showing everyone her drawers. Forever telling her that she was *just a girl*.

"Why aren't you inside with the others?" she asked, jerking a nod toward the sprawling brick house on the hill.

"Oh, they're all talking about old Boney again. And nothing interesting like preparing for battle or sending in the regiment. No," he said with the same exhausted roll of his eyes that he often gave to her. "They're only talking about his wedding—a *marriage alliance*, they call it—to that Austrian lady and the *rammer-fications* it'll have for England. And it's all so boring that I decided to walk home."

He bent down, a hank of straight brown hair falling over his brow as he snatched a rock from the ground. Tossing it in the air a few times, he caught it handily with a muffled slap into his fist. But he grew bored with this too and reared back to launch the stone in an arcing path over the wrought iron fence.

"What's a *rammer-fication*?" she asked, wondering if that was the reason he'd come to the graveyard instead of going back to his own house.

"Everyone knows what a *rammer-fication* is," he said with a mocking smirk. "It's what happens when you do something bad and your tutor makes you write out sentences. It means that marriages are bad, too. And so are the little girls who like to play pretend and hold weddings in the garden and dress up their dolls like brides."

She hated the way he snickered at her. Hiking up her chin, she set her hands on her hips and said, "Weddings are romantic, not bad. You don't know any better because you're just a boy. Just an orphan boy."

The instant his brown gaze flashed to hers, she wished she could take it back. She didn't know why she always taunted him in return. It only inspired him to say the meanest things. He liked to tell her that her eyes were the yellow of tree sap or dead leaves in mud puddles, and that her hair was the color of fresh horse dung.

She waited for him to say something horrible.

"Well, you're an orphan now, too," he said, but his words weren't spiteful. They were quiet and sad in a way that made her eyes sting and her throat tight. "That's your mum over there, isn't it?"

Her gaze followed his gesture to the headstone beside her father's yawning grave, where the name *Elodie Parrish* was chiseled into an arch of white marble. It was like having her own gravestone before ever having a chance to live.

Already, she didn't like being an orphan. She wanted to cry about it but, with her dreaded neighbor here, she couldn't.

Tears clogged her throat, gripping like nettles into her flesh as she swallowed, but she stubbornly held them back. Standing tall, she believed herself to be quite grown-up, indeed . . . until a stuttering breath shook her, making her sniffle wetly.

She darted a hateful glance to George, daring him to laugh at her. If he did, she'd push him into that hole.

But instead of teasing her, he surprised her by walking over and handing her his handkerchief. "Here. You should probably blow your nose or something."

"Thank you," she said with a polite sniff and turned away. Then she gave the damp, dirt-smudged square of starched linen back to him.

He crammed it into his pocket then stood beside her for a full minute before talking again. And there was something almost comforting about having him near. But she'd never tell *him* that.

"So, why are you still in the graveyard?" he asked. "Are you waiting for something to happen?"

She slid a wary glance his way, wondering how he could know such a thing. "What would make you say that?"

"Dunno," he said, his attention suddenly fixed on the moss underfoot. He scuffed the toe of his shoe against it, flipping it over to expose the wormlike tangle of milky roots beneath. "When my father died, I thought for sure he wasn't inside the coffin. I mean, what man goes off on a little hunt and never comes back? Besides, they wouldn't let me see him. And since he was always the kind to pop out from around corners for a scare and a laugh, I waited. Figured you were doing the same."

Again, he shrugged. But his shoulders seemed broader now, worldly even, fitting smartly into the seams of his coat. She blinked and stared at the bane of her existence as if seeing him for the first time.

"I am waiting," she admitted with whispered trust, "for Papa to cough. He often holds his breath forever but he always comes out of it."

To her surprise, George did not laugh at her. In fact, he appeared thoughtful as he stared toward the grave. "What's his record?"

"Well, a few days ago, it must have been a whole hour before he took a breath. I was holding mine the whole time, too, so I would know."

"Impressive." He nodded, stepping around her toward the elm tree. Finding a foothold above the hollow, he continued to talk as he climbed like a brown-haired ape in a suit. "I held mine for *two* hours once. But I'm supposed to be better at things like that. I'm a marquess now, after all. And your father was only a baron."

Considering the level of confidence in his declaration,

she believed him. The aunts often spoke with similar conviction when telling her that drinking every last drop of warm milk before bed would help her to sleep. It usually worked.

Except for early this morning when the terrible nightmare came.

She'd pictured her father waking, all alone and unable to breathe. There wasn't any air inside the dark silk-lined coffin. And no one could hear him shout or thunder his fists against the underside of the lid.

She'd jolted awake, screaming and clawing at the bed-curtains. And when the aunts rushed into her chamber in their dressing gowns with ruffled caps askew, she'd begged them to let her kiss her father one last time, just to be sure.

But it had been too late. The undertaker had already nailed the coffin shut.

Even now, a shiver stole through her as the ghost of her dream lingered, but she did her best not to show it.

A faint drizzle fell from the gloomy clouds overhead. Looking up, she shielded her eyes to find George straddling a large gray limb and scooting toward the narrow end.

"What are you doing?" she asked, perplexed by his need to climb a tree at such a time. Boys were such odd creatures.

"I'm looking down into the hole to see if the coffin is wobbling, of course. If it is, then I'd say he's trying to get out. You listen for his cough and I'll keep watch from here."

Elodie felt the slow upward curl of her lips, her misted cheeks lifting. Until this moment, she'd never realized how clever her neighbor was. "Be careful, George."

He flashed that teasing grin that she'd hated all her life . . . at least, up until now. "Worried about me, are you?"

"No."

But they were both smiling when she said it, as if they'd formed an alliance. And Elodie, feeling very mature now, wondered what *rammer-fications* it might have if they did.

The two of them held their vigil for some time. Hours and hours, at least. Or however long it was taking the grave diggers, who were waiting down the hill by their dray, to finish smoking their cheroots.

As time passed, the only sounds she heard were the creakings of the branch overhead and the hollow patter of icy rain against the cold earth and wood. But not a single cough.

Doubt started to creep in. She hugged her arms tightly around her middle, trying to shield herself against it, but it took hold nonetheless.

Her father wasn't coming back, was he.

"Being an orphan isn't so bad," George said from above as if her dismal thoughts had floated up to him. "You'll still have servants to bring your tea."

"And I have my aunts."

"But they're old. You can't count on them being around much longer."

She nodded glumly. It was true. Aunt Maeve was forty-six and Aunt Myrtle was forty-two. Practically mummified.

"And you're just a girl," he added as if that was the worst thing a person could be, "so you won't inherit your house like I did mine. You'll probably be sent away."

She looked vacantly to the brick house on the hill and thought of being taken away from everything and everyone she knew. To be all alone in the world, without anyone at all, would feel just like being trapped inside a coffin and buried underground, she was sure.

A flood of hot tears filled the lower rims of her eyes, turning the world blurry and bleak. Her breath stuttered. Then the sob she'd been holding back all this time finally broke free.

"Here now, have a care. I didn't mean to make you cry," he said, shimmying backward. "You won't be alo—*ohhh!*"

Without warning, the branch suddenly cracked. A terrible crunching followed. Then it snapped.

Everything happened so fast. One minute George was in the tree and the next he was falling in a tumble of splinters, arms and legs. He hit one branch after another, landing so hard against the ground that she felt the quake through the soles of her shoes.

Elodie rushed to him and collapsed to her knees. His body was stiff, eyes startled wide. Beneath her hand, his chest shuddered up and down, but he wasn't breathing. His mouth gaped open on a scream, but no sound came forth.

It was just like her nightmare.

Bending over him, she smoothed the hair from his forehead, his skin pale and pasty. She wasn't sure why she pressed her lips to his brow and cheek and then to his nose and chin, but she couldn't seem to stop.

She spoke in frantic whispers. "Please, George, please. Take a breath. I can't lose you, too. It wouldn't be fair when I don't hate you anymore. Talk to me. Say something. Tease me. Anything. Just please—"

All at once, he dragged in a hard, wheezing gust of air that sounded like chair legs screeching across the floor. Then his arms wrapped around her, clenching fistfuls of her awful dress as he pulled her close.

Squeezed tightly to him, she could feel his chest shudder. Hear the breath whoosh inside the column of his throat.

Elodie clung to him in return. A fresh wash of tears fell down her muddied cheeks. And, for reasons beyond her understanding, they both started to laugh.

Soon the somber cemetery was filled with hearty belly laughs and bright, pealing giggles that bounced off the headstones of her ancestors. But she didn't think they would mind under the circumstances. It wasn't often a person escaped the clutches of Death in such a place, she was sure.

Eventually, she sat up and looked down at him, smiling. "I saved your life."

"Thanks," he said with a crooked grin, reaching up to

brush the tears away from her cheeks with the cuff of his sleeve. "You're stuck with me now, I guess. I'll always be around to pester you. And if someone threatens to send you away . . . well . . . I'll just marry you and keep you with me. We'll have a marriage alliance between houses."

"What if I shouldn't want to marry you? You are terribly reckless, after all, climbing trees and such."

"Oh, you'll marry me, Ellie. Just wait and see." As if to ensure it, George rose up on his elbows and pressed his lips to hers.

The kiss was brief, wet and startling. She hardly knew what to make of it.

Before she could figure it out, he bolted through the open gate and ran toward home.

Dazedly, her fingertips came up to trace the tender skin of her lips. They were still damp. The realization made her heart squish warmly inside her chest. She suddenly knew that, with George, she'd never have to worry about being an orphan and all alone. He was her neighbor, so he'd always be there for her. And as she watched him disappear beyond the hill, she already began to wonder how long she'd have to wait to become his wife.

Chapter 1

Spring, 1828

> "Patience is a debutante's greatest asset . . . even if
> it should kill her."
>
> —A NOTE FOR *The Marriage Habits*
> *of the Native Aristocrat*

Elodie Parrish was still waiting for George to propose.

Meanwhile, betrothals were descending on the Baxtons' garden party like cannon fire.

The first hit a debutante in an explosion of giggles as her gentleman sank on bended knee by the roses. The second young woman was lost in a sudden onslaught of tearful happiness, her parasol toppling to the base of a bronze sundial as she fervently nodded to her genuflecting beau. A third was struck near the fountain, swooning into the arms of her beloved.

And Ellie interrupted every one of them.

She hadn't meant to, of course. She'd been searching for George, who'd promised to attend the tea with her and her aunts. But he was late, as usual.

Being a romantic at heart, however, she hadn't been able to deny the impulse to loiter long enough to hear the passionate declarations from the would-be grooms.

The first couple caught her sighing beside the arbor.

The second sent glares as she tsked in disappointment. But, really, he could have tried harder.

And the third, well, she couldn't resist clapping and saying, "Bravo! Best of the day! I almost wish *I* were marrying you."

Since his affianced had fainted into his arms, the comment was likely inappropriate. This assumption was quickly confirmed when the bride-to-be lifted her head and scowled over his shoulder.

Ellie felt the pink flush of embarrassment creep to her cheeks. "Not that I would, of course. I already have a gentleman of my own. Or, at least, I will have. And, I daresay, his speech will be just as pretty or even—"

The young woman sighed loudly, eyes flaring.

Ellie took the hint and disappeared between a pair of spiral topiaries. Besides, she had no time to dawdle, she needed to return to the house posthaste while these proposals were still fresh in her mind. They were wonderful bits of research for the book that she and her friends were writing on the marriage habits of the native aristocrat. And while Winnie and Jane had done their fair share of studying scoundrels, it was up to Ellie to write about marriage-minded gentlemen.

The only problem was, she wasn't an authority on the subject. At all. Otherwise, she'd be married already.

Nevertheless, she was determined to finish her portion of the book this Season, and the sooner the better. After all, both Winnie and Jane had found wedded bliss by the time they'd finished their research. And Ellie had every belief that it would be the same for her.

Encouraged by the thought, she hurried, practically skating in her slippers along the path toward the tall hedgerow that bordered the garden. As she reached the intersection marked by a pair of arrow-wielding cherub statues, she lifted her face, offering them a hopeful smile and a wish in passing. Then she turned and—*Oof!*

She came to a sudden, bone-jarring halt.

Of the countless ways Ellie had imagined she would die—fever, lingering illness, run down by a wayward stagecoach, unexpected avalanche of books at the Temple of the Muses, just to name a few—a full-body collision with a gentleman in the Baxtons' garden wasn't one of them. She wasn't at all prepared.

She felt her heart stop and her lungs shrivel. The force even knocked the soul completely from her body. It hovered above her, suspended and weightless, no longer attached to this earthly plane.

This was it, she thought, the untimely end of her unremarkable life.

It seemed rather unfair to arrive at Death's door so soon, and so dreadfully unmarried. But it was happening, nonetheless. There was nothing she could have done to stop it. So she bid a fleeting adieu to her loving aunts, her supportive friends, and especially to—

"*Bloody hell*," she heard muttered with vehemence. Hardly the chorus of angels one expected at a mournful time like this.

Then Ellie felt the grip of hands on her hips. The firm pressure of thighs and torso against her own. The sturdy cage of arms anchoring her. And the hot drift of breath against her cheek.

At once, her soul plunged back into her body. Her feet found terra firma. Her lungs drew in a new breath, filled with the appealing aromas of spring air, warm cedar, and starched linen. There was another scent as well, some unidentifiable and enthralling spice that compelled her to lean forward and take a deeper breath.

But then the gentleman released her. Too quickly, in fact. She wobbled on her feet. Reflexively, her hand latched onto the nearest solid object—*him*—or rather, his firm forearm, which she may or may not have squeezed to affirm her findings.

Jolted by the near-death experience and somewhat giddy, she blinked down at the brushed gray broadcloth beneath the grip of her ivory kid glove. Her gaze shifted to the cashmere waistcoat where she saw a loose thread that needed trimming. Distracted, she gave her head a shake to clear out the cobwebs and felt the staggered slip of her straw hat, listing toward the left side of her head.

"My apologies, sir. I did not see you there." With her unoccupied hand, she groped for her hat before it fell, all the while knowing that chivalry would demand that he take full blame for the practically fatal event, as any true gentleman would. "To be sure, I'm not usually so nearsighted, or . . . ungainly, or . . ."

She faltered. Why wasn't he interrupting her?

Ellie lifted her gaze to the starched cravat and stiff collar points, to the chiseled jawline and the shallow cleft in his chin, to the uncompromising mouth and aquiline nose, and finally to the shadowed ashy gray—*no*, mossy green—eyes beneath the broad brim of his hat.

A frisson of recognition darted all the way to her toes.

Even though they had never been formally introduced, there wasn't a woman in society who didn't know of *London's most elusive bachelor*, the Marquess of Hullworth. And from this close proximity, he was even more handsome than rumors credited him.

He wasn't as handsome as George, of course, her conscience prodded. No man was.

And yet, this man exuded a certain aura of self-assured masculinity that would be undeniably attractive to most women. Just not to her.

"My arm, if you please, ma'am," he said, accusation etched in his cool articulation. His jaw was already tight with patent exasperation as he flicked an impatient glance down to her hand. "That is, if you find yourself steady enough to stand on your own."

She barely lifted her hand before he took an immediate step back. He tugged sharply on the cuff of his sleeve, then on the hem of his trim waistcoat as if attempting to erase the encounter completely.

Ellie tried not to take offense. Though, to her, he was quite determined to give it. He acted as though she'd committed a crime upon his person. *Attempted wrinkling*— punishable by public flogging.

Nevertheless, she hadn't been looking where she was going, nearly killing them both in the process. Such an event could put anyone in a less than ideal temper. And, perhaps, the elusive bachelor simply hadn't had an opportunity to exhibit his renowned gallantry. Therefore, she decided that a little leniency was necessary for the moment.

Spying a familiar square of embroidered lace on the grass, she found the perfect means for the marquess to improve her opinion of him.

"Oh, dear. I seem to have dropped my handkerchief," she said with a polite smile, raising her *offending* hand to reset her hatpins.

He gave the fallen object no more than a cursory glance and said, "So you have."

Then, the rudest fellow on the face of the earth tipped his hat and stalked off.

Of all the unchivalrous nerve!

Bending down, Ellie swiped at her handkerchief, only to sully her fingertips in the process. *Splendid*, she thought crossly. Now she would need to restore her soiled glove before tea was served.

After sending a much-deserved glare to the retreating figure, she stalked off in the opposite direction. As far as she was concerned, she never wanted to see that ill-mannered, overbearing, odious man ever again.

By the time she reached the terrace doors of Lord and Lady Baxton's grand house, her aunts were nowhere to be found. Though if she had to guess, they were likely lingering somewhere near the kitchens and bribing a scullery maid.

No one amongst the *ton* knew it, but Aunt Maeve and Aunt Myrtle were thieves. Wherever they went, they stole recipes from everyone else's cooks. They'd done this for the past three years. And at home on Upper Wimpole Street, there were drawers upon drawers brimming with pages of their ill-gotten gains.

Ellie had asked them what purpose it served on several occasions. In response, she'd only received shrugs and blank looks of innocence, leaving her to presume that her eccentric aunts had become squirrels in their dotage.

Choosing to seek them out later, she found her way upstairs to the retiring room. As she drew near, the white-glazed door flew open and a dour-faced Lady Doyle barreled forth with a huff, heaving displeasure from her rather imposing bosom.

"Eugenia," the lady barked, "we shall not waste another instant inside repairing our hats while Lord Hullworth is *out*side and on the loose. Why, he is likely being pursued and charmed by our hostess and her simpering twit of a daughter as we speak!"

"Yes, Mother," a young woman of similar bearing said, marching closely behind. She rolled her eyes and issued a haughty toss of her coiffed blond ringlets.

"Mark my words, you *will* be a marchioness by Season's end," the lady said resolutely, both chins raised. She sniffed in Ellie's direction by way of greeting, then cast a disparaging glance over her shoulder. "Dash it all, where *is* that useless maid?"

"Coming, ma'am," a harried mop-capped girl said as she rushed behind, her arms overladen with a shawl, two straw bonnets and a plethora of ostrich plumes. In her haste, she lost half of her burden along the way.

Sympathetic to her plight, Ellie picked up the fallen

bonnet and handed it to her. "Here you are, dear. I quite like what you've done with this one. The ribbon is in a lovely Gordian braid that's difficult to master."

The maid's cheeks lifted, a mouthful of pins clamped between her grinning lips. Before she hurried off, she bobbed a curtsy and mumbled a happy, "*Fank you, ma'am.*"

In Ellie's opinion, no one deserved to suffer obnoxious fools during one's all too short existence. Unfortunately, insufferable people were everywhere. Case in point—Lord Hullworth in the garden. As far as she was concerned, he deserved a mother-in-law like Lady Doyle.

Stepping through the door, both she and her temper found the airy retiring chamber blessedly vacant. The pale azure-painted walls and the breeze drifting in through diaphanous ivory drapes provided her a moment's peace to put the garden collision far from her mind. Even so, she found herself muttering "hateful man" under her breath as she proceeded toward the washstand in the corner.

Fortunately for Ellie, the Baxtons spared no expense on their soap. They had an oval bar of Pear's in a ridged porcelain dish, which proved more effective than a more caustic paste in a jar would have done.

Satisfied with her scrubbing, she stripped off her dampened gloves and laid them near the windowsill to dry. But then she cast a disparaging glance at her bare hands and sighed in dismay.

Oh, they were fine enough as far as hands went, both pale and smooth with manicured fingernails. And yet, there was a glaring flaw on the left one.

It was still ringless.

This circumstance might have been a mere trifling matter if she were, in fact, the twenty-three-year-old debutante the *ton* believed her to be. Only the aunts knew her secret—that she was approaching spinsterhood at the alarming rate of a velocipede careening down a steep hill.

As of today, she'd passed a quarter century without a gold band on her wedding finger. Nine thousand one hundred and six unmarried days, to be exact.

Twenty-five pathetic years.

An impatient breath left her as she reached up to take the pins from her bonnet and set it aside. As far as she was concerned, her research couldn't be finished soon enough. She needed all the insight she could garner to finally get George to propose.

One glance at the disheveled slattern in the looking glass and she gave Lord Hullworth more of her ire. *High-handed popinjay.* She huffed. Here she was, repairing her coiffure when George might very well have been in the garden waiting for her. Turning her head, she stabbed her tortoiseshell comb into the twisted configuration of her ebony curls. But when she caught sight of a faint shimmer of something silver, she went stock-still.

Was that a . . . a . . . *gray* hair?

She gasped in utter mortification. It was official—she was ancient. A foot in the grave. A single stitch away from a burial shroud.

George would never marry her if he saw *this*. The Marquess of Nethersole would require an heir from his bride. One look at the gray-haired hag she'd suddenly become and all he would think she could offer would be a knitted shawl.

Ellie had to do something, and quickly.

She wanted to yank out the offender but her aunts were forever saying that, whenever they plucked one gray hair, four more sprouted up in its place. One was bad enough, but four? She might as well start walking with a cane and flirting with octogenarians.

Her gaze darted around for a way to conceal her shame. A pot of ink, perhaps? Just a little brush of black in the right place would allow her to return to the party as if nothing were amiss. As if she weren't as old as Methuselah. A veritable crypt-keeper.

But there was no writing desk in this room and no ink. Drat!

Distractedly, she reached for her bonnet only to realize it had slipped from the arm of the chaise longue and fallen against the wall. Crouching down to retrieve it, she heard the chamber door open, then close, on the far side of the room.

"If I hear the happy news of one more betrothal, I'm going to scream," a feminine voice muttered, her statement punctuated by an exasperated growl and the stomp of a soft-soled slipper.

Even in her agitated state, Ellie smiled to herself. Apparently, she wasn't the only one a bit tired of everyone *else* getting married.

She delicately cleared her throat to make her presence known, then stood and arranged the broad-brimmed straw to keep the unsightly, hoary coil hidden from view. It was safer that way. For all she knew, it held Medusa-like properties and gazing upon it could turn one's person—and one's marital hopes—to stone.

"Oh! I beg your pardon," the young woman said, her uncommonly clear blue eyes widening behind a frame of black lashes. "I didn't realize anyone else was in here. The maid told me she would return to mend my dress as soon as she finished her task with Lady Doyle."

Ellie flitted her fingers in a gesture of little consequence and set her hatpins. "Think nothing of it."

The young woman nodded. She tugged smartly on the ribbon of her bonnet, lifting it to reveal spills of inky hair a shade darker than Ellie's. It was so black it had the bluish tinge of a raven's wing. She was lovely, too, her skin unblemished by either sunlight or age. She couldn't have been more than twenty years old, at most.

Ellie sighed inwardly, remembering those youthful days long past. Before the gray hair.

The young woman turned to set her hat and gloves on a satinwood demilune table. The motion revealed a large rip in her cerulean-dyed muslin. A commiserating gasp left Ellie.

The young woman nodded, twisting to look over her shoulder. "Dreadful, isn't it? I fear it's ruined and I'll have to endure my brother's questions and disappointed glowers for days to come when I tell him how it happened."

"Well, I know little of brothers, but enough about needle-work to know that the maid will likely not be able to mend this properly. At least, not without calling attention to the stitches in such a delicately woven muslin," Ellie said with the experience gained from a lifetime of sewing alongside her aunts. "Of course, she could attempt to darn it if she has this particular shade of blue in her sewing box. Here, allow me to check."

Crossing to the tufted stool in the corner, she retrieved the basket beneath it. Upon opening the hinged lid, however, she saw the contents were as she suspected.

Peering inside, the young woman shook her head. "This is my punishment, I suppose, for setting the wolves on Brandon. I just wanted to elude his overprotective gaze for a moment. How was I to know that my escape would nearly have me interrupting not one but *two* proposals? Which, consequently, is how I ended up in a battle of thorns beneath the rose arbor. I was trying to sneak away without disturbing the turtledoves."

They must have been within a few paces of each other, Ellie thought with amusement. "Then it is fortunate you were not near the third by the fountain, or else you might have come in here decidedly wet from head to toe."

"*Three* betrothals at one party?"

"There appears to be an epidemic," she said with a grave nod. "However, on the bright side, I believe I can assist you,

I've been told that I'm rather nimble with needle and thread, especially during times of dire circumstances."

"Then you are an angel!"

"Well, before you say that, I should tell you"—Ellie hemmed, eyeing a length of red ribbon from the box—"in order to mend such a sizeable tear, we will need to be rather unconventional."

"I despise convention." The young woman flashed a grin. Then she held out her hand. "I know this isn't done but I feel as though we should introduce ourselves. I'm Margaret Stredwick, but please call me Meg."

"Very well, Meg. I am Elodie Parrish, *Ellie* to you."

They shook once, firmly as if embarking on a business venture. And the fix would require a bit of daring on both their parts. Nevertheless, she had the utmost confidence that it was the right decision.

"I don't suppose"—Meg hesitated abashedly—"there's any point in pretending that I didn't say such a horrible thing when I first entered the room. By the by, you're not one of the contented brides-to-be, are you? I should hate to have insulted you."

A breeze blew in through the open window, lifting hair from Ellie's nape. In that instant, she was reminded of her speeding course toward spinsterhood.

"Fear not, I am one of the *un*-betrothed." *As ever,* she added silently as she made herself comfortable on the stool to begin the repair. After threading the needle, she began with a quick slip stitch to hold everything in place and spoke conversationally. "Truth be told, the man I've set my cap for is not even here today."

"Ah," Meg said thoughtfully. "Then you cannot be one of the hopefuls vying for Lord Hullworth's hand."

A huff of indignation escaped her. "No, indeed. I do not find him agreeable in the least. Though I've not met him formally, he seems a rather cross, unmannerly and vain fellow. At parties he is ever surrounded by his adoring followers. A veritable King Goose among his gaggle."

Meg laughed brightly. "Surely, you mean *Marquess* Goose instead. My brother is not a king, no matter what he thinks of himself."

"Your broth—" Ellie pricked the tip of her finger. She instantly put it to her lips as a rush of heat rose to her cheeks. "I've stepped in it, haven't I? Please know, I meant no offense."

"No offense directed at me, you mean. Oh, don't be embarrassed. It's rather delightful to meet someone who hasn't set her cap for him." Her laughter ended on a sigh. "Almost every debutante to befriend me has had an ulterior motive to get closer to Brandon, including the two newly betrothed young women I nearly interrupted today. I suppose I was a ninny to have believed otherwise."

Ellie felt an instant pang of sadness and irritation on behalf of this young woman. She couldn't imagine entering a London Season without having any friends to rely upon. As for herself, she'd been fortunate in that regard, having met Jane, Winnie and Prue at finishing school eons ago.

"Nonsense," she said to Meg. "Everyone deserves a friendship founded on trust. And I would be honored to be yours, if you would have me after I've made such a cake of myself."

"Unfettered honesty—especially at my brother's expense—is at the very top of my list of requirements."

"Well . . . you may wish to delay your decision until after you've seen what I've done to your dress."

Meg peered over her shoulder. "Just how unconventional is the repair?"

"Terribly," Ellie said with mock severity. "How do you feel about dragons?"

Meg giggled. "I can honestly say that this is the most fun I've had all Season."

"Surely not. I imagine you've had scads of gentlemen callers."

Her slender shoulders lifted in a graceful shrug. "I suppose. Dancing with them is quite thrilling, but they are all fusty conversationalists. My brother seems determined to introduce me only to the dullest, most insipid men, the majority of whom speak to me with marked condescension as if I have no brain of my own." She sighed. "Just once I want a man to look at me with unquenchable desire. Surely, that isn't too much to ask, is it?"

"No, indeed. Every woman deserves a man who gazes upon her with such passion that she can feel the heat of it from across the room." Ellie spoke the words with such conviction, one might imagine she were an authority on the subject. But the truth was she hadn't even been kissed since her twentieth birthday. Five years ago—and one fewer gray hair—to the day.

"Precisely," Meg agreed. "The only problem is, Brandon believes that no man who would look at me in that manner could have honorable intentions."

"*No man?* That is quite untrusting of his own sex."

"Indeed. He is a veritable sentry. If a gentleman so much as smiles in my direction, he is there to act as a blockade. Is it any wonder I try so hard to elude him at parties?"

Ellie turned thoughtful as she finished the last stitches. Perhaps the Lord Hullworth she'd encountered in the garden had been the overprotective elder brother, distracted by concern for his sister, and not the gallant gentleman the *ton* professed him to be?

Even so, he was still rude. And now she understood him to be a curmudgeon, too, stealing the enjoyment of the Season from her new friend.

"I wish you did not have to endure such restrictions," Ellie added with sympathy. "It is a great pity that my friends and I have not yet completed the book we're writing. *The*

Marriage Habits of the Native Aristocrat will be a guide to aid debutantes in determining the differences between gentlemen and scoundrels."

The inspiration had come to Ellie, Jane and Winnie when their dear friend, Prudence Thorogood, had been exiled from London after being caught in a compromising situation in the gardens at Sutherfield Terrace. She'd been away for a year now and Ellie missed her terribly.

"That is the cleverest idea I've ever heard. It would not only educate young women but their stuffy chaperones as well." Meg smiled broadly. "All I ask is that you finish this book without delay so that I can shove it beneath Brandon's nose."

Ellie laughed as she reached into the box for a small white button. "I should like nothing more. However, I must confess that my research into the actions of the marriage-minded man has been rather . . . limited. After all, if I understood their mindset, I'd likely be married already."

"As selfish as it may sound, I am glad you are still unwed because you are here with me. I've so enjoyed our meeting."

"As have I." It was a rarity, indeed, when making an acquaintance felt more like meeting a long-lost friend. That hadn't happened since she'd met Jane, Winnie and Prue. And with the absence of so many dear friends, Ellie did not take the kindred feeling for granted. "Well, just one more stitch now . . . and there. Finished."

Closing the lid, Ellie stood and dusted her hands together.

Meg dashed toward the standing mirror in the corner and twisted to look over her shoulder. Then she gasped. Her gloved hand flew to her mouth, her clear blue eyes glistening with unshed tears.

Ellie's heart was in her throat. She'd clearly made a serious error. "Oh, Meg, please forgive me. I've overstepped and I—"

"It's *perfect!*" Meg exclaimed, clapping happily as she

twirled in front of the mirror. "A bright red kite on a sky-blue dress, and it even has a tail of lace and a little button."

Ellie's shoulders sagged in relief and she swallowed down her worry. "I'm so glad you like it."

"I love it! And, for once, I don't think anyone will be paying attention to my brother." With a little hop, she enfolded Ellie in a brief, exuberant embrace. "I don't know how to thank you. Oh, and you must let me introduce you to Brandon. I know I've said some terrible things about him, but he is actually a wonderful brother. And I know he has my best interests at heart—just don't tell him I said that."

"If you like," Ellie said, wary at the thought of meeting Lord Hullworth. Again. "However, there is no need to introduce us. Truly. In fact, I should be perfectly content without any further discourse between us whatsoever."

But Meg paid no attention to the small protest. Her enthusiasm could not be contained and she tugged Ellie out of the retiring room without delay.

And, for a short time, the dreaded gray hair was completely forgotten . . . at least until she met Lord Hullworth.

London's most elusive bachelor, though he may be, he was also arrogant, suspicious and determined to make her feel every day of her twenty-five years.

Chapter 2

"A true gentleman will never make note of a flaw
on a lady's person. If he should commit such a
heinous crime, then the unmannerly beast is better
off forgotten."

—A NOTE FOR *The Marriage Habits
of the Native Aristocrat*

Brandon didn't know who had first saddled him with the
moniker of *London's most elusive bachelor,* but he'd like to
strangle that person.

For two years, he hadn't had a moment's peace. What he
did have, however, was a list of all the cunning tricks that
women liked to use to bait would-be grooms to the altar.

Some preferred simple methods: come-hither smiles,
batting eyelashes, and tittering laughs at his most banal ut-
terances. Others were more direct by dropping articles of
clothing at his feet: handkerchiefs, gloves, shawls, and even
garter ribbons. Some boldly touched him, proclaiming innocence. *Dear me! I beg your pardon. Is this your shoulder/
arm/hand/thigh?*

There were those who feigned injuries. He couldn't count
the number of times he'd driven Meg through the park only
to have a woman hail him from the path, claiming an injured limb and begging him to drive her home.

And there were even those who popped out of nowhere
to ensure a collision. This was usually followed by a witness

to the event who would hint at having seen a clandestine embrace, attempting entrapment.

Thankfully, keeping his own reputation above reproach had saved him from the nuptial noose five times over by such ploys. Or rather, five and a half if he counted his clash with *Miss I did not see you there* a few moments ago.

She'd nearly bowled him over.

He'd caught her reflexively, fully intending to release her at once. But the impact had forced the air from his lungs. So he'd drawn in a necessary breath, never suspecting that the sudden immersion into a fragrant cloud—fresh and sweet like clover bathed in midnight dew—would leave him rattled.

That was the only way to explain why he'd held her for too long. Why his gaze had drifted, transfixed, to the suffusion of pink watercolor rising to the flawless porcelain canvas of her cheeks. And why a strange sort of restless impatience filled him as he'd waited for her to meet his gaze.

It had seemed to take forever. He should have been looking for her presumed cohort hiding behind the hedgerow or a topiary. Instead, his sole focus had been on those lashes. The fringe was so dark and sooty that he imagined one brush with the pad of his thumb would leave a permanent stain. Then they lifted to reveal a pair of almond-shaped eyes, the amber color pure and clear like cognac in the firelight. And heat pooled in his gut as if he'd drunk a whole snifter of that libation in one swallow.

Clearly, the collision had addled his wits.

He'd nearly forgotten that it was all just another ruse. A snare. Another woman who thought that marriage was merely a game. But then he saw the alert blink of recognition in her eyes, her lips tilting in a practiced smile as she'd offered an all too familiar excuse.

My apologies, sir. I did not see you there . . .

A swift flood of irritation had brought him back to his

senses. She was just like all the other husband hunters, cunning and manipulative. Never to be trusted.

At four-and-thirty, he was certainly no longer the callow youth he'd once been. No longer the man who'd so easily fallen for deceptions and machinations. So it cost him nothing to dismiss the deceiver. Before she could spring her clever trap, he'd turned on his heel and resumed his search for Meg.

His young sister was the only reason he endured the Season at all. To his way of thinking, in order for her to gain the proper understanding of the type of man she wanted to marry, then she had to be introduced to a number of them. And if attending balls and parties kept her from suffering any regret over her choice of spouse, then he would bear the agony of a thousand London Seasons.

Though, clearly, the affection between siblings was one-sided. Meg had been only too happy to leave him in the company of wolves a short while ago, skirting merrily away when a legion of rapacious mamas and their coquettish daughters had cornered him—quite literally against a column—on the terrace. A cacophony of invitations followed, along with list upon list of feminine accomplishments.

If it hadn't been for an exhausted bumblebee landing upon Lady Doyle's bonnet and the subsequent limb-flailing hysteria that followed, he might never have escaped. Though, little good it had done him to break free, only to head into the garden with *Miss I did not see you there* lying in wait.

The encounter still rankled him. Why hadn't he shrugged this one off like all the others?

Perhaps, the simple explanation was that he was tired of it all. Exhausted from exhibiting every ounce of gentlemanly decorum to women who merely saw him as *London's most elusive bachelor.* Yes, that must be the reason, he decided.

Thankfully, this afternoon would be over soon.

A short while ago, he'd caught a glimpse of his sister hurrying through the terrace doors. Since gentlemen were disobliged to enter the corridor designated for the female guests, he waited in a gold chintz antechamber off the main hall, concealed from direct view while keeping a close eye on the staircase.

Outside, tea was being served on the lawn. Dozens of linen-draped tables waited beneath striped canopies as the melodies of a string quartet drifted in through the open French doors on the late spring breeze.

Inside, his attention briefly veered to a pair of older women emerging from belowstairs. They passed by his alcove but were too absorbed in conversing over scraps of paper to notice him. Once they reached the doors, they exchanged quick, furtive glances around before stuffing those folded missives down their bodices and then snickering to each other like a pair of criminals.

Peculiar, he thought as he watched them steal out toward the lawn.

Hearing Meg's laugh, however, he quickly forgot them and turned his gaze toward the staircase. She was talking animatedly to someone not in his field of vision, her gloved hands moving in excited gestures, as was her habit. The instant she saw him, her eyes brightened with mischief. She gave a jaunty salute as if declaring herself the victor in her game of *escape-the-chaperone*.

"There you are, Brandon. I'd wondered where you'd gone," Meg teased with a cheerful grin.

No matter how hard he tried, he couldn't be cross with her. So, he smiled with wry fondness in response. But his amusement abruptly faded the instant he saw her companion.

It was *her*, the amber-eyed viper from the garden. Apparently, the cunning debutante had moved on to other tactics.

Of all the ploys for his attention, the worst was any attempt to befriend his sister under false pretenses. Meg's heart had been broken by too many would-be acquaintances. It made his blood boil to think of her suffering over someone's scheme again.

Though it took effort, he subdued the anger rising beneath a polite mask. "Thought I'd take a turn about the garden. You know how much I enjoy these parties."

"Sarcasm hardly makes for a good introduction to my new friend." Meg tutted in mock reproof.

He flicked a glance to the supposed friend and said, tightly, "We've met."

"But not formally. At least, that's what Ellie says."

"Oh?" His gaze shifted to those cognac eyes, heat roiling in his gut. "And what else does *Ellie* say?"

Meg sidled up to him, grinning. "As to that, I refuse to betray her confidence. However, there is a chance that you did not leave her with a very good impression of you."

Her companion's eyes went round as saucers and her cheeks paled. "Meg, I—"

"Oh, don't worry. Brandon is relieved by this. Are you not, brother? You see, he's positively hounded wherever we go. At least, with you, he can have a respite. And that is why I am determined we shall all be the best of friends," she said, reaching out to take the other woman's hand to tug her closer. "Brandon, I should very much like to introduce you to Miss Elodie Parrish. And Ellie, this is my often-smothering but usually quite amenable but *ancient* brother, Brandon Stredwick, the Marquess of Hullworth."

The interloper dipped into a curtsy, her cheeks abruptly saturating with the color of guilt and deception. "My lord."

"Miss Parrish." He bowed stiffly, then proffered his arm to Meg. "We shouldn't wish to keep you any longer."

"Brother, that is rather abrupt. I thought we might tour the garden in companionable conversation."

"Tea has already been served. Our table awaits. If Miss Parrish likes, we could escort her to her own. I'm sure there are those among her party looking for her. A chaperone, perhaps, or even"—he paused to scrutinize her critically—"a charge. Are you governess of one of the young debutantes in attendance?"

She stiffened on a blink, then speared him with a look of such contempt that he knew, at once, he'd insulted her. It was ingrained in him to make amends. After all, his father had been an impeccable example of how a gentleman ought to behave. And yet, Brandon did not apologize. Acting the gentleman would not dissuade a schemer's plot. He knew from experience that it only encouraged them. And he refused to see his sister hurt again.

He would willingly endure dropped handkerchiefs, feigned injuries and even accidental collisions. But not this.

Knowing it was better to end this farce now, he held his tongue and met her flinty gaze with his own.

"You are not yourself, Brandon. I fear the sun has singed your manners," Meg said curtly, then dropped her arm from his. "Ellie, I must apologize. He does not know what an angel you've been to me."

The schemer shook her head and prettily offered, "No, Meg. I am the one who should apologize. I kept you too long upstairs when your brother was obviously worried about your welfare. Think nothing of this introduction. I'm sure *I* will not." She cast one final disdainful glance his way before smiling at his sister. "But I look forward to seeing *you* again this evening at the Easterbrookes' ball."

With that, she left. And with each step she took, he exhaled a taut breath that seemed to burn the lining of his lungs.

Once they were alone, Meg swatted his arm. "I cannot believe you! I meet one person who enjoys my company—without any designs on you whatsoever—and you do your best to insult her. I've never been more embarrassed. And that is saying a great deal considering the fact that you are out to steal all the joy from my Season. I thought that was the point of it. After all, you and the high and mighty Mr. Prescott both declared that I wasn't ready for marriage until I experienced more of life."

"And you clearly are not ready. Marriage requires you to have your eyes fully open."

"That's peculiar. Our father always said it was the heart, not the eyes, that needed to be unhindered by obstructions."

"Then allow me to weed out those who are unworthy of you," he said patiently.

"Father wanted *both* of us to marry for love."

"For me to marry, it would take an act of divine intervention."

Years ago, Brandon had given up any hope of finding a wife. He easily recalled the day when he'd been standing at the base of a set of stairs similar to these, pleading with Miss Phoebe Bright after she'd just said the words that had ripped out his heart.

"I cannot marry you. The Duke of Horsham has offered for me and I have accepted. My father is drawing up the contract."

"But we've pledged ourselves. We love each other."

"You're appallingly naive, darling," Phoebe had said with a pat of her gloved hand to his cheek. *"That is how the game is played. For a time, you had a pretty girl on your arm, which made you look all the more desirable, while I had a handsome young buck thoroughly besotted with me, which made the older, fat-pocketed nobility who sat at your uncle's table take notice. Now I am going to be a duchess, and a rich one at that."*

"Money and status will not make you happy. But I would, every day of your life," he promised, taking her hand to press it against his chest. *"You have my entire heart."*

With a tittering laugh that had once been music to his ears, she slipped free. *"If you truly care for me, then you would never wish for me to have a poor, simple life with merely the nephew of a noble when I could have so much more.*"

Brandon shrugged out of his thoughts as if it were a hair shirt on his back.

His experience with Phoebe had taught him a great deal, as had his encounters with women *after* he'd inherited an unexpected title and immense wealth, which had come at great personal cost to him.

He cast a hard glare to the door where Miss Parrish had gone. Oh, he knew her game. In the past decade, he'd seen every ploy under the sun. But he would be damned before he'd ever allow his sister to feel that her worth could be summed up in an accounting ledger.

"Then I hope *divine intervention* knocks you over the head one day." Meg huffed and resignedly took his proffered arm. "You're wrong about Ellie, you know."

In order to end the disagreement, he offered no response. After all, he knew that, sooner or later, Miss Parrish would reveal her true self.

AFTER THE tea concluded, Brandon watched as an army of admirers gathered around Meg, and all because of a kite on her dress.

According to his sister, Miss Parrish had saved her *and* her gown from societal scorn with the whimsical applique but wanted no credit for it. Instead, they'd agreed to spin a story about Meg employing a personal, highly praised modiste. Now, dozens of women were clamoring for the name of this dressmaker goddess.

To be honest, he hadn't even noticed the difference. Female fashions had never been a priority. Whenever his sister came into his study to twirl about in a new frock, he would always tell her that she looked pretty. But if she went on and on about ruffles and flounces and the quality of lace, he felt as though his lifeblood were slowly draining out of him, drop by agonizing drop.

All he cared about was knowing what color it was so that he could spot her from a distance. Today, she wore a blue dress . . . and Miss Parrish wore clover green.

He saw her near the fountain. She was smiling toward Meg's admirers with all the *appearance* of altruistic gladness for her new friend. But Brandon remained suspicious of her motives. And since all the attention was on his sister, he took the rare opportunity given him and slipped away for a little interrogation.

Miss Parrish frowned at his approach, her gaze wary. Part of him felt a trifle guilty for being so direct with her earlier. Normally he was more diplomatic, even with those who'd pretended an affection for his sister. He didn't know why he'd been unforgiving with this one.

Stopping in front of her, he inclined his head in greeting and came straight to the point. "My sister believes I owe you an apology, Miss Parrish."

"But clearly, you do not share that belief, otherwise you would have simply offered one," she said with her chin held high.

Brandon opened his mouth to object, but she lifted her hand and continued.

"Fear not, I should never ask it of you. All you owe me is your absence. Or better yet . . ." She pivoted on her heel and walked away. Again.

He frowned, disliking the fragmented pattern of these encounters. The abrupt endings left him without a sense of satisfaction or conclusion. And besides, he still had questions for her.

So he followed and fell into step beside her. "I do appreciate what you did for her, with the kite and all. It seems that Meg is determined to keep you. However, I am equally determined to prevent her from being hurt."

"Your affection for her is your sole redeeming quality."

"Not so. I'm quite charming when I choose to be."

She huffed and rolled her eyes, her pace quickening along the mossy avenue between hedgerows. "And quite insulting by choice, as well."

"Come now. There is no cause to be so cross simply because you've been caught at your game," he said, easily matching her stride. So when she hastened, so did he. And when she slowed, he did the same. It was as though they were in a race, each determined to best the other in whatever sport this was. And when she growled and glared askance at him, he didn't know why, but a grin tugged at his lips. "Tell me, Miss Parrish. Why is it that we have never met before? Surely, this is not your first Season."

At this, she stopped abruptly. Facing him, her features were set in porcelain, amber eyes afire. "Is that another remark on my age?"

It wasn't, but he didn't tell her that he was genuinely curious about why their paths had never crossed. Instead, he blinked with owl-eyed innocence, pretending to misunderstand.

"Earlier, you called me a governess," she supplied, tugging on the cuff of her buttoned glove as if it were a wayward pupil she had by the ear. "You were either implying that I am shabbily dressed or too old to be considered a debutante in my own right."

"Your dress is quite pretty," he said by rote and earned another heated glare that sent a flick of pleasure through him.

The majority of women he met were so bent on being agreeable that their saccharine sweetness nearly gave him a toothache. But her ire was genuine. In fact, Miss Parrish's utter dislike of him practically made the ground quake. He had no doubt that if she could conjure a hole that would split apart the earth beneath his feet and swallow him up, she wouldn't hesitate to do so.

Strange as it was, he took a moment to savor the animosity directed at him.

His gaze skimmed over the sanctimonious arch of her black winged brow, and the crowding of her thick lashes as she narrowed her eyes. He could find no pinched disdain in her nose, for it was perfectly straight and slender. The pursing of her mouth offered little chastisement. The action only made it appear softer, her upper lip plumper than its counterpart by the barest degree. But her chin was stubborn, indeed, and her jaw well-defined, angling toward ears that were slightly flared. The very tips peeked out from a tumble of glossy ebony curls. And there, he caught a glimpse of something. Something in her hair that gleamed silver.

Without thinking, he took a step closer. Reaching up, his fingertips delved into tendrils that were so exquisitely soft and lush it was as if they'd been brushed a thousand times each morning.

The errant thought caused an image to form in his mind, of Miss Parrish seated at her vanity, wearing nothing more than a gauzy shift as she attended to her coiffure, slender arms raised to secure her combs, milk-white breasts lifting with the motion—

Her sudden gasp made him aware of his actions.

His gaze darted to her wide eyes as her pupils spilled like dark mercury to nearly engulf the pale irises. Her lips parted and twin spots of pink crested her cheeks. The color fascinated him. It looked as though it would be downy to the touch and taste like those little glazed cakes they'd served with tea. At the thought, an unexpected jolt of heat staggered through him.

"My lord . . . I had no intention of . . . that is to say . . . you are quite . . . most definitely . . . but I seem to be . . . light-headed . . . and my heart . . . too fast . . ."

Her statements were incomplete, her voice raspy and insubstantial. And yet, Brandon understood her perfectly, as if all the missing words were inside him.

Unaccountably, every fiber of his being urged him to take her in his arms, to shore her body against his own, to lower his mouth to hers and help her form a complete sentence. But before he gave in, a bumblebee buzzed by. The low hum snapped him to alertness, reminding that they were standing in the Baxtons' garden. Only steps away from discovery.

At once, he withdrew, then released the clover-scented air trapped in his lungs.

Across from him, Miss Parrish labored for breath as well, confusion stamped on her expression.

Before she could ask what he'd been about to do—the answer of which astounded him—he quickly raised his hand between them. "You had a thread in your hair. I merely removed it."

She blinked. As she looked from him to the object dangling between his thumb and forefinger, her hand absently flitted over the tendrils above the heart-halved peak of her ear. Then her shoulders seemed to sag with relief. "A silver thread. Thank the saints, I thought it was a—"

She broke off at once.

He wondered what she'd been meaning to say. But as she averted her embarrassed gaze and another wash of color tempted his sweet tooth, he surmised the rest.

"Did you think this was a gray hair, Miss Parrish?" he teased.

She gave her answer by quickly pulling the string free and casting it to the grass before dusting her hands together in brisk agitation. "You find this amusing, do you?"

"Immensely."

"And, no doubt, you would have laughed over my inert form lying on the grass after I fainted. I nearly did, you know. And not because of the thread, but for the way you crowded me so," she said, fanning her fingers in front of her face as she drew in a staggered breath. "I'm having the most adverse reaction to your presence. I can feel it in the way my head is still spinning. My skin is hot as well—sure signs of fever—and my palms are damp beneath my gloves. Worst of all, my pulse is pounding so hard it will likely break through my skin at any moment."

She pointed to the place and, there it was, hopping like a rabbit. His own thrummed in response, then rapidly descended lower.

"I am quite certain that I am on the verge of heart seizure," she rasped, "and all you can do is stand there with that sleepy grin on your smug face."

He quickly schooled his features. "Because you're being ridiculous. Those aren't signs of a heart seizure but of something else altogether."

"Oh? And I suppose you've studied medicine at university. No? Well, then, I think I should know what is happening to my own physiology."

"Actually, I don't think you do. What you're feeling is physical attraction," he supplied with firsthand knowledge, unwilling to sugarcoat the truth for either of them.

She stared at him as if he'd grown two heads. "Astounding. You would like to *think* that is the cause, only because your vanity demands it to be so."

"Of the two of us, *I* am not the vain one worried about a gray—"

"You needn't mention it again," she said sharply, cutting him off as her cheeks flushed once more, from porcelain to pink in the blink of an eye.

It was fascinating to watch.

He took an unthinking step toward her again—couldn't

seem to help himself—and she squeaked in response, skirting out of his reach. Then she hurried past him.

At the edge of the row, she straightened her shoulders and looked back at him with a mixture of confusion and irritation. "By the by, the primary reason we have never met before is because I never desired an introduction. As impossible as it may be for *you* to understand, my marital interests lie elsewhere. I have absolutely no designs on you. And now I take pity on any woman who does."

As Brandon watched her walk away, he felt a strange ailment come over him as well. Not a heart seizure, exactly. But, perhaps, something just as lethal.

Chapter 3

⌒

"A debutante should never enter a garden alone, for *alone* is likely not how she will remain."

—A NOTE FOR *The Marriage Habits of the Native Aristocrat*

At the Easterbrookes' ball that evening, Ellie watched George dance the quadrille. For her, no one else was on the ballroom floor.

He was such an athletic dancer, broad-shouldered and quick on his feet. Enjoyment gleamed in his treacle-dark eyes and, when he laughed, he still reminded her of the boy he'd been. The boy who'd both teased and charmed her over the course of her life.

George would play terrible tricks on her, like putting worms in her sewing box. But then he'd be terribly sweet, too, like the time he'd climbed the chestnut tree to bring down a nest of newborn hatchlings for her to see.

She remembered every moment with him—every clasp of his hand, every shared dance at the village assemblies, and every kiss. It was important to keep these memories close to her heart in order to recount them to their future children.

Of course, their sons would roll their eyes and pretend boredom with stories of a love that had blossomed decades before they were born. But their daughters would listen raptly with starry eyes and sighs, and learn the valuable lesson that sometimes it takes a bit longer for a man to fall in love than it does a woman.

Ellie knew it would be like that, one day. Preferably one day soon. After all, she wasn't getting any younger . . . as Lord Hullworth had so *subtly* pointed out.

A taut, peevish huff slipped out between her lips at the mere thought of him. At the same time, an ominous shiver cascaded over her skin and made her shift with restless agitation.

"Are you unwell, dearest?" Aunt Maeve looked over at her with concern. Her features were as sharp as her intellect, and her wizened brown eyes the very picture of Papa's. Even her hair was the same shade of iron gray.

Before she could answer, however, the younger of her aunts began to fuss over Ellie, hands fiddling with the flounces at her sleeves. Aunt Myrtle was a walking confection, petite and softly plump with flossy silver hair and eyes the milky lavender of elderberry jam mixed with clotted cream.

"It might have been the salmon *vol-au-vents* at the Baxtons' this afternoon. They were not nearly as delicious as they were reputed to be." She clucked her tongue in dismay. "A wasted use of our recipe espionage, I'm afraid."

Ellie shook her head. "It cannot be that, for I had no appetite by the time we sat down."

"Then you must be famished. Here, I've just the thing. Maeve and I took the liberty of stealing into the dining room as the servants were setting up the buffet and I found the most delicious little . . . Oh, where are they? I know I put some in here, just in case I became hungry on the journey home."

But even as Aunt Myrtle fished through her reticule, Ellie already knew the cause of her ailment. The culprit was that boorish Lord Hullworth. She hadn't been the same since she'd left the tea this afternoon.

Her agitation and symptoms had increased by degrees as

the hour drew closer and closer to the Easterbrookes' ball this evening.

She knew she would see him again. Tonight. Meg had told her as much in a missive she'd sent, thanking her again for the kite and her friendship.

Even though the words were cheerful, Ellie had felt a pang of sadness for the one who'd held the pen. The poor creature was left to endure a lonely Season without true friends. And all because half the *ton* wanted to marry that ill-mannered brother of hers.

Ellie sighed.

So did her aunt. "Oh dear. It seems I've already eaten them all."

"Myrtle," Aunt Maeve said with exasperation. "You promised to save one for our cook, as well. I never could trust you around cheese, or pear tarts for that matter. You were in such a hurry to gobble it up that a footman had to come to your rescue with a wallop to the back."

"Who's to say I didn't choke on purpose? He was a rather handsome young fellow. Did you see the size of his calves beneath those snug liveried breeches?"

"And you've always been too quick to swoon over the nearest male, whether you're old enough to be his grand—"

"Now that is the pot calling the kettle black. What about your ongoing flirtation with—"

"Fear not," Ellie interrupted as they continued their back-and-forth squabble. "I'm not hungry."

In the very next instant, her stomach flipped most alarmingly and she wondered what life-ending ailment was the cause. But then a sinking suspicion set in as the hair on the back of her nape lifted. And all at once, she knew.

Lord Hullworth was here.

She heard it in the hushed whispers that fell over the crowd. Then heads began to turn in a rolling wave toward the bank of open French doors along the far wall.

But Ellie refused to look. She knew precisely what he would think if she met his gaze. The vain peacock would assume she was seeking him out, unable to resist the supposed *attraction* between them.

Ha! The man knew nothing about the ailments she'd suffered earlier. For all he knew, she might have been bitten by a venomous snake, there on the garden path, with the poison leeching into her veins and making her light-headed. Attraction, indeed!

Keeping her slippers planted on the parquetted floor, she refused to give him the satisfaction of turning around. But there was a queer fluttering inside her midriff. Worriedly, she splayed her hand over it. This wasn't a mere case of nerves, she knew. And it certainly wasn't as tame as butterflies. No, indeed, for the spasms were escalating in intensity as the seconds ticked by. If the sensation could be likened to any winged creatures, flapping about inside her stomach, then they were large, rapacious flesh-eaters. *Vultures*, she decided.

She had vultures inside her stomach and it was all his fault.

Needing comfort, her gaze found George just as he was escorting his partner to her chaperone across the room. After another set, it would be her turn. He'd signed her card for the waltz. Soon, she would be swept up in his arms and anyone who happened to see the delight in her face would never believe that she could prefer *London's most arrogant bachelor* to her George.

The happy thought subdued the carrion birds for the moment and she dropped her hand to her side.

In the next instant, however, it was snatched by Meg, who sidled up to her with a happy whisper. "Ellie, you are a marvel! How can I ever thank you?"

Ellie squeezed back and looked at her beaming friend. Meg took the opportunity to stand apart and swish her skirts. Perched atop the puffed rouleau hem of her gown, sat a colorful parrot that Ellie had stitched years ago from leftover pieces of silk, along with a half dozen dye-dipped feathers. The latter pieces were sewn in a whimsical cascade from the sash at her waist. It was precisely what Ellie had hoped Meg's maid would do when she'd sent the appliques and a letter over by messenger that afternoon.

"There is no need, truly. I sew little odds and ends all the time and keep them tucked away in a box. You are more than welcome to come over and sift through them at your leisure," Ellie said. The truth was, her collection had started with the hopes of, one day, adorning her wedding trousseau. By now, she had at least a hundred. After all, she'd been waiting an exceedingly long time for George to stop being such a dunderhead and finally propose.

"Though, now that you are here," Ellie continued, "I should like to introduce you to my aunts, Maeve and Myrtle Parrish. And this, dear aunts, is Margaret Stredwick."

Maeve's smile softened her angular features. "Such a pleasure to make your acquaintance. And just look at how pretty you are. I don't believe I was ever so young and full of life."

"I'm certain you never were, sister. In fact, you've always been rather old," Aunt Myrtle teased, sidestepping away from a playful fan-swat that Maeve was about to deliver. Then she addressed Meg. "How lovely to meet you, at last. Elodie told us all about you. However, she was quite agitated when we returned home from the party. Apparently, she'd had this terrible encounter with an overbearing gentleman."

"No, I believe 'odious' was the word she'd used, sister."

"*Aunt* . . ." Ellie said, feeling her cheeks color.

Even though Lord Hullworth had not approached, she could still sense that he was quite close. Looming like a dark, disapproving cloud.

"Hmm. I think we are both correct," Myrtle mused with

a nod. "He was both odious *and* overbearing. Otherwise, I'm sure she shouldn't have been so distracted while unwrapping the shawl we gave her."

"Our niece is always one to notice and praise our handiwork, whether my sister deserves it for her part or not." Maeve cupped a hand to one side of her mouth and said in a stage whisper, "The fringe was uneven on her side."

Meg giggled. "It's very nice to make your acquaintance. Ellie didn't tell me how amusing you both are. She only said that you are very dear to her."

"What a darling gel! Elodie was quite right about you. She said you have the sweetest disposition and are positively brimming with gladness."

"If I am, then it is all her doing. She is the cleverest, most generous soul in all of creation and—" She broke off as her brother discreetly cleared his throat. Casting an unrepentant grin over her shoulder, she said, "Are you still hanging about, brother sentry? You were such a clock-watcher, I should have thought you'd already be about the business you were so eager to attend." She turned back to Maeve and Myrtle with a laugh. "I've never seen him so enthusiastic about a ball before, but he was quite cross that we did not leave on time."

"Perhaps, dear sister, I am precisely where I wish to be, among the loveliest ladies in all of England," he said, earning a roll of the eyes from Meg and two fan-to-bosom sighs from the aunts.

Then he stepped forward into their group. But instead of standing next to his sister, he stopped at Ellie's side. Her skin reacted to his nearness in a wash of disconcerting tingles. Her pulse leapt much too quickly, every beat belabored. And, drat it all, the vultures were back.

Ellie flicked a dismissive glance to him, noting that—without the obstruction of his hat—she could see the curl in his neatly trimmed hair, the color like burnished bronze.

Some of the tendrils caught the light of the chandelier and gleamed copper.

Other women might have found that quite appealing or even have felt an urge to run their fingers through those locks. Not her, of course, she thought as she curled her tingling fingertips inward to her palms. She preferred George's hair, dark and straight. Some men simply didn't need the superfluous adornment of curly hair to be attractive.

Lord Hullworth looked down the perfectly sloped edge of his nose at her, a sense of patient expectation in the subtle lift of his brows.

Apparently, he was waiting to be introduced. Ellie supposed she couldn't avoid it. At least, not without appearing rude. But when she opened her mouth to speak, her words suddenly faltered as her gaze connected with his.

For those next infinitesimal seconds, she was held captive by those irises. The color that appeared ashy gray at a distance turned silvern green up close, like the shifting warp and weft of velvet under the smoothing pass of a hand. And she was struck by the strangest urge to hold his face in her hands to see if they would alter again if she stood on tiptoe to peer even closer.

Those eyes crinkled at the corners in amusement as he spoke next, his voice low and intimate as if they were sharing a secret. "Shall I introduce myself to your aunts, Miss Parrish?"

"Elodie!" Maeve chided, and Myrtle joined in. "You did not tell us you were acquainted with the Marquess of Hullworth."

Tongue-tied, Ellie started to ramble. "Well, I . . . didn't suppose . . . that is to say . . . I thought perhaps . . . you were already . . ."

"Lord Odious and Overbearing at your service," he supplied with a courtly bow to her tittering aunts. The action caused his sleeve to brush the bare skin of Ellie's arm, inciting a rise of gooseflesh that covered her entire body—even *inside* her clothes—and stole her breath. "I had the pleasure of meeting your niece earlier today. Though, I must admit, my manners were sorely lacking. I do hope, however, that she will consent to a dance with me so that I may make amends."

"How prettily said and not the least bit overbearing," Aunt Maeve fawned.

Clearly won over, Myrtle gave him the saucy wink she usually reserved for wealthy octogenarians or the nut vendor in the park. "Or odious."

"And yes, I'm certain our niece would love to accept."

All eyes turned to her.

But no one seemed to realize that Ellie was on the verge of an apoplexy at the thought of being in his arms. Then again, she bore the symptoms—accelerated heartbeat, shriveled lungs, spinning pia mater—with the grace demanded of a public forum. Never let it be said that Elodie Marie Parrish would humiliate herself by dying in the middle of a crowded ballroom.

Glancing down to the hand he extended, she felt her fingertips heat and pulsate—a new ailment already upon her!

Carefully, she closed her hand at her side. "This set has already begun."

His gaze shifted to the dancers and back to her. "A problem easily remedied—then, let it be the next."

The next was the waltz. Her throat went dry at the mere notion of twirling and tangling in his closed embrace, the brush of his thigh against hers for every turn . . . And, quite perplexedly, she found herself curious about what it would be like, despite every ailment he caused.

But then—*thank the saints*—she remembered George.

"I apologize, my lord, but I've promised the waltz to another."

Lowering his hand, he studied her shrewdly. "Have you,

indeed? Very well, Miss Parrish. Perhaps another time, then."

He inclined his head, but with a smirk lifting the corner of his mouth as if he didn't believe her. The same way he'd smirked when she told him of her other marital prospects, earlier in the Baxtons' garden. Did he imagine her too old and unappealing to induce another man to sign her card?

That smirk seemed to say as much.

Rankled out of her apoplexy, she clenched her teeth. "Truly, I am obligated for the waltz."

She would produce her card as proof, but she didn't want to reveal that there were no other names on it aside from George's.

"I have no doubt of it," he said with a careful blandness that practically oozed with doubt. Then he proffered his arm to his sister. "Meg, I see Lord Butterfield beckoning me. If you'll recall, I promised to introduce you to his son."

"I was hoping you'd forget." Meg rolled her eyes and heaved out a sigh. Then to Ellie she whispered, "I've heard that young Lord Percival tends to salivate a great deal when he speaks."

"Regretfully, I must inform you that the rumor is quite true. Here," Ellie said, withdrawing an embroidered lace handkerchief from her sleeve. "Even if you already have one, you'll need another."

Meg laughed brightly. "I'm truly terrified."

She took her brother's arm and they parted with all appearances of affability between new acquaintances. And yet, there was an underlying tension between Lord Hullworth and Ellie.

It abraded her skin to watch him leave. So, she turned to her aunts, who were studying her with peculiar expressions. "What is it?"

"It was quite an honor for Lord Hullworth to ask you. You needn't have refused him."

"Of course, I did. I already gave the waltz to George."

"But George would have understood. Besides, it was clear you wanted to dance with Lord Hullworth."

She blinked. "It was not clear. Not clear at all. I didn't want to dance with him and I still don't. At all."

"If you say so, dear."

Aunt Maeve patted her arm. "It's your birthday, after all. You can believe anything you like."

At the reminder of her approaching descent into old age and an early grave, Ellie's gaze veered to George.

Just then, he bowed across the aisle to his partner and a hank of dark hair fell across his forehead. Unconcerned, he shook it back with a devil-may-care grin, barely missing a step. He was so full of life. So eager to enjoy every moment. And seeing him made all of Ellie's ailments disperse on a smile.

There was no need to think of Lord Hullworth for another instant.

Unfortunately, her gaze did not heed her resolve. It flitted toward the adjacent wall, where the arrogant marquess stood with Meg, Lord Butterfield, his son . . . and a beautiful woman.

Until that moment, Ellie had forgotten the mention in the gossip pages of Butterfield's ward, an orphaned ingénue from a distant Scottish cousin. It was said that she'd lived her life in a quaint rural village and all the *ton* marveled at her grace, despite her rusticated upbringing and misfortunes.

Miss Carmichael possessed a wealth of cornsilk hair coiffed in an elegant twist and adorned by a spray of pearl-headed pins. Her features were striking, her form willowy in her ivory taffeta, her movements graceful . . . even as she *accidentally* brushed Lord Hullworth's arm, then dropped her handkerchief directly at his feet.

Ellie felt the flesh around her eyes tighten as she observed the pretty display. And she heard herself growl in disgust when he bent down—without any hesitation whatsoever—to retrieve Miss Carmichael's fallen lace and *oh-so* gallantly return it to her.

If she were making a note of this for the primer, she would compare his actions to a gentleman who was intrigued and most assuredly *attracted* to his companion. The exact opposite of how he had acted toward Ellie. She added this to his list of offenses, which included rudeness, accusing her of deception, not to mention calling her old *and* vain.

At once, she decided that she hated him. In fact, she would hate him until the last dying breath left her body. And, perhaps, she would even hate him long after that.

Turning her seething attention away from the loathsome man, she took an avid interest in her aunts' discussion on the merits of the pilfered canapes and looked forward to her dance with George.

Unfortunately, when the time came, she watched in dismay as George took the floor with another young woman on his arm. Not Ellie.

Truth be told, it wasn't the first time he'd forgotten an obligation. He tended to be led by impulse, living moment to moment. She admired his *joie de vivre* and, therefore, always forgave him for these lapses in memory.

But it was particularly humiliating tonight, with Lord Hullworth across the crowded room. She didn't have to look to know that he was likely smirking at her. And, oh, she couldn't stand the idea of being on display for his amusement!

Since Maeve and Myrtle had already slipped away for another stealthy reconnaissance of the dining room, Ellie stole out onto the terrace.

The midnight air was cool, perfumed by the lilies of the valley and white anemones that bordered the broad stone steps leading to the garden. She followed them down and stood on the verge, where the glow from the windows faded to a dusting of gold against the Vandyke hem of her skirts.

When the music began, part of her longed to slip further into the dark shadows beyond the pruned spires of juniper. But after Prue's expulsion from good society, Ellie knew the dangers of being caught alone in a dark garden. There would be talk. And she would not risk her future marriage to George by having her reputation called into question.

Just as the thoughts traversed her mind, she saw the shifting shadow of someone stepping out onto the terrace. Hoping George had remembered his promise, she turned with a smile.

But it slipped the instant she saw Lord Hullworth instead. "Oh, it's you."

"I merely wanted to ensure that you were well," he said with a curl of smugness in his voice, his hand resting on the balustrade as he looked down at her. "After all, it surprised me to see you skulking out of the ballroom when you were so eager for the waltz. I told myself that Miss Parrish surely must be enduring some grave illness for her to miss the opportunity to dance with her mysterious partner."

She scoffed. *Skulking, indeed.* "And why are you not dancing with Miss Carmichael? You seemed quite eager to play the gentleman for *her*."

"Does it bother you that I picked up her handkerchief?"

"Of course not," she said without hesitation, watching warily as his foot landed on the first step. "It seems to me you play the gentleman quite well, when there is an audience you want to impress."

"And you're cross because you wish that I tried to impress you." Slowly, he descended to the garden and did not stop until he was within arm's reach.

"No, it's just . . ." She swallowed as his nearness caused a wash of awareness to shiver across her skin. And for some strange reason, she couldn't stop herself from noticing the way his shoulders filled the tailored dark blue coat as if it had been stitched directly onto his form. But he was odious and arrogant, she reminded herself. Hiking her chin, she refused to be intimidated by handsomeness. "You never answered my question."

"Do you mean, why am I not dancing with Miss Carmichael?"

She offered a stiff nod.

His gaze held hers, steady and resolute. "Because I'd already given my waltz to you."

When he presented his open hand to her, all the breath fell out of her lungs like a stone dropping between them. Did he truly expect her to dance with him now? She wanted to laugh in his face.

And yet, there was something about the expectant, almost impatient, look in his eyes. It caused a queer heavy sensation to shift in the pit of her stomach. It affected the beating of her heart, too, for the organ stuttered to a halt, then started back up again, beating faster than ever before.

"But . . . but you don't even like me. For all I know, you followed me out here to question my motives again," she said in a panicked rush, dazedly watching her arm lift. Then she felt her fingertips slide into the warmth of his waiting palm. Clearly, her body and her mind were not on speaking terms.

"True," he admitted. "However, I can interrogate you just as easily while you're in my arms."

Before she could take offense—before she was even aware of moving—Lord Hullworth drew her into his frame, his hand splayed over the center of her back. And there, at the base of the terrace stairs, they danced in the shadows on the manicured lawn.

It was as terrible as Ellie imagined. She could scarcely breathe. Her head spun in a thousand more revolutions than their bodies. She tried to remain stiff and formal, but her bones seemed to dissolve into dust with every brush and press of his thighs against hers. So, he was forced to pull her against him, their hips and torsos intimately locked.

His steps never faltered. His form was a sinuous arrangement of firm muscles that knew precisely where to tread. Because of his secure hold, they glided over the grass, their every movement in perfect symmetry. Even their breaths were in tandem. Quick and shallow and hot.

Unable to bear the overwhelming rush of sensation, she melted against him, supple silk melding with taut wool, their garments interlacing with enthralling friction. Her flushed cheek fell to his shoulder. His scent tasted like cedar and rain on her tongue. She swallowed, vaguely aware of how scandalous this would appear to anyone who found them in the garden. They would have no idea that the dancers despised each other.

Then the music ended and they stopped, both panting near an arch of wisteria that had yet to bloom.

She dragged in a quick breath. "You forgot to . . . interrogate me."

"So I have," he said, holding her for a moment longer, his heart pounding against the cage of her corset and ribs. "Are you suffering any ailments, Miss Parrish?"

"An exceeding number of them, my lord."

"Another heart seizure?" he asked, the hint of a smile in his voice.

Her forehead brushed his cravat as she nodded. "I do believe so. And I'm quite certain I shouldn't survive another dance with you."

"Mmm," he murmured in thoughtful agreement, his hand drifting soothingly down the ladder of her spine. "At least not with your reputation intact by the end of it."

She lifted her gaze to his, confusion furrowing her brow. "Whatever do you mean?"

He didn't answer. Instead, he glanced to the terrace and

slowly exhaled. Then he cupped her shoulders and eased her apart from him, ensuring a proper degree of space between them.

Her mind thought this was sensible. Her body protested, however, listing toward him until she staggered to find her feet.

"Steady now?" he asked. Once he gained a baffled nod, he released her.

Gradually, the rhythm of her heart slowed into something more recognizable and less alarming. Even so, Ellie didn't know what had come over her. Perhaps it was the lateness of the hour taking its toll. She'd been awake since half past five this morning and now she felt as though she were coming out of a dream state.

Dazed, she walked beside him to the base of the stairs and watched as he bent to pick a white anemone. He looked down at it with a bemused grin, twirling the blossom between thumb and forefinger.

Then he surprised her into full wakefulness by presenting it to her. "For your birthday, Miss Parrish."

"But how did you . . . that is . . . I never told . . ."

"Your aunts mentioned that you'd unwrapped a shawl earlier today." He shrugged. "I surmised the rest."

"Thank you." The words came out on the barest breath as she tentatively took the gift. Their fingertips brushed and, even beneath her glove, hers tingled.

She stared down at the white petals in bewilderment. He was full of surprises, one after the other. She wasn't entirely sure she liked it. Then again, she wasn't entirely sure she disliked it either.

He looked toward the house and back to her. The golden glow from the windows silhouetted his head and shoulders but left his eyes shadowed. And she couldn't help but wonder what color they were in this moment—a distant gray or that velvety green?

"To guard your reputation," he said, his low voice sending ribbons of warmth cascading through her, "I shall return to the ballroom first and ensure that your entrance will go unnoticed."

She felt a slow smile dawn on her lips as he mounted the steps to the terrace. "How very gallant of you. Planning to create a spectacle?"

After such an inauspicious beginning, she could never have imagined the first day of their acquaintance ending like this. There was a distinct possibility that she would *not* hate him forever after all.

At least, that's what she thought . . . until he looked down at her and spoke again.

"No indeed. I plan to ask Miss Carmichael to dance."

A swift, scalding heat scorched the insides of her veins at once. She wasn't sure what was causing such an intense reaction. Why should it matter to her with whom he chose to dance? It didn't at all, she assured herself. They were veritable strangers and nothing more.

And yet, when he dared to flash a grin an instant before he turned to head inside, she couldn't seem to stop the impulse to pluck every petal off the flower and toss the bare stem to the ground.

Whatever this unwelcome feeling was, she would have to make note of it for the primer. It would serve as a warning for debutantes to stay far away from gentlemen who had unwelcome effects on one's physiology.

Chapter 4

"When suffering the unwanted attentions of an undesirable gentleman, avoidance is the surest remedy."

—A NOTE FOR *The Marriage Habits of the Native Aristocrat*

"Pray, walk slower, Brandon," Meg said with a frown the following day. "It is no use trying to outrun them, you know."

He grunted in displeasure, but slowed nonetheless.

They'd only been in the park for a quarter hour and had already encountered three handkerchief droppers, two *accidental* stumblers, and one limping debutante hoping to play upon his sympathy to drive her home. He'd gritted his teeth while politely assisting the first five, and hailed a hackney cab for the sixth.

"These constant efforts to gain my attention have become suffocating," he grumbled under his breath.

His sister clucked her tongue. "It is your own fault. After dancing with Miss Carmichael last evening, you've created a frenzy. Even the society pages are speculating whether or not *London's most elusive bachelor* is finally ready to tie the knot."

Brandon hated that moniker. He was just a man. And he longed for the simple pleasures that any other man might take for granted—a walk through the park without being accosted by husband hunters, a dance with a lovely woman without it appearing in the papers, or simple companionship without ulterior motive.

"But what I cannot understand," Meg continued, "is why you danced with that vainglorious ninny at all. She is beautiful, to be sure. But I knew you didn't like her the instant she'd purposely dropped her handkerchief to cause a stir that would link her name to yours."

He certainly hadn't intended to resume his acquaintance with Miss Carmichael after their initial introduction had ended. But he'd suspected that his absence had been noted from the ballroom and, if Miss Parrish and he had walked through the same door—even minutes apart—he knew all too well that rumors would quickly abound.

The article in the gossip pages this morning would have been ruinous.

"And there you have your answer," he lied. "Perhaps, my displeasure over the utter monotony of these games has frayed the last coils of my civility, and so I felt obligated to make amends for any curtness I displayed."

It was a plausible excuse. In fact, it was the very excuse he'd given himself before he'd danced with Miss Parrish. The same dance that he'd lain awake thinking about all night, replaying every touch, breath and sigh, his head spinning as if he were standing on the diorama platform in Regent's Park.

"Fear not, your gallant facade was convincing enough for the others. Only *I* know when you are displeased with your company," Meg said with a smug purse of her lips as they walked along the path. "Though it has been such an age since I've witnessed enjoyment from you that I might mistake it for something else. Last evening, for example, I thought I saw a glimmer of *contentment past* when we were speaking with the three Miss Parrishes."

"Must have been an aberration," he said, but his thoughts ventured again to the dance in the garden.

Even now, hours upon hours later, his muscles contracted with the memory of her body pressed against his. He could still feel the weight of her head nestled against the crook of his shoulder. The supple cushion of her breasts. Her heart pounding hard against his own. It was as though she'd been stitched against his skin like a suit of clothes.

As he walked, his shoulders shifted in restless agitation. He wanted to be rid of these sensations.

This confounding desire for Miss Parrish made no sense. After all, she'd been playing a coy game with him from the beginning, much like Miss Carmichael. And the last thing he wanted was to allow himself *or* his sister to be taken in by another deceiver.

"An *aberration,* hmm?" Meg mused. "That is a pity, indeed, for I believe my new friend is on yonder bench."

Distracted by his own thoughts, it took a moment for him to realize what his sister said. He absently followed her gaze to the figure seated up ahead. Then he jolted to a halt.

In the same instant, Miss Elodie Parrish looked up sharply from a pocket-sized book in her gloved hands, like an angler startled to attention when a fish snagged the lure. Her gaze widened on him, a flush rising to her cheeks. Beneath the ribbon of her bonnet, he saw her throat constrict on a swallow. And beneath his cravat, his did the same. *Damn this infernal attraction!*

Meg tugged his arm, propelling his steps forward. "Good day, Ellie. What a lovely coincidence that we should meet in the park today."

"Good day," she rasped, her voice as insubstantial as it had been last night after the music had ended.

For some unholy reason, the sound of it made him want to soothe her. To close the distance between them in two strides and hold her like he had in the garden.

Thankfully, she dragged her gaze away from him to look at Meg. After a delicate clearing of her throat, she said,

"Though, I couldn't call it a complete 'coincidence.' That word implies no foreknowledge. And I must confess that, when I read your correspondence aloud this morning, my aunts were compelled to choose this park in the hopes of seeing you again. We normally walk in Regent's Park which is a stone's throw from Upper Wimpole Street, of course."

At once, Brandon felt a surge of scalding irritation.

This meeting was no more happenstance than the sun rising in the sky each morning. Not only that, but he knew this game, too—the ever-sly mention of her address in hopes of luring him into her trap by inciting his curiosity.

Polite conversation dictated that he was now supposed to tell her of some familiarity with that street. Perhaps even mention an acquaintance who lived there. To which she would respond with practiced surprise, marveling at happenstance, before inviting him to pay a call whenever he should find himself in the vicinity.

But Brandon, seething through gritted teeth, refused to play his part. "At least you openly admit to plotting this time, unlike our first meeting."

"To plot—" Miss Parrish stopped on a scoff. Her cheeks abruptly cooled. "Oh, yes. I forgot how we're all trying so desperately to marry you."

"As you say," he added coolly.

She squinted at him, the warm brandy fire of her gaze turning hard as brass ingots. "'Tis no wonder you chose to walk out of doors today, my lord, for it seems the only venue capable of housing your immense ego."

"No truer statement has ever been spoken, I'm sure." Meg slipped her arm from his. Sitting down on the bench beside Miss Parrish, she glowered at him as if he were in the wrong for speaking the truth and her duplicitous companion was wholly blameless.

"Well, that is fine, indeed," he said to the little traitor. "Have you not said, yourself, that you are tired of the ceaseless methods used to gain my attention? For all we know, your supposedly faultless friend was sitting here alone and waiting for the opportunity to claim an injury and beg a ride home to *Upper Wimpole Street.*"

Meg linked arms with Miss Parrish in a show of solidarity. "Ellie would never do such a thing. Now, I insist that you apologize and invite her to walk with us."

"Actually, Meg . . ." Miss Parrish began with something of a rueful laugh. "While I am not opposed to a much-deserved apology, I cannot walk with you. I did, in fact, turn my ankle—"

"Ah ha," Brandon interrupted smugly.

"—whilst descending from a phaeton's perch a short while ago," she finished, darting an irritated glance to him. "Nevertheless, you may rest assured that your brother would be the last person I would ever prevail upon to assist me in any way whatsoever."

Meg issued a sympathetic sigh and nod. "I do not know what has befouled his manners, but I should rather wait here with you than go another step with him."

"You are too kind," the friend replied with a sniff, pretending as if he wasn't there. "However, you must forgive him, I suppose. His dance last evening must have put him in the path of Cupid's arrow, and now he is forlorn that it isn't Miss Carmichael on this bench. Obviously, his grumpy little heart simply cannot take another moment without her."

Meg tried to smother a surprised laugh with her gloved fingertips but failed miserably, her eyes dancing.

Brandon's attention fixed on Miss Parrish and the peevish edge to her tone. If he didn't know any better, he'd think she was jealous. She'd sounded the same last night when bringing up Miss Carmichael's handkerchief, without seeming to realize that she'd essentially admitted to watching him across the ballroom.

Truth be told, her admission was precisely the reason he'd

chosen to dance with Miss Carmichael in the first place. In-
voking Miss Parrish's ire helped to keep a necessary barrier
between them. Because the more she adamantly refused to
acknowledge that her *symptoms* stemmed from a basic attraction, the more he wanted to prove it to her. And that was
a temptation he would not give in to.

She was still the enemy, after all. Not to be trusted.

Even so—and despite his own suspicions of her ulterior
motives—bantering with her caused a grin to tug at his lips.
And since he couldn't very well leave his adversary feeling
as if she had gained the upper hand, he said, "You are quite
clever, Miss Parrish. I did enjoy the ball *and* the partner in
my arms . . . for the first dance."

Her eyes went round as gold guineas. Then, he had the
immense pleasure of watching her blush anew, color slowly
blossoming on the crests of her cheeks like the petals of a
peony opening to sunlight. With such a fair complexion and
expressive features, there was little she could do to conceal
her true thoughts. And that, he decided, was a quality in
her favor.

"Don't pay any attention to him, Ellie. Brandon only had
the one dance," Meg said. "It is a pity you had to leave early,
though. I do hope your aunt has recovered."

Miss Parrish blinked and turned toward Meg. "She has,
thank you. Aunt Myrtle sampled one too many canapés
before dinner, but she is hale now. In fact, that is her over by
the nut seller's cart." She gestured with a nod, then flicked
a defiant glance to Brandon. "Aunt Maeve is riding in the
phaeton I mentioned a moment ago."

There was blatant challenge in the arch of her wispy,
black-winged brows. That look said, *Call me a liar. I dare
you.* She even pursed her lips and waited for his response.

And Brandon—damn it all—felt an annoying impulse to
take her by the shoulders, lift her from the bench, and kiss
that provoking mouth in front of the entire *ton*.

These urges were getting out of hand. Clearly, he needed to think of a new tactic to expose her scheme before he did something to make the two of them the latest *on-dit* in the scandal sheets.

But she was skillfully subtle in the way she upheld her pretense. It was almost as if she'd expected her pursuit to meet with obstacles, and had contrived to wear him down bit by bit each time they met. The thought was unsettling. He'd barely known her above a day and she'd already gotten beneath his skin. There was no telling what state she'd have him in by week's end.

However, if he was correct about her tactics then, theoretically, the only thing she couldn't anticipate was a quick surrender.

Hmm . . . Perhaps that was the answer—upset the plot altogether. And the surest way to take her off guard was to appear to give her precisely what she wanted.

"Very well, Miss Parrish," he said. "You win."

She hiked her chin. "And *what*, pray tell, have I won?"

"Meg and I will drive you home."

His sister gasped in surprise and grinned up at him in frank approval. "Well done, Brandon. You are, once more, my favorite brother. See, Ellie? I told you he could act the gentleman and be agreeable when he chooses. And a drive home is the least we can do, after all you've done to keep me from fading into obscurity as a mere shadow that once lingered in the vicinity of London's favorite bachelor."

"Quite so," he agreed with a grin, feeling his own victory close at hand. "The attention and admiration my sister's frocks have garnered have also provided me with a few moments of respite, and for that I am in your debt. Name your recompense for my boorish suspicions and it shall be yours. Within reason, of course."

"Of course," she parroted with all seriousness. "My goodness, what a prize indeed. I hardly know what to demand." A conspiratorial glint lit her eyes as she turned to his sister. "What do you think, Meg? Should I ask for a trip to Paris for you and I, along with my aunts?"

Meg coughed to cover a laugh. "That would be lovely!"

"Indeed, it would. Then again"—she tsked and issued a sigh—"surely it is too late in the spring to see Paris at its best."

"Oh, quite so. A deplorable city unless one visits between the end of April and the beginning of May," Meg agreed with mock disenchantment.

"Perhaps theatre tickets, do you think? That is assuming your brother holds a box."

"I do," he answered quickly—half with impatience and half with something he could not name—waiting for her demand. *Hell*, he was actually eager to hear it, if only to end this torment of not knowing what she would take from him.

"Hmm," she murmured with a *tap-tap-tap* of her fingertip against the corner of her mouth, and cast him a sly sideways glance. "For such an *elusive* gentleman, you were certainly easy to capture under my thumb."

"As you say," he offered again, his pulse thrumming, itching beneath his skin.

Considering her options, she pursed those lips again.

He took an unconscious step closer before he caught himself and curled his hands over the lapels of his coat, rather than her shoulders. He felt as if he were on the verge of going mad from waiting.

Then, at last, she lowered her hand in her lap and looked up at him, her expression open and seemingly guileless. "I should like to be your friend, Lord Hullworth. No more of this 'she's plotting to marry me' nonsense."

Brandon simply stared at her. For a moment, he couldn't form a coherent response. Of all the requests she might have made, *this* was all she wanted?

He was ashamed to admit that part of him believed her.

But that was the fool talking, the part unaccountably attracted to her.

The rest of him, however, thought it highly suspect. A new kind of plot. Oh, and she was clever, too. The minx.

But so was he.

"If friendship is what you ask, then you shall have it beginning this very instant," he said, deciding to play this *let's pretend to be friends* game. For a time. Though he wouldn't allow it to drag on for too long, for Meg's sake.

Miss Parrish exhaled slowly. A soft—perhaps even victorious—smile played on her lips as she extended her hand.

Without hesitation, he took hold of it. He felt the mutual squeeze run in a warm current through his entire body, and saw it glowing in her cheeks. He couldn't help but wonder if this blush was brought on by guilt, attraction, or some combination of the two.

Withdrawing her hand, she averted her gaze, then startled slightly as she looked past his shoulder. "Aunt Maeve, you've returned," she said, tilting her head in perplexity. "But . . . where is George?"

The older woman stepped crisply toward their group and waved a hand in the air in an absent gesture. "Oh, you know how he is, flitting off on a moment's notice. But he did lend me this for you to use."

Brandon frowned at the ebony walking stick and watched Miss Parrish take hold of it, her palm curving over the faceted obsidian hilt. But why would she require . . . ?

He knew the answer in the same instant. *Damn!* She truly was hurt. And he was ashamed and disconcerted to realize that all he'd done was to offer her mockery.

He was ready with a humble apology. Considering how their prior conversation ensued, he wouldn't have been surprised to see a look of superiority on her face at the confirmation that she had, in fact, turned her ankle.

But Miss Parrish became unaccountably shy and refused to meet his gaze, as if embarrassed. Either that or she'd been expecting the owner of the walking stick—this *George*—to accompany her aunt and was disappointed by his absence.

Brandon wasn't certain which possibility bothered him more.

While he mulled this over, Maeve Parrish greeted him and Meg with easy familiarity.

"Lord Hullworth. Miss Stredwick. How good you are to keep my niece company. I see that Myrtle has abandoned her for the sake of flirting with another nut seller, tittering and batting her lashes." She cupped a hand to the side of her mouth. "Between the three of us, she has half the vendors in London thoroughly besotted. Needless to say, we are never in want of nuts or muffins." She waggled her eyebrows with meaning before turning back to her niece. "I have a hackney waiting near the gate. Do you think you can manage the distance, dearest?"

"I believe I am able," she said with a comical sigh. "The question is whether I want to hobble around appearing infirm and feeble."

"Then take my arm," Brandon offered, coming to her aid after assisting Meg to her feet.

Miss Parrish held up a hand to him. "Thank you, no. I do not wish to end up in the late edition of today's scandal pages."

"I insist."

"And I insist more. Stand aside or I shall throttle you with my cane," she said, brandishing it with a laugh that ended on a hiss the instant she attempted to rise on her own.

Brandon did not move away. Instead, he leaned, so close that the brims of their hats rasped intimately together. So close that he tasted her sweet fragrance in the air. "Allow me to assist you or you'll soon find yourself carried through the park over my shoulder."

She gasped. Even he was startled by his determination to follow through with his threat, his hand already splayed against the small of her back. She seemed to have awakened some strange and primitive side of his nature. But there was still enough of the gentleman in him to wait for her murmur of acquiescence.

"Careful now," he said, settling his other hand beneath her elbow as he drew her up beside him, giving her time to find her footing.

She bit down on her lip, her brow furrowed as she tested her weight, her hand gripping his forearm tightly. With a nod, she lifted her gaze to his, her irises soft and warm. "I think I can manage."

"Are you certain?"

"She said she could," Meg said softly in singsong, her teeth clenched in an imitation of a smile. "And you have an audience, Brandon."

One glance proved she was right. *Damn it all*. A crowd of parasol-wielding busybodies had formed, gloved hands lifted to hide the whispers that their scandalized arching eyebrows could not.

"Let them look," he said, keeping her hand on his arm. "The more they do, the more they will see that circumstance demands it."

"Of course, *we* know that," Meg said from the other side of her friend as the three of them made slow progress along the path. "But your gaggle will surely use this as a script to follow. I doubt we'll ever be able to walk in the park again."

"*Gaggle?*" he asked, perplexed.

The corner of Miss Parrish's mouth twitched. "Your followers," she supplied dryly. "I may have referred to you as 'King Goose' before I realized that Meg was your sister."

"Don't forget about calling him odious and overbearing," her aunt reminded with a lilting laugh as she veered toward the nut seller's cart to tug at her sister's arm.

Miss Parrish offered a sheepish glance. "Under the circumstances, I should likely recant two of those." Then she added under her breath, "Though you're still being rather overbearing."

He grinned, unapologetic. "I'll claim it. And, actually, I rather like 'King Goose,' as far as monikers go."

Meg expelled a dramatic sigh. "I told you it would go to his head."

"I suppose, that leaves but one," Miss Parrish said. "And I'm discovering that you're not nearly as odious as you were before, my lord."

"Just somewhat odious," he offered ruefully.

"As you say," she mocked.

They reached the waiting hackney far sooner than he'd expected. And he was forced to relinquish his claim on her when Maeve and Myrtle appeared at his side.

Once she was settled snugly in the dark interior of the carriage, he said, "We'll call on you later to see how you are faring."

She shook her head instantly. "I . . . I feel much stronger after the short walk." Looking past his shoulder to those who were still watching, twin spots of color rose to her cheeks. Then she continued in a whisper. "I appreciate your assistance, of course, but there is no need to continue our spectacle."

"You are so right, Ellie," Meg said, her voice rising to reach the crowd. "It is terribly rude when the snootiest members of society refuse to mind their own business. Instead, they linger like white-gloved vultures waiting for the feast of rumors to begin."

She turned to glare at Lady Doyle and her daughter. The ladies dispersed on a sniff.

"Meg, you are positively incorrigible," Miss Parrish said with affection that had all the appearance of being genuine. Perhaps it actually was.

His sister beamed brightly. "You'll have to get used to it, I'm afraid." Meg waggled her brows then waved her fingers, oddly keeping one hand behind her back. "Ellie, I'll send you a missive later and tell you all about how my brother enjoyed eating his crow for dinner after accusing you of feigning this injury."

"Splendid. I look forward to it," she answered, her laughing amber eyes flitting to him.

He cautioned himself not to be taken in by her charms. After all, just because he'd been mistaken about her ankle, didn't mean he was wrong about everything else.

Realizing his hand had been lingering on the open door all this time, Brandon closed it. Then he inclined his head and sent the driver on. But as he and Meg began walking on the pavement toward their town house, he felt his brow furrow as he reexamined everything Miss Parrish had told him, albeit from a slightly less suspicious viewpoint.

He didn't particularly like where his thoughts took him.

"Who the devil is this George fellow?" he grumbled under his breath. And what kind of gentleman would have left her in such a state in the first place without bothering to see her home? No gentleman, at all, in Brandon's opinion.

"I believe he is the man for whom she has set her cap, brother. You see? I told you that you could trust her motives."

"Hmm . . ." he murmured, stubbornly holding on to skepticism. "You *believe* he is, but have you met him? No. I thought not."

"Do you doubt his existence simply because Ellie hasn't introduced me to him within the first twenty-four hours of our acquaintance? Or is it because"—she eyed him impishly—"you're jealous of his claim on her affections?"

He ignored the idiocy of her comment. "I am only looking out for your best interests. You deserve someone who is honest and forthright."

"And so do you," she said as if it were that simple. But he

knew better. "Surely you're not going to let a bad apple spoil my chances of my becoming an aunt one day. I should like to be the kind who flirts with street vendors when I'm in my sixties and rides in phaetons until my gray hair is mussed."

It wasn't just a bad apple. His decision came from something far more serious than that. From something he'd lost years ago and, unless he found it, he'd never consider marrying. "And I think that you should focus on being twenty and enjoying your Season."

Meg shrugged in response and began whistling a tuneless melody.

He looked over at her skeptically. "You only whistle for one reason. Tell me, what mischief are you up to this time?"

He didn't have to wait or prod her, for she was all too eager.

From behind her back, she produced a familiar leather-bound booklet and feigned surprise. "Dear me! I seem to have forgotten to return Ellie's book. I suppose, we'll simply have to pay a call on her."

He snatched it out of her hand and tucked it inside his inner coat pocket. "I'll send it by courier."

"Likely for the best," she said with the scholarly air and severe expression she employed when attempting to imitate him, walking with purposeful clipped strides, her shoulders plank straight. "After all, she'll have *George* paying a call on her instead, I imagine. And we wouldn't want to interrupt them."

Brandon's step faltered. Nothing more than an errant stone on the pavement, he was sure. But beside him, Meg started to whistle again.

Chapter 5

"A debutante should view a gift with a degree of skepticism before heaping too much favor upon the gentleman. After all, the Trojans accepted an impressive offering once, too."

—A NOTE FOR *The Marriage Habits of the Native Aristocrat*

"I came to see the ungainly creature from the park," George said with a dark-eyed wink as he swaggered through the parlor doorway later that afternoon.

Ellie beamed from ear to ear. Until that moment, her thoughts had been rather maudlin. Seeing herself dressed in cream muslin on the red caffoy settee with her shawl-draped legs stretched feebly across the cushion, she'd felt like a sacrificial offering, laid out and waiting for Death to ride his horse through the doors to carry her unmarried soul off into the veil.

But now her spirits and her heart were bright and airy, like the lemon souffles in her aunts' collection of stolen recipes.

Ellie knew he couldn't have simply forgotten about her. Well . . . not like he had at the Baxtons' or the Easterbrookes'.

Nevertheless, she refused to hold on to disappointments. After all, men of his ilk often had pressing matters to attend. It would be wholly selfish of her to expect him to drop everything over trifling matters like garden parties or turned ankles. He certainly would never want a wife who couldn't manage on her own. No man would.

Striding into the room, he paused by Aunt Myrtle's and Aunt Maeve's chairs to buss their cheeks in greeting. And hanging at his side, he held a string-tied cone of jonquils.

Ellie's breath stuttered happily in her lungs. He'd never brought her flowers before. When they were children, he'd presented her with pretty rocks and foundling buttons—all of which she still kept stored in a blue glass vase on her bedside table—but nothing since he'd left for university or after.

This, however, filled her with so much hope that her little souffle heart could barely contain the joy rising within it. Surely a gift of flowers meant something.

She pressed her top teeth into her lower lip to keep from smiling too broadly. "Are those for me, George?"

"Just thought I'd bring them for all my best girls." He lifted his shoulders in an absent shrug and with each step he took toward her, she could see their future unfold, their wedding, their first child, their second . . .

Then he dropped them unceremoniously onto the low oval table.

A few of the yellow petals fell off and scattered over the polished rosewood surface. Her souffle deflated a bit. And then a bit more when she saw the pitying glance the aunts exchanged.

Ellie couldn't help but compare this lackluster flower presentation to the startlingly romantic one from Lord Hullworth after their unexpected dance. But that was unfair to George. After all, he had come here to see her when he might have been off at his club or on whatever errand had drawn him away from the park earlier. Not only that, but he'd gone out of his way to purchase flowers. Lord Hullworth had merely plucked a convenient blossom from the ground.

So, surely, this gesture from George meant something, she thought again. Progress in the right direction.

This was definitely worth noting for the primer. Only, as she looked toward the table, she didn't see her little pocket ledger. *Hmm . . . where could it have gone to?*

Well, it didn't matter at the moment. She would focus instead on seeing if she could glean any other positive signs from his visit. And she likely wouldn't have long because he was already milling around the room in his usual restless fashion.

"The flowers are lovely. Thank you." She twisted and stretched, trying to pick them up, but they were just out of her reach. Just like George.

At least, for now.

Aunt Maeve stood and nodded with encouragement, her eyes bright as she bent to retrieve the bundle. "I'll just go put these in water and return straightaway."

"I'll come with you, sister," Aunt Myrtle said with excitement, drawing her hands together in a cascading clap of fingertips before bustling out of the room. "I've always had an eye for arrangements."

George studied them with a wry smirk then turned to look at Ellie. "This reminds me of the time you fell off that swing on the hawthorn tree. Cried like a little girl the whole time I carried you inside."

"Well, I was a little girl at the time and you'd pushed me too high," she said with mock scolding, remembering that day.

It had felt exhilarating at first, the swooping sensation, her plaited hair lifting in the wind as if she were flying. But then she reached the pinnacle and caught a glimpse of the cemetery on the hill. The wrought iron fences. The grayed marble headstones. In the same instant, the ropes had fallen slack, as insubstantial and limp as hair ribbons. It only lasted a second. Perhaps less. Yet, it was enough time for her to see how high she was, to imagine her own small coffin and the piles and piles of worm-smelling dirt the grave diggers would shovel on top of her. The same things that still gave her nightmares to this day.

She recalled how the ropes had suddenly jerked taut, startling her. Panicked, she'd leapt off the swing to safety, to reassurance. To George.

"I told you to hold on," he said, standing with his hand resting over the back of the cream upholstered chair and wearing a grin of boyish remorselessness.

"I believe what you said was that I was too afraid to jump."

He chuckled. "And I was right. You fell like a lump of coal and were abed for almost a month. Now, look at you. Can't even hop down from a phaeton without someone to catch you."

"Perhaps I should have been born with a stronger skeleton to be around the likes of you," she said, the words a little sharper than she intended.

In truth, part of her was cross that he'd insisted she ride in the phaeton at all. It had frightened her to be up so high. When she'd said as much, he'd laughed and told her to hold on. But there'd been nothing to hold on to. The spindly rail on the side of the bench was no higher than her hip. One turn or bump would have sent her flying toward a most awkward demise.

With George, there were times when Ellie still felt like she was holding on to the ropes, never knowing how high she would go.

But seeing a confused frown corrugate his brow, she tucked those thoughts away. The last thing she wanted was to mar their time together by making him feel guilty. So, she offered, "I'm sure it isn't as bad as all that. In fact, it's hardly swollen at all."

He issued an absent murmur of agreement while his attention skimmed over the slender writing desk in the corner. "I see you've got some letters to keep you company."

"Yes, indeed. One just arrived with splendid news," she said, glad that she could so easily share it because he was well acquainted with all her friends. "Winnie sends word from the south of France that she and Asher are now the proud parents of a healthy baby boy. They've named him Marcus. And even better, they plan to return to England by midsummer. Also, Jane and Raven will have a new little bundle by year's end. All my friends are starting their families. Isn't that wonderful?"

Ellie knew she was piling on the enthusiasm like clotted cream over a dust-dry scone. But what else was a debutante hurtling toward spinsterhood supposed to do when given the perfect opportunity to plant the seed of wedded bliss in her intended's mind?

In the waning afternoon light sifting in through the window, he looked over his shoulder and gave her that boyish grin again. "*Wonderful* for them," he agreed wryly.

"Surely, enduring a few balls and parties hasn't turned the fearless boy I knew into a man afraid of the idea of a wife and children."

"Not afraid. It's just that I like women too much. You're all so pretty and so soft and—" He stopped and cleared his throat as if he remembered his audience. His gaze turned serious when he looked across the expanse at her, his tone gentle. "I'm not ready to make wedding plans quite yet, Ellie. Be patient, hmm?"

She nodded, having heard this before. He just wasn't able to picture how happy their lives would be. At least, not yet.

Her gaze slid to the stray petals on the table and she wondered if progress might require a little shove for the up-swing. "I imagine that both Asher and Raven had felt the same way before they married Winnie and Jane."

George sighed. "Don't you have any news about friends who *aren't* married?"

Ellie took the hint.

"You might recall my friend Prue, who has been away these many months."

"Not sure I do," he said with an absent pass of his hand over the surface of her desk, scattering her stack of letters. "Oh wait. The shy one with the blond hair. Miss . . . Thorogood, I think?"

Distractedly, Ellie murmured *Mmmhmm* . . . as she watched him at her desk, trying to recall if she'd already sent off the letter she'd written to Prue, telling her all about meeting the pompous Lord Hullworth, or if it was still there in plain sight. She wouldn't want George to read it. He might wonder why she'd dedicated so much ink and paper to another man and believe there could be interest in that quarter. Which there wasn't, of course. Her accounting of *Lord Goose* had been less than favorable.

When George turned around, however, she recognized the folded foolscap in his grasp as the letter from Prue. This was even worse!

Ellie gave a start, jolting forward on the cushions, hand outstretched. "You mustn't"—she broke off on a hiss, wincing as the sudden movement caused a twinge of pain in her ankle—"read that. It's confidential."

"Confidential," he scoffed and unfolded the letter with a single shake. "I imagine you've read the contents to your aunts or else it wouldn't be here in the parlor."

"Well, yes, but that's different. We're all women and we confide in each other about certain personal things."

He lifted his eyebrows in a wounded expression. "Are you going to start keeping secrets from me? Is that the kind of life I'm to expect in the future?"

"Of course not," she said, both flustered by the casual mention of their long awaited *happily-ever-after* and frustrated that he wasn't listening. "It's just—"

"'Dear Ellie,'" he began with a roguish wink over the open page. "'I have, indeed, heard the happy news about our friends. Your letters as well as theirs have been my companions these long months. And I hope you can forgive me for not being as diligent in responding. I find lately that the right words simply will not come. As to your numerous queries regarding *Lord F* and his efforts for a clandestine meeting . . .'" He lowered the page and his lips curved in a conspiratorial grin. "Ah ha! I knew I'd find a juicy tidbit in here."

"George, I really wish you wouldn't—"

"'Pray, do not fret on that account,'" he continued, splaying a hand over his heart as if he were reading the script of a melodramatic play. "'He has made no further attempts to see me in all these weeks since my last letter. I have been quite alone. I need not worry about his presence in the village any longer. He went away, and his lack of correspondence indicates that I shall never hear from him again. I am relieved, of course. Indisputably relieved. My conscience can be clear, once and for all. Your friend, Prudence Thorogood.'"

He lowered the letter to his side, appearing almost thoughtful for an instant. Until he adopted a bored expression. "Wasn't quite as interesting as I'd hoped."

Ellie glared at him with her arms crossed. "It wasn't meant to be riveting entertainment. It was a *private* letter, and now I feel as though I've betrayed a friend."

After all, George didn't know Prue the way Ellie did and might take the wrong impression of her character. Prue was of a reserved nature. She was good-hearted and never deviated from propriety, especially since her father and stepmother were notoriously critical of her actions. And Ellie was sure that, whatever had transpired the night that Prue's father found her and the mysterious *Lord F* in the gardens at Sutherfield Terrace, she was not at fault.

"Come now, you're making far too much of it. Why, it's only right that you share everything with me, considering what we are to each other. That means your friends are mine, too. And I seem to recall this one," he said, gesturing with the letter before he dropped it, unceremoniously, back on top of the desk with the others. "You've mentioned something about her living in the country with her aunt and uncle, I believe."

She nodded tersely, still sore at him. Though, she was glad he didn't appear to be judging her friend on the contents therein. Which meant it was likely that he wouldn't have any qualms over having Prue as a guest in their future home. Therefore, she supposed it was no monumental transgression that George had read the letter. And it did cheer her to hear him say that he wanted her to share everything with him.

That statement seemed like something a marriage-minded man might say.

She wished she knew for certain. Wished she understood what force took a gentleman from fondness and onward to affection, then tipped him over the edge to inspire him to drop on bended knee and offer up his heart and soul.

Once she could spot the signs of a man driven to propose, she could help so many women like herself—those trying to figure out how long they would have to wait. And so many women like Prue—those who put faith in a man only trifling with their affections.

But Ellie was not short on hope. She would keep trying and, one day she would have the answers. And she would have George, too.

"Yes, Prue is in the country with her aunt and uncle," she reiterated. "Though, the letters she seldom sends are written with such loneliness that I cannot wait until the Season is over so that my aunts and I can visit her, at last. I'd wanted to last year, but then Aunt Maeve had taken ill."

After a short stay in the country, they'd ended up returning to London in order to be closer to her physician. Thankfully, all had turned out in their favor and she was healthier now than ever before. But by the time she recovered, it was too late in the year to take a chance on travel. Prue had understood.

However, considering the forlorn quality in this last letter, Ellie wondered if she had made the right decision. Surely Prue was lonely for the society of true friends, instead of being constantly shamed and beleaguered by her disapproving Aunt and Uncle Thorley.

"Well, that's a fine thing, indeed," George said, drawing her out of her musings. He faced her with a disapproving frown. "Here you are planning to flit across the countryside and you never invited me."

Ellie's breath caught again, her heart in her throat. "I was unaware that you would wish to join us."

"And just what, pray tell, am I to do at my country house without my best girls next door? This summer would be a right solid bore, wouldn't it?"

She nodded, unable to form words. Was it possible that he couldn't imagine spending so much time apart from her?

Her aunts arrived in that next instant and George proceeded to give them a mock-scolding. "I've just learned of your great plot to abandon me next month. I'll have you know that I am sorely tempted to take a tour of the continent now that I've realized how little I'm regarded by those residing beneath this roof."

They just laughed and issued an invitation for him to join them. Though, Aunt Myrtle wasn't opposed to traveling with *him* to France for croissants and a flirtation with a Parisian nut seller, instead.

Ellie held her breath, waiting for George's response. Waiting for their eyes to meet.

He cast her another wink and there was a new grin on his lips that made her heart swoop. Then he took a step toward her. To do what—to press her hand? To kiss her cheek? To declare that he couldn't imagine spending those days apart from her, or any days for that matter?

She wondered if she should toss a pillow to the floor, just in case he was compelled to kneel.

He leaned in and then—*oh, this was all happening so quickly!*—picked up the walking stick propped against the arm of the settee.

"I shall consider it. But, for now"—he paused to twirl the ebony stick like a Catherine wheel—"I am off."

When he turned to leave, Ellie blinked in surprise as if someone had splashed water in her face. She watched as he stopped once more to buss the aunts' cheeks before tromping down the stairs without a backward glance.

There was a time when he used to buss *her* cheek, she remembered on a sigh. He'd made terrible raspberry noises that always made her swat playfully at him.

But that had been long ago, before his years at school had changed him from a boy into a man who enjoyed all the pleasures and carefree pursuits of town life. Aunt Maeve referred to it as a man needing to *sow his oats* before he was ready for marriage. Ellie wondered if all men were that way.

Aunt Myrtle waggled her brows as she set down a cream-ware vase, brimming with heavy-headed yellow blossoms. "Well, that was a surprise. Seems like a certain gentleman cannot bear the idea of retiring to the country without his favorite neighbor in the vicinity."

Ellie kept her expression neutral as she plucked at the pillow fringe, feeling foolish for letting her imagination run away with her. "Meanwhile, in London, he hardly knows I exist."

"You hold your heart in your eyes, dear. George would have to be blind not to see it. But some men simply aren't comfortable with showing their own affections openly. The important thing is, when he thinks of hearth and home, you are the one he pictures."

Aunt Maeve pursed her lips thoughtfully as she swept up the scattered petals with a brush of her hand. "Perhaps it wouldn't hurt if she kept *some* of her heart secret. It might be better if George had to question her devotion."

"But that isn't in her nature, sister. Our Elodie is unreserved in her emotions, and all the better for her. We were well into our forties before we sloughed off the skin of diffidence we'd inherited from our parents." She sighed, her gaze distant and unfocused. "I can only imagine what our lives might have been if we'd learned it sooner."

"To my way of thinking, a man should have to work for a woman's affection, not simply expect her to always be there for him."

"Quite true." Aunt Myrtle nodded in agreement then turned to look at Ellie. "Fear not, dear. George will come around. It's like I've always said, the Fates will have their way no matter what."

Strangely, as soon as the last word left her lips, a knock sounded on the door below and the mahogany longcase clock in the corner chimed the hour. In the same instant, a warm breeze unsettled the drapes over the open window and stirred the wispy tendrils at Ellie's nape in a shivering caress.

It seemed peculiarly prophetic.

Aunt Myrtle's brows inched toward her hairline. "You see, my dear? He has returned already. The Fates will keep putting the right one in your path, over and over again, until *both* of you finally realize that it was destiny all along."

"And that, sister, is a sentiment we both agree upon," Maeve said, then turned back to Ellie, whispering, "But try not to look so besotted. Make him come to you, because you deserve a man who puts forth effort."

She nodded. That was such a good point, she should write it down for the primer. Her gaze drifted to her writing desk in a cursory search, then swept over the ormolu table. Drat! Where was that ledger?

Hearing the steps growing closer and closer, her breath quickened. It would be difficult to keep her heart out of her eyes when she saw him, but she would do her best. And she dropped the pillow to the floor beside her. Just in case.

Mr. Rivers stood in the doorway, but it wasn't George he announced.

It was Lord Hullworth!

Ellie's heart jolted. She stared at her aunts, both mute and agape like her.

Then the man himself appeared and her throat went dry . . . before she remembered to close her mouth with a snap.

He filled the doorway, dangerously handsome in his tailored sable broadcloth. She'd seen advertisements for men who wore corsets and needed padding for their shoulders and calves. But after her much-too-close dance with him last night, she knew that he required no such artifice. He was solid and firm and had held complete mastery over his own form . . . *and* hers.

She swallowed at the recollection. Her hand lifted reflexively to cover the harried pulse fluttering on the side of her neck. His erudite gaze tracked the movement, missing nothing. And reclined as she was—with the shawl over her legs and stockinged feet—she felt peculiarly undressed in a way that she hadn't when George was here. As if Lord Hullworth had just walked in on her during a bath.

"My lord, I . . . did not . . ." Ellie began, but was saved the task of stammering on awkwardly when Meg appeared and summarily nudged him aside.

She swept into the room as if she'd been here to call a hundred times. "It seems like only hours since we last met," she said cheekily, her cheerful greeting settling some of Ellie's frazzled nerves.

"Minutes, even," she answered with a smile. To Meg, at least. To Lord Hullworth, she still wasn't sure how to arrange her features or what to say, other than, "Please do come in."

Just then, another gentleman appeared in the doorway, handsome and vaguely familiar with brown hair and round spectacles, and carrying a black valise at his side.

"Forgive the intrusion," Lord Hullworth said with an apologetic bow. "I hope you don't mind, but I brought a friend of mine from university to call on you. Miss Parrish"—he nodded, addressing the three of them in turn—"I should like to introduce Doctor Aiden Lockwood."

The man in question smiled cordially and bowed. "A pleasure."

After the introduction, her aunts quickly dragged Meg over to the corner curio cabinet, where they began wafting dimpled glass dishes filled with nougats and jellied comfits beneath her nose that she *simply must sample.*

"Dr. Lockwood," Ellie said, realizing where she'd seen the man before. "I believe we've met, during a time when you'd been called to Lord and Lady Hollybrook's house to tend one of their eleven rambunctious children. I know the eldest quite well."

His blue eyes brightened beyond the lenses with recognition. "Ah, yes. I knew you looked familiar. You're Miss Jane's friend—or rather, that would be Lady Northcott now."

She nodded, and her gaze darted between the two gentlemen, surmising the reason for the unexpected visit. "I hope you weren't prevailed upon to call on me over a simple misstep. It's hardly bothersome, truly."

"Not at all. Hullworth and I are old friends. And when he expressed concern over the damage to your limb, I was more than happy to offer my services."

Feeling that nervous rush inside her, she slid a wry glance to the marquess. "*Damage to my limb*, Lord Hullworth? Good gracious, you've made me sound quite like a fallen tree."

A grin quirked at the corner of his mouth. "Lockwood is the best lumberman I know."

"Well, I don't believe I'll need the axe this time," the doctor said genially as he approached. He tossed a glance over his shoulder and said, "Nevertheless, if you wouldn't mind waiting in the hall, Brandon . . ."

"Yes, of course." But he hesitated, his gaze colliding with Ellie's again. He seemed to be asking for permission to leave her with the doctor.

A bit of an afterthought, don't you think, she mused with the quirk of her brow. He shrugged in response as if she'd spoken aloud. When she nodded her acquiescence, he withdrew without delay.

Ellie expelled a breath. Her shoulders sagged as if she'd just been released from his embrace and couldn't support her own frame without him. And yet, hearing the creak of his footstep in the hall, just out of sight, kept her from giving in to the urge to rest against the concave corner of the settee.

This was all rather odd. She couldn't imagine why any of it was happening.

"If I may, Miss Parrish . . ."

Turning her attention to the doctor, Ellie bobbled her head in consent and fumbled under the shawl to slide down her stocking. Seated at the far end, the doctor examined her ankle with the remote efficiency that gave one comfort in such circumstances, even if one still suffered a case of acute embarrassment.

"Does this cause you pain?" Lockwood asked with concern.

Realizing that her brow was puckered, she schooled her features. "No, indeed. At the moment, I'm more confused than in discomfort. It's just that I shouldn't know why Lord Hullworth would trouble you over something so trifling. I'm practically a stranger to him." Her gaze shifted to Meg, who was walking toward her, leaving Maeve and Myrtle to argue the merits of candied orange peel over almond nougat. "I can only surmise that I made too much fuss at the park to cause needless worry to Miss Stredwick and, for that, I apologize."

"Not so," Meg insisted with a shake of her head. "Brandon was quite determined all on his own. In fact, we even went to three different shops to find a—"

From the hall, Lord Hullworth cleared his throat.

His sister quieted instantly, albeit with a roll of her eyes and a twist of a key at her lips as if there was some unspoken agreement of which she could not speak. "Nevertheless," she said cheerfully, "we are not strangers. After all, we have known each other above twenty-four hours. Were we mayflies, we would already be enjoying a second lifetime of friendship."

Ellie laughed but abruptly hissed when Lockwood found a rather sore spot.

"My apologies, Miss Parrish," he said and lowered the hem of her gown before draping the shawl over her bare foot. "On the bright side, no irreparable damage has been done."

"No need for the axe, then?" she teased.

He smiled affably and shook his head. "There is, however, evidence of a rather substantial bruise. By any chance, were there stones on the path where you turned your ankle?" When she nodded, so did he. "I'd thought as much. The contusion appears deep enough to cause tenderness for a while. There is a slight swelling but nothing unmanageable with plenty of rest, elevation, and a strong poultice."

"I have the perfect poultice recipe," Aunt Myrtle declared merrily.

Meanwhile, a ridiculous vision of attempting the quadrille whilst wheeling about in a Bath chair entered Ellie's mind and her spirits plummeted.

"That news does not bode well for the end of my Season." *Or marital prospects*, she thought, especially considering that this was her last foray into society before she was firmly on the shelf. And the odds of George remembering to visit the invalid, when he had so many other amusements to distract him, were slim indeed.

"If you do have an obligation to venture out, I suggest walking boots with firm laces and the aid of a cane if you have one," the doctor suggested passably, as if he hadn't just doomed her to spinsterhood.

"A cane." She sighed with utter despair at the prospect. Out of the corner of her eye, she saw Lord Hullworth emerge with unpardonable amusement lingering in that velvet gaze of his. She adjusted the shawl over her legs and shifted her attention to the doctor. "Thank you, Dr. Lockwood. I greatly appreciate the time you've taken out of your day to see me."

"I'm afraid I'm off as well," Meg said with obvious regret. "Brandon and I are attending dinner with the Dowager Duchess of Heathcote, and I must wear the blandest, most uninspiring white gown in my wardrobe or else earn her displeasure."

Dimly, Ellie found herself wondering if Miss Carmichael would also be attending the dinner and whether or not Lord Hullworth would sit beside her. Then she shook herself free of the thought. It did not matter in the least, she told herself.

Wanting to think about anything other than her random musings, she tapped her finger beside her mouth and considered the contents of her sewing basket. Then her gaze lifted to Meg's and she lowered her voice. "If you happen to have a tiny rebellious streak that you cannot tamp down for the life of you . . ."

"I do, very much," she said, eyes dancing.

"Then it just so happens that I stitched a small white crane the other day. The wings are ever so slightly lined with silver. And if you stitch it in place right about . . . here, I should think," she said, twisting to reach over her shoulder to tap a portion of the scapula, "it would hardly be noticed at all. Then again"—she shrugged and lifted her brows in impish challenge—"it might be noticed quite a bit."

Hearing the conversation, Aunt Maeve was already at the sewing box, opening the lid to retrieve the crane. Meg went to her and waved the little bird like a victory flag. "Thank you, Ellie. I'll call on you tomorrow with a full report."

"I look forward to it."

Before she could leave, Aunt Myrtle put a few comfits inside a handkerchief. Then Ellie watched Meg take the doctor's arm as they stepped into the hall. The aunts followed, chatting animatedly.

Ellie was surprised, however, that Lord Hullworth lingered behind.

He said nothing at first, but merely waited in the doorway, watching the others depart. Then he went back into the corridor only to return an instant later, holding a box. A rather long, rectangular box like the ones containing long-stemmed flowers. And it had a red ribbon on it as well.

She blinked up at him in confusion. "Did Mr. Rivers carry up a package during Dr. Lockwood's examination?"

"Not exactly," he said mysteriously and proceeded to place it across her lap. "Just open it, Miss Parrish."

"Overbearing," she muttered in singsong under her breath. Even so, she felt a thrill rush through her as she untied the ribbon and lifted the lid.

Inside the red velvet lining, lay a frilly lace parasol with a thick ivory handle, carved in the shape of a cockatoo's head, set with glittering amber eyes. It was surprisingly heavy. And beneath, she noticed the small white card.

As sturdy as a cane, but disguised as a parasol to shield your vanity.

She gasped and looked to Lord Hullworth, only to discover he'd moved to the doorway, ready to take his leave. "From *you*?"

He inclined his head. "Considering the fact that we are friends, I wanted to make amends for my skepticism regarding your injury."

There was something in the way he held her gaze that made her feel flushed from head to toe. Perhaps, it was merely the warm temperature of the room. Or perhaps . . . it was because Meg mentioned they'd visited three different shops. And all for her.

"This is an awfully pretty apology."

"As you say," he said simply.

She averted her face so he would not see her blush, and traced the delicate featherwork with the tip of her finger. "Does this mean I've managed to quell *all* your suspicions where I am concerned?"

Neither his answer nor the curl of amusement in his voice surprised her when he said, "I'm afraid not."

She nodded, believing him to be a hard-won skeptic. But she would convince him in time. "I really shouldn't accept this. There are rules of decorum that one must abide. After all, I cannot imagine you would allow Meg to accept such a thoughtful present from a gentleman, no matter what his reason."

He didn't respond and, when she looked again to the doorway, he was gone.

Ellie sank back against the settee on a sigh, wondering what this meant. But surely, considering the parasol came from *London's most elusive bachelor*—a man who was neither interested in marriage nor willing to trust his sister's newfound friend—it meant nothing at all.

Even so, the episode might be something worth jotting down in her ledger. If only she knew where it was.

Chapter 6

"Gentlemen are perplexing creatures. A debutante must resign herself to this irrefutable fact."

—A NOTE FOR *The Marriage Habits of the Native Aristocrat*

Brandon didn't know why he hadn't returned Miss Parrish's little ledger yet.

It had been a week since he'd first tucked it inside his inner coat pocket. A week of Meg visiting the town house on Upper Wimpole Street. In the very least, he could have given it to his sister when dropping her off from the carriage for her morning call, or left it with the manservant at the door when arriving to escort her home again.

And yet, he never remembered to do so.

Therefore, each night he would remove the palm-sized booklet from his pocket and place it on the marble top of his bedside table. Then, each morning, he would tuck it into a fresh coat and tell himself that he would see it returned promptly.

He never intended to read it.

After all, he had agreed to be her friend. He shouldn't have invaded her privacy. Or in the very least, the instant he realized that the pages contained Miss Parrish's private thoughts—instead of the collection of poetic verse he'd expected to find—he should have closed it at once.

But he had not.

He'd like to tell himself that he first opened the sueded

leather cover while alone in his study out of a sense of obligation to his sister, a need to protect her from a stranger he knew very little about. Since he valued honesty, however, he refused to lie to himself.

The truth of the matter was, he was curious about Miss Parrish. And not just in regard to her friendship with Meg.

He wanted to know more about her: the inner workings of her mind, how she passed her time, and why the color of her blush made his mouth water. His thoughts had become consumed by the shape of her mouth, that enticingly plump upper lip, and with the need to feel how their flesh would fit together. He wanted to taste her gasp, her tongue, that tiny fluttering pulse on the side of her throat.

But most of all, he wanted to know why he still felt this way *after* he'd read the damned ledger.

He still wasn't entirely sure about the purpose of the contents written on the pages in a neat, feminine scrawl. Though, it seemed to be a collection of her observations of gentlemen. Quite a number of gentlemen, in fact. Pages and pages of how they stood and talked and gestured with their hands.

But it was the last entries that left him the most irritated of all. They read:

> *Proposals*
> *The first, behind the hedgerow:*

> "I cannot let lack of fortune stand between us any longer. I care not what my family says; I must make you my wife."

> *What it lacks in forethought, it excels in passion—two sighs, zero swoons.*

> *The second, beneath the arbor:*

"I find myself inexplicably in love with you. Please do me the honor of becoming my wife."

A bit cliché and not quite as romantic as one would hope—zero sighs, zero swoons.

The third, by the fountain:

"You encompass every ray of sunlight and moonbeam. You are in every drop of rain that falls from the heavens. You are in my every breath and beat of my heart. And if I allow another moment to pass without securing your hand, then there is nothing left in this world for me."

Best of the day!—three sighs, one swoon.

Brandon had read the words so many times, they were now burned into his cornea and crammed inside his gray matter like wadding down a musket barrel.

If he'd wanted proof of her duplicitous nature, it was written on the pages—pages that were, even now—tucked inside his pocket. He felt the slap of them against the left side of his chest with every hard, agitated stride down the wet pavement near Regent's Park.

It was no more than an hour after dawn. The rising sun was trapped somewhere behind an impenetrable fleece of soot-gray clouds pressing down on the city. The air was heavy, charred and ripe, which seemed the perfect counterpart for the devil of a mood he'd been in all week.

Countless times, he'd wanted to show Meg the contents of the ledger. To prove that her *supposed* friend was obviously just another husband hunter. But he hadn't.

It was possible that Miss Parrish felt genuine fondness for his sister. In fact, if the ledger was any indication, she was quite capable of holding affection for a great number of people at once. *Quite capable, indeed*, he thought bitterly.

Three! Those poor sods. They likely had no idea that she'd moved on to another target, and had set her trap for *London's most elusive bachelor* instead.

Clearly, this meant she was just like all the others—a woman well practiced in artifice, who delighted in ensnaring men for sport, fully intending to rebuff their offers until the preferred one came along.

He couldn't help but wonder which one of these declarations had come from the mysterious *George*.

Beside the arbor?

Behind the hedgerow?

Or by the fountain?

Or . . . was *George* just a ploy she used to make a man believe she had no ulterior motive when she claimed to want nothing more than his friendship?

Brandon's hands curled into fists. He hated that her seemingly guileless request had intrigued him. Why had he allowed himself to be taken in by her, like a fly snared in a pretty spider's web? What a fool!

"Is that you, Lord Hullworth?"

He jolted, recognizing the soft voice. The hard soles of his boots skidded to a halt the instant his gaze alighted on the very tenant of his thoughts.

"Miss Parrish," he said to the face framed by the open window of a parked carriage. "Whatever are you doing out and about at such an hour?"

A pair of dark brows arched at the accusatory edge in his voice. "I was unaware, my lord, that you held dominion over the dawn, as well as the geese I was observing by the pond just now."

"I meant to say," he amended, "that I thought you would be resting as Lockwood suggested."

Beneath the curved brim of a straw bonnet tied with a red ribbon, she studied him shrewdly as if contemplating whether his brusqueness was a front for genuine concern—which it wasn't, of course—or if he was displeased to see her.

She must have decided on the former, for she inclined her head in quick forgiveness. "I am much recovered now and required some fresh air after an idle week. And to aid my first foray, a . . . *friend* of mine lent me the use of a rather sturdy parasol."

She lifted the handle of said object into view as if the carved cockatoo head remained a constant fixture in her grasp.

The thought warmed him . . . Until he felt the press of the booklet in his pocket.

Before he was drawn in too much by her well-rehearsed charms, he removed the small leather tome and lifted it toward her. "I forgot to return this to you when last we met. Apparently, my sister had carried it when you were injured."

"My ledger!" Miss Parrish clutched it in her hand, then against her shapely bosom. "Thank the saints. I've been searching for this all week. I thought I'd lost it."

Her unreserved show of gladness did nothing to alter his mood. In fact, it darkened ever more, resonating in a low thunderous growl.

"No, I'm sure you would not want to lose an accounting of your many conquests."

"My con—" She broke off. Her mouth pinched shut and her lashes scrunched together in perplexity. Then, suddenly, her expression opened, her lips parting on a startled bubble of laughter. "You thought that this was . . . that I kept . . . a tally of some sort? Oh, that is too diverting."

"Is it?" Unmoved by the gilded glint in her gaze, he felt his jaw harden to steel.

After a moment, she sobered and expelled an exhausted sigh. "I find your mercurial nature quite puzzling."

"I'm sure you do," he said. She was likely used to men grinning sappily as she went about spinning her silken cocoon around them.

"Yes, indeed," she assured tersely. "You are capable of such gallantry and generosity as to leave me speechless. And yet, for more than half of our acquaintance, you've been unreasonably cross with me. If that were not confusing enough, this morning you seem to be under the impression that I am capable of turning so many heads that I have the skills of a plate-spinning circus performer. I suppose I'm expected to thank you for the flattery. But I will not. I will say only that *this*"—she gestured with the ledger—"is my research for a book my friends and I are writing."

He crossed his arms, unwilling to be taken in yet again. "A book."

"*The Marriage Habits of the Native Aristocrat* to be precise," she said with a succinct, perturbed nod. "These are my observations of gentlemen who have matrimonial inclinations. Nothing you would be interested in, I'm sure." She huffed. "And shame on you for reading it."

Something niggled at the back of his mind.

He had a vague recollection of Meg going on and on at dinner one evening about Miss Parrish's numerous accomplishments, among which were kindness, generosity, seamstress extraordinaire, and . . . authoress of a guide for debutantes and their overprotective brothers. At the time, however, he'd just finished perusing the pages of the ledger and, piqued as he was, had refused to hear any praise regarding the inhabitant of Upper Wimpole Street.

But now he wondered . . . Could it be that the contents of that pocket ledger were merely a study of some sort?

If that were true, then she hadn't been toying with those men—or with him—after all. Perhaps there was no web.

Unfolding his arms, he stepped closer to the carriage. "I've been rather boorish again, haven't I?"

"Quite so."

The flesh between her wispy brows knitted with continued irritation. Her scolding tone was likely meant to put him in his place. However, unbeknownst to her, it had the opposite intended effect.

At once, his cerebral dark cloud dissipated. From the brassy glare in her eyes, he felt the first rays of amber sunlight warming him like a dram of cognac on a rainy evening.

A debutante who intended to ensnare him would not have passed up this opportunity to pout coquettishly or bat her eyes in order to suggest that a pretty display of temper was the worst he could expect from any discord. But Miss Parrish did nothing of the sort. She expressed her every thought and emotion candidly. Hiding nothing.

He found that inordinately appealing.

"I imagine that my behavior this morning would earn"—he darted a glance down to the ledger—"zero sighs and zero swoons."

"Indeed," she said, but the corner of her mouth twitched ever so slightly, telling him that he was on the road to forgiveness.

He likely didn't deserve it after harboring such animosity toward her. He'd been furious over her deception in a way that rivaled any he'd felt for other women in the past. And he wasn't even certain why it was different with her in particular.

All he knew was that being in London and enduring the tedium of the Season this past week while dwelling on her ledger had been utterly exhausting. In this moment, however, a charge of reinvigoration filled him. It rushed through his veins with new life.

"It seems that I have need to make amends once more. Name your recompense. The use of my box at the theatre? Trip to Paris?" he asked, only half teasing.

"You owe me naught, my lord. I suppose everyone is

entitled to a few moments of capriciousness, though *some* more than others."

As she spoke, an impish glint in her gilded eyes compelled him to step closer still. Close enough to catch the sweet clover fragrance that surrounded her. He inhaled deeply as his hand curled over the window casing.

Looking down, he noticed that his gloved fingertips rested on her side of the door with her red bonnet ribbon dangling just a scant inch or two away. He was struck by an uncanny urge to tug on it. To unknot her. To draw her to the opening between them and press his lips to hers.

"Then spend the day with me," he said, his voice low and intimate as his index finger extended to brush the angled edge of that ribbon.

Her gaze wandered dazedly over his face, her lashes drifting lower, her voice breathy. "With . . . with you?"

"We'll have a picnic. Nothing too taxing, of course. I know of a perfect glade just out of town. And while we're there, I'll even help you with your book."

She blinked in slumberous confusion like a dreamer waking. "My book?"

"You desire to know more about the ways of men and I," he said with a grin, "just happen to be a man."

Twin spots of color crested her cheeks, tempting his sweet tooth. "I'm not sure it's wise for us to be . . . quite so alone . . . together."

He hadn't meant the invitation to sound as if he planned a scandalous interlude. *Or had he?*

Regardless, an image of just the two of them flashed in his mind. Of her lying back, ebony curls spread over a blanket on the grass, her rosy lips swollen from his kiss, and her gaze filled with the desire she simply couldn't hide. A pleased hum of approval growled in his throat.

Without conscious thought, he took hold of her ribbon. But when their fingers briefly tangled, as she pulled the red silk from his grasp and withdrew into the carriage, he realized that he was being a bit forward.

Strange. That wasn't like him at all.

In fact, the more he thought about it, the more he realized he hadn't been quite himself since they'd met. He'd been ungentlemanly, surly at times, and now he felt strangely . . . *primitive*.

With a shake of his head, he called to mind the lifetime of manners and politesse reared into him. "Forgive me for not mentioning my sister in those plans. I know that Meg would love to spend more time with you and your aunts. The three of you are all she can talk about."

Miss Parrish expelled a breath of relief, lowering the shield she held over those ribbon ends. "I should have realized you were including all of us. It's silly but, for just a moment, I thought that you were actually"—she swallowed—"oh, never mind."

"Then it's settled. Shall I call on you in one hour or in two?"

"So soon? But it's still early morning and the weather doesn't appear to be in our favor and this is all quite unexpected," she said in a flustered rush and he could see the enticing flush of her cheeks even in the dark recesses of the carriage. "I'm not entirely sure what my aunts have planned and . . . Oh, but wait. I just recalled we have a prior engagement."

"Come now, Miss Parrish," he said with a tsk, "you need to be more convincing than that. It's far too late to begin playing coy with me. Besides, I'm quite determined to ignore any and all missishness."

She sobered at once and scoffed. "Playing coy, indeed. I'm hardly a member of your gaggle, Lord Conceit. The truth of the matter is, my aunts and I have already accepted an invitation to tour the Zoological Society Gardens."

"Clearly, the holder of your obligation does not know

that you were recently injured. I'm sure, whoever this person may be would readily postpone this outing for another day," he challenged with a flick of his brow, already feeling triumphant.

She held his gaze and said, matter-of-fact, "Oh, he knows."

"He?"

"Mmmhmm," she hummed with a decidedly smug nod. "I already assured him that I am hale enough. It would be unpardonably rude of me to accept another invitation."

Brandon studied her with acute scrutiny, remembering a similar expression the night he'd asked her to dance and she'd gladly refused him. He'd seen it at the park last week, as well. "And would this be *George*, by any chance?"

The same mysteriously invisible man who never claimed his waltz, nor bothered to appear in his phaeton? Who apparently had no surname or title?

The more he thought about it, the more he was inclined to believe that *George* had been invented by Miss Parrish to put Brandon in his place. And now, she must have felt the need to continue on with her charade. It was a ploy he could easily forgive since it did nothing to dampen his spirits.

"You needn't say his name in that manner," she said.

"I don't know what you mean. That is how I've always said *George*."

She pointed at him, her eyes narrowing. "There it is again. Your *G*s are very hard, indeed."

"Dreadful, I know. A failure of mine since my school days," he agreed in mock self-reproach. "I was forever disappointing my elocution master. Oh, the knuckle-rapping reprimands I suffered whenever I spoke of our king, not to mention *giants*, *giraffes*, and especially *gingerbread*. Even now, years later, I still shudder."

"You're being silly. From this point forward, I will not mention his name again in your presence."

Better and better, he thought, but nodded as if in solemn contemplation. "Likely for the best. It does make planning our picnic rather awkward."

"We are not having a picnic," she declared, but the firmness of her argument was lost in the midst of her reluctant puff of laughter. "I'm going to peruse the animal cages and likely be trampled to death by the Brahmin bull. It will be in all the papers tomorrow—*Unmarried Woman Dies Horrifically on First Expedition to the London Zoo*."

"*First expedition?* That cannot be true. Meg and I have been a number of times and it seems that all of England is there, too."

"Perhaps, but I've never been. I typically prefer events with far less likelihood of being crushed or eaten."

He was certain she was teasing, but the ludicrous portrait she painted just gave him an idea. Normally, he abhorred attending functions where society's unmarried female population gathered in droves. Today, however, he was going to make an exception. Then he would see firsthand who this *George* was. Or rather, if the man existed at all.

"Ah," he answered vaguely. "Well then, I suppose our picnic will have to be postponed . . . for now."

After bidding adieu, he tipped his hat to her and walked on, knowing that both he and Meg would be seeing her far sooner than she expected.

Chapter 7

"Debutantes, be on your guard. Some gentlemen
are little more than wild beasts in fine attire."

—A NOTE FOR *The Marriage Habits
of the Native Aristocrat*

Within five seconds of stepping beneath the arch at the Zoological Society Gardens, Ellie knew that some sort of unexpected calamity was bound to happen. She hated arches. Their shape reminded her of gravestones. And, therefore, everything she saw from that point on was bound to make her think of her own demise.

She wished George were here. A short while ago, he'd popped by the town house to tell them he'd thoughtlessly driven his high-perch phaeton without considering the number of passengers he would have. With a hapless shrug and a wink, he'd asked if they wouldn't mind taking a hack and meeting him by the bear pit.

By the bloodthirsty *bear*, of all things!

Her aunts had agreed without batting an eye. And so here Ellie stood, separated from that very beast—and certain death—by a flimsy barrier of wrought iron fencing and a low stone wall.

Eyeing the small rectangular enclosure with skepticism, she watched as the black furry creature scrambled up the pole in the center of his pen with alarming speed. No one told her that bears were so adept at climbing! What was to stop him from scaling the bars, escaping, and then eating the person who'd unthinkingly dressed herself in a walking costume the color of honey?

Nervously, she retreated a step.

Aunt Maeve and Aunt Myrtle returned from the nearby stall that sold little buns for the purpose of feeding the bear and elephant. Ellie didn't even want to think about the elephant!

Aunt Maeve studied the confection shrewdly. "Doesn't seem natural to feed buns to a bear."

"Aren't many *wilderness buns* that I know of," Aunt Myrtle agreed, leaning in for a sniff. Then she pinched off a corner and sampled it. "Not half bad."

"A little on the dry side," Maeve said, her lips undulating in appraisal. "But a pleasant enough flavor. Certainly better than those dust motes Lady Walmsley served us at tea the other day."

The bear shimmied halfway down the pole. His rapacious onyx eyes shifted to the bun her aunts were appraising, mouthful by mouthful. She could have sworn she heard the creature whimper with longing. Or perhaps that was her . . . because George was still nowhere in sight.

"He'll be here, dear," Aunt Myrtle said, but her voice canted downward slightly in an unmistakable admission of doubt.

Ellie pretended not to hear it. She responded with a hopeful nod and scanned the surroundings again.

Not far beyond the llama exhibit, a crowd formed, clotting the thoroughfare that curved around the pond. She worried briefly that something wild was on the loose. It wasn't unheard of, after all. Just two years ago there was an ill-fated elephant escape from the Exeter Exchange in all the papers. A shudder trampled through her, compelling her to sit on the stone wall.

George, she thought crossly, *why did it have to be the zoo?*

Absently, she glanced over her shoulder to the growling

bear, only to be startled half out of her wits. The terrifying creature was right beside her! She leapt up with a squeak, gripping the handle of the parasol to defend herself in her last moments on this earthly plane. Death by exsanguination was surely only moments away!

Standing in the pit on his hindlegs, Toby the bear reached up with his lethal paws and long, curling black claws toward a fallen cluster of crumbs at the wall's edge.

"Shoo! Shoo!" As she spoke, she pushed the crumbs with the tip of her parasol and into the kennel, watching as the bear sniffled the ground hungrily, exposing rows upon rows of sharp, debutante-devouring teeth. "You, sir, are a danger to society."

"Are you talking to that bear, Ellie?" a familiar voice asked from behind her.

Meg. Ellie's lips curved instantly. Just as quickly, and peculiarly, she also felt a thrill clamber through her at the thought of Lord Hullworth standing beside his sister. *But no, no, no,* she told herself. She should not be pleased to see him here. After all, his only reason for coming would be to spy on her. And shame on him!

However, instead of being perturbed, she was looking forward to scolding him. She did her best to hide her grin as she backed away from the pit and slowly turned. "I am, indeed. This bear deserves a proper setdown, much like your—"

She stopped short when she found Meg, and *only* Meg, standing there.

"My brother?" Meg asked, her blue eyes sparkling with undisguised mirth. "I couldn't agree more. After the way he pounded on my door, and far too early this morning, he deserves to be throttled for waking me from a perfect slumber to inform me that we had an urgent appointment to keep. He bid me to make haste, returning to my chamber every quarter hour to check my progress. Then, once I finally reached the bottom of the stairs to face Brandon the Clock-watcher, he surprised me with the news that we were on our way to the zoo. And, as you can see by my everyday bonnet and flourishless dress, I am not properly adorned for promenading."

Aunt Maeve clucked her tongue and Aunt Myrtle came forward to give her hand an affectionate pat. "Men can be so inconsiderate."

"Brothers especially," Meg agreed with a nod. "Adding to my confusion, he ordered the kitchen to pack a large picnic basket, which is waiting in the carriage as we speak. I honestly don't know what to expect next."

Aunt Myrtle was delighted. "A picnic! How splendid for you!"

"I do love a good picnic," Aunt Maeve agreed, "especially one abounding with an assortment of cold meats, minced pies and sharp cheeses."

"Oh, and you mustn't forget the tarts, sister, perhaps with hautboy strawberries. Or cherry would be lovely with a nice brandy glaze. And I simply adore fig with . . ."

Meanwhile, Ellie was fuming. Why, that presumptuous popinjay! "And where is he now, pray tell?"

Meg pointed toward the single brown beaver top hat amidst a throng of ladies and their plumed bonnets. "Getting his just deserts. He's currently holding court at the center of a rather rapacious gaggle."

"Good heavens!" Aunt Maeve declared. "Have they no shame?"

"Apparently not, sister. Why, there's one with her arms hanging about his neck who clearly knows nothing about the subtleties of successful flirting. She'll never charm a muffin man that way."

Meg sighed. "I suppose we should rescue him. Rumors about him being ready to marry have been abounding ever since his dance with Miss Carmichael. The methods of gaining his attention have been even more outrageous than before."

As they began to walk toward the horde, Ellie pushed aside her pique—at least for the moment—and observed the shocking spectacle. It was a wonder the women hadn't started to leap onto his back.

She'd seen him surrounded on multiple occasions, but his followers had never seemed so desperate. Part of her was angry on his behalf, while another part was angry *at* him for allowing this pawing. Why didn't he simply say that he wasn't interested in marriage? After all, he'd suffered no qualms about flatly telling *her*.

"Has he always had to deal with this attention from the fairer sex?" That would explain his conceit, she thought.

"Oh, no. Until recently, we lived a quiet life in Northumberland. We come from a respectable line, but not a very fashionable one. Our father was a younger son whose wealth was more in the contents of his heart than in his bank account. It was his elder brother, my uncle, who held the title, with my cousin to inherit."

Because the aunts made a point to acquaint themselves with details regarding every unmarried male in the aristocracy, Ellie had heard that some sort of tragedy surrounded Lord Hullworth's succession to the title, nearly ten years ago. However, she had not realized that he'd lost so many members of his family. And so had Meg.

Reaching out, she gave her friend's hand a squeeze. They shared a commiserating look between them that required no words, as if their friendship spanned years instead of days.

Meg smiled softly before she continued. "So when Brandon was younger and without title or great fortune, he only had aspirations to marry for love and have a family of his own. Unfortunately, the local beauty who'd stolen his heart had much loftier ambitions."

Ellie nodded. Everyone in the *ton* had heard the rumor of Lord Hullworth and *the one who got away*. That was all she knew of the matter. And yet, she wondered if there was a bit more to the story.

Her gaze strayed to him. Seeing him standing there, so straight and tall and handsome, it was almost impossible to think that any woman would have broken his heart. "I imagine she's filled with regret now."

"Perhaps," Meg answered thoughtfully. "Although, I do worry that he's never found anyone else. Our family comes from a long line of love matches. We are firm believers that, when we meet the one person we're going to marry, we simply know. We feel it from the roots of our hair to the marrow in our bones. It's called the *Stredwick certainty*. According to lore, it's supposed to work with both parties, overwhelming the destined pair with a sudden and irrefutable sense of *knowing*."

"And yet, your brother's certainty led him astray," Ellie said, understanding a bit more about his standoffishness.

Meg sighed. "I often wonder if Brandon and I didn't quite get our fair share of the fabled certainty."

Ellie had no opportunity to comment or reassure her friend due to the din of voices as they reached the outskirts of the mob, hearing seemingly respectable ladies practically offering up their daughters in sacrifice.

"You enjoy dancing? My Agatha is as graceful as a swan!"

"My Cordelia is a diamond of the first water and it's only her first Season. Just look at her. Prime pickings, my lord!"

"I have three daughters. Take as many as you like! Or take me, instead."

Lord Hullworth, who'd kept his expression remote until this point, looked aghast when the woman launched herself at him.

"Control yourself, madam." He turned sideways to wedge through a portion of the throng. "I've no intention of marrying any of your daughters."

As he spoke, his gaze was ever searching for an escape . . . until it collided with Ellie's. And held.

In that same instant, her heart gave the most disconcerting squeeze. There was an odd quickening in the pit of her stomach, too. She settled a hand over her midriff to quell this foreign ailment. Dimly, she wondered if she might have contracted some sort of bear fever from standing too near the bun-crazed beast.

Lord Hullworth took two steps but jerked to a halt when a girl was thrust in his path. "My Beatrice can heal your broken heart. Sweet as a lamb, she is!"

He blinked at the young woman whose white-blond hair was a fleecy mass of curls that, sadly, resembled a sheep in need of a good shearing. Then he looked at Ellie over the top of the frothy configuration. When his eyes widened, she knew they were sharing the same thought.

The entire episode was so comical that she forgot all about contracting bear fever, and her shoulders began to shake with insuppressible amusement.

Then Aunt Myrtle suddenly cried out, "Gracious sakes! Is that an elephant on the loose?"

Said at any other time, by any other person, Ellie would have been alarmed. Yet, when she saw Myrtle nudge Maeve in the ribs with her elbow, she knew it was only a ruse to cause a distraction. They were trying to save the marquess. And Ellie laughed behind her glove.

Aunt Maeve adopted the appropriate expression and truly looked surprised. "An escaped pachyderm! And he's coming this way!"

"Where? I don't see it?" Beatrice's mother asked skeptically.

Aunt Myrtle pointed vaguely behind the crowd. "Just beyond the hill and that copse of trees."

"I think I see it," first-water Cordelia said, after affixing a pair of spectacles to her nose. "Dear me! It *is* an elephant!"

At this, Ellie glanced absently over the hill, believing that there must have been a mistake. There couldn't actually have been an elephant on the loose. Surely, someone would've taken measures to prevent . . .

She stopped cold. It was true. The aunts weren't dreaming it up, after all. And the gray beast was headed their way.

"Oh, he's just a baby. And isn't he adorable with those floppy ears," Meg said, but then emitted a startled squeak when the creature lifted his trunk and trumpeted as he came charging toward them like they were the pins in a game of lawn bowling. *Baby*, though he may have been, he was still the size of a curricle.

One woman shouted, "Elephant on a rampage!" while another cried, "We'll all be crushed."

The mothers and their sacrificial daughters flurried about, knocking into each other before dispersing in a disorderly frenzy.

Ellie's humor at the situation vanished on a tremor of icy dread. This was how she was going to die, she realized. She would end up as some mangled victim of an elephant attack. She never should have come to the zoo. Drat it all, George!

Lord Hullworth found his way to her, Meg and the aunts, crowding closer with his arms spread to shield them from the ensuing melee. "We're going to have to run for it."

Aunt Maeve and Aunt Myrtle each linked arms with Meg. "We're a rather large target together. It will be better if we separate."

He agreed and settled his hand to the small of Ellie's back. She was stiff and unyielding, frozen in place. But the instant she felt the warm solid strength of his hand she moved reflexively, hurrying beside him without knowing where they were headed.

"Saved by a rampaging elephant calf," she heard him say but kept her gaze straight forward. "And you were quite the giggling spectator,"

"You should sell tickets for the next act and provide seating and refreshments," she said in a startled rush as another bleat trumpeted behind her and the ground thundered at their feet.

Lord Hullworth glanced over his shoulder. "Damnation, he's a fast little beast," he muttered under his breath. Then he cinched an arm tightly around her waist, shoring her against his side and supporting most of her weight. Under any other circumstance, their proximity would be quite scandalous. "This way, Miss Parrish. I don't wish to alarm you, but our friend seems to be following us. It must be how fetching you look in yellow."

Ellie tried to focus on her steps and *not* look at the alarmed faces of the people staring in horror at what was directly behind her shoulder. But she could feel her blood turn colder, her limbs stiffening, her hand numb around the handle of the parasol.

"I wish . . . I had my . . . embroidery," she panted inanely. "I always embroider when the world is coming to an end."

He chuckled as if he thought her jesting. "No need to fret. Just think of this as having your own personal guide through the zoological gardens. Ah, here we are passing the parrot exhibit. They're in fine feather today. And next we're approaching the giraffes. Would you like to stop there on your pell-mell tour?"

She cast a wary glance toward the pair of tall spotted animals as their heads tilted, following her every movement with their large dark eyes. "Please don't. Quite honestly, I stayed awake half the night worried about something terrible happening . . . like being eaten by a giraffe."

"I believe they are herbivores."

"Sure, that is what everyone thinks. But how does anyone really know? Have you ever asked a giraffe if he wouldn't prefer a filet of beef over a bowl of lettuces?"

"Now that you mention it, no, I have not," he answered,

his tone light with amusement just as he darted behind one of the brick shelters. Stopping for a moment, he peered around the corner, still holding her firmly at his side. Then he set her on her feet. "The little beastie turned off in another direction and there's an army of caretakers right on his heels. We should be safe here for a moment or two."

"No one . . . can promise that. Especially not you. Why, you cannot even protect yourself from husband hunters."

Ellie leaned stiffly against the support of the brick wall at her back, her lungs tight from oxygen deprivation. First, it was death by trampling, and now by suffocation. Either way, she was never going to make it out of the zoo alive.

Her body would likely be picked apart and eaten by carnivores and *supposed* herbivores alike. At her funeral, her aunts would wail and mourn and surely demand that a bench be erected in her honor for all who visited this terrible death trap. A bench, so that future victims could be presented on a convenient platter, instead of forcing the animals to chase after them.

Lord Hullworth set the crook of his finger beneath her chin and tilted up her face for scrutiny. Then he frowned. "You really are afraid, aren't you?"

Much to her dismay, she felt the mortifying prickle of tears behind her eyes. "Only of dying . . . and of all the things that cause one to die prematurely . . . and of being closed in a coffin . . . with heaps and heaps of dirt and worms shoveled on top of me. I know it's irrational but I can't seem to help it."

"Miss Parrish," he said softly. "Nothing terrible is going to happen. I won't allow it."

Ellie had no idea how he could make such a promise, or why he felt the need to take hold of one of her hat ribbons as he had done early this morning. This time, he tugged the knot free. Blinking up at him in question, she wondered at his intent as he eased her hat away and let it fall to the grass beside them. Her gaze followed the bonnet where it rested on the ground.

"There now," he crooned, gathering her in his arms.

A shuddering sigh left her as he pulled her rigid body against his solid form. Not too far off in the distance, chaos ensued. She could hear the bleats of the elephant, the quick padding of footsteps on the path, men shouting and a few female shrieks.

But here in the shelter of his embrace, her focus lingered on the steady drumming of the heart beneath her ear. The warm breath that drifted across her temple. The splayed hands stroking down her shoulders and along her spine in a soothing rhythm, coaxing the air back into her lungs.

She inhaled deeply. Beneath the faint fragrance of the collective horde's cloying perfumes, she found his scent. How peculiar that it was already familiar to her. And he smelled exceptionally good. The combination of cedar, fresh linen and spicy clove—perhaps from his shaving soap—blended together with the heat of his body to form a heady elixir that made her drowsy and relaxed.

She melted against him, forgetting about the rest of the world. In her mind's eye, she pictured the two of them huddled close together in the middle of the zoo, barely hidden from the crowds. It would be scandalous if they were caught. And yet she couldn't summon any desire to separate herself from him.

"How is your limb faring?" Lord Hullworth murmured, the vibration of his voice tunneling warmly inside her.

"If you want the truth," she said gravely, "at the moment, I'm not certain that I still have limbs."

Her entire being seemed comprised only of the portions pressed to him—her cheek, stomach, breasts, hips. He drew back marginally and began a careful assessment. Nothing untoward. And yet, she gradually became more aware of other parts as if she was being reanimated into being by the brush of his hand on her hip, his palm trailing upward along her side to her shoulder, and his tactile fingertips skimming over the fragile curve of her neck to settle gently beneath her jaw.

He must have removed his gloves, for she felt the touch of his skin against her own, welcome but also startling in the way the sensation fizzed through her.

He lifted her face, those gray-green eyes studying her with the close inquiry of a physician gauging the severity of this new ailment. "You're still quite pale. Are you in any pain? Did I jostle you too roughly during our escape?"

"No," she said at once in reassurance. "You've done nothing wrong. It's just . . ." She felt her brow pucker in bewilderment over these foreign sensations. "I'm strangely light-headed and buoyant. And I don't wish to alarm you, but the blood in my veins feels rather effervescent, like champagne bubbles in a fluted glass. My bones are as insubstantial as feathers."

She felt a coil of tension roll through him, and watched as his pupils expanded in spills of inky black. Then he crowded ever closer as if he feared she would float away on the barest breeze.

"And is your pulse racing?" He didn't wait for her answer. Instead, his fingertips drifted down to the quick hummingbird wingbeat at the side of her throat. "And has your mouth gone dry just now? Your lips plump and tender?"

She nodded, mystified. "You're very good. Doubtless, you could have become a physician. Do you think we should summon Doctor Lockwood?"

"No. Lockwood cannot help you with this," he said, his tone edged with a low growl that left her to wonder if this was far more serious than she thought. Before she could ask his opinion on her chances for survival, he leaned in and said, "Only I can."

And then he eased his mouth over hers.

Chapter 8

"A debutante must hold fast to her wits, especially when a gentleman is determined to scramble them into oblivion."

—A note for *The Marriage Habits of the Native Aristocrat*

Ellie was stunned. A fatal prognosis would have been less startling. But Lord Hullworth didn't seem shaken at all. He simply drew the sound of her gasp into his mouth as his lips took firm possession of hers. Then he fed her a hum of approval as if sampling something lush and decadent, and the intimate vibration made her heart quicken to a perilous speed.

Flustered, she didn't know what to think. *Or* what to do. Her hands flitted at her sides like scattered leaves caught in a sudden whirl. She should have pushed him away. Reminded him about George. But as he continued his tender assault on her lips and senses, smoothly taking hold of her hands to drape them over his shoulders, she could not fight the unfathomable pull to stay in his arms.

The warm press of his broad, enticingly firm mouth over the tender flesh—which had been sorely neglected these past five years—sent a staggering zing of pleasure all the way to the soles of her feet. Then the sensation traveled back up through her veins in lovely spiraling tingles. It filled her with a sort of restless urgency that demanded more. So she rose up on her toes and pulled his mouth harder against her own.

She felt the curve of his grin beneath her lips. It was likely one of his smug grins, where he was all too pleased with himself. But she didn't care. She simply wanted this to last a bit longer. In her experience, a kiss never continued past the time that it took to inhale the moment. Such a brief delight destined to fade like the sweet brandied steam of a pudding under a silver cloche.

But, surprisingly, Lord Hullworth lingered, nuzzling into one corner of her mouth and then the other. Her heavy-lidded eyes drifted closed as his hands skimmed along her back. She felt the slightly roughened pads of his fingertips trace the delicate curve of her nape, sifting lightly through the downy hairs. A contented purr escaped her at his touch. And she smoothed her palms over the expanse of broad-cloth, stretching like a cat against the hard planes of his body.

A soft grunt of surprise left him. The thin summer wool of her frock was now clenched in his fists, drawn taut over her frame. He angled her head beneath his, taking her mouth in impatient tugging sips, first the bottom lip and then the top. He coaxed her mouth open, the tip of his tongue nudging inside to explore the dewy shallows in slow massaging licks.

Again, she gasped. The contact was shocking, indeed, sending darting pulses on a deep descent into the pit of her stomach, liquid and heavy. She'd never experienced kisses like this. At least, not in her waking life. Sometimes in daydreams, she imagined being thoroughly ravished and breathless to the point of fainting, like the heroines in the torrid novels she borrowed from Aunt Myrtle. But she always felt a trifle guilty and embarrassed afterward. She never imagined it would feel this good.

So she licked into his mouth, too. She tasted heat and salt and some unknown delicious spice that she suddenly needed more than anything else in the world. *More. Please. Yes.* He growled, the sound low and hungry and urgent. And the kiss deepened, his tongue tangling with hers as he searched the silken recesses of her mouth.

Curls of illicit pleasure spiraled through her, dragging a strange—decidedly wanton—mewl from her throat. Ellie felt sampled and savored like a sumptuous dessert buffet. The well-bred, respectable part of her knew she should demur and protest his advances, but it wasn't in her nature to put up a false show. This felt too good. Too right. And, besides, it was just one kiss, after all. It meant nothing. So she gave herself over to it, her neck arching in complete surrender. He could be as smug as he liked . . . as long as he didn't stop.

Then he drew her closer still, their bodies falling into an unexpected, but blissful, alignment. And in the frenzied, clinging moments that followed, all the activity of the surrounding world seemed to fade away.

On a gruff groan, he broke the kiss, soothing her flesh with the tip of his tongue along the swollen seam. His open mouth drifted along the unexplored underside of her jaw to that pulse on the side of her neck, sending a lovely clench of pleasure to her midriff.

"It's no use," he said, his voice hoarse, his breath falling heavily against her lips.

Dazedly, she stretched upward, seeking his mouth like a ravenous nestling. "What is *no use*?"

"I cannot fight this any longer. I'm going to start paying calls on you, Miss Parrish . . . Ellie," he said against her lips. Then smoothed the dark fringe away from her forehead to kiss along her brow, her closed eyes, and her flushed cheeks. "Mmm . . . You do taste sweet here, like those little cakes covered in pink icing."

"Petits fours?"

"Yes, those," he said, returning to her mouth. "I'm going to take you to the theatre, on drives through the park, out for ices on hot afternoons . . ."

Something about his declaration didn't make sense. But she was so distracted by these knee-melting kisses that she couldn't put her thoughts together.

Once she did, however, she realized her confusion stemmed from the fact that he was *London's most elusive bachelor* and paying calls on a young woman was something only a man interested in marriage would do. Wasn't it?

She withdrew slightly, her hands shifting from his nape to his shoulders, and she blinked up at him. "To be clear, you mean to *pay calls* as one friend to another?"

He gazed back at her thoughtfully, seeming to ponder his response with the gravity of a man questioning the state of his own existence. After a moment, he simply said, "Yes."

His tone was so sensible, so matter-of-fact, that it should have settled her confusion. And yet, it didn't. For some strange reason, her mind conjured an image of him dancing with Miss Carmichael and a peculiar ailment began to twist hotly in her stomach.

Ellie frowned. "And just how many other female *friends* do you kiss?"

Brandon gave her a small laughing smile as if she should know the answer. Then he stole another kiss. "There's just you."

His straightforward reply loosened the knot in her stomach, but something else lingered in its stead. She realized at once that it was guilt.

Remember George? her conscience prodded.

"And when you call on me, you'll be assisting with my book," she added, almost as if she were trying to give herself permission, the way she did when she allowed herself to have a second slice of cake on Sundays. "Therefore, I'll simply explain the situation to *G*—or rather—to the person whose name I cannot say. I'm sure he'll understand."

Lord Hullworth chuckled. "Tell the truth, Ellie. Isn't this *George* just someone you made up in order to incite my interest?"

"Whyever would you think that?" Yet, as she asked the question, she realized her fingers were threaded in his hair while her body was molded against his. Somewhere, pressed between them, were the blurred lines of their burgeoning friendship.

Gradually, she lowered her hands to his broad chest to put distance between them. "I suppose I must take partial blame for making the mistake of referring to him with the familiarity gained by a lifetime of acquaintance. From this point forward, however, I will refer to him as—"

She didn't have a chance to finish.

In the same instant, Meg's voice interrupted, calling out her brother's name.

The sound was near enough to send alarm sprinting through Ellie. Oddly, she hadn't felt so exposed while *in* his embrace. *Out* of his embrace, however, she understood what it must have been like for Eve, the moment she realized that she'd been frolicking naked out of doors.

Ellie wrapped her arms around herself. "Good heavens! Your sister! My aunts are bound to be with her. They'll know everything at a glance."

He quickly scrutinized her face, expelling a rough exhale with a shake of his head. "You're quite right. Your cheeks are flushed, your lips bee-stung, and with your propensity to stammer when nervous—"

"I do not," she protested.

"—there'll be no disguising the truth. And yes, you do," he said softly, daring to reach out to brush the pad of his thumb into the divot between her chin and her mouth, his gaze lingering there. "Though, if I'm to be honest, it's quite charming."

She felt her cheeks catch fire when he leaned in and took one last fleeting kiss.

Flustered, she said, "You must stop doing that. I'll surely die of self-combustion. My aunts would never forgive you if I disintegrated into a pile of ash. And what in the world are you doing with my hat?"

She watched as he snatched it up from the ground, then sent it sailing with a swish of his arm. Turning to her, he held a finger to his own lips and whispered, "Just follow my lead."

Then in a robust voice, he called out, "Ah ha! There is your hat, at last. It appears as though the wind has whipped it into that tree."

Hardly convincing since there was scarcely a breeze, but Ellie went along with the charade to save her reputation.

Unfortunately, her acting ability left much to be desired. "Dear me! What a terrible turn of events. Whatever will happen to my poor hat . . . which is now dangling from that . . . um . . . branch?"

He cast a dubious glance over his shoulder, his mouth quirked in reluctant amusement. "Fear not, Miss Parrish. I shall recover it."

Just then, Meg rounded the corner of the brick building. "There you are, Brandon! I've been looking everywhere. And poor Ellie," she said rushing to her side. "You've had to endure his company all this time. Was he a terrible grump to you?"

Conscious of her kiss-swollen lips, she pressed her fingertips there as if she were studiously contemplating her answer. "I wouldn't necessarily call him a . . . that is to say . . . he was actually quite . . . unexpectedly . . ."

"I believe Miss Parrish is trying to say"—he broke in, returning with her manhandled hat and presenting it to her with a gallant bow—"that she enjoyed our sojourn off the beaten path immensely, believing that it far surpassed all others."

She would have surely blushed anew, giving them both away, if not for his smug smirk. "*All others?* A very bold statement, indeed. Some might even call it an arrogant assumption."

"As you say," he offered with a nod.

Though it would have been better if he didn't hold her gaze for so long and if the low timbre of his voice didn't curl warmly inside her. Her gaze flitted to his mouth and her lips tingled with longing.

Yes, she admitted to herself, it had surpassed all others. In fact, she wanted to kiss him again. This instant. Drag him into the nearest copse of trees and fling her arms around him.

What in the world was wrong with her?

"Oh, dear! I'd better fetch your aunts," Meg said hastily, withdrawing. "They'd just spotted an acquaintance before I heard Brandon's voice and I scampered off. They're right around the corner."

As her friend left, Ellie helplessly met Lord Hullworth's gaze. "You cannot look at me. When you do, all I can think about is . . . well, you know . . . and if I think about that . . . then this"—she pointed to her reignited cheeks, casting all the blame on him—"will happen again and again."

His grin returned as he took a half step toward her. Stripping the hat from her hands, he situated it with care on her coiffure, his voice low and intimate as he said, "That's going to be a problem. Knowing the reason for your blush only makes me want to kindle it all the more."

She didn't have a chance to reprimand him or even take a breath to fight a sudden rush of giddiness. Because, in that very same instant, she heard his sister speaking to her aunts nearby.

Then came another voice, one that was nearly as familiar to her ears as her own. Ellie shifted uncomfortably as the deep baritone filtered in through the surrounding shrubbery.

"Oh, dear," she whispered, guiltily worrying the corner of her well-kissed mouth. "It's George."

Lord Hullworth whipped around so fast she felt the breeze stir her bonnet ribbons. And just as the party entered the clearing, he looked down at her, his brow furrowed. *"Nethersole?"*

"Don't tell me you failed the letter *N* in elocution class as well," she muttered under her breath as the others aimlessly made their way toward them, chatting amongst themselves.

Out of the corner of her eye, she observed a change in Lord Hullworth. His posture, though always impeccable, became stiff and strained as if he'd been posing for a statue for hours, his profile chiseled out of granite. And while he was—only moments ago—warm, playful and passionate, he was now decidedly cold and distant.

Ellie frowned. As startling as it had been to lose herself in his embrace, to have been pressed so ardently and intimately against him, she found this sudden alteration even more disconcerting. It was like stepping barefooted from burning coals to a frozen lake. And the uncertainty of it all bothered her more than she cared to admit.

So, she pushed the thought aside, adjusted the seam of her gloves and pasted on a smile for those who were far more constant in their temperaments.

"George, you're here at last." Hearing a growl from the man beside her, she cast an uncertain glance to Lord Hullworth to see a muscle ticking along his jaw. "I mean, Lord Nethersole, of course. Are you acquainted with Lord Hullworth and Miss Stredwick?"

"Indeed," George said with his usual affable grin. "Hullworth and I have been known to frequent the same parties. As for Miss Stredwick, she and I were introduced at Broadhurst's ball last month. Unfortunately, I arrived too late to snag a dance, as her brother had so quickly informed me that her card was full." He cast a playfully dubious glance toward Lord Hullworth, earning a giggle from Meg. Then he turned his attention to Ellie with a dramatic shake of his head and a hand to his heart. "And since you weren't present either, I was set adrift on a sea of desolation. I barely summoned the will to venture into the cardroom."

George finished his monologue with a wink to her and she rolled her eyes at his silly flirtations. "Well, I'm certain Lord Hullworth will have no objection to leaving us in your care."

"But I would," Meg interjected before her brother could offer his opinion. "Brandon, you cannot allow them to leave us. With such an adventurous start to our day, I'm eager to see how the rest of it will fare. We're bound to have something even more monumental happen by day's end."

The prospect of something *more monumental* terrified Ellie, and she wasn't even thinking about the elephant. No, her thoughts were solely on that kiss. Her body issued an immediate pulse-fluttering, head-dizzying, stomach-tilting response. She was sure that such sensations weren't beneficial to one's longevity.

Helpless, her gaze strayed to him. He looked back at her and, for an interminable moment, said nothing, his expression inscrutable. But, drat it all, she felt the slow saturation of heat rising to the crests of her cheeks. To hide her blush, she turned her head under the pretense of tying the ribbons of her bonnet.

"You're quite right, Meg. My apologies, Nethersole, but I simply cannot relinquish my claim on Miss Parrish"—he paused long enough for her attention to whip back to him—

"and her aunts. I plan to take them on a picnic this afternoon. You are welcome to come along, of course."

His manner was perfectly genial as if they'd discussed this and she'd agreed. As if they'd spent all those moments alone having a friendly chat and making plans instead of learning the taste and texture of each other's tongues. And not only that, but in his tone there was a palpable edge of unspoken tension that Ellie did not quite understand.

George seemed to, however. He chuckled but his grin didn't reach his eyes. "The way I see it, their plans for the day were with me. So if anyone is going to take them on a picnic, it shall be I. Though *you* can come along, of course."

"Have you plans, then?" Lord Hullworth inquired with a lift of his brows. "Because I have a basket packed to the brim and waiting in the carriage already. There will be plenty enough for all. And you can drive that *phaeton* I've heard so much about, while I take the ladies in the comfort of my open landau."

Ellie could have sworn she heard the combined growls, roars and snarls from every single male animal in the zoo at once.

Wondering if anyone else noticed the peculiarity of the exchange, she looked past George to her aunts. But they were distracted in conversation, animatedly whispering, likely about the contents of said picnic basket.

Meg, on the other hand, was staring at her brother as if she'd never seen him act this way before. Hmm . . . Perhaps Ellie wasn't the only one wondering where the next step would lead.

George magnanimously offered, "Far be it from me to spoil a perfect picnic. However, since I had intended to have the ladies over for tea this afternoon, then I insist"—he paused to flash a smile—"that you and your sister join all of *us* at my town house. Bring your basket, if you like."

The marquess nearest to her inclined his head in agreement. And it seemed as though George had had the last word on the matter. But Ellie was proven wrong in the next moment.

Lord Hullworth stepped around her to retrieve the fallen parasol. Yet, instead of offering it to her, he proffered his arm. "Miss Parrish?"

She accepted without realizing it would cause one marquess's eyes to flash with annoyance while the other grinned back smugly.

Chapter 9

"A debutante must never miss an opportunity to exhibit her charms."

—A NOTE FOR *The Marriage Habits of the Native Aristocrat*

So the renowned *George* was real after all.

Brandon should have known. Everything he'd learned about Miss Parrish suggested that she couldn't tell a lie to save her life. She'd been honest with him from the beginning.

There was truth in the way she responded to every situation, and truth in her words. Which meant that, when she'd told him she'd set her cap for George, she'd had no ulterior motive. She'd simply been stating a fact.

Then, why had he so adamantly refused to believe her?

As he sat on a garden terrace in Grosvenor Square, listening with half an ear to the Marquess of Nethersole recount the endless tale of how he'd outbid all competitors at Tattersall's for the finest grays in all of England, the answer came to Brandon in disgruntled self-mockery. Because at some point over the past few years he'd grown so used to the sly machinations of women trying to marry him, that he actually started to believe that *every* woman was trying to marry him.

How ridiculous that sounded to him now! And he knew that if Miss Parrish were privy to his thoughts in this moment, she would call him *arrogant* and there would be mirth dancing in her eyes.

Imagining such an exchange, he felt a grin tug at the corner of his mouth. His gaze drifted to the occupant of the chair at the far corner of the rectangular wrought iron table.

In the same instant, her hat tilted away from the speaker and she glanced alertly at him as if he'd called her name aloud. He hadn't, of course. He didn't know why she turned just then. But their gazes caught and held, nonetheless.

His pulse raced, blood burning through his veins. And he wasn't alone. Her cheeks colored swiftly with her own inner heat, as if she couldn't stop thinking about their kiss either. Couldn't stop tasting him on her tongue. Couldn't stop wanting to relive those stolen moments over and over again . . .

Her lips parted on a breath. He exhaled his own. Then he reminded himself that thoughts like those would do him no good. And, at the opposite end of the table, she turned away, the brim of her hat shielding that pink-icing glow from him.

Brandon noticed that Miss Parrish didn't blush at all when she looked at *George*. She merely wore a soft smile like a woman admiring a basket of puppies. He was partly gratified by this knowledge, especially when he recalled how unfamiliar those *ailments* were to her when he'd held her in his arms. Which clearly meant that Nethersole had never stirred her passions in the way that Brandon had.

Yet, in the end, that knowledge didn't matter in the least. She had made her choice, and he felt five times the fool for not having believed her from the start. Perhaps then, he might have saved himself the embarrassment of declaring his intentions to court her. Saved himself from entertaining the fleeting notion that, perhaps, he'd finally found—

No. He refused to finish the thought.

"It seems that Ellie is quite at home here," Meg whispered from the chair beside his.

Brandon shifted in the ironwork chair, feeling as though

it was a cage forming around him as he acknowledged the truth. "She does, indeed."

Their host concluded his tale but quickly began describing his most recent race on Rotten Row. If the past hour was any indication, this was going to take a while.

"If not for her," Meg added, "I daresay, we would be returning with a full basket *and* our tails between our legs."

He, too, had witnessed the quiet exchange between Miss Parrish and the housekeeper when they'd first arrived and the subtle instruction for the footman to carry his basket to the kitchens. Not long after, the servants brought out silver trays carefully adorned with the picnic food as if it were being served during a seven-course service.

Though it was clear that Nethersole remained oblivious. He'd boasted that no other cook knew how to assemble such an excellent meal in great haste like his very own.

Miss Parrish had the grace, not only to leave Nethersole uncorrected but to give her compliments to Brandon when she'd said, "I'm certain no picnic has ever been more thoughtfully provided or filled with such a variety of sumptuous fare."

In short, she was an ideal hostess . . . but for a house that was not hers.

Nethersole didn't appear to mind, however. In fact, as far as Brandon could tell, he didn't truly run his house at all. He offered no direction to his servants, but left them floundering.

Both the butler and housekeeper were visibly relieved when Miss Parrish had taken charge, informing the staff of the impromptu picnic on the terrace. She ensured that umbrellas were set in place, that rose-patterned china dressed the table, and sent instructions to the kitchen to bring tea and lemonade but to wait for coffee until the end.

Brandon knew from years of managing his own house

that the servants had enough to do without having to wonder about place settings and menus and the like. And so he admired the ease with which she saw to these tasks.

But it grated on his nerves to see her playing the part of a wife for a man who behaved like a spoiled child.

"Our host is terribly charming and handsome," Meg offered thoughtfully. "But what I don't understand is why you do not like him. Even from the moment I was first introduced to him, you were all gruff-mannered. You even lied about my dance card being full."

"Perhaps I find him a bit *too* charming."

By all accounts, Nethersole was a veritable tomcat. Whenever a rumor went flying about illicit trysts behind closed doors, he was the first to take credit by boldly proclaiming innocence with a sly grin on his face. And he lapped up the accolades from his lordling sycophants like a bowl of Devonshire cream.

Brandon wasn't certain if Nethersole was an actual libertine or just pretending to be, out of some misconstrued notions about proving his manhood. For the sake of caution, however, he was keeping Meg far from the likes of that notorious flirt.

"Ellie doesn't mind."

"No, she doesn't." That also bothered Brandon.

She seemed blind to George's shortcomings in a way that reminded Brandon of himself when he'd been besotted with Phoebe. She, too, had been an outrageous flirt. But he'd found her bold and carefree nature utterly entrancing. It had never entered his mind that she'd been toying with his affections. That it was all just a game to her.

Then the shades had been stripped from his eyes. And, unless he was wrong about Nethersole, that same thing would happen to Miss Parrish one day.

Not that it was his concern. He'd learned long ago not to trifle with a woman whose affections were not his to claim.

"All this talk about racing is quite thrilling," Myrtle Parrish interjected during one of the scant moments Nethersole drew a breath. "And your new phaeton and horses are quite the thing for a young bachelor, I'm sure, gadding about town, the envy of all . . ."

Maeve Parrish cleared her throat and quickly added, "But for a man with his eyes on a happy future and a glowing bride by his side, perhaps he might make his next purchase one that is a bit more sedate."

Nethersole laughed with mock alarm. "Don't saddle me with a perambulator quite yet, ladies. There's plenty of time for all that fuss and bother. Right, Hullworth? *London's most elusive bachelor* certainly isn't rushing to the parson for the ole shackles."

"No, indeed," Brandon said, as if by rote. But when he saw the look of commiserating triumph on his host's face, he felt it necessary to add, "However, I'm not opposed to the institution of marriage. My own parents were quite content. Their example of genuine affection, mutual trust and support left a lasting impression on me. I will not settle for less. And I wouldn't want my sister or any friend of hers"—he glanced to Ellie—"to either."

"No one could find fault in such an admirable pursuit," she said to him with a warm smile.

"No one?" his sister interjected. "Ellie, you're supposed to be my friend first. And this *admirable* brother of mine refuses to believe I can make my own decisions regarding my own future."

"Forgive me, Meg. I forgot myself for a moment," Miss Parrish said, pulling her gaze from his to grin conspiratorially at his sister. "You are right, of course. Any man who doubts a woman's right to choose her own happiness is a veritable ogre, mercly disguised in gentleman's attire."

"Even if said *ogre* wants to ensure that his sister has experienced enough of the Season to make a well-informed choice?" he asked, having heard this argument from Meg countless times before. When she was eighteen years of age, his sister believed she'd found the one she was meant to marry. But since Brandon had firsthand knowledge of how foolish one could be at that age, he'd asked her to wait and experience more of life. Thankfully, the man she'd set her cap for had agreed.

"After all," he continued to Miss Parrish, "is that not your intention with the guidebook you're writing?"

She inclined her head in agreement and then the corner of that tempting mouth curled up wryly. "But I do not intend to beat future readers over the head with it. After all, there is a lesson in self-discovery as well, my lord."

Even though it wasn't her intention, his thoughts traversed beyond the walls of this garden and dropped back into an empty glade when he was making some indisputably enjoyable discoveries of his own. Like the way her plump upper lip nestled perfectly between his own, and the way wanton sounds spilled from her lips when his tongue found that delectable fluttering pulse at her throat.

And just like that he was more than half-aroused. *Bloody hell.*

Shifting uncomfortably, he cleared his throat. "Point well made, Miss Parrish."

Brandon really needed to banish that memory from his mind permanently. But that would be impossible, at least for the remainder of the Season. They were bound to attend the same events. Her close association with Meg would ensure that they were in the same company, as well. Therefore, he would simply have to school his responses. Imagining the difficulty awaiting him, he reached for his glass of lemonade and drained the last of it.

"Speaking of new ventures, I have an announcement of my own," George interjected proudly on his favorite topic—himself—and waited for every eye to fall upon him in rapt anticipation. Once satisfied, he drew in a great lungful and said, "I am taking a house in Wiltshire. My steward has been scouting properties for the past two weeks. That will give the four of us a fine place to rest our heads when we journey there, and a capital spot for my hunting trips."

Myrtle gave an excited clap. "George, that's wonderful!" And Maeve clucked her tongue fondly. "Such a dear boy to think of us."

Ellie's brow furrowed. "That is a surprise. You gave no indication that you were already planning a trip to Wiltshire when we spoke of it a few days ago."

Nethersole shrugged and gave her an easy smile. "Must have forgot. I thought you'd be pleased by the news."

"Renting a house is a lovely thing to consider," she said kindly. "However, it may take a good deal of time to conclude the leasing of a property. Not to mention, readying it for habitation and hiring a staff."

A sensible argument, Brandon thought.

But further proof of Nethersole's immaturity was his immediate reply of "I'm sure it will all sort itself out."

Ellie issued an uncertain nod, then turned to Meg and Brandon, graciously opening the conversation to include everyone present. "I have a friend in Wiltshire whom I have not visited for far too long. My aunts and I were planning to venture there at Season's end. We hope to tour the county. I've heard of its beauty. Have you ever been?"

"The lands are simply breathtaking," Meg supplied eagerly with a little hop to the edge of her chair. "In fact, Brandon holds an estate there."

"Does he, indeed?" Nethersole asked tightly, his puffed chest losing a bit of its air as he flicked a glance to Brandon. "Capital."

Brandon inclined his head but made no comment. The vast property was one he'd inherited after a wave of typhus fever had claimed the lives of his uncle, cousin and father.

After such a great loss, it was not a possession that he would ever boast about, even if to take Nethersole down a notch or two.

"What a coincidence that you should mention traveling there, when we are doing the same," Meg continued. "We will be staying at Crossmoor Abbey for a few weeks before venturing north to our main residence."

Ellie's eyes brightened at the mention. "I have heard the name—or read it, rather. My friend, Miss Thorogood, writes of seeing the abbey far up on a hill when she goes on her walks. Her descriptions have been so poetic and picturesque that I've often wondered if such a place could be real. Now, when I visit her in a month, I will be able to tell her that I am acquainted with the inhabitants."

"You must drop by and see us, too," Meg said with enthusiasm.

"Oh, but why stop there?" Nethersole asked in a sardonic drawl. "We should all just travel together in the splendor of Hullworth's open landau."

Ellie slanted him a mortified look as if she'd never heard *George* speak so childishly. Her face drained of all color when she turned to Meg and Brandon. "I must apologize. I hope you know that it was never my intention to invite myself."

"Nonsense, Miss Parrish," Brandon said smoothly, which was quite a feat since his blood was currently boiling over Nethersole's tantrum and the subsequent humiliation it caused Ellie. "You've done nothing of the sort. I'm sure he was only jesting in good humor." He flicked a warning glance to the head of the table.

Nethersole lifted his palms up and shrugged in a gesture of feigned innocence. "Already, you know me so well."

That's what Brandon was afraid of.

Learning that Miss Parrish was intending to travel in such company—even with her aunts alongside—did not sit well with him. This concern, he told himself, was nothing more than he would have for any friend. And he had agreed to be her friend, after all. Therefore, it was a matter of upholding the dictates of his own conscience when he made his following decision.

"Nethersole's suggestion does pose the notion of practicality, however," Brandon said, easing back into the chair. "It would only make sense if we did travel together. And you shall be my guests at Crossmoor Abbey."

A sudden wash of pink flooded Ellie's cheeks and she shook her head. "That is most generous of you to offer. But . . . but I'm afraid that . . . would be . . ."

"Splendid!" Myrtle chirruped.

And Maeve added, "Absolute perfection! We'd be delighted, my lord."

"Then it's settled," he said, holding Ellie's round-eyed gaze in an effort to reassure her. "Just a nice, friendly holiday."

And all Brandon had to do was remind himself that she was his friend and nothing more.

Chapter 10

"A debutante mustn't exaggerate the significance of random encounters."

—A NOTE FOR *The Marriage Habits of the Native Aristocrat*

Ellie spent the following few days trying not to think about Lord Hullworth, the kiss, or the upcoming trip to Wiltshire in June. Unfortunately, it proved impossible.

He was everywhere.

On Sunday after church service, she'd just reached the carriage when she realized that she'd lost her ledger again. Making a quick excuse to the aunts, she went to retrace her steps. However, she hadn't taken more than a half dozen— her head bent to survey the pavement—when she encountered a pair of gentleman's shoes blocking her path. She stopped, and even before he spoke, she knew.

"Were you looking for this, Miss Parrish?" the all too familiar voice asked as he held her ledger in view.

She looked from the gloved hand and up the tailored lines of his waistcoat past the crisp folds of his cravat, to the smirk tucked into one corner of his mouth, and finally to a pair of amused gray-green eyes. At once, her pulse leapt. Then her stomach fluttered. And she had the most disconcerting impulse to touch him. It didn't matter where—his sleeve, his chest, the back of his nape. She just wanted her hands on him.

She felt terribly guilty about that.

Believing it best to end this encounter with utmost haste, she curled her hands around the book instead. "Thank you, my lord. I'm much obliged that you rescued it, yet again."

She gave a quick curtsy and meant to withdraw. But he held fast, stalling her retreat.

"I found this on the stairs and thought it looked familiar," he said conversationally. "Then I began to wonder what research you could possibly be up to in the church of all places."

"I was attempting to make note of the gentlemen's reactions to the reading of the banns. I thought that if I saw either eagerness or nervousness, it might offer some insight into their thought process."

"And what did you discover?"

She glanced down to where his black-gloved thumb rested on the worn brown cover, a thread's breadth from her ivory kid leather. They were so close she would swear she felt the heat of him. How simple it would be to accidentally brush against him . . . just a small touch . . .

She shook her head. "Nothing. I spent the whole time searching for my pencil."

"Ah. Well, perhaps I could offer a bit of assistance in your studies. Your first lesson, as it were." He inclined his head with a scholarly air. "A gentleman worth his salt would take special care to, at least, *appear* steady and collected so as not to alarm his bride-to-be with his eagerness."

She grinned. "Are you saying that gentlemen are always eager? I would have thought that some would merely be resigned to the institution of marriage."

"If he is resigned—or too immature to understand how fortunate he is—then he isn't worth setting your cap for." As he spoke, his expression darkened and appeared accusatory.

She stiffened at once. "And is that second lesson for the book . . . or for me?"

"I was under the impression that the book was for you, as well as others like you, who require an understanding on the differences between gentlemen and scoundrels?"

He didn't say George's name outright, but he might as well have done.

She glared at him. Lord Hullworth's gaze flashed in return, roving hotly over her cheeks and then her mouth. Her lips tingled in response.

Strangely, she could still feel the searing pressure of their kiss as if they had just broken apart. As if no time had passed at all and they remained secluded in that cozy glade in the center of the zoo. He seemed to read her thoughts and growled low in his throat. The deep sound made her aware of all the places her undergarments clung to her most sensitive skin, the air crackling with a static charge between them.

How could she feel this inexplicable pull even when she was irritated with him?

"I never kept anything from you," she said quietly.

His gaze softened with understanding as if he could see the confusion roiling inside her. "I know and I wish I'd believed you. But now . . ." He exhaled slowly, leaving his statement unfinished as he released his hold on the ledger. Then he touched the brim of his hat. "Good day, Miss Parrish."

Watching him go, Ellie was determined not to wonder what he might have said. She would be better off not knowing, she was sure. And better off not thinking about him at all. Well, at least for the remainder of the day.

But early that afternoon, a package arrived. Within a wrapping of brown paper, she found a small rectangular box with a sliding lid. Inside was a stack of pencils from the stationers, along with a single card that simply read: *Your friend, B*

Friend.

She stared at the card for a long while, tracing her finger-tip over the letters. She wasn't sure why that word seemed so strange and foreign to her now when it never had before. It was like reading *friend* in another language and she was left to decipher the meaning on her own.

On Monday, Ellie was off to a better start. She hardly thought about Lord Hullworth or the kiss at all. It only entered her mind a dozen times. Every hour. Nevertheless, she considered it progress.

At least, until the collision in the park.

After suffering an episode of acute embarrassment due to the flirtation between Aunt Myrtle and the nut seller, Ellie decided to slip away quietly and observe the geese in the pond.

Unbeknownst to her, in that very same moment around the corner, Lord Hullworth was making a daring escape from a rather rapacious gaggle of the featherless variety.

Neither he nor she were looking where they were going. Then suddenly . . . *oof!*

Their bodies slammed together. He was quick to react with a pair of steadying hands as her own gloved palms fell against the firm expanse of his chest. Then came the wide-eyed recognition. His grip on her hips tightened. She pressed closer instead of pushing away. It only lasted an instant. Just long enough for their combined breaths to catch, for their pupils to spill darkly, for heat to wash over her skin, and for his low grunt to draw her attention to his mouth.

Oh, how she wished she could stop thinking about that kiss. Stop reliving it in her daydreams and nightdreams. Her lips were beginning to ache every time she saw him, as if they suffered an ailment that required a compress comprised of his lips and to be applied in frequent doses.

They were both so addled that neither one spoke or

moved. Not until they heard his sister's approach. Then they sprang apart just before she found them.

Meg rolled her eyes and huffed in exasperation, speaking as if the three of them were already in the midst of a conversation. "Seven handkerchiefs, Ellie. Six accidental stumbles. And four—count them, *four*—turned ankles."

Lord Hullworth took a breath and kindly said, "There appears to be an epidemic of improper footwear."

"An epidemic of something, to be sure," Ellie muttered, her mood shifting to storm clouds as she imagined all those women falling against him. Laying their hands on him. Sighing in his embrace. "Honestly. They should be ashamed of themselves."

He quirked a quizzical brow. "You are rather vehement in your disapproval of them."

"As I would be for any friend," she responded instantly, albeit tersely, not liking the accusation in his tone.

Truth be told, she wasn't certain why she felt a hot surge of peevish irritation just then. It wasn't as though he didn't know how to manage the wayward attentions of the female sex on his own. He was a grown man, after all.

"Ellie's quite right," Meg said, coming to her side. "As far as I'm concerned, her statement only proves her devotion to your cause, which is far more than I can say for you. Frankly, I'm appalled by what you permit. An outside observer might think you actually enjoyed the attention. Perhaps even"—she slid an impish glance to Ellie—"call you arrogant."

Having a sense that Meg was in the mood to tease her brother, Ellie played along, preferring a playful air over whatever it was she felt toward his gaggle. "Indeed. Some might even think that you were at fault for provoking them, strutting around as you do, stealing the attention from your sister. In the very least you might try to disguise yourself in public."

"Excellent point," Meg agreed with a nod and a purse of her lips. "I think you'd make a fine little old man. At your age, it wouldn't take much. You could powder your hair."

"Wear spectacles and smoke a pipe."

"And there's no need to put stuffing inside your shirt, because you are well on your way to having a paunch."

Ellie tsked. "A shame, really."

"I beg your pardon," he said, affronted and frowning as his hand patted his perfectly taut abdomen.

"Vanity, thy name is Lord Hullworth," Ellie said under her breath, concealing the fact that she wanted it to be her hand that had done the patting.

He squinted at her but a grin lurked at the corner of his mouth. "Now that you've sufficiently shredded my *amour propre,* are you finished having a go at my expense?"

"Are we?" Ellie asked, turning to her cohort.

Meg nodded. "As much as it pains me to end this repartee, I fear we must. If I'm not mistaken, the gaggle is headed our way."

The three of them peered past the shrubbery that had been doing a fair job of concealing them for this long, only to see a half dozen debutantes and their conspiring mamas marching steadily on the path. Like a hunting party without horses.

Ellie laid her hand on his sleeve. "You'd better leave while you have the chance."

He glanced down, and only then did she realize what she'd done. She withdrew at once, curling her fingertips into her palm. And he gazed at her in a way that caused a quick escalation in her pulse.

He lingered a second longer, long enough for Meg to turn back with exasperation as she tugged on his arm. Then, just before they made their escape, he touched the brim of his hat. "Until our paths cross again, Miss Parrish."

Heaven help her, Ellie was already looking forward to it.

But, surely, that didn't hold any significance. Nor did it mean anything when she sent a parcel to his residence later that afternoon.

For your next foray out of doors.

> *Your friend,*
> *E*

IN THE privacy of his study, Brandon unwrapped the small package with eager curiosity. What might Miss Parrish have sent him? Then, as he lifted the object within and held it up for inspection, he couldn't help but laugh.

Draped from his fingertips was a finely stitched scrap of black silk, sporting two almond-shaped slits and a length of ribbon on either side.

He immediately penned a response.

Dear E,

Now I can finally live out my dream of becoming a dashing highwayman.

> *Your (masked and soon-to-be infamous) friend,*
> *B*

He surveyed the card for several minutes. Should he send it? Or did it seem too flirtatious for one friend to send to another?

Over the years, he'd engaged in other acquaintances with women. But they were typically the wives and close relations of his friends, and solely platonic.

He never wanted to kiss them so much that his teeth ached. Never wanted to run his hands over every inch of their flesh. Never wanted to swallow down every softly whispered sigh from their lips as if it were ambrosia.

His *friendship* with Miss Parrish put him in a completely foreign territory, one that he would have to navigate with extreme caution. After all, she'd set her cap for Nethersole, he reminded himself. That, in and of itself, made his own choice all the clearer.

Therefore, he would merely keep to their bargain, offering his experience and knowledge to aid in her research. There would be no more kissing.

Feeling confident in his decision, he sent the missive. Now, if only he could stop thinking about her.

The problem was, Miss Parrish was everywhere.

On Tuesday, he saw her at a bookseller on Finsbury Square. He was walking down the stairs with a book in hand when he spotted her standing near the carousel in the center of the main floor, the clerk handing her a paper-wrapped purchase.

For an instant, Brandon contemplated slipping stealthily into the stacks. He didn't know how often a man could tempt the Fates before they rebelled against him. But even as the thought entered his mind, he saw her head lift in a graceful arc, her hat tilting in his direction, her gaze drifting across the green carpeted room, searching as if she'd heard the whisper of her name, and then . . . she saw him.

She smiled at once. So did he. And yet, beneath his cravat, the cording along his neck tightened and his throat went dry.

As he started to cross the room, he swallowed. However, this particular thirst remained—and would always remain—unquenched.

"Miss Parrish," he said, stopping beside her. "It seems as though we are of like mind, yet again."

Her wispy dark brows arched, a glimmer of something playful in her butterscotch eyes. "Lord Hullworth, it is indeed quite the coincidence that I should see you just now." The statement held an aura of mystery that tempted him to ask what she could mean. But before he could, she moved a scant degree closer to peek at the gold lettering on the leather tome in his grip, her sweet fragrance spinning a tangible web around him. Then those sooty lashes lifted in curiosity. *"The Gardener's Labyrinth?"*

"A book for my aunt Sylvia," he supplied after clearing his throat. He was especially proud of the fact that he did not allow himself to glance down to her lips. Well, no more than three or four times.

A small laugh escaped her. "Then it is even more of a coincidence, for I have just purchased a silver-fork novel for Aunt Maeve and a gothic novel for Aunt Myrtle. I am due to pick them up from their Lady's Society tea. So, I'm afraid, I must bid you a hasty adieu."

He inclined his head in farewell, but wished he felt relief. Wished he felt something other than the desire to tug sharply on those bonnet ribbons, tilt back her head and devour her mouth. Right there in the Temple of the Muses. "Until our next chance encounter."

She sketched a quick curtsy. But before she took a step, she turned toward the young bespectacled clerk across the sales counter and said, "Mr. Wood, in regard to that other book I inquired about—" She darted a glance to Brandon and then leaned on tiptoe over the counter to whisper the rest in the clerk's ear. Straightening, she concluded her tête-à-tête with, "And that should be all. Thank you ever so much."

"My pleasure, ma'am," the clerk said with a broad grin that Brandon sorely wanted to wipe off his face.

Instead, his attention followed Miss Parrish to the door, waiting to see if she would turn once more.

"Beg your pardon, my lord. But the lady bid me to give you this." The clerk snared Brandon's attention by lifting a cloth-covered book into view. It bore the title *Humphrey Clinker*. "And wished me to tell you that it has highwaymen in it."

Brandon's gaze shot to the door just in time to hear the bell tinkle overhead and to see her look over her shoulder. She flashed a smile that would surely linger in his thoughts for far too long. Then the door closed.

"I'll take that one as well, Mr. Wood," he said, wishing Miss Parrish didn't make the task of not thinking about her so utterly impossible.

⚜⚜⚜

PROOF OF that came Thursday, when he saw her yet again.

Brandon and Meg spotted the three Miss Parrishes on the pavement outside the milliner's shop. After stopping for a brief chat, and revealing that he and his sister had been on their way to Gunter's for ices, Brandon insisted that they join him. It was what friends did, after all.

Or so he told himself.

However, if he thought seeing Miss Parrish in the park or the bookshop tested the limits of his control, then he was sorely mistaken. Because watching her eat a dish of burnt filbert ice cream had him behaving like a madman.

It might have been the way she closed her eyes with each taste. Or the way her upper lip nestled the bowl of the spoon as she dragged it from her mouth with exquisite slowness. Or perhaps it was the way she sighed, ever so softly, right before she declared she couldn't eat another bite.

But the next thing he knew, he was reaching across the small round table for her dish. Without a by-your-leave, he proceeded to devour every last bite, barely restraining himself from licking the beveled glass dish clean.

Thankfully, his episode went unobserved by his sister and the elder Miss Parrishes since they were absorbed with sampling the various flavors in each other's dishes. Maeve declared that parmesan was superior. Myrtle disagreed, preferring the sweetness of royal ice cream. While Meg liked pineapple.

Brandon couldn't even remember what had been in his own dish. All he knew was that burnt filbert was on his tongue, just as it was on Ellie's.

He gazed at her burning cheeks, at the quick rise and fall of her breasts with every breath as she stared back at him, her eyes dark beneath the brim of her bonnet. And he made no excuse as he slid the dish back across the table.

She swallowed and looked down at the spoon. Her delicate hands curved around the dish and pulled it closer. Without lifting her gaze, she softly asked, "Are you fond of burnt filbert ice cream, my lord?"

"So it would seem," he said, his voice steady and matter-of-fact, as if the lunatic he was a moment ago had been an aberration.

She glanced up at him, her brow knitted in a confusion that he understood all too well.

"Brandon, did you hear that?" Meg interrupted with an excited chirrup. "Our friends are to attend a concert at Hanover Square this evening."

Both he and his sister had another obligation. It would be rude to cancel at such late notice. Aside from that, tickets to the performance would be nearly impossible to garner. But as he was about to mention those obstacles, Ellie spoke the words that guaranteed his efforts to move a mountain, if he must, to attend the concert.

"Indeed," she said. "Lord Nethersole has invited us."

Chapter 11

"A true gentleman honors his obligations."
—A NOTE FOR *The Marriage Habits
of the Native Aristocrat*

The Hanover Square Rooms were a place of entertainment and exhibition. Society was on display in all their finery beneath the vast vaulted ceiling and glow of the chandeliers. There were those who attended for the delight of the music and sat amidst the long horizontal rows of straight-backed benches facing the vast stage. Then there were those who delighted in watching, whispering, and waiting for the barest hint of a scandal. These voyeurs typically sat in the gallery along the far wall, facing the listeners.

Situated near the stage, and ever-aware of his audience, Brandon took care not to appear obvious as he glanced back to the doorway. Miss Parrish and her aunts were late. The musicians had begun to warm up their instruments, the discordant strains of violin and cello filling the hall. The lamps were being dimmed, the scent of candle smoke filling the air. Throats were cleared for one last time. Programs ceased rustling. Gradually, the entire assembly quieted in anticipation for the concert to begin. And he expelled a breath of disappointment.

But in the next instant, he felt a tingling sensation skim along the nape of his neck and a taut coiling burrow deep in his gut, and he knew that she'd arrived.

From his seat beside Meg, he observed Ellie's agitated

search of those in attendance, the nervous fidgeting of her white gloved hands against the broad sash of her diaphanous lavender silk gown, and the heavy breath she expelled when she realized Nethersole was not among them. Clearly, the man had neglected to honor his commitment. Again.

Her gaze alighted on Brandon. At first, she offered a smile of relief. But then she frowned, her brow furrowing. He didn't take offense. She likely didn't want to be glad to see him, or to have him bear witness to Nethersole's abandonment.

Brandon understood the conflict within her. He, himself, did not want to be drawn to a woman who had no intention of choosing him above all others.

Nevertheless, here they both were in this unwelcoming hinterland between desire and reality. As her friend, he would demonstrate what a young woman should expect from a gentleman who respected her.

With a lift of his fingers, he hailed the usher and arranged for the three Miss Parrishes to be escorted to the finest seats—which, as it happened, were near him. At least, *after* a few subtle displacements.

A susurration of rumors cascaded through the crowd, building to a crescendo, until Maeve Parrish bracketed a hand by her ear and loudly proclaimed a temporary ailment that required her close proximity to the stage. Spoken with such uncompromising conviction, she subdued the gossip to a dull murmur. He would have to thank her later.

Pink with embarrassment, Ellie acknowledged him with a nod and sat stiffly beside his sister, her aunts filing in along the row.

"You're late," Meg whispered playfully to her friend from behind a fan.

Ellie lifted her shoulders in a delicate shrug. "When George did not arrive at our town house, I thought, perhaps, that I misunderstood our plans and we were meant to meet him here."

Meg cast a surreptitious glance over the assembly and shook her head. "I do not see him."

"He must have been detained."

Brandon gritted his teeth when he heard those words from Ellie. True to form, she made excuses for Nethersole. It seemed the man-child could do no wrong in her eyes. She merely accepted the meager offerings given to her.

Didn't she realize how much more she deserved?

He brooded over the answer for the first four movements, the dips and swells of the music roiling inside him as he recalled making that same mistake long ago.

When the intermission came, he went to the refreshment table and waited for the punch. Of course, he could have had the footman bring it to his party, but it was better this way. Brandon needed the distance between himself and Ellie. Not only to quiet the lingering rumors, but to ensure he wouldn't forget himself. Standing too near her brought out an overwhelming temptation to touch her, to brush the bare strip of skin between her elbow-length glove and the ruffled cuff of her sleeve, to lean in and—

"Why, Lord Hullworth, I thought that was you."

He stiffened reflexively at the sound of the familiar voice, but carefully schooled his features before he turned. "Lady Chastaine."

The woman he once knew as Miss Phoebe Bright flirtatiously roved her gaze over his form. "How absolutely scrumptious you look this evening. If you'll recall, I always did like you in blue."

"I was sorry to hear about your second husband's death," he said blandly, wishing he'd remained with his party.

Her fingers flitted in the air. "Yes, yes, well, I'm more apt to say good riddance to the old devil. He left me without a penny. Or not enough pennies, rather. I barely survived a year out of mourning."

She pouted prettily, her face still a reflection of the one he'd spent years dreaming about. Before he'd spent years despising it.

"I'm certain you'll land on your feet, my lady."

"Will I, Brandon?" She issued a sigh, her dark sapphire eyes peering up at him through her lashes. "Of course, I know that my face and figure still appeal to most men, but there comes a time in a woman's life when she wants more. Lately, I've been filled with so many regrets for losing my one true love." She laid a hand on his sleeve and when he did not remove it, she smiled sweetly. "I was far too young to understand what I had. Surely, you couldn't hold that against me."

"No, indeed. I doubt there is anyone present who couldn't claim a youthful blunder or two." He lifted her hand and summarily passed it to the late-arriving gentleman who came to stand at her side.

Phoebe startled as Lord Savage clasped her fingers and pressed a kiss to them. It was well-known amongst the *ton* that she was his current paramour.

Brandon, on the other hand, was far more discreet in affairs with the fairer sex. Unless . . . he was in the middle of a zoo . . . or seated at a table in a confectioner's emporium . . .

Apparently, there was something about Ellie that made him lose his head.

"Darling!" Phoebe said in breathless surprise. "I thought you would still be at Sterling's, enjoying an evening at the tables. You've often told me how these concerts are so much of a bore."

In response, Savage smiled with his usual unaffected air and curled her arm into the crook of his as he tucked a lock of hair behind her ear. "What you were saying about mistakes, Hullworth, I couldn't agree more. The marvelous thing is that, once you learn from them, they lose their ability to affect you in any way whatsoever. After all, when a candle flame burns out, you don't simply sit in the dark. You find a fresh taper and light it. There are dozens more just like it to be had."

Brandon made no comment. Even though his *tendre* for Phoebe had dissipated years ago, he wasn't going to belittle her.

He couldn't help but recall the young man Savage had once been decades ago, well before untold betrayals had turned his heart to stone. He'd always been a solid friend—as long as you stayed on his good side—and he had a robust appetite for all the pleasures that life could afford. And with his fortune, he could afford them all. But that dynamic, untamable zeal that had always shone like a beacon from his eyes had gone out somewhere along the way, snuffed like a candle flame. And while the ladies of the *ton* considered Savage dangerously handsome, Brandon saw a man who was dead inside.

There were many similarities between them. Too many, in fact. An unwelcome shiver rolled down his spine at the realization.

Once upon a time, both men had been blinded by love. Both men had lost a vital part of themselves—their trust and faith—when their eyes had been opened. But, for Brandon, it was even more than that. He'd lost the potent sense of certainty that ran deeply through his lineage.

But as his gaze shifted to Ellie and then back to Phoebe—who was busily making excuses and using her wiles on Savage—Brandon discovered a pleasant sort of peacefulness wash over him. He could now look at her without feeling the old bitterness that had plagued him, as if she'd been nothing more than a passing acquaintance. A part of his past that was not even a ghost that could haunt him any longer. It was freeing.

"My lord," a footman said from beside him, his gloved hands holding a tray with five crystal cups of punch, the bright color of one of Ellie's blushes.

Brandon gestured toward the ladies gathered in conversation on the opposite side of the room, and the footman left to deliver them. With a bow, he addressed Savage and Lady Chastaine. "If you'll forgive me, I'm going to return to my party."

Savage glanced over, his brows inching upward in inquiry. "So the rumors are true, then? You *are* courting."

"No," he answered succinctly, feeling Phoebe's interest heighten. The last thing he wanted was to encourage her machinations, or have her decide that Miss Parrish was an obstacle to be destroyed. "I am merely escorting my sister, who is enjoying the concert with her friend and her friend's aunts. That is all."

"Well, just be careful, old man. You never know when they'll turn on you."

Brandon inclined his head in farewell. As his steps took him across the hardwood floor, he understood how Savage could become cold and bitter over time, especially considering his choice of companions. But where Savage was content to continue on his jaded path, Brandon was not.

He wanted more for his life. More for Meg's life. And yes, more for Ellie's, too.

Even though he was just her *friend*, it irritated the hell out of him that she didn't seem to want more for herself than Nethersole's inconstant attention. And even if the Fates never chose to smile upon Brandon in regard to his own contentment, the very least he could do was ensure that she made her choice with her eyes fully open.

❧❦❧

"DOES HE have to be everywhere I turn? And why did he have to bring us punch?" Ellie groused, jerking off her gloves as they stepped into the foyer late that night. They'd told Mr. Rivers not to bother waiting up.

"Who dear? Lord Hullworth?" Aunt Myrtle asked, untying her bonnet.

Ellie nodded on a huff and cast a disconsolate glance toward the parasol waiting in the urn.

"He is a gentleman in every sense," Maeve added, matter-of-fact. "Surely, you didn't expect him to bring a glass for his sister and not for the rest of us."

"Well, no," she said. "It's just that I wish George was the one who brought us punch, took us out for ices, met us in the park . . ." *and danced with me in the moonlight,* she thought, *and kissed me breathless in the zoo.*

Oh, why couldn't she just forget about that kiss!

Aunt Maeve chuckled. "There are worse things than attracting the notice of an absurdly handsome gentleman. Any other young woman would be over the moon."

"I'm merely his . . . friend," Ellie said, but the word felt tangled on her tongue, and so she added with more force, "That's all. Just his friend."

More than anything, she had wanted George to come to the concert. She was beginning to feel so unguarded without him around, like a ripe apple dangling on the very tip of a branch where anyone might simply reach up and . . .

She shook her head, refusing to finish the thought.

"Then perhaps, you've solved the riddle of the ages, dear," Aunt Myrtle said, tugging on the knotted configuration she'd made of her bonnet ribbons before Maeve came over to drag her closer to the wall sconce.

Ellie glanced at the squinting pair. "What do you mean?"

"Well, if George is truly the one you want, perhaps you should treat him as you do Lord Hullworth."

Maeve agreed with an absent nod. "And treat Lord Hullworth with the familiarity you would with George."

Ellie considered that prospect and felt a frown knitting

her brow. "Oh, I couldn't do that. And I certainly could never treat George with indifference."

"Is that how you think you are with Lord Hu—"

Aunt Maeve tugged a bit harder on Myrtle's ribbons and stared at her thoughtfully. "Of course she is, sister. And I think we need not interfere."

"You are both so dear," Ellie said fondly and stepped over to them to work the knot free in a trice. "Pay no attention to me. I'm just sore at George, that's all. But I will be in better spirits tomorrow evening when he escorts us to dine at Lady Millington's. And then everything will return to the way it ought to be."

There would be no Lord Hullworth there to crowd her until she felt every finely woven thread within the fabrics that lay upon her skin. No Lord Hullworth there to cause her throat to be so parched that her glass of punch could not quench it. No Lord Hullworth there to offer his own cup for her to drink her fill—*and she had accepted it, drat it all!* No Lord Hullworth there to hand her into the carriage and bid her a good night with that warm knowing gleam in his eyes, as if he knew very well that she would dream of him.

It was a relief that *he* would not be there. She'd learned from Meg that she and her brother were set to dine with Lord Butterfield instead. *And* Miss Carmichael.

Of course, it didn't bother Ellie in the least to think about it. No, she was far too thrilled by her own plans to give a passing thought to his. Let him dine with all the Miss Carmichaels of the world.

"Dear, are you feeling quite well?" Aunt Maeve asked with quiet concern.

Aunt Myrtle brushed her cheek. "You do look a bit peaked all of a sudden."

"Perfectly hale," she said immediately. "Simply tired, that's all."

Tired of being left in the lurch by the man she wanted to marry. Tired of Lord Hullworth doing everything she wished that George would do. Tired of this ripe-apple feeling. And tired of worrying that, if she didn't snare George this Season, she would end up being left on the branch to rot, drop to the ground, and then decay into nothingness.

Please don't leave me dangling, George, she thought as she mounted the stairs, looking forward to Lady Millington's dinner, albeit with a bit of trepidation.

Chapter 12

"A debutante must always be on her guard from wayward advances *and* from thieves of the heart."

—A NOTE FOR *The Marriage Habits of the Native Aristocrat*

At Lady Millington's dinner party, nothing was turning out the way Ellie wanted.

George had sent his regrets, without even bothering to give a reason. Aunt Maeve had begged off, claiming a headache. The gentleman seated to her right was a complete lecher. And Lord Hullworth was here.

Would the Fates ever allow her a single day without seeing his damnably handsome countenance?

And it was impossible not to look at him, for he was seated across from her in the perfect patch of light. The same glow from the chandeliers that gilded the burnished bronze curls, artfully swept back from his forehead, also accentuated the chiseled edge of his jaw and naturally drew the eye to the shallow cleft in his chin and up to his unbearably well-formed mouth. The sight of it only reminded her how it had felt against her own, thereby setting off a tumult of escalating ailments, among which included wayward tingles, a racing pulse and a weighted sensation deep in her middle. She would likely never survive the night.

To his credit, however, he did not gloat over George's absence. There was no smug smirk on his face whenever his gaze brushed past hers as he turned his head in conversation with the women seated on either side of him. Which was another thing that irked Ellie to no end. Honestly, did Lady Millington have to seat him between such celebrated beauties?

The young woman to the left of him was Lady Elise—a duke's daughter in her first Season—and on the right sat Miss Carmichael.

She'd heard it whispered in the parlor earlier that, upon gaining Lord Hullworth's attendance, Lady Millington had invited Miss Carmichael only minutes before the dinner this very evening. A clear attempt at matchmaking! It appalled Ellie. Not for her own sake, of course. But for his. As his friend, she didn't want him subjected to the attentions of these husband-hungry women. He deserved better than to be manipulated by his hostess. But now the question foremost on the *ton*'s lips was surely, which one would ensnare London's most elusive bachelor?

Ellie couldn't give a fig. She and her quarter-century-old, shriveling body were content to wait for George.

With that thought in mind, she tried not to look across the table at all. Instead, she focused on her own seat partners, the handsome Lord Savage to her left and the tipsy Lord Bassingstoke to the right. While the former was shifting away from under-the-napkin advances from *Lady* Bassingstoke on his other side, the latter seemed fascinated by the subtle touches of needlework Ellie had stitched along the edge of her bodice.

"Does your wife enjoy embroidery, my lord?" she asked through her teeth.

This wasn't the first time she'd inquired after his wife, hoping the gentle reminder would bring him to heel. But his two—well, perhaps three—interests seemed to be in discovering the mysteries at the bottom of his wine goblet and whatever lay beyond her pale apricot gown.

She'd thought the stylish cut was modest when she'd

peered in the looking glass earlier. Sitting down, however, caused the bodice's lacy edge to lower slightly—but not indecently—and the ivory swells of her breasts to rise like twin souffles, baked in the gusseted cups of her corset.

Lord Bassingstoke's gaze gradually lifted quizzically. "What was that, Miss Parrish?"

Thankfully, the appearance of a footman and a fresh decanter at his other elbow distracted the lecher for the moment.

"Admirable effort, Miss Parrish," Lord Savage murmured beside her. "But there are some gentlemen and ladies alike who simply enjoy being naughty. I fear the only way to deal with one deep in his cups is with"—stealthily he slid his fork to her, his tawny brows arching over clear, emerald green eyes that flickered with cynical amusement—"gentle persuasion."

"Thank you, my lord," she said. "I shall use this *advice* wisely."

"Don't keep it for long, hmm? Otherwise, I'd have no way to defend my own honor."

She laughed softly. The statement was all the more comical coming from a man of Lord Savage's powerful physique. Rumor had it that, for a time, he even ran a pugilism club out of his ballroom. And yet, he moved with the grace of a golden lion and seemed equally as dangerous to know. After all, he was well-known amongst the *ton* for being something of a scoundrel.

He was another wealthy bachelor who openly professed to never marry, much like Lord Hullworth. However, Lord Savage's reputation for having a slew of indiscreet affairs kept *him* from being dubbed a prime catch. As far as the *ton* was concerned, any marriage of his would be nothing short of scandalous.

"I wonder if I might bend your ear, my lord," she said

quietly, not wanting to arouse any interest in her topic or accidentally incite a scandal of her own.

He leaned a fraction closer and whispered, "You have me at your disposal. Do with my ear—or any other part of me—whatever you desire."

"Now who's being naughty?" Of course, she blushed. Especially when he unleashed the full potency of his rakish grin. Coupled with the drowsy, devilish gleam in his gaze and she was in desperate need of a fan.

"Forgive me, my dear. I spend so little time with innocents that I often forget how easy it is to make you blush. Fascinating to watch, really. It's like you're coming into bloom. No wonder Hullworth cannot take his eyes off you."

She turned sharply, but only to see her *friend* angle his head in conversation with Miss Carmichael. And whatever he said made the young woman titter and look up at him shyly through her lashes as she responded.

A discomfiting burst of fire filled Ellie, scorching the inner lining of her lungs. And when she exhaled, she was surprised flames didn't spew from her lips. "You're mistaken."

"And you're not paying attention to the way his white-knuckled hand is gripping his goblet stem, or to the tense twitch at the hinge of his jaw." As her tableside companion spoke, Lord Hullworth's gaze swung back across the table, transforming at once to a dark glower that fell on Lord Savage, who apparently found the entire episode amusing. "See the murder in his eyes? I daresay, it won't be long before he leaps across the table and pummels me to a permanent good night. However, I do hope it's not too soon. The dessert course is next. And I firmly believe that one should never meet one's maker before partaking in any and all indulgences." He paused to poke the bear by raising his glass in a mock toast. "Tell me, Miss Parrish, why do you think he reacts this strongly to seeing the two of us enjoying a pleasant conversation?"

"I should hardly know. We are only acquainted through his sister."

"Interesting. That is precisely what he said." He let the statement hang in the air while he took a long swallow, studying her over the rim of his goblet. "But I think you're both lying to yourselves."

She shook her head in adamant denial, her pulse unbearably quick. "There is nothing more between us. He knows that I've set my cap for another man."

"Ah. Now I understand. The root of all that anger stems from his own desire. He wants you but you're not his for the taking, and he isn't about to make that mistake again. Poor sod," he said as he set his glass down. "I suppose I'll stop tormenting him now. And so, what was your question, my dear?"

Ellie could hardly recall it at the moment. Both her brain and heart had stopped functioning the instant she heard the words *he wants you*. And when they started up again it was with an unwelcome rise of warmth and lightness that felt far too like exhilaration, giving rise to an entirely new series of ailments to worry over.

"It was in regard to a book that my friend, Lady Northcott, and I are writing," she said, her voice sounding far away to her own ears. Dimly, she nodded toward the far end of the table where Jane sat. At the same time, she discreetly reached under the table to stab Lord Bassingstoke's thigh as he slid his knee along hers. "Its primary focus is to identify the differences between the gentlemen who marry and the scoundrels who don't. And I was wondering what your views on marriage are?"

"As a confirmed scoundrel, I will say that marriage is an affair that's overstayed its welcome," he said succinctly. "There's no need to get the vicar involved for something that's bound to end in misery. But to each his own." He shrugged and his pointed gaze fell to Lady Bassingstoke's wandering hand as she pretended to be absorbed in the conversation on her other side. "Case in point, my dear."

Ellie frowned. Not because she was distressed over Lord Savage's rather grim outlook, but because she was still thinking about what he'd said about Lord Hullworth.

He couldn't want her. Not really. He knew she was George's. So the glower across the table must have been due to the fact that he was simply looking out for her, as he would do for any of his sister's friends. Wasn't it?

❧❧❧

AT THE conclusion of dinner, Ellie found Jane waiting in the corridor to walk with her and the other women to the parlor, while the men lingered in the dining room over port and tobacco. Aunt Myrtle was already far ahead and doing her best to ferret out recipe secrets from their hostess.

Jane twined arms with Ellie as they meandered along the blue lias stone tiles, their skirts slowly swishing together in shades of apricot and plum. Her friend's sapphire eyes blinked drowsily while she reached up to brush an errant brown curl from her cheek.

"Just so you know," Jane began, then paused to stifle a yawn, "coming back from the brink of ruination isn't as grand as it might seem. I cannot wait until the Season is over so I can take a good, long nap."

"If you're tired, then why not send your regrets? Our hostess would have understood. And I'm sure your husband would have agreed. He must detest these obligatory parties to introduce him to society."

"Unfortunately, most of these are for *my* benefit—all part of Lord Herrington's campaign to have society forget about my sojourn into a brothel last fall. Though, since he was the one who brought it out into the open, it's hardly fair that I am the one losing sleep. But I appreciate his efforts to make amends and become a true family, nonetheless. As

for Raven," she said with a very un-Jane-like wistful sigh as
if the very mention of her husband's name stole the breath
from her body, "he doesn't want to disappoint his grandfather by refusing the invitations. There are still too many
who believe him to be a feral creature. They're correct, of
course, but only in the best possible way." She bit down on
her bottom lip to hide a grin and passed a caressing hand
over the barely noticeable swell of her midriff. "So tell me,
how is your progress with Lord Nethersole? Any new devel-
opments for our research?"

"Well, I had thought things were finally progressing
when he'd offered to travel to Wiltshire with my aunts and
me," Ellie said, having already told Jane about the entire
ordeal. "However, I have seen little of him since."

"From your description of how he'd practically dared
Lord Hullworth to offer his carriage and house, I'd spec-
ulated that George's unexplained display of agitation was
indicative of jealousy," Jane said, lighting a candle of hope
inside Ellie. But then she dowsed the flame on the next
breath. "But his absence would indicate he wasn't afraid of
losing his hold on your affections at all."

At once, Ellie felt like that apple again, dangling at the
very edge of a branch. In her mind's eye, she pictured a
hand reaching up to pick the ripe, red fruit. But the most
disconcerting part of that vision was . . . it wasn't George's
hand she saw.

"And he wouldn't, of course. Certainly not to Lord Hullworth, who has no intention of marrying."

Yet, as she recalled what he'd said on the terrace last
week about his parents having a partnership based on love
and trust, she wondered if her statement was entirely ac-
curate.

I will not settle for less, he'd stated plainly. Such a con-
fession didn't sound at all like a man who never intended to

marry. Instead, it sounded like a man who was searching for someone to change his mind. Not that it mattered to her.

Jane stared at her quizzically. "There was a downward cast to your voice, just now, as if Lord Hullworth's intentions, or lack thereof, bothered you."

"No, indeed." She swallowed, wondering why the avowal tasted strangely flat and formless on her tongue, like sampling a spoonful of pavlova only to realize that the cook had left sugar out of the meringue. "We are nothing more than friends to each other. In fact, he could be a trifle more elusive for my tastes. Every time I turn around, he's there."

Jane lifted her slender shoulders in an offhanded shrug. "Ours is a smallish society. In a week's time we see many of the same people. In fact, in our previous Seasons, you and I have attended dozens of events where he was also a guest and surrounded by his followers."

"The gaggle," she supplied with an absent nod, her brow knitted. "But it's a bit different now, and it has been ever since our encounter at the Zoological Society Gardens."

She didn't particularly want to talk about it, but it was important that Jane understood the severity of the conundrum Ellie found herself in.

"What happened at the zoo to bring about this transformation?"

"Well . . ." She leaned closer and cupped her hand to the side of her mouth to whisper into Jane's ear. "He might have . . . um . . . kissed me."

Jane gasped. "Newton's apple!"

"Hu-ush," she answered in singsong through her teeth as she smiled at Miss Carmichael and Lady Elise, who glanced back over their shoulders. Both were whispering like a pair of vipers in a basket, doubtless pretending friendship while scheming against each other for Lord Hullworth's attention. Ellie slowed her steps until she and Jane trailed all the others, then continued sotto voce. "It only happened because I was in a panic due to an elephant on the loose. You know how I can be when on the precipice of death. And I'm sure he wouldn't have done anything so drastic if he hadn't still believed that I'd made up George to make him jealous." She shook her head. "It all sounds too ridiculous to speak aloud."

"No, not at all. In fact, this is an inspiring development for our research. By all accounts, he is a gentleman who values his privacy. Not only does he shield his younger sister from scoundrels, but his own liaisons are quite discreet."

Ellie's spine stiffened ramrod straight. "What do you mean *his own liaisons*?"

"Precisely," Jane said with a scholarly nod. Then, clearly unaware that she'd just tied her friend's stomach in knots with three words, she continued. "So, one could only imagine the numerous options he might have chosen to employ to subdue your dread. A 'there, there, Miss Parrish' and a pat on the hand might have sufficed. And yet"—she paused to lift her pointed finger and arch her brows—"he chose to kiss you. *In public*."

"You're making too much of it. We were well hidden," Ellie groused, still wondering about those liaisons.

She supposed that it wasn't beyond the realm of possibility that he, like George, had oats to sow. But quite suddenly she hated the thought of oats, sown or unsown. If she never saw or heard of an oat again, it would be too soon.

"Very well," Jane said a bit too easily. "Then tell me what happened directly following this apparently insignificant moment."

"He declared his intention to call on me. But it meant nothing. Truly."

Ellie did her best to keep her expression neutral but Jane's erudite eyes gleamed in triumph like a cat who'd caught a mouse by the tail. Thankfully, she kept her cunning thoughts to herself.

Pursing her lips, Jane looked down to fish a tiny ledger and pencil stub from the placket sewn into her skirts at the hip. Turning to a blank page, she asked, "And was this said in the obligatory 'I kissed you and, therefore, I must behave like a gentleman now' sense? Or was he rather demanding and animalistic? Did he growl at any point?"

Knowing it was important to document her findings for research, Ellie was straightforward and completely honest. "It must have been obligatory. However, since he was still holding me at the time, I cannot make an unequivocal statement to that effect." She paused to gather in a breath, wondering why she was suddenly light-headed, her chest tight—likely a collapsed lung, her death imminent. It could have nothing to do with the fact that she was recounting the most intimate experience of her life, she was sure. "There may have been a growl, but we were in the zoo so that hardly signifies."

"Everything signifies. One must explore all avenues," Jane said with a tap of her pencil to the paper. "But the most important thing to note for the primer is, what did it do to your physiology?"

The recollection caused her pulse to quicken. Dragging in a sip of air, she settled her fingertips against the insistent fluttering on the side of her throat in order to keep it from bursting through her skin and causing some sort of disastrous arterial damage. "I don't really . . . that is . . . it was all so . . ."

Jane closed the ledger with a snap and grinned. "Inordinately interesting, indeed. Tell me this—how much embroidery have you done ever since the zoo incident?"

Knowing that her friend would make too much of it, Ellie was about to deny that she'd done any. And yet, in that precise instant, she noted that her free hand was on a fidgeting spree, unfastening and refastening the pearl buttons of her glove. She'd even loosened one.

"I can't seem to stop," she admitted on a reluctant sigh. "Even now I wish I had a needle and thread just to keep myself from thinking about it. Dash it all. I'll need to mend this straightaway. Let's go to the retiring room."

"Left an impression, did he?" Jane asked as they took the corridor away from the parlor.

Ellie nodded and lifted her hands to cover her scorching cheeks. "He did things that I never knew were part of kissing. Wondrously delicious things. I even forgot where I was."

"Then it stands to reason that he would be an exceptional lover."

"Jane!" She gasped and glanced around the empty hallway. "You're a married woman. You shouldn't think about those things."

"On the contrary, as a woman married to a visceral man with unassailable stamina, I am delighted to be distracted by *those things* several times a day. I have no doubt that you will be, as well. When you marry, I daresay, you'll have little time to embroider then," she added with a waggle of her brows.

Ellie's mind immediately conjured a picture of Lord Hullworth, interrupting her needlework to haul her into his arms and . . . satisfy his appetite.

The thought caused her blood to simmer like mulled wine in a pot over the fire. Her lungs were left burning for a breath of cool air and a fine sheen of perspiration bloomed on her skin.

She fanned herself surreptitiously with a wave of her hand, and belatedly realized that it should have been George's face that her mind conjured. George that tossed aside her tambour and pulled her into his embrace. And when she purposely put him in those imagined scenarios, her blood cooled to its appropriate temperature and she breathed much easier.

"I wish George was ready to marry. It would help to settle my mind, I think. And yet, I fear I'll be as old as the aunts by the time he proposes. If I even live that long."

"Why not consider Lord Hullworth as a viable candidate?"

"I couldn't do that!" she declared on a misstep, stumbling forward a bit before she regained her bearings.

"Are you afraid of being attracted to him? Perhaps afraid that someone other than George could claim your heart?"

"That simply isn't possible. I've always loved George, and I always will."

Jane gave her a dubious look. "Regardless of the outcome, I hope you've written all this down. It will be perfect for our book. On one hand you have a courtship between two people who have professed no desire to marry each other and yet find themselves inexplicably drawn together—"

"It meant nothing," she insisted again.

"—and on the other hand, you have jealousy serving as the impetus to prod an unyielding party into action."

"Jealousy?" She scoffed. "I could not care less about Lord Hullworth's liaisons."

"I find it quite noteworthy that you concluded I was referring to you in regard to Lord Hullworth," Jane said with a grin and continued before Ellie could offer an excuse about anyone making a similar assumption. "I'm certain your trip to Wiltshire will provide all the answers you need."

"For the book, you mean," Ellie clarified sternly.

"Of course." Jane blinked with owl-eyed innocence that wouldn't even convince a vicar that she was in earnest.

But the very thought of traveling with Lord Hullworth, of sleeping beneath the same roof, brought back that sense of heart-racing panic. It was surely not an ailment she could survive all the way to Wiltshire. It would be better if things went back to the way they were, a simple trip with her aunts and George. That was all she needed.

"Lord Savage said something interesting at dinner," she said, glancing sideways at Jane as they continued to walk. "He thinks that Lord Hullworth might want . . . to pursue me. At least if I were available to pursue. Which I'm not, of course."

"Hmm. So that's what you were talking about at dinner. I was afraid that I'd have to send Raven after the scoundrel to warn him away from trying to seduce my friend."

"Don't be ridiculous."

Jane shrugged. "It isn't the first time I've thought that he might have been the one in the garden at Sutherfield Terrace with Prue."

"But that was *Lord F* not *Lord S*?"

"It could be that Prue is trying to protect the man from being discovered by using a different letter."

Ellie shook her head. "Scoundrel though he may be, Lord Savage confessed that he was only trying to goad his friend into ill humor. In fact, he appears to have no interest in what he mockingly referred to as *innocents*."

Jane made a note of that in her ledger and then lifted her questioning gaze. "What if Lord Hullworth does want to pursue you?"

"He doesn't," she said quickly, practically shooting the words from her mouth. A small laugh erupted from Jane's throat as she eyed her dubiously. Ellie's shoulders sagged. "Well, if that were true—though it's entirely doubtful—I would have to make an excuse to travel without him. In fact, I might do that regardless. It's just that I feel a sense of imminent doom whenever I think about the trip."

"You've always felt that way about everything."

"This is different." After all, it couldn't be conducive to longevity if her pulse always leapt at the sight of him. It filled her with the strange urge to run—though in which direction she was never sure. Away from him? Or toward him? Neither choice seemed appropriate. She was his friend, after all. One did not run from friends *or* rush into their arms.

Jane reached out and set her hands on Ellie's shoulders. "Perhaps, it is time to face your fears head-on."

Ellie didn't think there was ever a good time for that.

"Speak of the devil," Jane said with a grin.

Then, she spun Ellie around to find none other than Lord Hullworth at the end of the paneled corridor!

In the sconcelight, his lean form strode toward her with purpose, his black tailcoat parting to reveal the outline of firm thigh muscles encased in supple gray woolen trousers. The sight left her abruptly breathless and flushed as if she were seeing him in a silk banyan and nothing more, just like in one of the scandalous daydreams she'd been having all week. She blamed Aunt Myrtle's latest novel for the inspiration.

Unable to look away, Ellie's gaze wandered upward in slow, unladylike appreciation beyond the intriguing, heavy form beneath the fall front, up the flat expanse of his satin paisley waistcoat—of the same smoky silver and mossy green hues that matched the shifting colors of his irises—and up along the folds of his white cravat to the chiseled features that looked especially dashing this evening.

She swallowed and briefly wondered if the servant at the end of the hall would think her mad if she just lifted her skirts and began to run as fast as she could.

Likely so.

"Miss Parrish," he said with a formal bow.

"Lord Hullworth," she answered inanely, somewhat breathless. Flustered, Ellie barely remembered her manners. "Have you met Lady Northcott? You may recall that Doctor Lockwood's residence is neighbor to the home of Jane's parents."

"Ah, yes. A pleasure," he said with a bow to Jane.

"Would you also happen to be one of the friends with whom Miss Parrish is writing a book on the subject of matrimonial habits?"

Jane nodded. "Very astute observation, my lord. And what a coincidence that you stepped into the hall just now. We were just discussing—"

"Our book," Ellie interrupted, feeling as if a swarm of bees suddenly descended into her stomach with the intention of turning it into a honeycomb. "But not the . . . matrimonial parts . . . of course."

"Of course," he parroted, amusement lingering in his eyes. Then he sobered. "I came to bid you a good night."

Her surprise subdued the buzzing hive. "So soon?"

"I fear, I must," he said. "As you doubtless noticed, I was added to Lady Millington's party at the last minute. I had intended for my sister to join me—as her ladyship made it known that she had two available places for dinner—but Meg begged off, claiming a headache."

And thus, leaving the perfect opportunity for Miss Carmichael, Ellie thought peevishly.

"I hope Meg is feeling better soon," she said and would be sure to send her well wishes and a cheerful sampler.

"I have a slew of experimental remedies for headaches," Jane interjected. "And, I'm proud to say, that not a single one has ever exploded. I'd be happy to send them over."

Lord Hullworth's brow furrowed over the bridge of his nose in uncertainty. "Thank you, my lady. However, I'm of a mind that she will be hale once more after a night's rest. Much like Lord Bassingstoke, I imagine," he added turning his attention again to Ellie. "I just saw him to his carriage and he will be of no further nuisance to you."

A shock of bewilderment temporarily robbed her of speech and she blinked at him.

It was one thing to glower across the table. But to *act* on her behalf? That was rather presumptuous. After all, there'd been no need. She'd handled the situation effectively with the aid of a few fork tines.

She felt her spine stiffen.

Beside her, Jane murmured a *hmm* of intrigue while biting her bottom lip. Then abruptly, Jane said, "I beg you would excuse me for a moment. I was just on my way to fix a button on my glove. Dratted things always come loose when you least expect it."

Jane, clearly sensing her friend's need to set matters straight, cast her a sly wink and sauntered down the corridor.

Left alone with him, Ellie drew in a measured breath. "You needn't have interfered with Lord Bassingstoke. I am not wholly incapable of dissuading unwanted advances, nor was I living beneath a rock before you took notice of me."

The corner of his mouth quirked in amusement, setting a spark to her ire. "I've no doubt of your abilities, or the likelihood that you have tempted your fair share of gentlemen. But what kind of man would I be if I merely stood by and watched, when I could easily settle the matter between Lord Bassingstoke and Lord Savage?"

"Lord Savage?" she gasped, embarrassed and furious now.

He lifted his shoulders in an inconsequential shrug. "Merely a discreet word between old schoolmates. Savage actually assisted me in seeing Bassingstoke to his carriage."

"You had no right, you overbearing, pompous, stuffed—"

"Though, in the future, if you are interested in conversing with a research candidate for your book, you might consider one with actual marital intent. That is your aim, is it not? It is sad, however, that *Nethersole* has never provided inspiration on that particular topic. A marriage-minded gentleman should always provide support and encouragement to the woman who holds his affections."

She was seething now, shooting flinty bronze daggers with her eyes. "I cannot fathom how the matter has anything to do with you. Good night, my lord."

She turned on her heel, only to feel a warm hand on her arm, staying her. A glance confirmed that he wasn't wearing a glove. He was touching her, skin on skin. And all at once every sensation and every emotion seemed to amplify inside her as if she were trapped inside a bell tolling the midnight hour.

She could hear everything. The sound of a single footstep. The quiet rasp of superfine wool against linen as he shifted closer. And she could feel everything. Her nails biting into her palms. Her heart hammering. The strained tightness of her corset. The heat of his body at her back even though she wasn't pressed against him. The soft brush of her lashes as they fell against her cheeks as she closed her eyes to absorb it all.

"We are friends, are we not?" he asked quietly, as if he was just as uncertain as she. "And you would do the same for me, I should think."

"Do you mean, would I escort Miss Carmichael to her carriage because she laid her hand on your sleeve?"

"I wish *someone* would," he said dryly, and the vision it created in her mind, of her doing just that, was so ludicrous that a rueful laugh escaped her.

She turned to face him. In doing so, his hand naturally fell from her arm, leaving the flesh tingling and wanting. And he stared down at his own fingertips as if he didn't recognize them. But when his gaze lifted to hers, his eyes were darker, more green than gray. The same ravenous color they'd been at Gunter's as he'd eaten her last bites of burnt filbert ice cream.

Her stomach gave a funny little hop and a sudden rise of gooseflesh prickled along her arms. It made her want to step forward, to press against him in order to quell the sensation.

She chafed her hands over her arms instead. "I don't understand our friendship."

He stared back at her quizzically as if she'd spoken a language he'd never heard before. Tension emanated from his rigid form. His nostrils flared. His fists were clenched tightly at his sides like a man straining to keep them there.

Then, after a moment, he finally said, "I'll give Meg your best. Good night, Miss Parrish."

With a stiff bow, he turned on his heel and left her standing alone in the corridor, listening to the hard echo of his retreating footfalls.

Behind her, she heard the quick patter of steps and soon felt Jane slide her arm through hers, elation fairly vibrating from her frame. "There's no question about it, Ellie. I think Lord Savage had it right all along."

Chapter 13

"Do not trust your heart, for there are times when said organ is being ridiculous."

—A NOTE FOR *The Marriage Habits of the Native Aristocrat*

By the middle of the following week, Brandon was convinced he was going mad.

His sleep was fitful. His appetite altered from none at all to a ravening bottomless pit. His clothes were too warm. His cravat was too tight, even though his valet had assured him several times that he hadn't altered his method of tying the preferred mathematical knot. His windows offered no view that pleased him. And he couldn't stop hearing Miss Parrish's soft plea, "I don't understand our friendship."

He didn't either.

At Lady Millington's dinner, Lord Savage had laughingly accused him of behaving like a man who'd staked his claim. Or even like . . . a jealous husband. Brandon had assured him that was not the case at all. He was merely looking out for Miss Parrish's reputation as he would for any friend of his sister's. Then Savage had clapped him on the shoulder and bid him good luck against the demons he would soon be wrestling.

Soon be? No, Brandon was already in the midst of the tussle.

He wanted her so badly that he dreamt of her all through the night, every night. The visions tempted him to linger abed and take this consuming desire in hand. To be rid of it, once and for all. He'd even been tempted to pay a call on one of the dozens of women who'd offered to be his mistress. But he knew it was no use. He knew that there was only one woman who could satisfy this maddening hunger.

He couldn't explain it. No matter how many times he reminded himself that she and Nethersole had something of an understanding. No matter how many times he vowed to never entertain the idea of courting a woman whose affections lay elsewhere. No matter how determined he was to be her friend and *only* her friend, some other, strangely primitive, part took over when she was near.

He needed to put an end to it. And if that meant complete absence from her presence until the demon wrestling was over, then so be it.

"I will conquer this before we travel to Wiltshire," he said into the empty study, absently wondering if he should lock the door and toss the key out the window, just to be safe.

❦❦❦

ELLIE DECIDED to stay home that week and sent her regrets for the dinners and parties on her schedule. When the aunts fretfully inquired after her health, she merely said that she desired some evenings to herself.

It was true enough. She'd been tired of late, and wanted to turn in at an earlier hour than societal events allowed.

"And besides," she'd added to ease the worry-knitted brows that lingered, "with George out of town, there's hardly a point in dressing in all my finery for a ball that he isn't going to attend. After all, the purpose of this final Season is to snare him, is it not?"

It was a plausible excuse, and the aunts accepted it without any further questions. But deep down, Ellie knew that she was only trying to avoid Lord Hullworth.

He was the reason that her sleep had been interrupted,

appearing in a constant series of dreams that left her heart racing and her skin damp. And she was desperate to finally rid herself of the churning, tingling, palpitating restlessness she suffered when he was near.

So, she was grateful that he never came to call with his sister. Meg had been over nearly every day, declaring that her brother was too busy with estate matters, even to take a drive. Assured that there was no chance of running into Lord Hullworth, Ellie readily agreed to shopping excursions, tours of the museums and walks through the park.

Her days were filled with activity, but her evenings were subdued. While the aunts enjoyed the parties, Ellie occupied much of her time with embroidery and letter writing.

> Dear Jane,
>
> Have you any recent news from our dear Prue? It has been more than a fortnight since I've received a letter and I am worried. You and I spent so much time chatting about a certain marquess that I neglected to ask if you also thought her letters seemed more melancholy of late.
>
> Your friend (the worrier on Upper Wimpole Street),
> Ellie

> Dear Worrier,
>
> You needn't. I have had a number of letters in the past fortnight and I detect no great sadness from our friend. In fact, her letters seem somewhat hopeful, at least to my eyes. She is asking about marriage. Queries along the line of: when I was certain that Raven cared for me and how he proposed.

I see this as promising. Perhaps she has met some-one who has taken her mind off Lord F?

> Signed,
> Jane, the apparent optimist

Ellie decided to be optimistic as well and allowed herself to imagine Prue being wooed by some handsome gentleman. She hoped that was the case.

Then, near mid-week, she finally received a letter from Prue.

Dear Ellie,

Forgive me, again, for being so negligent in my correspondence. With the days growing longer of late, I have extended my walks. I wish I had the words to describe the beauty of the grounds of Crossmoor Abbey. If I did, however, this letter would be far too large to fit on the mail coach.

But please know that you and our friendship are ever in my thoughts, and your letters are most welcome. In that regard, I have noticed that a certain gentleman has not earned mention in your correspondence of late and, with that said, I offer my sincerest hope that you are in good spirits.

> *Affectionately,*
> *Prudence Thorogood*

Dearest Prue,

In regard to the matter of a certain gentleman, the reason he has not earned mention in my last few letters is because there is nothing to report. G—is no closer to proposing to me than a squirrel to a peahen. I am nearly resigned to it.

Thankfully, I have made a new friend and I know you would like her, too. My aunts have all but adopted her, and would have done if she did not already have a brother to look after her (a certain not-so-elusive marquess that I may have mentioned a time or two). Where she is all effervescence and light, he is mercurial and bewildering. I never know which disposition to expect whenever we should meet. So you can imagine that my head has been awhirl.

Did I mention that he is also the very one who holds the deed to the property you so admire? Therefore, I am quite eager to learn more about your walks, even if it takes four mail coaches to bring your letter.

Your friend,
Elodie Parrish

Dear Ellie,

I just received the enclosed letter this evening from our friend. I now believe you were correct to have concerns.

Jane

Dear Jane,

I hardly know how to write this letter.
Lord F—has returned. And he seems so earnest in his pursuit, proclaiming a genuine regard for me, that I am questioning my reasons for ever trying to avoid him.

Could it be that I have misjudged him all along? I am both afraid that I have and that I have not.

After reading your last letter, regarding your own courtship, I am wavering on a dreadful pendulum between believing him and holding firm to my resolve.

I know that, either way, nothing good will come of my decision. I will surely lose something dear in exchange for whatever I may gain.

Your friend,
Prudence Thorogood

Dearest Prue,

I am heartsick over the trials you are suffering. And I hope you do not mind that Jane shared your last correspondence. We are all like sisters, after all.

Please hear this again—that my aunts and I would welcome you to stay with us.

I know what you have said before, that you would not sully our house with your reputation. But I do not care a whit about that. No matter what event occurred that night at Sutherfield Terrace all these many months ago, it does not alter the bond we share.

Ever your friend,
Elodie Parrish

Even as Ellie looked down at the letter, she doubted Prue would accept her invitation. And it was clear that her friend needed someone to confide in, to help her through this trial.

Mere ink on paper would not do.

When the aunts returned from cards, Ellie asked if they would be willing to leave for Wiltshire within a few days, as soon as they could arrange it. As she knew they would, Aunt Maeve and Aunt Myrtle immediately agreed.

That left only one thing to do—tell Lord Hullworth that his escort was no longer required.

Ellie felt relieved by the decision. Soon, she would not have to endure any encounters with him that made her question what they were to each other. The restlessness and ardent dreams would no longer plague her. And she would never again have to be held in his arms and kissed witless.

Never again.

She frowned at the thought, strangely wishing that *never* didn't seem like such a terribly long time.

Chapter 14

~

"A debutante must never trust herself in the moonlight."

—A NOTE FOR *The Marriage Habits of the Native Aristocrat*

The gardens at Sutherfield Terrace were beyond compare. In daylight they were a splendor of color for the eye to behold. But at night, they held a mysterious allure. There were winding pathways between lush hedgerows, whimsically sculpted topiaries, and fountains that sparkled like diamonds in the moonlight.

It was easy to imagine someone getting carried away in such a place.

Ellie turned from the rain-dappled window to face the grand ballroom. She took little notice of the surrounding opulence, the ornate arches over Corinthian columns, the alabaster walls richly decorated with gilded scroll-work pargeting, or the wealth of colorful silk gowns and waistcoats, blurring together over a vast expanse of gleaming carrara marble.

Instead, her gaze landed directly on Lord Hullworth.

It was no wonder. He was a sight to behold, handsome and broad-shouldered in tailored dark broadcloth that hugged the perfection of his fine form. And no feminine eye could resist admiring the tousled configuration of his bronze curls or the flawless taut skin of his freshly shaven jaw above the impeccably folded lines of his snow-white cravat.

As usual, he was surrounded by his gaggle. Beside him, Meg earned her own following of admirers, as well, young women and gentlemen pausing to admire the subtle alterations to her gown.

But there was another reason why Ellie had spotted him so quickly. Because every time her gaze strayed to him, *he* was always looking back at her.

She felt the tug of it deep inside, as if there were some invisible filament connecting them. This sensation puzzled her all the more when she thought about how they hadn't seen each other in a sennight. Surely, whatever this was should have dissipated by now. And yet, even this evening as they'd spoken no more than four words in greeting—a mere "Miss Parrish," and "Lord Hullworth"—the mysterious tug was still there.

It left her with an unfinished feeling. A need for more.

Of course, the simple explanation for that was because she had yet to speak to him about canceling their joint trip to Wiltshire. Once that was out of the way, this unwelcome sensation would abandon her, surely.

However, instead of putting one slipper in front of the other and speaking with him now, she made an excuse to her aunts about needing a bit of air, then headed in the opposite direction.

Slipping through a side door, she made her way to the wraparound terrace. The rain had just ended, leaving the air damp and the stones slippery. She was cautious of every footfall while descending the rounded stairs. After all, one would rather die of old age than of a cranial impact that turned one's encephalon into jelly.

Standing in the gauzy golden light spilling out from the ballroom windows, she wasn't certain where to go next. Although, she was thankful she hadn't chosen a satin gown tonight, for it would have been spotted and revealed her sojourn. This evening, she wore tiers of ruffled Bengali muslin, a fabric so diaphanous that it rustled in the faintest breeze. But it was also so pale that it appeared almost silver in the light of the crescent moon, so she ventured toward the shadows to avoid discovery.

Up ahead, the garden was dark, the torches having extinguished into hissing spirals of smoke. It was surely hazardous to one's health to be out of doors in such moist environs. However, at least she wouldn't encounter another soul.

In the very same instant, she heard a sure-footed step on the terrace behind her and, even before he spoke, she knew. She felt it in the way her body instantly became alert. Every downy hair on her skin seemed to lift, sensing the breeze like a butterfly's antennae.

"Taking the air, Miss Parrish?" Hullworth asked, his low voice sending a wayward shiver through her—also known as *the first symptom*. "Or was your withdrawal from the ballroom a calculated effort to lure me to your side? After all, you had to know I would follow."

Pushing aside her ailment for the moment, she rolled her eyes and turned to face him. "Such an arrogant presumption. There is every possibility that I am merely *taking the air*, as you said."

"*Hmm . . .*" he murmured dubiously, stepping down into the garden. "I would wager that you've already thought of at least two different ways that a calamitous injury might befall a person from slipping on these wet stones."

Seven, actually, but she wasn't about to admit it. "So, as my friend, you ventured outside to ensure I was safe, from stumbles and rapscallions alike?"

"As you say," he offered and proceeded to join her on the graveled path.

"Well," she began, "since you are here by chance—"

"*Ah ha*. I knew it."

"—there has been a new development I need to share with you." As soon as she finished, the smug arch of his brow fell into a flat line.

Something dark flickered across his gaze. "Nethersole has proposed."

"*What*? Whyever would you . . . No." Ellie shook her head, both startled and confused. She couldn't fathom why that would have been the first thing he imagined or why his statement seemed so clipped and forced, like an accusation. So, again, she said, "No."

He stared back at her for a moment, then jerked his head in a quick nod before turning to look over his shoulder. The shifting of his soles on the rock nearly covered up the rush of his exhale. But not quite. She still heard the unmistakable sound of relief.

His reaction did nothing to ease her bewilderment. In fact, quite the opposite. Why should he care either way? After all, George would propose eventually.

"Then what is your news?" he asked.

She put her own questions out of her mind as she followed his gaze toward the shadows falling on the terrace from the guests milling near the open windows. It wouldn't take more than the turn of a head to peer through the glass and see them together. Alone in the garden. Their names would be on society's lips, the scandal in bold black ink in tomorrow's paper. "Perhaps it would be best to tell you in the garden."

Returning his attention to her, a smile drifted over his lips as he offered his arm. "This mysterious development must be quite important if you would risk whatever fatality might arise from a damp hem."

"Tease all you like," she said curling her hand along the inside of his sleeve, keeping a fistful of skirts in the other. "But one of these days you'll wish you had someone to warn you of every potential calamity."

She expected him to laugh at that. Instead he nodded contemplatively, his focus toward the moon-white stone path ahead. The walkway canted on either side, with a sloping ridge down the center to draw water away. It worked perfectly for keeping rain from saturating her shoes and skirts.

"First of all, I want to thank you for offering to escort my aunts and me to Wiltshire. You were most generous to do so after being practically forced into a decision you had no time to contemplate."

"It did not require overthinking," he said with the matter-of-fact air of a man who, once decided, held fast to his commitments. The thought did not sit well with her.

"Even so," she continued, "you will be glad to know that you are no longer under any obligation. You see, my aunts and I need to leave sooner than the end of the Season."

An unexpected tension collected in the corded muscles beneath her hand. "When?"

"As soon as we can arrange it. No more than two days hence, I should think."

Ellie expelled a breath. There. She'd said it. His next response could only be a nod of understanding, followed by his blameless termination of their agreement. It was all for the best. She'd been spending far too much time thinking about him when she should be thinking about George.

"Very well. I can manage that."

"Quite understandable. No one would expect you to—" She stopped abruptly, her heels digging into the gravel. Surely, she hadn't heard him correctly. "You *can . . . manage that*?" At his nod of affirmation, she shook her head at once. "No. That isn't necessary. I wasn't asking for you to alter your plans. In fact, I insist that you do not."

"I don't mind. And I'm certain Meg wouldn't either."

"But . . ." She stared up at his steady countenance, at a loss for how to proceed. "But you don't even know the reason we're leaving early."

"It doesn't matter."

"It might," she argued inanely, her hands dropping to her sides, fists clenched in increasing agitation over his inability to see a perfectly acceptable escape for them both.

"Then tell me your reason," he said, drawing in a patient breath. As he exhaled, he reached up to tuck a wayward curl behind her ear. "So that I can tell you it still doesn't matter."

Drat this man! Why was he making it so difficult for her? He was supposed to be just as eager as she to end their travel plans. To want as much distance between them as possible. Instead, she had a dizzying impulse to close her eyes and lean into his touch—the sure signs of a fainting spell.

Thankfully, before she collapsed in a heap of muslin, he withdrew.

Readying her excuse, she cleared her throat and absently skated her fingertips over the tingling sensation he left in his wake. "Here it is, then. There's a distinct possibility that a blackguard is in pursuit of my friend and I must save her."

His brow furrowed instantly. "Then I am most definitely escorting you."

"What I mean is," she hurried to say, while inwardly groaning at her poor choice of words. "I'm not certain he is a blackguard. Neither is she, for that matter. You see, she is the dear friend who has inspired Winnie, Jane and me to write our book. In fact, it was right here in this very garden where her father discovered her with a man. I do not know the whole of it, only that she was sent away the very next morning to live with her aunt and uncle. Now, even if she is wholly blameless—of which I have no doubt because Prue, by nature is shy and reserved—her father's rash actions cast a tarnished light upon her."

"Perhaps," he said, "your friend's father objected to the gentleman in question and sought to protect his child by removing her."

"Doubtless, that is what you would do for Meg," she said with a reluctant measure of fondness. Hullworth would choose to shield and protect those he loved rather than allow them to come to harm. It had a terrible effect of making her like him a good deal more than she wanted to. "Unfortunately, her father has always been unduly severe in his judgements upon her. Although, that is not to say that he didn't have a stronger objection to the gentleman, who must possess an awful reputation as to sully her by acquaintance. Not even Prue has revealed his name in her letters, but refers to him as *Lord F.*"

"And you say the blackguard has followed her?"

"All the way to Wiltshire. And now," she said on a heavy breath, "you know the reason why my aunts and I are leaving *without* your escort. After all, you must think of Meg."

He gave her a pointed look. "Contrary to your opinion, I have not placed my sister in a glass box, high upon a shelf. Believe me, when she thinks I'm being overprotective, she tells me. I, in turn, remind her of how young women who are used to doing as they please in the country cannot do the same in London. As her brother, my only wish is to keep her from harm and from regret, not to rob her of experiences. And as for your utterly transparent attempt to compel me to rescind my obligation, for shame, Miss Parrish."

"I—" she began, wanting to tell him how wrong he was, but her guilt was already flaring in her cheeks and he tsked her playfully. It was no use. Hullworth knew her too well, it seemed.

Smiling down at her, he lifted his hand and curled his index finger beneath her chin. "You failed on two counts," he continued with mock sternness. "First, in believing that Meg and I are the fair-weather variety of friends. And second, that I made the decision lightly. You should know that I never make any decision without giving it . . .

careful"—he stopped and glanced down to see that his thumb strayed to the verge between her chin and bottom lip and his teasing grin abruptly faded—"consideration."

His gaze darkened and Ellie's breath caught. She knew that hungry look. It caused all sorts of ailments. Right this instant, it filled her with a terrible impulse to wrap her arms around him. And she really shouldn't do that.

Oh, but it would feel so good to give in. The pulsing tingles that were sparking to life in her body told her so. Told her that he was solid and warm, and that all his hard places would line up perfectly with her soft ones.

"I . . . I think we should turn back. The damp air, you know. It's been known to cause all sorts of illnesses." As she spoke, his thumb grazed her bottom lip and a shiver rolled over her.

He crowded closer. "Are you cold, Ellie?"

The delicious scent of him made her mouth go dry. So she nodded, believing he would suggest that they adjourn to the ballroom. Instead, she felt his hand skirting over the curve of her hip to the small of her back, drawing her against his warmth.

Resisting only made her head feel giddy and too heavy to support, so she allowed her body to tilt naturally toward him, her hands coming to rest over the granite hardness beneath his satin waistcoat.

"Better?" he murmured, his breath drifting against her temple as he nuzzled into her fragrant curls.

She closed her eyes in an effort to ignore the tumult of harried pulses happening inside her. "I'm not certain. It seems that I have a list of entirely new ailments. Now, I feel flushed all over." Especially wherever her body was pressed to his.

He tensed at hearing her admission, his grip tightening as if attempting to keep both of them perfectly still. Then he muttered a low oath.

"I wish you hadn't told me that," he said, his mouth drifting over her brow. "You don't know how the thought of your skin—glazed pink like iced cakes—tempts me beyond reason, makes me wonder how sweet you would taste . . . *all over.*" He trailed kisses down to her cheeks, from crest to crest. "This color, right here, haunts my dreams. Are your lips flushed, too? They are. Mmm . . . so warm. Give them to me. I'll take care of them. Yes, yes, so sweet . . ."

He took her mouth with impatient, searing sips and a helpless mewl escaped her throat. She arched into his embrace, unable to fight the assault on her senses as he nibbled and tasted her, pleasuring her relentlessly. Her palms glided to his shoulders, fingertips digging into the fine wool for purchase.

"But I thought we were friends," she said weakly, her pulse heavy and thick, like her blood had turned to rivers of thick icing. It was having a terrible thudding effect on her heart.

"We are," he said with convincing certainty against her lips. "But sometimes friends just need to kiss in order to purge the overwhelming urge for more."

More? The mere idea caused her knees to tremble.

In response, he pulled her closer still, shoring her lower half against the solid girth of his thigh. She jolted at the intrusion, but he soothed her with sure deep kisses, his hand splaying firmly into the curve of her lower back.

Ellie clung to him. She felt scattered and ready to fly apart, her breaths too quick and shallow to fill her lungs. Why were her symptoms so horrendous when he was near? They transformed from almost unbearable agony to the most exquisite torment she'd ever suffered.

He offered her beleaguered senses a slight reprieve as his lips grazed the delicate shell of her ear, trailing to the place just behind the bare lobe. Then he opened his mouth over her, tasting the sensitive skin. And *oh yes* that was lovely.

"Your pulse is quite fast," he murmured against the harried flutter.

"If it bursts through my skin, my death will be on your hands."

"Well, we cannot have that," he said, laving that tender place with the flat of his tongue, lifting her higher along his thigh.

A soft, surprised moan escaped her and he growled in response, taking her mouth again. He gripped her hips, his kisses deep and drugging, as if he were feeding his own patented cure-all directly into her veins. And she suddenly felt alive, infused with vitality in the tight cinch of his arms. She wiggled, struggling to get closer, to rise up the length of the leg he braced between hers.

But just as she was starting to enjoy her symptoms—especially if this was the prescribed medicine—he stopped.

Abruptly, he lifted his mouth from hers, tucked her head against his panting chest and whispered, "We're not alone."

She startled, trying to hold her breath.

Sure enough, on the other side of the hedgerow, the sounds of another couple's amorous encounter drifted to them—a lilting feminine giggle, then a low masculine chuckle.

"Phillip, not here. We shouldn't."

"My love, I need to be inside you again. To feel your wet flesh clamp tightly around my aching—"

"Shh! You're such a naughty boy. But I'll not let you ruin my dress. No, no. I mean it this time."

The statement was followed by a giggle, then the quick patter of receding steps. A gruff chuckle answered as heavy footfalls followed in pursuit.

Hullworth shifted his hold, moving his thigh to the outside of her own. But he still held her close—close enough that she felt the hardness of his body, the imposing ridge pressed against her soft midriff. And all at once she understood what he'd meant by *more*.

With arms helplessly entwined around his neck, she lifted her gaze, uncertain. "I don't think kissing was a very good idea."

"Likely not," he said on a taut exhale.

She nodded, believing it was for the best that they abandon any thoughts of *purging the overwhelming urge for more.* "Just as long as we're both aware of what's between us."

"It is utterly undeniable," he said, easing his mouth over hers briefly for one more searing kiss before setting her apart.

Her head was still spinning by the time she got home that evening. And it wasn't until much later, when she was alone in her bed, that she suddenly realized the real reason she didn't want to travel to Wiltshire with Hullworth. Because it meant that she would be side by side, between the man she planned to marry and the man she couldn't seem to stop kissing.

Chapter 15

"Take heed—a marriage-minded gentleman may darken your door when least expected."

—A NOTE FOR *The Marriage Habits of the Native Aristocrat*

The following morning, Mr. Rivers handed Ellie a missive from Lord Hullworth. She accepted it with a mere nod of thanks, but inside her heart suddenly burst into a ramshackle rhythm that threatened to bore a fatal hole through the cage of her ribs.

Stealing upstairs to her bedchamber, she pressed the folded letter to her bosom and closed her eyes, willing herself to live long enough to read it. And she wondered if, perhaps, it contained another startling admission like the one he'd confessed about her pink skin last night.

But in the minute that followed, as she greedily skimmed the efficient scrawl, she realized there were no such passionate declarations on the page. Which was a relief, of course. Because she should only want love letters from George.

The contents pertained to their travel arrangements. She was both awed and amazed over the amount of work he'd managed to accomplish in the matter of a few hours. Apparently, they were set to leave the day after next. He even offered the use of his own serving staff to aid the preparations of her and her aunts, if need be.

And then the letter was signed: *Your friend, B*

Somehow the mere mention of the word *friend* caused

her body to react with a flood of heat and heady pulses that left her in need of a cool breeze. But the morning air through her open window was stifled and humid, frizzing her hair. She had to settle for splashing water into the basin to dampen a square of flannel, wringing it out before she bathed the perspiration from the surface of her skin.

She couldn't stop thinking about the kiss last night. It had become part of her being, as identifiable as the color of her eyes. Her tongue knew his taste. Her nose knew his scent. And her body knew the feel of him against her as if he'd left an indelible imprint behind.

This intimate knowledge was something she would have to accustom herself to as the years passed. And when she married George, she would just consider this her one and only, well-sown oat.

By the time afternoon arrived, she managed to pull herself together enough to agree on taking a jaunt with her aunts. However, that didn't mean her thoughts weren't still lingering in the gardens at Sutherfield Terrace. In fact, as she left her bedchamber, she realized she was dressed in a walking costume of mossy green velveteen that suspiciously resembled a certain gentleman's eyes. She only hoped no one else would notice.

Coming down the stairs to the foyer, Ellie stopped short when Mr. Rivers opened the door to Lord Nethersole.

"And don't you look fetching," George said, causing her heart to leap guiltily in her throat as he swaggered toward her. "Your eyes are bright, cheeks aglow. You must be thinking about me, hmm?"

"Of . . . course . . ." She swallowed, gripping the banister. "My thoughts would be on you since I haven't seen you in more than a week. Doubtless, you've come to discuss the changes in our travel plans." When he stared back at her blankly, she added, "I wrote about it in the missives I sent to your house."

Removing his gloves, one after the other, he shrugged. "I just returned yesterday to find heaps upon heaps of letters and ledgers that my steward is waiting for me to read through. But I ask you, Ellie, what's the point of paying his salary if I have to do all the work? One of these days, I'll just leave all that up to you."

Usually, when he mentioned *one of these days,* she could picture their life together—their wedding, their children, their house in the country with a familiar view from every window. But that didn't happen this time. Her mind remained blank, like an empty slate.

Surely, that meant nothing. Her hopes for a future with George were still the same. She simply had other things on her mind, like packing for the trip and closing up the house and midnight kisses . . .

She cleared her throat. "Well, if you haven't come about the letters, then what brings you here?"

"What else but my need to see your smiling face?" Stopping at the bottom step, he took her gloved hand and brought it to his lips. "I was out for a ride and my first thought carried me to your door."

The news brought a pleased smile to her lips. It was definitely progress in the right direction. "Is that so? Well then, I must know what this thought is so that I might encourage more of them."

"It's this damnable button. Apparently, my valet missed the fact that it's loose. I certainly don't look smart enough to dandy about town with my button bobbling."

She glanced dutifully at the coat button. "And . . . would you like me to mend it for you?"

"You see, Ellie. That's precisely the reason your name popped into my head."

Oh. So that was the reason for his visit. She turned away, carefully concealing her disappointment as she headed back upstairs for her sewing basket. Doubtless, her aunts would see this in a positive light, stating that he thought of her when he imagined the perfect *someone* to mend his buttons.

In the next moment, she heard them chatting about the confectioner's shop they planned to visit, and whether or not they could finagle the recipe for custard tarts from him before they left town.

The instant they saw George pacing impatiently in the parlor doorway, they erupted with bright cheerful greetings. "George!"

"My darling boy!"

"Whatever brings you here today?"

Threading the needle, Ellie exhaled a slow breath as she heard him say, "What other reason than to see your smiling faces?"

As she had done, they also fawned over him. Only, in her case, she was left feeling foolish.

"And how did your estate business fare?" Aunt Maeve asked.

Seeing his brow knitted in confusion as he shrugged out of his coat and absently tossed it to Ellie, Aunt Myrtle supplied, "Remember, dear? That was the reason you've been gone for over a week."

"Oh, *that* estate business. Right. Well, funny thing is, I'll have to go out of town again tomorrow morning for the same reason."

"But we're leaving earlier than planned for Wiltshire. Lord Hullworth and his sister will be here the day after next. Didn't Elodie mention it?"

"I didn't have the chance yet," Ellie interjected as she continued her task, not bothering to mention the three letters she'd sent to George's town house, informing him of the abrupt decision to travel ahead of schedule.

"No need," George said, dusting his hands together. "If it's settled, then all the better for me. The last time I traveled with the three of you, we had to go back a half dozen times because of something you'd forgotten." He chuckled, not remembering the story correctly. The trip they'd taken together was to leave him at school, and the reason they'd gone back was because *he* had forgotten his favorite riding crop. "I'd sooner give Hullworth the onerous task of wrangling you lot into a carriage and save the fun for me."

"George!" Aunt Maeve said with a playful swat on his shoulder. And Aunt Myrtle did the same, saying, "Incorrigible, boy!"

Ellie frowned down at the button, tying the brown thread before she snipped the end cleanly with her scissors. "All finished."

George moved toward the settee and took the coat but then set his finger beneath her chin, tilting up her face. "What's all this gloom about? Is it that you find Hullworth's company abhorrent?"

"No. Not at all," she said honestly, ignoring the wayward flutter in the pit of her stomach at the thought of their escort. She stood and smoothed her skirts in place.

"Then you're just pouting because you prefer mine, isn't that right?"

She smiled at him, but it felt as if it were an applique she had to stitch in place. "Of course."

He shrugged into the garment and grinned back at her. "I knew I was right to come here instead of going back to my valet. He's as slow as treacle in February and I have important places to be." Then he did something that surprised them all. He leaned in and kissed her cheek. "Thanks, Ellie. That's so you won't forget about me in the meantime. See you in three days, hmm?"

She touched her cheek and nodded. "Three days."

George winked and sauntered out of the parlor. The aunts waited until the door closed before they made a fuss over his thrilling, yet unexpected, display of affection. They began discussing her wedding cake and whether or not it should be apple and pear, or fig with walnuts.

But meanwhile, Ellie was distracted by the peculiar realization that the cheek beneath her fingertips remained perfectly cool, and not flushed pink at all.

ⷯⷯⷯⷯ

ELLIE DECIDED not to join her aunts when they went to the confectionary shop for recipe espionage. After George's visit, she didn't feel like venturing out. Her thoughts were too preoccupied by his impulsive kiss.

George lived on impulse, often flitting off at a moment's notice. It was impulse that had brought him to her doorstep to mend his button, and impulse that would likely compel him to marry her. One day.

The thought usually brought her a measure of comfort. But after last night, she was beginning to wonder if she might not want . . . more.

She immediately shook her head in denial, chiding herself firmly as she began to stuff her sewing and samplers into a woven valise. "No, Elodie Marie. George is all you've ever wanted. As for Hullworth, he isn't even looking for a wife." She stopped at once. *A wife?* Now where had that come from? What part of her own overblown ego believed that she, out of scores and scores of debutantes, had snared London's favorite bachelor? Ha! Again, she shook her head. "Not that it should matter to you either way. You're just friends. Friends who . . . really enjoy kissing each other," she said, her words trailing off on a sigh, until she pricked the tip of her finger on a needle.

She hissed and drew back sharply as a tiny red dot welled to the surface, then put it to her lips before she bled to death, albeit slowly. Though, an agonizingly lengthy exsanguination would serve her right for spending so much time thinking about the wrong man.

"Forgive me for coming in unannounced, Miss Parrish."

Ellie turned with a start as the man himself stood in the doorway. Her finger jerked out of her mouth with a *pop*. "Lord Hullworth?"

"Mr. Rivers is discussing the luggage and trunks with my butler in the foyer and I thought I'd see myself up. I hope I haven't come at an inconvenient—" He broke off, glancing down to her finger, and strode into the parlor without delay. Brow knitted, he withdrew a handkerchief from his pocket and took her hand in his, pressing the folded linen to her wound. "Surely, you have a thimble to save yourself from injury."

"Had I known you would come all this way merely to scold me, I'd have donned a thimble on every finger and thrown them at you, one after the other," she said with equal curtness, even as her pulse quickened.

A reluctant grin quirked at the corner of his mouth, his gaze meeting hers and warming as it brushed her cheeks. It was only then that she realized she was blushing. Again.

"I also came here for another reason." Leaving the handkerchief in her grasp, he reached into his pocket, then withdrew a small paper-wrapped parcel. "For you."

A mixture of uncertainty and anticipation filled her as she stared at the mysterious object. It would be highly improper to accept anything else from him. And yet, the desire to discover the contents therein filled her with such childlike glee that she couldn't contain it. Absently, she tucked the square of spotted linen up her sleeve, the tiny puncture in her skin indiscernible, and likely not fatal. She took the package. Her fingers trembled as she opened it. Spreading the paper, she found a fresh ledger, the leather cover smooth and warmed from the heat of his body.

"I hardly know what to say. You have given me so much already . . ." She smoothed her hand over the surface and brought it to her nose to inhale the rich fragrance, feeling a sharp tug on her heart. Looking into Lord Hullworth's gaze—nay, *Brandon's* gaze, for he could only be Brandon to her now—she said, "Thank you."

He inclined his head, appearing almost shy. "Open it. There's something more inside."

She complied, unbuttoning the clever fastening to find a thick pad of blank pages, bound and stitched into the spine. He leaned closer to point out a small loop of sueded leather on the side, and said, "That is for a pencil. I thought you would like a fresh ledger for our journey."

She gazed at him in speechless wonder, an overwhelming rush of tenderness filling her with that alarming effervescence. It did terrible things to her conflicted heart. And he looked back at her with such intensity that she was sure he was an instant away from pulling her into his embrace.

He took a step back and shook his head. "I know what you're thinking."

"I'm not certain you do."

"You think it would be perfectly natural to rush into my arms and show your appreciation by showering me with kisses. But I won't have it."

Caught off guard, a laugh bubbled out of her. "You won't?"

"No, indeed," he said with mock severity. "After your behavior last night, I must admit that I've become worried that you would try to seduce me again."

"You're calling *me* a seductress?"

"How else can a man describe a lovely young woman who boldly lures him out into a garden to take advantage of the first opportunity to scramble his wits."

"Mmm . . . yes, I see. Have I scarred you, then?"

He issued a solemn nod. "I may recover; however, there is no guarantee. All I know is that there will be no kissing on our travels, no matter how much you plead with me. I understand how tempted you are. I am London's most elusive bachelor, after all."

"London's most elusive lunatic, you mean. You are positively mad," she said, grinning broadly.

"Then, this madman bids you adieu," he said with a formal bow and a smile that displayed sprays of the most attractive crinkles beside his eyes.

For a breathless moment, she couldn't help but wonder what his smile might look like in twenty years, or in forty. And with her mind wandering—somewhere near his eightieth birthday where she envisioned the most appealing wrinkles of all—he turned and left.

Alone in the room, Ellie realized that he didn't call on her to give her the ledger. He came to ease her mind, in case she had any misgivings over traveling with him after their kiss.

It would likely be prudent of her to cry off . . . but she no longer wished to avoid him. In fact, she was looking forward to the trip.

That strangely light, unidentifiable sensation bubbled inside her as if her blood were filled with pockets of air, ready to lift her off the ground. A body could explode from such an ailment. And yet, it didn't cause her a moment's panic.

Chapter 16

"It is entirely possible that Pandora's box was, in reality, a picnic basket."

—A NOTE FOR *The Marriage Habits of the Native Aristocrat*

On the afternoon of their journey, Meg poked her head outside the carriage window, shielding her eyes from the bright sunlight. "Brandon, could we stop for a picnic soon? Not for me, of course, because I enjoy sitting perfectly still for hours upon hours and never have any appetite whatsoever"—she grinned impishly when he cast a dubious glance down from the seat of his stallion—"but Ellie's groaning stomach is not nearly as stalwart. In fact, I think she might be tempted to eat the bluebird on Aunt Myrtle's hat if we do not stop soon."

Through the opening, he heard laughter and saw Ellie reach across the seat to playfully swat at his sister. Then her face appeared through the frame, her cheeks flaming pink. "Pay no attention to your sister, my lord. I am perfectly content. Please do not alter your plans any more than you already have done on my account."

"I happen to be famished myself," he said and couldn't resist a glance down to her lips. "There's a glade not too far ahead with a brook nearby. We'll stop there for a spell."

He spurred Samson forward and informed the driver. Thus far the roads had been clear and dry and they were making excellent progress. There was plenty of time for a picnic.

But surprisingly, Brandon didn't feel the need to rest. He was filled with an inexplicable surge of energy, as though he could ride all day beside the landau. Hell, he could *run* the whole way to Wiltshire without tiring. He just felt good. Damn good, in fact.

He didn't quite know the reason for this but wondered if, perhaps, it had something to do with Nethersole's absence. That alone had a way of making the warm, luminous day all the more perfect. The only thing better would be to have him change his mind altogether.

It was no secret that he didn't like Nethersole. But it was an absolute mystery what Ellie found appealing about him. Clearly, she couldn't see what an utter nodcock he was. But Brandon hoped that would change. She deserved more than someone like Nethersole.

That very thought had been with Brandon for days, pestering and irritating him constantly. In his opinion, there was nothing worse than being blinded by love. If he could, he would save her from that.

Leaving his horse in the care of one of the groomsmen, Brandon joined his party in the clearing. Ellie and Meg laid out a cluster of shawls amidst an archipelago of oxeye daisies. The elder Miss Parrishes unloaded the hamper. And for the better part of an hour, they enjoyed fine fare and easy conversation.

After their repast, the aunts went to forage for berries and his sister followed. But he was glad that Ellie lingered in his company. Gladder still that she'd abandoned her formal use of *my lord* when they were alone.

"Brandon, I have something for you," she said, reaching into a tapestry-covered satchel beside her. "I just thought, with the others away, that it would be the best time to give this back to you." She reached across the fringed border, holding out a folded square of white linen. "It's your handkerchief, the one you left with me the other day. I washed away the blood and well . . . you can see the rest."

He did see, indeed. She'd embroidered one corner with a looping letter *B* in green thread, trimmed with silver to give it a shimmering effect in the shifting light. And right on the very edge, rested a tiny clover.

"It's remarkable," he said without any exaggeration. As a gentleman, it was his duty to admire needlework of all sorts but he rarely, if ever, saw something truly stunning. Even with this small sampling, he could see that she had an exceptional hand.

She nodded as one did when grateful for a compliment while, at the same time, knowing her own skill. There was no false show of modesty and he liked that about her.

"To be perfectly honest," she said, "I was going to come up with a story of how I'd mistakenly began an *M* for your sister only to find it a trifle too large and was forced to transform it into a *B*."

"Quite the elaborate falsehood," he said with a grin.

"Of course, I never would have been able to say it without stammering and giving myself away," she admitted ruefully. "So I must be truthful and tell you that I made this for you because I wanted to offer a small token of appreciation for escorting my aunts and me to Wiltshire. And to tell you that . . . I'm glad we are friends."

"As am I," he said, tucking her gift into the inner breast pocket of his coat and patting it fondly.

He watched as she absently plucked one of the nearby blossoms. A scattered collection of white petals already lay in front of her, as if those pale, delicate hands required an occupation at all times. And there were many nights that he'd envisioned those hands being *quite* industrious, over his clothes, over his flesh . . .

"I imagine you are eager to return to your estate," she

said, drawing him away from dangerous musings. "It must be difficult to be away for long intervals when you have so much to oversee."

"My uncle employed an exceptional steward, who stayed on after I inherited. Mr. Weymouth keeps Crossmoor Abbey running like clockwork and my aunt Sylvia is there, as well, to confer with the housekeeper on a daily basis."

Her gaze turned tender as it drifted over his features and she said softly, "I am truly sorry for how your inheritance came upon you."

He responded with a solemn nod, knowing that it wasn't said out of pity but out of an understanding of great loss. "I only wish that Meg had had more time with our parents. With so many years between us, you can gather that she came along as quite the surprise to them. But Mother had not fared well having a child at her age and declined in the few years following. Father, of course, was the best of men and taught me the importance of living for each day."

"You are too modest with your own accomplishments, not only in handling a title you were never prepared to attain, but accepting the charge of your younger sister," she argued.

As always, she gave her opinion openly, and it pleased him to know that her thoughts regarding him had greatly altered from their initial encounters.

"Hmm . . . strange," he said. "I seem to recall a certain young woman casting the labels of *odious* and *overbearing* upon my shoulders."

"And you still are those terrible things. You're quite the conundrum," she said, swiping up a few petals and tossing them in his direction.

He brushed at the ones that landed on his waistcoat and glanced to the figures of his sister and her aunts collecting berries in their bonnets a distance away. Leaning back casually on one hand, he propped the other over his bent knee and twirled a single petal between his fingers. "Then I shall endeavor to be more transparent, like you with your blushes."

His statement instantly rewarded him with a view of pink saturating her porcelain skin and she threw another handful of petals at him.

He merely smiled and looked up at the blue sky through the kaleidoscope of leaves overhead. It was so good to be away from London and the constant siege. He felt more relaxed than he had in months.

Somewhere in the back of his mind, it occurred to him that everything he could ever want was right here within easy reach. He looked across the little shawl island to Ellie and she smiled, her eyes glittering like gold in the sunshine.

In that instant, a warm, lighter-than-air feeling swept through him. It was a strange sensation, like a nudge in the center of his chest, or a whisper in his ear with an answer to the most rudimentary question, as if he'd been asked *What's two plus two?* There was no need to count on his fingers. He just knew the answer was four. It took no calculation or thought at all.

And with Ellie, he realized, every question was like that. So simple it took no thought at all.

Should I waltz with her in the moonlight? Yes.

Should I tease her to make her blush? Yes.

Should I kiss her? Yes.

Should I kiss her again? Hell, yes. You'd be a fool not to.

Should I cancel every obligation to take her to Wiltshire? Yes.

Should I steer her away from marrying a man who doesn't deserve her? Yes.

Should I spend this day and all the days for the rest of my life with her?

That answer was the same as all the others.

Unquestioningly, yes.

And all at once, Brandon knew that his sense of certainty had returned.

For years, his faith in other people and his ability to rely on his gut instinct had crumbled. Every time a passing acquaintance approached to ask him for money, or a young woman decided she wanted to marry him—knowing nothing at all about his character or whether or not he was a murderer in the dark of night—he was confronted by greed and manipulation.

Perhaps, if he'd been raised with the belief that he'd inherit one day, he might have become numb to the machinations. But because he'd thought of himself as a gentleman farmer who merely wanted a contented life, it bothered him that he couldn't find anyone he could trust.

Until now.

Perhaps this feeling had been with him all this time, ever since he'd collided with *Miss I did not see you there* in the Baxtons' garden. Perhaps the only reason he hadn't recognized it was because what he'd once felt for Phoebe wasn't like this at all.

He'd never been consumed with the need to touch her, hold her, talk to her and kiss her constantly. Never had the pattern of his breathing altered when he sensed her nearby. Never felt as if his entire body had been tuned by a piano fork to vibrate at the same pitch.

He only felt that way with Ellie.

The realization sent a surge through him. He wanted to breach the slight distance between them, ease her down onto the shawl and kiss that smiling mouth thoroughly. He wanted the welcome of her arms around him, the taste of her sigh on his tongue. And the only things in his way were a clover-scented breeze, that flower in her hand and . . . Nethersole.

Damn!

It was utterly maddening to finally have this realization,

only to be reminded that Ellie wanted to marry someone else.

"Are you trying to wilt this daisy with your sudden glower?" she asked with a small laugh and waggled the bare stem at him. "I daresay you would have succeeded, had I not plucked the petals already. But it does make me wonder where your thoughts had gone just now."

"Not far," he answered distractedly. Leaning across the fringed border, he brushed the tip of the petal in his grasp over the flawless surface of her hand, and then lingered to paint a horizontal line over her ring finger. "Do you have your new ledger nearby?"

She tilted her head, a puzzled smile on her lips as she reached inside her satchel. "Are you about to impart wisdom on me?"

"I am, indeed." He waited for her to open the book and carefully smooth the page with the flat of her palm. When she was poised and ready, he said, "The thought that occurred to me just now is that a marriage-minded gentleman will surmount any obstacle in his path in order to win the woman he wants. To make her his, and his alone."

Her cheeks abruptly flooded with more pink, her pencil stalling on the open page as if she sensed that his declaration wasn't necessarily for her book, but to inform her of his intentions. She delicately cleared her throat, then prompted, "'. . . to make her'?"

"His," he repeated helpfully as he pointed down to the page, "and his alone."

She scribbled with haste, finished, then tried to return the pencil to its sheath. But she fumbled a bit. And with his mind on a course of wooing, winning, and claiming, all it took was the sight of the tip nudging into the tightly closed loop to send his mind on a salacious track. His mouth went dry as he watched her careful prodding. When it finally slipped inside, he nearly groaned on an errant surge of arousal, his pulse thudding thick and low. And he felt more than a bit depraved at the moment.

She looked at him with uncertainty, covering the ledger with both hands as if she was afraid that the latest entry might escape. "Is that all you wished to tell me?"

He took a breath to cool his ardor, reminding himself that he still needed to convince Ellie to choose him, instead of Nethersole.

With a glance toward the berry-pickers, he saw that they were already heading up the hill toward the picnic site. Meg gave a merry wave, lifting her bonnet like a prize cup. Turning back to Ellie, he held her gaze and said, "For now."

❦❦❦❦

UNFORTUNATELY, BY the time they arrived at the cobbled courtyard of the coaching inn a few hours later, Brandon realized that telling Ellie he wanted more than friendship between them would likely send her scurrying off in the opposite direction. She was easily alarmed by anything new and unexpected. Understanding this, he knew he would have to ease her into the idea of a future with him. In other words, he needed to win her heart.

The way he saw it, he had two advantages over Nethersole—her trust and her desire.

Ellie wouldn't have accepted his friendship or his escort if the former wasn't true. As for the latter, she'd proven that she was just as overwhelmed by the scorching heat between them as he was. And given the innocence of her response, he knew that he was the only one who had ever inflamed her passions.

This knowledge awakened a primitive side to his nature, one that was determined to keep it that way. She was his. The only problem was, *she* didn't know it yet.

Brandon considered a number of delectable ways he'd like to enlighten her, demonstrating how good they could be together. Of course, it probably wasn't wise to allow such thoughts to distract him as they entered the tidy, Tudor-style inn where they would both be sleeping this evening.

The innkeeper, Bertie, was a lively fellow, ready with a cheerful welcome and a pumping handshake. He offered them his finest rooms upstairs, which included two bed-chambers and the common room that separated them. The latter was furnished with a small, round table and chairs near a blazing stone hearth that banished the evening chill from the air. And after freshening up from their lengthy journey, the five of them enjoyed a fine meal from the inn-keeper's wife.

Seated next to Ellie, Brandon was frequently called upon to pass a bowl or platter to her. Each time his fingertips brushed hers, the contact jolted through him. And he wasn't alone. He heard her breath catch and watched as her cheeks turned icing pink.

While he listened to the elder Miss Parrishes discuss the merits of the menu, he caught himself glancing to the door that would be Ellie's for the evening. A mere nineteen steps from his own. Not that he'd counted.

He didn't know how he was going to survive the night with temptation so near.

So he made the absolutely brilliant decision to get drunk. Well, he had only intended to have one glass of brandy to help his frustrated body find sleep. But the innkeeper was so thrilled to have a marquess under his roof that he was all too eager to share his homemade cider.

The cloudy brown liquor was known as *rough* in these parts because it was pressed from the apples or pears that had either dropped to the ground or were left on the branch due to their less than appealing qualities. And after the first biting swallow, Brandon was sure he'd been hoaxed into drinking turpentine furniture polish.

But Bertie reassured him with a hearty slap on the back

that it was *first-rate rough*. So Brandon had another glass. He had to sample the pear, after all. Of course, his taste-buds had disappeared by then and all that remained was the flavor of oblivion, which was precisely what he needed.

An hour or two later and truly tap-hackled, he mounted the steep stairs, ready to find his bed.

But what he found instead was Ellie.

Her door opened as soon as the top stair creaked beneath his footfall. Then she appeared in a white ruffled nightdress tied in a tiny bow at the neck, a gauzy wrapper with more frills, and the plaited length of her hair draped over her shoulder. He stood stock-still, and blinked several times to ensure she was real.

Then his gaze returned to that little insignificant bow. He wanted to take hold of it with his teeth. Tug it loose. He wanted that more than anything.

"Brandon," she said with a start, her hand gathering her wrapper closed, the soft fabric clinging to the luscious teardrop shapes of her unbound breasts. "I thought . . . perhaps . . . that you were a maid."

"Left my frilly cap belowstairs, I fear," he teased, his voice husky and in need of another drink. Or in need of something else. Something soft and frilly and warm under-neath. "Issthere something I can do for you?"

His tipsy slur caused her lips to curve invitingly. He wished she wouldn't do that. In his current condition, the gentleman's code of honor that had been ingrained in him since birth seemed to be sleeping quite soundly. And she was too tempting when she smiled. He knew the flavor of her mouth so well by now that his own watered at the mere thought of kissing her . . . and of doing much more than kissing her.

"I was going to ask the maid for a glass of hot milk. I'm having trouble sleeping." As she spoke, a very loud snore drifted through the crack in the door. Stepping out, she closed it quietly behind her and shook her head. "My aunts. I honestly don't know how Meg can suffer through it."

"Noise has never bothered her," he said conversationally, his legs staggering a step or two toward her without the permission of his brain. "Even as an infant, Meg would cry *incessan—incessant—*quite a lot when the nursery was peaceful. But put her bassinet next to the chaos of the kitchen and she slept like a babe. Well, she was a babe at the time so, you can just about imagine the rest."

That smile appeared again, along with a small laugh as she tilted her head in inquiry. "Are you feeling quite well?"

"If I say I'm not, are you going to cure what ails me?" he said with a rakish lift of his brows.

She covered her mouth, her eyes dancing with mirth. "I'm not certain I can."

"Oh, you can, you can. I'm sure of it."

"Well . . . if I help you to your bed, will you behave yourself?"

If she helped him to his bed, he wasn't sure he could let her leave it. Yet, as appealing as the thought of spending hours, days, weeks, years with her arms and legs wrapped around him was, the last shred of chivalry that wasn't completely foxed made him shake his head.

"'Fraid not. You'd better stay by the door, Ellie. That tiny little bow right there"—he pointed to the lovely bare column of her throat—"it'd never survive what I've got planned for it."

Chapter 17

"A debutante who flirts with temptation is as if Eve had said, ''Tis only one little apple.'"

—A NOTE FOR *The Marriage Habits of the Native Aristocrat*

Ellie didn't sleep at all. But as much as she wanted to blame it on her aunts' nocturnal symphony, she couldn't.

She'd lain awake the entire night thinking about Brandon and wondering why every conversation with him left her with that unfinished feeling. It was as if there was always something just out of reach, and yet she didn't know what it was.

All she knew was that it made her restless and drew her skin uncomfortably tight and achy over her frame. A dreadful ailment.

The following morning, she repeatedly caught herself staring dreamily out the carriage window, where Brandon rode on horseback beneath an overcast sky. She couldn't stop thinking about their encounter last night. For a man who was always so steady, self-assured and capable—the ideal for countless young debutantes—it had been shocking to see him jug bitten. She doubted that many others had.

She'd seen George drink to excess on numerous occasions. Whenever he came to her country house for dinner, actually. And he was never shy about relying on one of her footmen to see him home at the end of an evening. In fact, his drunk self wasn't all that different from his sober self.

He was just . . . George, a man who was impulsive and rash and frequently laughed at his own jokes.

But with Brandon, it was unexpected. There was something almost charming about seeing him a bit worse for wear.

She'd wanted to go to him, to untie his cravat, to help him off with his coat and boots, to see that his pillow was fluffed and his linens were cool. And she'd wanted to do these things even *after* he'd warned her away.

The only thing that had kept her bare feet rooted to the floor was the way he'd looked at her. There was something altogether untamed in his gaze. And she was quite certain that, if she had helped him to his bed, that she would have found herself in it.

Even now, a terrible thrill tore through her at the thought. It was shameless to admit, but he could have easily coaxed her. Especially if he'd kissed her and held her the way he had in the garden at Sutherfield Terrace.

She wanted that again. It made her feel terribly guilty. She should be thinking about George. She could picture their life together so easily it was as if it had already happened and she had the memory of each day tucked inside her heart.

And her heart was filled with George. There simply wasn't room for Brandon.

Well . . . perhaps a little room. After all, she still planned to be part of his life. His sister was a dear friend. And there was no question in her mind that she would always be his friend, too.

However, once she married George, Brandon would have to stop saying things about little bows on her nightdress, how her blushes tasted, and how a man would *surmount any obstacle to win the woman he wants. To make her his, and his alone.*

Because then she could stop wondering what it would feel like to be that woman.

Just then, a rumble of thunder called down from the skies, as if heaven were damning her for her thoughts.

Duly reprimanded, Ellie sat up straighter. She forced her gaze from the window and her thoughts on something—anything—other than Brandon.

Unfortunately, in the next minute, that proved impossible.

It began to rain in curtains of diaphanous silver, requiring Brandon to come inside the carriage. Then, by a series of seat changes, choreographed by her aunts, Ellie ended up sharing a bench with him.

At first, Meg was on the other side of her brother, but she complained that his coat was too damp and that she wanted to sleep. Aunt Myrtle, who was looking a bit drowsy herself, invited her to their side. She bid Meg to stack the valises that held their sewing samplers where she had sat. Of course, Brandon could have easily situated the bags between them, but he left it as it was, staying close to Ellie.

It was pure torture. As the rain saturated the road and the wheels frequently slipped in and out of well-traveled runnels, it soon became apparent that they could not avoid touching.

Ellie tried not to think about how warm he was, or how solid his thigh felt whenever the carriage shifted and they bumped against each other. And each time, she heard the subtle intake of his breath, and saw the hand resting on that thigh clenching into a fist as if he was in torment, too.

Across from them, Meg and the aunts gradually dozed, lulled by the shushing rain, the dim light and the slow rocking motion of the carriage.

It had the opposite effect on Ellie.

With every touch and press, her senses became heightened. The scent of rain and saddle leather and Brandon's shaving soap filled her every breath. A fine sheen of perspiration collected on her skin, causing cambric and silk to cling and tug with each small shift of her posture. The sensations accumulated into low liquid throbs that compelled her to press her knees together. And by the time they pulled over at the nearest coaching inn for a change of horses, Ellie felt as if she were ready to fly apart.

Thankfully, the rain had passed and they would not be traveling in such close confines for the remainder of their journey.

When she stepped outside, the air was so thick and sticky that the last thing Ellie wanted to do was go inside a stuffy inn. Her nerves were strung tight as harp strings. She needed a moment to breathe, to collect herself.

Making her excuses to her aunts, she walked around the thatch-roofed coaching inn and found a gated kitchen garden, blissfully empty. She stole inside and drew in a deep breath of fragrant herbs and flowers, trying to chase away Brandon's intoxicating scent.

But she couldn't stop thinking about him. Her skin was on fire. Unbuttoning her spencer, she parted the fabric to invite a breeze to cool her.

She didn't expect Brandon to follow.

"Miss Parrish, it isn't safe to be out here"—his words faltered for an instant when she whipped around in surprise and his gaze darted down to the parted fabric—"alone."

Ellie didn't fumble to secure the buttons. Something about the smoldering hunger in his gaze, his heavy swallow that followed, and the hour she'd spent in close quarters with him all burst upon her at once.

She didn't even know what she was doing when she started to walk toward him, or even when she lifted her hands to his nape and tugged his mouth to hers. But when he caught her and pulled her flush against the wild pounding of his heart, she knew she would find the answer in his kiss and in the feel of his arms around her.

Ellie slanted her mouth beneath Brandon's, nudging his

lips apart with a hungry murmur of insistence. He answered with a gruff grunt of surprise and approval deep in his throat and hitched her higher until the toes of her half boots were dragged over the grass.

She clung to him, her tongue skirting over the edge of the broad, firm flesh of his lower lip to the heated, intoxicating interior. He tasted of the fresh water from the pail and ladle outside the inn's entrance and she wanted to drink him in. Every last drop.

She felt the inn's fieldstone exterior at her back. Brandon's firm body pressed and molded to all her fiery places as he kissed her in slow, deep pulls. But it still wasn't enough. She was afraid it never would be.

"This is all your fault. Every time I'm near you, I feel like I'm coming apart at the seams."

"I'll hold you together," he rasped, even as he tugged the high collar of her spencer away from her neck. His lips seared the exposed bare skin, burning a path of kisses down to the ribbon edge of her rose pink bodice. He inhaled deeply. "I dream of this sweet clover scent each and every night, then I wake up reaching for you. But you're never there."

"You shouldn't say such things. It makes me dizzy."

"Then hold on to me tighter and kiss me again. That is the only cure."

Her lips nudged eagerly against his. She grappled with his shoulders, half-crazed and needing to get closer. Frantic, her hands stole inside his coat to where his waistcoat and shirtsleeves were plastered damply to the broad muscles of his back, then up to his shoulders, gripping him and shamelessly urging her breasts against his chest. And then his hand was there, coasting over the curve of her hip, up the narrow cinch of her waist and corset ribbing to cup the aching swell. His mouth descended down her throat, skimming the fragile column until he breathed hotly over the muslin-clad center, drawing the flesh unbearably tight. And when his tongue laved the pebbled peak through the layers, she gripped the back of his head to hold him there.

His ardent attention turned the fabric a dark burgundy color before he nipped the taut bud of flesh with his teeth. She cried out from the spasm of pleasure shooting deep inside her, clenching where she was warm and wet between her thighs.

His mouth returned to hers. And he fed his patented cure to her, dose by dose, searching the inner recesses with his tongue. His hand cupped her breast with tender possession as his thumb spurred the tip and her hips tilted involuntarily. She startled at the feel of the heavy shape she met and the instant spark of pleasure that flared through her. It was in her nature to be wary of new discoveries, and yet, an age-old instinct compelled her to press closer.

Confusion and passion warred within her, but she didn't shy away. She kept him there, her body cradling the hard, imposing ridge of flesh. He growled deep into her mouth, rewarding her with the slow grind of his body against hers.

A shaking moan left her throat and she knew she was no longer in control of her senses. Perhaps she never was. And worse, she was starting to suspect that only Brandon could make her feel right again.

They were friends, after all, she told herself as they consumed each other. And friends helped each other find answers to mysterious ailments. They soothed each other when their every nerve was frayed and eager for something undefinable.

"Oh, please," she whispered. "*Please*, Brandon."

His grip descended down her rib cage, splaying possessively over her hip as he rocked against her, over and over, until her head fell back on a whimper of surrender. He rained hot kisses down her throat and murmured, "Tell me your symptoms, my lovely valetudinarian."

"Oh, no. I couldn't . . . they're just too . . . wicked . . . to speak aloud." Embarrassed and panting, she pressed her lips to his cheek, to his jaw, to the curling tendrils at his temple that were damp and salty with perspiration.

"I think I understand," he said, shifting slightly. His movements tugged at the length of her skirts, inviting a cool breeze against the thin cambric of her drawers. And then his large hand found her hip beneath the fabric. She jolted at the feel of his warmth so near her flesh.

"Shh . . ." he whispered in a brush against her lips, soothing her with tender passes. "I just want to touch you, that's all. I can't leave you like this."

Powerless to resist the potency of this terrible yearning, she gave him the barest nod. He kissed her again, his hand cupping the throbbing private place. She gasped, shamelessly arching against his palm. His fingers delved through the lacy slit to brush the damp curls, deftly navigating the secret recesses of her sex. He took her mouth again as he caressed and coaxed his way through her swollen folds to circle the tight, pulsating pearl. At that first scintillating touch, a helpless mewl tore from her throat. She held him tighter, her fingertips digging into the seams at his shoulders, her spine bending in a supplicant arch.

She couldn't stop the motion of her hips, pushing against his rhythmic strokes, sensations collecting and coiling in tight spirals behind that heavy throb. Her heart thudded thickly, rushing in her ears. She felt ripe and tender all over, a sense of desperation and imminent death building.

The world around them disappeared. And her entire focus centered on the heat between them, the sweet musky fragrance in the air, the taste of him on her lips and tongue, and his slow, circular caress.

"Just give yourself to me. That's all I ask." His voice was gravelly and strained. And it seemed as if there was something left unspoken, something urgent and all-encompassing that she should understand, but she couldn't think of what it might be. She couldn't think at all. Not with his hand on her, his tender rotations narrowing by degree, intent and unyielding. "Let me have you, Ellie."

Her heart lurched at the gruff command. And, all at once, she cried out on a sudden explosion of rapture that tore through her body in gushes of molten heat. She hunched into his embrace as blinding sparks lit the darkness behind her closed eyes for endless minutes, and she clung to him in shuddering, soul-splintering spasms that left her weak-kneed and exhausted.

Supporting her limp body, he lowered her skirts and smoothed his hands over her back, shoulders and arms, his lips pressed to her hair. She could still feel the hardness of him through the layers of their clothing and her body issued a sweet clench in response, like the last shard of glass to fall after a window had been shattered.

As he held and caressed her in slow passes, she gradually became aware of their surroundings—the nearby buzzing of a bee, the scent of tarragon and mint, the distant sounds of horses and rigging, the murmurs of indiscernible conversation interrupted by the clatter of pots and pans.

A glance along the inn's stone facade showed a cloudy diamond-paned window opened on a pair of hinges like the wing of a dark moth. She went pale, her hand flying to her mouth to stifle a sound of distress.

"No one saw," he assured her quietly. "The window is facing the garden, not us."

"But surely they . . . *heard* . . ." Mortified she buried her face against his shoulder.

He pressed a kiss to her temple, his lips curving in a grin. "I think we were both lost in the moment."

She peered up at him, uncertain. "This cannot happen again. I don't even know what came over me. Perhaps it was the heat of the day that put a fever inside me. Fevers are never good, you know. It made me feel so . . . And then suddenly you were there and I . . ." Recalling every moment, she turned poppy red. "We'll have to avoid carriage rides together and . . . and gardens . . . and . . ."

"And the inevitable?" he asked dubiously, brow arched. "We're right for each other, Ellie. I think you know it, too."

She shook her head, adamant, and issued a panicked pointing gesture between them. "No. We're just friends. Friends who"—she swallowed—"shouldn't be kissing each other."

He expelled a slow breath and pressed his lips to her forehead. "Very well, Ellie. We'll avoid carriages and gardens . . . for now, if that suits you."

An acceptance, but one with conditions.

She didn't want to think about what *for now* meant. So, instead, she simply agreed with a nod and tried to button her spencer.

Chapter 18

"A marriage-minded gentleman isn't above
resorting to murder."

—A note for *The Marriage Habits
of the Native Aristocrat*

Well, hell. Brandon hadn't meant to lose control like that,
or to rush Ellie.

But after enduring the agony of the longest carriage ride
of his life—most of which was spent with his hat on his
lap to hide the unmistakable outcropping of his erection beneath his buff riding breeches—he hadn't expected her to
launch herself at him.

Knowing that she'd done so out of her own desire for
him, he'd temporarily lost the ability to think. And, *damn*,
it had felt so good to have her willing body in his arms, her
eager, searching mouth beneath his.

But now, she was skittish. She wouldn't even meet his
gaze as her fingers fumbled with the fastenings of her little
jacket.

Knowing Ellie as he did, he feared that a declaration
from him would surely send her into a panic. She was like
a rabbit that twitched at the hint that any man other than
George might have an interest in her. And since rabbits
tended to scamper off in the opposite direction, he would
have to proceed with care.

But proceed he would.

He'd been scorched by love before and he hadn't found

anyone he'd risk getting burned over . . . until now. He had every intention of wooing her by slow degrees, so that by the time he proposed there would be no question in her mind. No *George*. Only him.

Brushing her hands aside, he deftly put her in order. He paused, however, when he noticed how her pretty blush had spread to the upper region of her chest, like rose-colored paint, sponged on a porcelain canvas. Understanding the cause made it impossible to resist pressing a brief kiss to that bare flesh.

She gasped, her lips parting—doubtlessly—to scold him.

Before she could, he secured the last two fastenings and said, "Just a taste to tide me over until next time."

"There isn't going to be a—"

He cut her off with a kiss. With his hands at her nape and hip, he eased his mouth over hers, proving that there was no denying the palpable force between them. He was rewarded by the feel of her arms around his neck, her body arching against him as she welcomed the tender plunder of his tongue into her sweet mouth.

He wanted her, all of her. Wanted to taste every inch of her petal-soft flesh. To lay her down in the grass and strip away all the barriers between them, exposing her fair skin to the sunlight and then to the shadow of his body over her, *inside* her, thrusting deep as she shuddered and rasped his name.

On her whimper of surrender, he realized he'd forgotten himself again. Lifting his head, he looked down at her plump lips and flushed skin, and felt the heat of her sex against his thigh, braced between hers. The swelling of his cock would never subside at this rate.

He kissed the tips of the sooty lashes resting on her cheeks and carefully set her apart from him. Her gaze fluttered up to his, her breaths shallow and quick. She looked so passion-drugged and confused that he was almost sorry for what he'd done. But not quite.

"We're good at being honest with each other," he said. "Let's not spoil it by claiming there's nothing between us."

She expelled a sigh. "Brandon, this shouldn't have happened. You know very well that I plan to marry—"

"Elodie!" Myrtle Parrish called from outside the kitchen garden, her singsong tone betraying a noticeable amount of worry. "Dearest, where are you?"

Eyes wide, Ellie looked to Brandon. "They'll know everything once they find us together. *Oh dear . . .* Is it possible to die from guilt, do you think?"

"It will be fine," he said soothing away the tension in her shoulders and nape with gentle massages. "I'll wait while you go out. I'm sure they imagine I'm at the stables. And here." He paused to gather a handful of nearby herbs and flowers and pressed the bouquet into her hand, easing her stiff fingers around the stems. "You won't have to say a word. They'll think you were merely walking in the garden."

"But my cheeks . . ."

"Explained by the fact that you left your bonnet behind," he said with a fond grin, fighting the urge to kiss her again. And when she lingered, likely imagining all the terrible things that might happen, he crowded closer and spoke in a low murmur. "If you'd rather have us caught, however, it wouldn't bother me at all."

That was all it took to startle the golden-eyed rabbit into motion.

She hastened around the corner to the garden entrance and was out of breath when she said, "Here I am. I was just . . . um . . . gathering some rosemary and chamomile for a tea, in case we stop for another picnic. See? The proof is in my hand . . . so there can be no question . . . regarding my . . . um . . . activities."

Standing at the gate, his lips curved in a wry grin as he listened to the hopeless liar.

"How thoughtful, dear. But that's tarragon, I'm afraid. Beneficial if you require a medicinal mugwort tea for certain ailments. It helped tremendously after the canape incident at the Easterbrookes' ball. You aren't feeling poorly, are you? Good. Then we'll use the tarragon for its perfume."

"Sister, stop stuffing those leaves down your bodice," Maeve Parrish interjected with a huff of exasperation. "The last time you put something other than a sprig of lavender in your décolletage, you had hives for a month."

Meg was the next to speak. "Ellie, have you seen my brother? I thought he was at the stables, but the hostlers haven't seen him."

"Your brother? Whyever would I have seen . . . I mean . . . after all . . . Lord Hullworth is hardly likely to spend time in gardens . . . which is precisely where I was."

"Your cheeks are quite flushed, Ellie. Are you certain you're feeling well?"

"It must be the sun . . . and well . . . my bonnet is . . . somewhere . . ."

"It sounds as though you could do with a spot of tea, dear," Myrtle added.

"Indeed," Maeve said. "For we have some splendid news. You'll never guess who surprised us just now."

"Oh, Aunt, please don't say that. My heart couldn't take another surprise today."

"Well, this is one of the good ones. It's George, of course! He came to meet our carriage on the road and found us here. And, what's more, he asked for you straightaway. Has something to tell you, apparently."

"Or perhaps," Myrtle interjected with a pleased hum, "something to *ask* you, hmm? He does seem to be terribly excited."

Brandon's hands closed into fists. *Nethersole!* Why did

he have to show up now? With Ellie back to being skittish, it was going to take a lot of coaxing to draw her out again.

He wanted her all to himself. That would settle her confusion. After all, if he was going to convince her that *George* wasn't the only man for her, then he needed to show her how good her life could be with someone else. To ease her into the idea that they were more than just friends who enjoyed kissing each other.

Glancing out through the opening, Brandon watched the four women skirt around the corner. He retreated with haste, striding around the back to encounter them by way of the stable yard.

By the time he arrived at the inn's entrance, he saw Nethersole twirling Ellie around in a circle, his hands on her hips. Brandon growled low in his throat, picking up the pace.

A startled laugh escaped Ellie. But he could see she was uncomfortable as her complexion paled, the hands clutching his shoulders white-knuckled from strain.

"George, put me down. This is utterly improper, not to mention dangerous. You could lose your balance and hit your head on a rock."

"Always the worrier." Nethersole chuckled and finally set her down. Though he released her so quickly that she staggered to find her feet. He didn't seem to notice or care as he turned away.

Brandon came to her side with a supporting hand at the small of her back. At his touch, he felt the quick contraction of the lithe, sinewy form beneath her dress. Felt the reflexive way she almost leaned against him. *Almost.* She stopped just shy of it, however, color flooding her cheeks.

Not wanting to give her any reason to balk, he withdrew the instant she was steady but remained by her side none-theless.

"I came to tell you all," Nethersole began as if he were

center stage, "that I have narrowed down my search for a house in Wiltshire to two potential properties. One is furnished, the other isn't. Although, I must say that I'm terribly partial to the unfurnished house, which would be a good deal of bother unless . . . I could talk my favorite girls into doing a bit of shopping." He chuckled and wagged a finger at the surprised expressions on the elder Miss Parrishes' faces. "*Eh, wot?* I imagine you didn't think I was serious about taking a house here. But I most certainly am. We could stay all summer, if you like. And where's Hullworth? Oh, there you are," he said with a smug glance over his shoulder. "Looks as though I'll be taking these beauties off your hands in no time at all."

When hell freezes over, Brandon thought but managed a clenched smile. "In the meantime, you're welcome to stay on my estate."

"No need. My steward has secured most excellent lodgings at the village inn. But I wouldn't be opposed to seeing how your pile of bricks compares to mine."

Brandon inclined his head, maintaining a reserved and humble expression. The grand manor house, extensive grounds and finest stables in this part of the country were not something he would boast about, but he was actually looking forward to seeing Nethersole's first glimpse of Crossmoor Abbey.

Chapter 19

"A debutante should never determine a gentleman's marriageability until she has seen the size of his house."

—A NOTE FOR *The Marriage Habits of the Native Aristocrat*

Ellie hated surprises. To her, they were like tempests and tornados blowing in from out of nowhere to bring about the end of things. In fact, she was fairly certain the end of the world would come as an enormous surprise.

But it wasn't George's surprise that bothered her. He was always doing the unexpected. Knowing that, she could anticipate he would invariably do something to shock her. Therefore, whatever it was, never affected her overly much.

Brandon, however, had taken her completely off guard earlier and left her insides rushing in a terrible, unexplainable tumult. She'd never cared for tumults either.

Let me have you, Ellie . . . We're right for each other . . .

As the carriage trundled along the road, she felt a tremor quake through her at the memory. No matter how hard she tried to simply stare out the window toward the picturesque scenery of the countryside and *not* think about what happened in the garden two hours ago, it proved impossible.

In every blade of grass on the rolling hills, she saw the striations of green color in his hooded gaze. In the thick trunks of the mature trees, she couldn't help but think of the imposing hardness he'd pressed against her. And in every wildflower, she felt the foreign, untamed part of her that had bloomed in a sudden, startling cataclysm.

Until today, she would have claimed a loathing for cataclysms, as well. But after careful consideration, she decided that those were tolerable. Quite tolerable, actually.

A sigh passed her lips as her gaze drifted to Brandon's fine form on horseback and to the hands that held the reins with such skillful and utter command. He had absolutely divine hands.

For the entire journey, he'd kept pace with the carriage on the side where she and Meg sat. And even now, as the landau slowed to turn off the main road, he stayed by her side as if in a proprietary manner, leaving George to trail behind on his own horse.

"We're here," Meg chirruped excitedly from the bench across from her. Beaming, she leaned out the window just as they drove between a pair of obelisk boundary markers. "Brother, can we not remove the hood for the rest of the journey so that we can take in the splendor of the grounds?"

He looked from his sister to Ellie. "What say you, Miss Parrish? I should hate for the sunlight to take advantage of your fair complexion, for it seems rather pink at the moment."

Beneath the brim of his hat, his eyes gleamed with smug pleasure as if he knew that her heightened color meant that she'd been thinking of their stolen moment.

Hating that she was so transparent to him, she reached for her bonnet and crammed it on her head with a curt, "I can bear it as well as you can, my lord."

"I am heartily glad to hear that," he said directly to her. But there was something in his expression that intimated a double meaning, which only made her cheeks flare hotter.

Leaving her with a grin, he spurred his horse forward and called out to the driver to make the adjustments. Then, when the carriage stopped, he dismounted to help.

"Ellie, I can hardly contain my happiness at finally having a guest of my own here," Meg said brightly, then issued an elfin squint to Brandon. "My brother has had his share of gentlemen over for hunting, but they are all fusty and reserved like he is."

In the beginning of their acquaintance, Ellie might have agreed with Meg. Since then, however, she'd come to understand that beneath his composed exterior lay a man with a passionate nature too potent to deny.

If only he *were* reserved, she thought. Then she might have stood a chance of resisting him.

Out of the corner of her eye, she saw George ride up, but he made no move to lend a hand to Brandon and his driver. She tried not to judge him too harshly for this. After all, he'd grown up under the steady counsel of a steward who always assured him of how important it was to be a marquess. Even so, she wished George would have at least *offered* assistance instead of merely observing.

As the partitions of the hood were systematically tucked away into their compartment, Ellie's view expanded to a perfectly situated lane, winding beneath the shade of leafy branches of thick oak, elm and ash trees. Further ahead, beyond the endless expanse of rolling verdant hills, a pale stone bridge with two arching pediments rose up from the dark waters of the river.

A cold chill of trepidation skated through her at the thought of crossing it. Drowning was very near the top of her list of most dreaded ways to expire.

"Is that your pile of bricks, then?" George asked, distracting her from her dire thoughts. He gestured with a lift of his chin toward the dark-tiled rooftop breaking above the tree line about a quarter of a mile ahead. "Seems a trifle small for such a grand entryway."

Ellie frowned at the way he chuckled. While she knew

Brandon wasn't bothered by trifling things, it was starting to bother *her* that George wasn't putting his best foot forward.

Brandon's expression remained placid as he issued an absent response. "That is Stredwick Lodge, the bachelor's quarters for whenever we have unmarried gentlemen visiting."

"And is that where you'll be staying, then?"

Aunt Maeve clucked her tongue. "George, of course Lord Hullworth doesn't reside in a separate house. He is the lord of the manor. It is his duty to look after the welfare of his guests."

"My privilege, as well," Brandon answered. He smiled politely, taking no offense to George's embarrassingly improper comment that a lesser man might have seen as an attempt to call his honor into question. "And, besides, my rooms are in a separate wing."

When it appeared as though George was readying to make another comment, Ellie shot him a stern look of reproach with a delicate clearing of her throat. Thankfully, he closed his mouth.

Soon they were on their way again, with Brandon riding ahead this time. As they neared the river, Ellie squeezed her eyes shut and listened to her aunts coo with pleasure at the idea of freshly caught trout for supper.

Across from her, she heard Meg's soft laugh. "Ellie, don't you like bridges?"

"I adore bridges," she said, her voice thready as cobwebs as she listened to the rush of the water, and the crunch of the carriage wheels over the cobblestone. "Just as long as they don't give way in a sudden calamitous erosion."

"Fear not, this one has been here for nearly two centuries."

Ellie awkwardly bobbled her head in a nod, refraining to mention how stone can deteriorate over time and, quite often, unexpectedly. It was only when she felt the road beneath them alter to the easy glide of hard-packed earth that she dared to open her eyes, and found Meg biting her lip to keep from smiling.

Ellie soon forgot about the bridge as they passed the brick and stone facade of the lodge, and her gaze was greeted by an awe-inspiring vista of vast parks. There were woodlands, grassy meadows, walking paths along shaded avenues, a pond dotted with water lilies, and little meandering brooks tucked inside this majestically informal wilderness. It was simply breathtaking.

She thought she had seen every imaginable delight. Yet, as they continued on the winding lane, she was proven wrong by the splendor of formal pleasure gardens. Every view surrounding her was like stepping into a painting. Definitely worth crossing a bridge to see. Perhaps even *two* bridges.

"What lovely grounds, my lord. I'm quite wonderstruck," Aunt Myrtle said dreamily when Brandon came to ride alongside them again.

He inclined his head with all modesty. "Thank you, ma'am. I give the credit to my groundskeeper and also to my widowed aunt, who lives on the estate year-round. He takes her ideas and sketches and turns them into what you see all around you."

"She must be quite an exceptional artist, then," Ellie said, her face lifting to see his lips curve in a tender grin as he nodded, clearly fond of his aunt.

"I've written to her," he said, "and she is looking forward to meeting you."

She knew he meant *you* in a figurative sense that included her aunts as well as herself. And yet, there was a certain warmth in his eyes that seemed to blanket her, and her alone, like a beam of sunlight breaking through the clouds to shine on a solitary sea bather.

Doubtless, most women would rejoice at such a feeling. But for her, that frightening tumult returned. After all, a sea bather must always be wary of the dark chasm of water approaching the shore.

Blinking, she turned away from his gaze before she was blinded by it and drew in a deep breath. "My aunts and I should like to meet her as well. It is a pity, of course, that our acquaintance will be of such a short duration."

She hated to admit it, but she was eager to leave here. To be far away from the unwelcome stirrings he caused. Oh, she hoped that George decided to rent the furnished house. The sooner she was staying beneath *his* roof, the sooner she would be one step closer to marrying him. Then, surely, she would begin to feel like herself again.

"Already planning a hasty retreat, are you?" Brandon said with that smug *I-can-read-your-thoughts* grin in his voice. "Well, perhaps you'll be willing to look the house over before you order the servants to keep your trunks packed."

Not likely, she thought, her heart rabbiting in a panic.

The carriage rounded the final bend and Aunt Myrtle gasped, pointing ahead. "Oh, sister! I think I must be dreaming."

They all turned to look and fell into slack-jawed speech-lessness.

Crossmoor Abbey was a veritable castle! A frontage of smooth ashlar stone stood three stories high, adorned with a plethora of tall, rectangular windows that glinted like mirror glass, along with rounded, crenelated towers on either side.

"Just imagine the size of the kitchen," Aunt Maeve murmured, her eyes as round as plum custard tarts.

Meg giggled. "There are actually four kitchens, including the scullery."

"*Four kitchens*. Good heavens, I am dreaming."

As the carriage came to a stop and Brandon dismounted, a team of servants bustled out to greet them and take hold of the reins. A footman appeared with a step and opened the door, assisting Meg to the ground. Brandon came over and spoke to the servant in a low tone, and the young man summarily stepped aside with a bow and made way for the marquess.

With her thoughts so distracted by the sights and splendor of Crossmoor Abbey, she thought little of the gesture and eagerly slid her hand into his waiting palm. Her eyes must have been dancing with dizzied delight because he smiled knowingly.

"Ah, such a pity. You don't like it at all, do you?" he teased, guiding her to the step.

As her feet settled onto the crushed stone drive, she wanted to laugh at the ridiculousness of his statement, but managed an offhanded shrug. "As you say."

He chuckled warmly and she beamed up at him.

It wasn't until she noticed a pair of waiting maids whisper and glance down, that Ellie became aware of her hand still lingering inside Brandon's.

Oh, bother! She heard the maids giggle as she hastily withdrew.

Blushing profusely, she refused to look at Brandon again. Her heart was fluttering in a confusing jumble of beats that would likely prove to be an ailment from which she would never recover.

Well, one thing was for certain. She needed to set matters straight between them, once and for all. At her first opportunity, she was going to remind him that she still had every intention of marrying George . . . whenever he got around to asking her.

THERE SHE goes again, Brandon thought wryly as Ellie quickly stepped apart from him. However, he wasn't overly concerned by her withdrawal this time. His confidence was leavened by her responses to him, not only at the inn earlier, but in her simple unconscious gestures—taking his hand, gazing at him as he rode beside the carriage, teasing and smiling.

She likely didn't realize it, but she'd spent more time frowning at Nethersole than not. And Brandon found tremendous promise in that.

He gathered that Ellie hadn't spent much of her life truly seeing Nethersole for the immature, spoiled man-child that he was. He kept to a circle of adoring sycophants, but was otherwise seen among the gentlemen of the *ton* as a cocksure noble with more bollocks than brains. And now Ellie was getting a glimpse of it.

Witnessing her displeasure at a number of Nethersole's comments and actions had given Brandon an idea.

"Nethersole, I insist you stay here instead of at the inn. That way, you'll save me from sending out a messenger whenever the ladies decide to have a picnic, a sail on the pond, or a ride on horseback through the—"

"You won't get Ellie on a horse," Nethersole interrupted with a laugh. "She's afraid of them."

"I'm not *afraid*. That would be silly, considering they're everywhere and provide our means of transportation. The reason I don't ride is more about"—she swallowed—"having no desire to fall from a great height while moving at an alarming speed."

Brandon felt the flesh of his brow pucker. "But what about the phaeton in the park?"

"Couldn't go through with it," Nethersole interjected with a chuckle. "Clambered down so fast the groom couldn't catch her."

A tide of anger swept through Brandon at the knowledge that Nethersole had known of her fear and had put her on the high perch of a phaeton regardless. It was quite clear that he'd done nothing to aid or reassure her. Because of that, she'd suffered a moment of panic and an injured ankle that day.

But what if that panic had overtaken her later, while Nethersole was driving her pell-mell through the park?

A shudder coursed through Brandon, white-hot and seething inside his veins. He clenched his fists, wanting to rail at Nethersole for putting her in danger. A turned ankle was the mildest of injuries she might have suffered. And now the unconscionable arse had the nerve to just stand there and tease her as if she were the butt of a long-standing joke?

This was the man she wanted to marry? Well, Brandon would see about that.

Drawing in a breath through his teeth, he cooled his temper enough to continue. "Aside from riding, there will be numerous opportunities for all of us to become better acquainted, not to mention the jaunts to the village to meet with Miss Parrish's friend." He turned his gaze to Ellie. "Of course, I plan to extend an invitation for her to stay here, as well, along with her aunt and uncle."

Ellie's eyes brightened, the corners of her mouth lifting. "That would be simply splendid."

"Well, I don't suppose it would be too much of an inconvenience to have my things moved," Nethersole said as if bored.

"Good. Then, I'll send a footman to the inn. In the meantime, I leave you in the capable hands of Mr. Tidwell. He'll see you to Stredwick Lodge for you to relax before dinner this evening."

Even though the courtesy pained Brandon, he no longer wanted to exclude the other man. Erecting a blockade between Ellie and Nethersole would likely compel her to latch on to the idea of marrying him all the more. And that was the last thing Brandon wanted.

She needed to see for herself and to choose the better man.

But that didn't mean he was simply going to sit as a passive observer. No, indeed. Brandon planned to help Ellie realize that the chemistry between them was undeniable and their future inevitable.

Chapter 20

"A debutante mustn't panic when her heart
stumbles."

—A NOTE FOR *The Marriage Habits
of the Native Aristocrat*

The aunts and Meg decided to rest after their long journey.
Ellie tried to nap as well, but there was no convincing her
eyelids to stay shut. The views from her perfectly situated,
cerulean-blue bedchamber were too beautiful to leave un-
admired.

The interior of her spacious room was lovely, as well. Her
canopied bed hosted an array of sumptuous pillows, and the
intricately embroidered coverlet caused her a pang of envy
as she passed her hand over the silken threads.

The tables and wardrobe were a smooth satinwood with
polished silver knobs, and the thickly woven carpet a delight
beneath her bare feet. The open window framed a lovely
picture of the cloud-dappled summer sky, as a gentle breeze
blew in the scents of fresh hay and honeysuckle. From the
colorful gardens, lush meadows and verdant woodlands
gilded by the late afternoon sunlight, every part of nature
blended seamlessly into the next like an intricately stitched
tapestry.

She wanted to see it all before evening fell, but it wasn't
in her nature to go off wandering on her own. Typically,
her friend Jane had to prod and cajole her into risking any
potentially dangerous escapade. But Ellie couldn't seem to

find a reason to linger in her bedchamber when a whole new world waited beyond the door.

Thankfully, the maid had already pressed her pale lilac and bronze striped evening gown and left it hanging on the wardrobe. If there was one benefit to Ellie's recurring nightmare, it was that she usually awoke before the servants and could manage the fastenings of her corset and dresses on her own. Her hair was another story. However, with a quick brushing, an artful twist and a few pins, she managed.

Pristine white wainscoted walls adorned with polished brass sconces led her through the guest wing and to the stairs. As she descended, she caught herself wondering about the other wing of the house where Brandon slept. A shameful rise of unmaidenly interest sparked at the mere idea of exploring that part of the house and *accidentally* stumbling upon his bedchamber.

Would he be resting now? Perhaps lying on his bed? Shirtless? And were the linens molded to all the hard planes and ridges of his body the same way she had been . . .

"Might I help you, Miss Parrish?"

She turned with a guilty yelp to find a maid standing there, her freckled face smiling beneath the ruffled cap. Then, true to her nature, Ellie tried to hide the embarrassment over her skittish outburst by nervously beginning to ramble. "Good day. I was just exploring a bit. But, of course, I wouldn't have gone anywhere that . . . would have been unseemly for an unmarried . . . um . . . How do you already know my name?"

"Oh, we've been all astir for your arrival, miss."

Ellie's heart gave an uncertain leap. Then, she told herself that it couldn't have simply been *her* arrival that set the collective "we" of Crossmoor Abbey astir. "I imagine that it's good to have Lord Hullworth and Miss Stredwick here again."

"Aye, miss," she agreed with a friendly air, tucking the

feather duster behind her back as her gray service dress swished about her legs. "His lordship doesn't stay all too often, just a few days a month to see to estate matters and visit the Dowager Lady Hullworth. But we're all hoping that'll change now. After all, it's been many a year since the abbey was a genuine home, filled with laughter and parties and the like."

Ah. It was precisely what Ellie feared. This maid had the wrong idea about the purpose of her visit. Not wanting to build up false hopes, she decided to state things perfectly clearly.

"This wasn't a planned holiday. In fact, it came upon us rather suddenly," she said. Yet, as the maid's smile only grew wider and wider, Ellie realized *it came upon us rather suddenly* could have been misconstrued to suggest an act of impromptu passion. Much like at the inn earlier. And all at once she was thinking about that wondrous cataclysm again. "Lord Hullworth . . . um . . . extended the invitation to my aunts and me out of generosity."

"Aye, miss. His lordship is generous, indeed. And fair-minded and good-natured, if you don't mind my saying."

"No, of course not," she said quickly. "He is, indeed, all those things and . . . has many other fine qualities, I'm sure."

The maid giggled. "You're blushing, miss. Me mam always says a girl knows it's true love when she blushes at the mere thought of her man, even when he's not around."

"Oh, but he's not my . . . You see, I blush all the time . . . a terrible failing . . ."

"Becca," a woman called, her voice gently chiding. "Leave poor Miss Parrish alone. And I believe that duster is required in the drawing room."

"Yes, my lady." The maid bit her lip, trying to hide her smile as she bobbed a curtsy. "It was a grand pleasure, miss. If you need anything at all, just ask for Becca."

Ellie wished her cheeks weren't aflame when she met

the woman who could only be Brandon's aunt, but there was no hope for it. Turning, she saw an older woman in a black dress and wide-brimmed bonnet cross the room in a graceful stride, while stripping off a pair of soiled gardening gloves.

"I know it isn't done this way, but I'm Lady Hullworth. You must call me Sylvia, Miss Parrish," she said with a warm, easy smile that creased the delicate ivory skin around her blue eyes.

"Ellie, please," she said, clasping the older woman's fine-boned hand.

With a gracious nod, Sylvia removed her hat and touched her pale hair, absently smoothing the wayward moon-silver strands that escaped her coiffure. Even though the widow was likely well into her fifth decade, she possessed the air of someone perpetually youthful.

"You must forgive the maids, Ellie. I'm afraid the belief that *spring is in the air* has been with us since the day I received Brandon's letter announcing his plan to bring you to the abbey. The instant I told them to prepare for female guests, they became all a dither, hoping that Cupid's arrow had finally struck." Seeing Ellie adamantly shake her head, she issued a light laugh. "Fear not, my nephew explained the whole of it to me just now when I met him in the stables."

Ellie expelled a sigh of relief and nodded. "I'm glad. I should hate for there to be any misunderstanding."

"I can see that you would," she said, gazing at her thoughtfully. "My nephew prefers certainty, too. I've found that those who've experienced great loss often dislike the unknown. After all, surprises can lead to all sorts of things that one couldn't anticipate."

"Precisely," Ellie agreed readily, glad to have found someone who understood.

Sylvia lifted her finger as one did when filled with sudden inspiration. Then she smiled again. "Speaking of surprises, there is one task I must see to before I dress for dinner. Would you care to take a walk with me?"

Even though the abrupt change in topic was a trifle puzzling, Ellie nodded without hesitation. "I'd be delighted."

"Two weeks ago," she began as they crossed the stately hall and entered an airy corridor lit by the warm glow of late afternoon sun, "a stray twig caught on the hem of my skirt and I unwittingly dragged it into the house. It wasn't until I plucked the interloper loose that I found the chrysalis attached. A perfect little silken pod. And I brought it in here, to the morning room."

Opening the door, she gestured to the array of potted plants and flowers in a row before a bank of mullioned windows.

"There. The third one from the left," she said closing the door behind them.

Curious, Ellie walked over and peered between the leaves. She spotted the chrysalis, but it looked rather wilted and collapsed. Perhaps the little pod had never survived the fall from the tree, after all.

"Oh, it seems we've arrived too late," Sylvia said, peering over her shoulder, but without any disappointment in her tone. In fact, she laughed again.

Puzzled, Ellie turned and saw Sylvia's gaze directed to the painting over the mantel. She gasped with delight. A golden butterfly was slowly flexing its wings.

Then suddenly, it lifted off, fluttering with haphazard graceful wingbeats.

"Quick. Throw open the window," Sylvia said, crossing the room.

Ellie scrambled for the handle and turned the latch, pushing one of the lead glass windows open on its vertical hinge. The butterfly fluttered past her, pausing briefly to perch on her flounced sleeve before venturing into the garden beyond.

Watching it alight on the dropping violet falls of an iris, she felt a wistful smile on her lips. "If only all surprises turned out so beautifully."

Beside her, Sylvia picked the twig out of the plant and twirled it in her fingers, looking down at it thoughtfully. "That is what loss has taught me—to never underestimate the importance of these little accidents or a chance encounter. Even the smallest of obstacles in our paths could very well lead to discovering something beautiful and wondrous. For you," she said, handing the twig to Ellie before she swept to the door. Smiling over her shoulder, she added, "I must go forth into my own chrysalis or else I'll never be presentable in time for supper."

Ellie stared after her hostess. She had the sinking suspicion that she'd just been passed a baton, of sorts, inviting her to open herself up to new possibilities. To Brandon.

What they didn't realize was that her connection to George had been permanently fused in her mind and in her heart when she was young. Knowing she would marry him had always given her a sense of lasting comfort. She couldn't simply change her mind and give up all the dreams she had.

With a shake of her head, she put the baton back in the dirt. She was going to marry George and it was time that everyone understood.

AT SUPPER that evening, Ellie endeavored to clear up any misunderstandings. But she wasn't certain how, other than raising her glass in a toast to George, her future husband.

Thankfully, when they were all gathered in the dining room, she didn't have to take such drastic measures. George offered her his unwitting assistance by sharing fond remembrances of his youthful days of living in the country, with each story featuring her.

". . . I'd likely be at the bottom of that pond if not for my Ellie," he concluded with a wink to her across the table.

That should settle things, she thought, as *my Ellie* lingered in the air. There should be no further question of who she intended to marry. And when she looked across the table to George, she expected her heart to hitch and her breath to catch. She knew it was bound to happen. It always did whenever he said *my Ellie*.

So, she waited for it. And she waited.

Seconds ticked by and his conversation resumed to the time he'd fallen from the ladder in his house's grand library and his Ellie rushed to his side. But still she felt . . . nothing. Her pulse didn't so much as issue a random flutter. Her lungs were adequately filtering air into the cavities and expelling it without interruption.

In fact, the only difference she noticed was the unpardonable peevishness she felt each time she heard George say li*bury* instead of li*brary*. She hated to admit it, but that had always grated on her nerves.

Her gaze wandered to the head of the table to see Brandon already looking at her and she felt that instantaneous tug. Disconcertingly, *that* was the moment when her heart decided to palpitate. Strenuously. Her veins flooded with warm currents of blood that colored her cheeks. Her lungs constricted to the point of aching beneath the confines of her corset as if she were trapped inside the woven silk of a chrysalis.

More than anything, she wanted to be free of it.

And yet, the terrible sensation stayed with her even after dinner, when they gathered in the parlor, waiting for the gentlemen to join them for cards.

Ellie caught herself holding her breath as she watched the door. She forgot to make her wager, and Meg had to prod her to slide a fish token to the center of the table. She missed countless tricks, her nerves twitching like a cat's whiskers at the slightest sound from the hall. She kept wondering when Brandon would come. Would he sit beside her? Would their hands brush accidentally on the table? Would she blush and give herself away? Would she ever be able to look at him again and not think of their illicit encounter?

A shadow crossed the open doorway. In the same instant, Aunt Myrtle emitted a happy chirrup, "I won! I won! I won!" and Ellie yelped, nearly jumping out of her seat.

"Gracious sakes," Aunt Maeve chided, a hand splayed over her bosom. "The two of you could deliver a heart seizure to a corpse."

Aunt Myrtle laughed merrily, greedily drawing the tokens toward her as if they were sugar-glazed comfits. "My apologies. I didn't realize I could be so invested in the outcome. But when Ellie kept discarding all the hearts, I got rather excited."

Ellie looked down at her pitiful hand and laid them out like a fan on the table. "I'm afraid I don't have a head for cards today. If you don't mind, I think I'll retire early."

"Are you unwell?" Sylvia asked with concern.

With a quick shake of her head, she eased her hostess's mind. "Perfectly hale. A bit tired from the travel, perhaps."

Just as she stood, George strode in and called out merrily, "I say, who's ready for a right proper trouncing at cards?"

Her aunts laughed, welcoming him over to the vacant chair.

As he ambled closer, Ellie noticed that his gaze was slightly pickled. She'd witnessed the sight too often not to recognize the signs of overimbibing. *Oh, George,* she thought despairingly, *why couldn't you be on your best behavior for one single night?*

She glanced nervously at the doorway, expecting their host forthwith. But when Brandon didn't appear, she stayed George with a hand on his sleeve. "Did Lord Hullworth not accompany you from the dining room?"

"Had a matter to attend in the stables," he said, then lowered his voice conspiratorially. "We chatted about you, though."

Her stomach gave a queer flip. "Whyever . . . would you . . . talk about me?"

"He wanted to know all about little Elodie Parrish and if she was always afraid of horses. And you know what I told him? That my Ellie was an adorable little coward in a pinafore and ringlets," he said with a wink and then turned toward the table, chafing his hands together. "Prepare yourselves, ladies. I take no prisoners, you know. Not even you, Miss Myrtle Parrish. I see all those fish you're hoarding. Well, they are about to find more welcome shores."

Ellie wanted to know what reason Brandon had for asking such a question. However, George wouldn't be able to answer that for her. Still, she couldn't help but wonder. Not only that, but whyever would Brandon go to the stables instead of joining the rest of them in the parlor?

Part of her was relieved, of course. And yet, it was with great dismay when she realized, *most* of her wanted to see him just once more. She wanted to see *his* face before she laid her head down to sleep. Perhaps if she did, she would dream of him, instead of her dreadful recurring nightmare.

The intensity of this unexpected desire frightened her. She felt as if she were teetering on the edge of an abyss. One slip and she could fall endlessly into a dark, consuming void.

The only problem was, Ellie feared that it would only take the smallest push to send her plummeting.

Oh, George, she thought, *won't you finally propose and bring an end to all this uncertainty?*

Chapter 21

"A debutante mustn't teeter too long on the edge of an abyss."

—A NOTE FOR *The Marriage Habits of the Native Aristocrat*

The nightmare came again.

Ellie awoke gasping for breath. Clawing at the coverlet, she shoved and kicked it away from her limbs, wanting to be free of the nightmare.

Sitting up, she drew in shuddering lungfuls of air and blinked at her unfamiliar surroundings. Threatening shadows seemed to grow and expand from the marble fireplace, hulking wardrobe and dressing screen in the corner. She scooted back against the bolster pillow, clutching the same linens she had just pushed aside.

At the sound of a low growl, her gaze shot to the slitted window where a dim, gray light bled into the chamber. Another distant rumble was accompanied by the patter of rain on the balcony. Gripping the counterpane, she felt the silken threads of the embroidery and, suddenly, she knew where she was.

Crossmoor Abbey. Her shoulders slumped with relief but it was short-lived.

She had hoped her nightmares would abate while she was here, beneath Brandon's roof. Why she dared such a dream, she did not know. But she felt the instant that it abandoned her on a weary sigh.

Burying her face in her hands, she mumbled, "I despise mornings."

BRANDON LOVED early mornings, especially in the country.

As was his habit, he awoke just before dawn and heard the last grumblings of a passing storm. After a splash of water on his face, he donned his shirtsleeves and a pair of trousers, then padded barefooted out of his rooms to watch the dawn break over the horizon from the best vantage point.

When he was younger and visiting Crossmoor Abbey with his father, the two of them would often sit together on the Eastern terrace and watch the sunrise in appreciative silence. Back then, he took those quiet, commonplace mornings for granted.

He never imagined the day when there would be no more sunrises for one of them. But after his father's death, along with those of his uncle and cousin, he thought about it a good deal. He understood how fleeting life was, and the importance of choosing the people in his own with care.

Mulling over that thought, he traversed the dark corridors with a lamp in hand, the flickering shadows on the wainscoted walls his only companion.

Truth be told, he'd thought about taking a wife a couple of years ago and letting a matchmaker decide. And yet, something inside him told him to wait. So he spent his time ensuring a solid foundation for Meg, teaching her all the lessons that their parents had taught him.

He didn't regret his choice. There had been no one to tempt him to follow another path. No one who had filled him with that sense of utter certainty.

No one until now.

Even so, it was strange to think that he would find someone who—like Phoebe—wasn't stricken with the desire to choose him over someone else. And only a fool would ever imagine pursuing such a woman, knowing full well that she could walk out of his life at any moment.

But with Ellie, he couldn't help himself. He wanted her despite the risk.

All he had to do was show her how good they could be together. The only problem was, Ellie was afraid of . . . well, just about everything under the sun. Including her feelings for him.

It might very well take a miracle to win her over.

A rueful laugh escaped him and guttered his lamp as he entered the long gallery. In the darkness, he heard a soft, startled gasp.

Hullo, he thought curiously, quite familiar with that breathy sound and from whose lips it came.

Eyes adjusting to a faint light at the far end of the room, he saw a lone figure holding a chamberstick, the silhouette of her dress, head and shoulders outlined by the gray curtain of approaching dawn behind her. "Ellie?"

"Brandon! Oh, I'm so glad it's just you," she said in a quiet rush and he chuckled wryly. "I mean, not *just* you . . . but I was afraid you were one of the servants who would, undoubtedly, think I'm barmy for roaming the halls at this hour."

"And you're not worried that I would think the same?"

He could hear the smile in her voice even before she spoke. "Well no," she said, "because you are roaming the halls as well. That could only mean we've both gone mad."

"Ah. Better the pair of us off to Bedlam than only one."

"Precisely."

If he needed proof that he was already in over his head, it came to him the instant he caught himself grinning at the thought of being locked in an asylum with her.

The notion seemed to brighten his path on the runner in the long gallery. He passed the gilt-framed portraits of his ancestors and scattered groupings of upholstered furniture that welcomed the living to gather in communal fondness with the dead.

He recalled when his father had once stood in this very room and said, *For what is life without the reminder of those who have gone from us to teach us how to live each day as if it were our last?*

"Of course, it could also mean that we both enjoy watching the sunrise," he said, drawing near enough to see the flame reflected in her eyes.

But then she looked down, her lashes creating dark, wing-like shadows over her lids. "I actually don't enjoy the sunrise. I would much rather sleep through it."

He took her brass chamberstick and set it beside his on the demilune table, then lifted his hand to cup the soft curve of her cheek. Only now did he see the purplish bruises beneath her eyes.

Tenderly, he traced the vulnerable skin with the pads of his thumbs. "Can you not rest in the country? I've heard that some people prefer the noise of town traffic to lull them into slumber."

"It isn't that . . ." she said but hesitated, worrying the corner of her mouth. "Oh, bother. I don't suppose there's a point in keeping this from you, especially since we're bound to bump into each other again in these early hours." She drew in a breath and when she continued, the lyrical quality of her voice turned threadlike and haunted. "The truth is, I'm plagued by horrible nightmares, nearly every night. Of course, no one else knows, not even my aunts, and I shouldn't want to worry them." Her gaze held his in a beseeching request as she rested her hand over his.

He nodded in swift agreement to keep their secret, but his brow furrowed with concern. "How long has this been going on?"

"Since I was young, when my father died. It began with the terrible certainty that he wasn't dead when they put him in the ground. In those dreams, I was always left to watch helplessly while he struggled to claw his way out of the coffin as the dirt rained down on him. Then, a few years ago, the person inside the coffin changed." She took a shuddering breath. "And I became the one being buried alive."

Brandon crowded closer, feeling the bone-deep tremor that rolled through her. He wished he could somehow protect her from these dreams.

"There are some days when I'm fortunate enough to awaken before the nightmare really takes hold." She shook her head. "It's silliness, I know, for a grown woman to admit such a thing. But there it is, nonetheless."

He tilted her face up to gaze into her eyes with utter earnestness. "It isn't silly at all. I can see by your pallor that they affect you greatly. And an Elodie Parrish with pale cheeks is not something I take lightly." Even though he was serious, it brought a soft smile to her lips. "You're not alone. After my father died, I had nightmares, too. Dreadful things that felt disturbingly real to me."

"What were yours about?"

"Mostly that something would happen to me and that Meg would be left on her own to fend for herself, without any protection from a world that I knew to be hard and cruel at times."

"It seems like a perfectly rational fear to me," she said. "How did you stop having those dreams?"

He felt the tender warmth of her hand as she laid it over his heart without any shyness, and he wondered if she was even aware of her actions. Likely not, he reasoned, or else she would be blushing.

"I sat her down and talked to her," he said. "I explained that, while I had no intention of disappearing through the veil quite yet, I was still going to see that she was well provided for. Then I drew up a set of contracts with my solicitor to ensure it. Once it was all settled, the nightmares never returned."

"It sounds as though I need to have a conversation with myself. Only, I don't know what I'd say."

"You will when the time is right," he said and pressed a kiss to her forehead.

She smelled so good and felt so warm that all he wanted to do was carry her to bed and give her something far more pleasant to think about.

Instead, he took a step back. If he wasn't careful, he'd forget himself again.

Ellie blinked up at him sleepily as if she, too, had been thinking about bed. Then her gaze drifted aimlessly down to his lips, the open neck of his shirtsleeves, and to the hand still lingering on his chest.

She snatched it back. Her cheeks flushed a bright magenta that rivaled the striations of color now on the horizon. "I . . . um . . ."

Before she could balk, he took that hand in his and stepped through the open door to the loggia. "Come. Let's watch this sunrise together, hmm? In the very least, it will help you forget about the nightmare."

He felt the reflexive grip of her delicate fingers curling into his palm, and so it surprised him that she didn't budge from her spot.

"I'd rather watch from here"—she swallowed audibly—"if it's all the same to you."

Her wide-eyed glance darted past him to the roofed stone terrace room and the seven open archways. She didn't appear to admire any of the faint stars still winking in a pale lavender sky. Or particularly care for the patches of mist moving silently over the gardens and the rolling hills, all the way to the riverbed. Instead, she looked as though she were seeing a mausoleum.

He felt another tremor roll through her. Stroking his thumb in soothing sweeps over the petal-soft ridges of her knuckles, he warmed her chilled fingertips in the cup of his palm. "You are quite safe, and I would not say that lightly. Is it the height that bothers you? If so, we can sit together on the bench by the wall."

She peered around the corner as if in consideration, but then shook her head. "It's true that I'm not overly fond of high places. However, you could say that I have . . . a somewhat unnatural fear of stone arches. Have you ever noticed that the void beneath it resembles a gravestone, as if the marker had been chiseled away and the remaining stones are waiting to collapse and bury a person?"

"I cannot say that I have," he said, but looked at the arches from the perspective of someone who had nightmares of being buried alive. He'd never noticed it before, but the void beneath did somewhat resemble a gravestone.

She slipped her hand free and wrapped her arms around herself as if to ward off the chill. "Of course, I'm perfectly capable of managing this phobia. Whenever I must step beneath an arch or travel over a bridge, I simply close my eyes and hold my breath until it's over."

Brandon wanted her hand back in his. He wanted this to be the first of many times that they sat together to watch the sun breaking over the horizon. And he hated the thought of her going through her life simply *managing* her fears instead of overcoming them.

Returning to her side, he absently brushed his fingertips across the soft blue muslin of her skirt. It was impossible not to be near her. And impossible to be near her and not to touch her. "Did you know that an arch can support more weight over a broader expanse than a standard, horizontal lintel? Without them, most bridges would require too many braces to allow ships to pass underneath."

"You're trying valiantly to make me feel better about arches *and* bridges, but it isn't going to work."

He watched her chin hike and felt his own stubbornness rise with determination. *Challenge accepted, Miss Parrish*.

"My father once told me that there is a reason arches resemble a pair of shoulders, for they carry more weight than one can bear by halves." As he spoke, he put his arm behind her, settling his hand into the small of her back to share his warmth. Then he smiled inwardly when she listed toward him ever so slightly as if she needed to be closer to him, too. "And like a pair of shoulders, they require a connecting component to hold them together, to keep them strong. That's where the keystone comes in."

He pointed to the angular ashlar stone at the crest of the arch, large and pale with decorative fan-shaped grooves chiseled into the surface.

She followed the gesture with her gaze, but swallowed again. "What's to keep it from suddenly giving way?"

"It's cut to fit perfectly, wider at the top so it won't slip free. Additionally, it has equal pressure from both sides. It bears a good deal, that keystone."

"Indeed, it does. And there are seven of them here," she said warily.

"Along with seven below it, where the lower loggia leads out to the garden." He kept his tone matter-of-fact and the hand at her back moving in slow, reassuring sweeps.

In an unobtrusive gesture, Brandon traced the fingers of her left hand, still curled over her arm, and slyly moved them into his grasp. As he spoke, he shifted her toward him by degrees, his fingertips skating along the ladder of her spine. It was highly improper to hold her this closely. He was the lord of the manor, after all. She was his guest and under his protection. But it was that very thought of wanting to protect her, to shelter her, that kept him on his course.

That very thought that compelled him to furtively guide her one step out onto the terrace.

"According to legend," he said, holding her gaze, "the Italian architect of this house designed these arches for lessons, of a sort. The lower seven are said to represent man upholding the holy sacraments of his church."

"And the upper arches?"

"The seven deadly sins bearing down upon him."

A startled laugh escaped her. "Goodness! Yet another reason to avoid standing beneath arches."

"Hmm . . ." he murmured thoughtfully, wondering if she realized that they'd taken two, *three*, steps. "But you know—at least, I hope you know—that I would not put you in harm's way."

She nodded, her gaze never straying from his. "That is the only reason I've allowed you this masquerade of luring me out onto the terrace."

He stopped in surprise. His brow furrowed even as a bemused smile curled the corners of his mouth. "I thought I was doing a fair job of distracting you."

"I tried to be distracted," she admitted shyly. "I don't like being afraid, Brandon. If I could do anything to be rid of the pins and needles of dread down my spine, I would. It is only because of the steady certainty in your bearing and in your tone that I made it this far. I know that, if you suspected even the smallest defect in the structural integrity of this terrace, you would never permit your sister, your aunt, or any of your guests to step foot on it. However"—she paused on a gulp of air, her hand gripping his—"to be perfectly honest, I have far more faith in you than in this pile of stone that's been here for nearly two hundred years."

Considering the fact that she was still afraid, her declaration shouldn't please him so much. But it did, nonetheless.

"Well then, allow me to take you back to safer ground."

He felt the stiffness leave her spine the instant they stepped back across the threshold.

She looked through the doorway and a soft smile brushed her lips. "Do you want to know something? It wasn't as awful as I thought it would be. And look. There's the dawn right now. It is quite lovely from up here." The light of it glowed in her eyes as she looked at him again. "Thank you for making this morning brighter."

"My pleasure."

As their gazes brushed and held, the connection they shared seemed stronger now, a tangible thing dangling between them. He could almost reach out and pluck it from the air.

"Well, I'd better be off before the servants . . ." Her voice trailed off as she glanced down to the hand that she'd laid against his chest again. Her eyes widened, and when her fingers flexed over the hard muscle beneath, she emitted a quiet sound of distress as if she couldn't stop her own response. "Oh, forgive me. I . . . didn't . . . you're in your shirtsleeves . . ." Deep pink color flooded her cheeks, expanding across the bridge of her nose as her fingers drifted higher, sifting through the thatch of hair rising from the open neck. "And you have all these crisp, little, perfect bronze curls . . . and um . . ." She swallowed. "I should . . . go. Now."

"Likely for the best," he rasped, her touch setting off quicksilver flares of sensation through his body even as she slipped out of his embrace.

He wanted to haul her back, to let her continue her exploration. But if he did, he knew he would kiss her. And if she kissed him back the way she did yesterday, well, his plan to woo her slowly would likely go up in flames.

Chapter 22

"One must cross a bridge when one comes to it,
or simply take the long way around."

—A note for *The Marriage Habits*
of the Native Aristocrat

Ellie hadn't intended to reveal so much this morning. She hated her fears. They made her feel inadequate, as if she lacked a vital component that other, more worldly and desirable, women possessed. In fact, she often thought that if she wasn't such a ninny about heights and arches—as well as scores of other things—then George would have married her long ago.

Of course, she couldn't be certain. However, she knew without a doubt that if she were to have told *him* about her nightmares, he would have teased her mercilessly.

But not Brandon. He hadn't made her feel the least bit odd or deficient in any way. He'd even shared his own fear, which told her that he understood and, more importantly, that she wasn't alone.

Usually, the nightmares left her with a sense of lingering exhaustion, but now a wondrous vibrancy hummed inside her. It felt liberating.

Stepping out onto the courtyard a few hours later, she breathed in deeply, tasting the sweet traces of morning dew on the air. Her heartbeat was as light and aimless as her steps upon the gravel drive, her spirit as weightless as the cottony clouds overhead.

It was a beautiful day, perfect for the open carriage that would drive them to Mr. and Mrs. Thorley's to visit Prue.

She caught sight of Brandon speaking to one of the grooms. Instantly, she recalled their early morning embrace and the fascinating texture of the bronze furring on his chest beneath her wayward fingertips. Her heartbeat quickened. But, this time, she did not disparage herself over her reaction to him. She was too content at the moment to let skittishness encumber her.

So when he smiled in greeting and he touched the brim of his hat, she did the same. Feeling rather playful, she added a jaunty salute.

She walked on ahead to where Meg was waiting for the step to be placed in front of the carriage.

"Have I mentioned," Ellie asked her friend, "that you look positively divine in that blue frock? I'm sure the sky is jealous and wishing it were just a shade brighter."

The younger woman raised her black-winged brows in teasing speculation. "Well, someone is certainly cheerful this morning."

"I am, indeed," Ellie admitted. "I don't know how to explain it. I just feel so"—she shrugged—"alive, I suppose. Must be the Wiltshire air."

"What about the air?" Brandon asked from behind her, sending a pleasurable shiver down her body that seemed to collect in her midriff, tilting and weighted.

"According to Ellie," Meg said as she settled her skirts on the carriage bench, "it makes a person feel alive."

"Is that so?" Brandon took Ellie's hand to assist her. But when she mounted the step and they were of a same height, he leaned covertly closer and drew in a breath that flared his nostrils. "I believe you're right, Miss Parrish. The air is intoxicating."

The words were said matter-of-factly, but the smoldering heat in the gaze beneath the brim of his hat turned her cheeks seven shades of red and made her knees wobble as she climbed into the carriage.

The arrogant man had the nerve to grin as he occupied the opposite bench. Clearly, he knew precisely how he affected her. Then again, it didn't take much. In fact, all she had to do was look at him and her heart palpitated queerly.

She was quickly learning not to be too alarmed by these sensations. And yet, they were still somewhat disconcerting.

She tried to pay attention to the scenery as the carriage trundled down the lane, but her gaze kept straying back to him. This morning, he was dressed in a pair of buff breeches that molded over the solid muscles of his thighs like a second skin, and he sat with his legs splayed in the relaxed confidence of a well-formed gentleman. His camel waistcoat was a shade darker and invited the eye to appreciate the drum-tight abdomen beneath. With his cravat so neatly tied and his green morning coat so smartly tailored, it was nearly impossible to imagine him in less civilized attire. And yet, after their dawn together, she could quite easily.

"Is Lord Nethersole not joining us?" Meg asked, jolting Ellie out of her musings.

She blinked with a start, only now realizing that George wasn't with them. And when her gaze met Brandon's, that knowing smile of his returned.

"Nethersole opted to ride instead," he said. "When we left, he was at the stables, taking me up on my offer to select a mount for his morning ride."

"Well, I hope he isn't taking my mount. Ophelia isn't overly fond of long rides."

"Fear not, your palfrey is quite safe. The stablemaster informed me that Nethersole had requested one of the Arabians."

"Just as long as it isn't Hamlet. Ophelia quite depends upon him and he is protective of her, always by her side."

She looked at Ellie with a wry expression. "If you cannot tell, I was reading Shakespeare when Brandon said I could name them."

"At least those names are cleverer than the one I'd chosen for my pet canary," she said. "Can you guess what color Goldie was?"

"Yellow, perhaps?"

"Why, no. He was as mossy green as your brother's eyes," she declared, all innocence. Then she spoiled her teasing fib by laughing. "Indeed, he was yellow from beak to tailfeather and I, obviously, lacked any imagination whatsoever."

Meg's gaze turned thoughtful and a touch sly as it shifted from Ellie to Brandon and back again. "That's peculiar. Most people are under the misconception that he has gray eyes."

"From a distance, perhaps, but—" Ellie stopped when she realized what she'd admitted. Heat rushed to the surface of her skin and she felt as if every intimate encounter were written on her face. "I believe . . . I caught sight of their true color . . . as he handed me into the carriage."

She didn't want to look at Brandon just then. But she couldn't help it. What made it worse was the way he was looking back at her, his irises all warm and velvety.

"That explains it then," he said quietly, holding her gaze.

"Yes, that must be it," Meg said, her tone tinged with sarcasm. "Oh, and don't look now, Ellie, but we're already on the bridge and you're not holding your breath."

Even though she and Meg were facing the rear of the coach, Ellie had known precisely when the horses' hooves and wheels had met with the cobblestone. But in the same instant, she had been looking at Brandon and felt his strength envelop her, just as it had early that morning on the loggia. And it was that same sense of certainty she felt now. She knew without a doubt that he wouldn't let the bridge collapse.

Yet, even if some terrible accident from her imagination befell them—a sudden gale force wind, rabid horses, a rare but not impossible Wiltshire earthquake, or any number of catastrophes that sent them careening over the side—she also knew that Brandon would find a way to keep the river from swallowing her whole.

At one time, she might have ascribed the confident quality in his nature to utter arrogance. But the more she came to know him, the more she believed that he was indisputably adept at everything he did. Therefore, if he had faith in the aging rocks beneath them, then so did she.

At least . . . as long as she didn't look away from him.

"My father called this the marriage bridge," Meg said, conversationally. "Because of the two arches and how they support one another. According to tradition, the titled lord takes his intended bride to the river. Their boat floats easily downstream through one arch. Then, through the second arch, they're supposed to paddle together."

"I quite like that." Ellie smiled. "It would make a splendid analogy for a book. In fact—"

"Tally ho!" The call rang out from the lane behind them, accompanied by the thundering of hooves.

She startled, head jerking sharply to see George charging forth on a spirited black mount.

Disconnected from Brandon's gaze, her vision rippled like the waves tumbling over the rocks beneath them. She wanted to close her eyes but she couldn't. All she could do was watch the horse approach at breakneck speed.

She knew in an instant that George wasn't going to slow down. He had that look of determination in his lowered brow and an all too familiar mischievous gleam in his dark eyes. He clearly wasn't planning to follow behind the carriage. And the bridge wasn't wide enough for the two to ride side by side.

Panic sluiced icily through her body, her breaths shallow

and quick. Meg stifled a terrified gasp. Brandon cursed and shouted to his driver. And Ellie squeezed her eyes shut.

The carriage stopped with a lurch on the bridge and she blindly gripped the edge of the bench. She felt the restless shifting of the horses. She heard the taut strain of the ribbons, the discordant jangle of rigging, the crunch of stones giving way beneath the ruthless plodding of the racing Arabian. And the sound of the rushing of the water beneath her.

The air smelled of wetness and worms. She could taste it at the back of her throat where a scream was lodged like hard-packed earth. It was suffocating.

There was movement beneath her and she was certain that they were all falling and falling and soon they would crash into the water and the bridge would break off into great chunks to bury them all . . .

"Ellie. Ellie, dear. Fear not. We are all fine," she heard Meg say through the terror roaring in her ears, and felt a small hand rubbing circles between her tight shoulder blades. "We are over the bridge now. See?"

But she didn't see. She couldn't open her eyes. She was still trapped in the darkness, her limbs frozen and locked in place.

"She isn't breathing properly," a gruff voice said. It was similar to Brandon's, but the sound was far too deep, too threatening, to be his. She felt a tug at her throat, then the weight of her hat lifting from her head. "Miss Parrish—*Ellie*—take a breath. Meg, unfasten those buttons. No, here, let me."

She felt swift, deft movements down the center of her fawn spencer, and she shivered when the warm air brushed her neck.

"Her lips are turning blue around the edges. Do something, Brandon."

The heat of a hand touched her cheeks, her lips, her throat, then settled on the upper portion of her chest, just above her bodice, and rubbed in rough circles. "Take a breath. Now, Ellie. No, a deeper breath. Come on. If you don't start to breathe properly, then I'm going to have to murder Nethersole. I'll likely murder him anyway. That's it, sweetheart. Nothing like a threat to the man-child to bring you around. Yes, take another. Slowly, now."

It hurt to drag in a breath. Her throat stung with the effort. But then the scent of Brandon's shaving soap and the warmth of his skin filled her nostrils, comforting her, easing the air into her lungs sip by sip.

Her lashes blinked open. Vision still gray around the edges, it took her a moment to focus on his face, to see the taut lines etched into the furrows of his brow and the hardness of his jaw. The penetrating heat in his gaze caused her pulse to accelerate in some unnamed emotion that teetered between elation and alarm.

She'd never seen him look so fierce before. And it seemed impossible that such a ferocious gaze could be paired with the tender brush of his fingertips over her cheek as he tucked a lock of hair behind her ear.

Gradually, she became attuned to everything around him—the stillness of the carriage beneath the shaded canopy of trees, the whicker of restless horses, the feel of Meg's small hand clutching her own.

All at once, embarrassment flooded her as she recalled every grueling moment. Mortified by her reaction, she closed her eyes. "Oh, bother. I cannot tell you how sorry I am for being such an utter ninny."

"No. *I* am the ninny," Meg declared. "How thoughtless of me to tease you about bridges. I had no idea they affected you so. If it wasn't for Brandon, I don't know what we would have done."

Ellie didn't know, either. Only now did she recall the gruff endearment he'd spoken—*sweetheart*—and her heart quickened painfully beneath her breast. And she had a terrible impulse to fling her arms around him, bury her face in his neck and never let him go.

What was happening to her?

As she glanced to Meg, a wash of guilt was added to this churning mix of emotions. Her friend would surely feel betrayed if she ever found out that Ellie was helplessly drawn to her brother, like so many others were.

So she looked again to Brandon, almost pleadingly, for him to stop this tumult just as he had done a moment ago. But he only gazed back at her with that new intensity that didn't resolve anything inside her. It only made it worse.

Lifting her free hand to cover his, she drew it away and kept her words simple, if not impersonal. "Thank you, my lord."

The alteration in him was subtle. A slow blink, a shift in his posture, then gradually the warmth receded from his gaze, and the air turned cooler.

"Think nothing of it," he said with a curt nod as he eased back onto the opposite bench before handing her hat to her. "And, pray, forgive my forwardness a moment ago, Miss Parrish. If you want to turn back, then I'm sure your friend will understand."

As any gentleman would do, he averted his face to look outside the carriage, thus allowing her a moment to compose herself and rearrange her clothing.

Ellie's stomach twisted in knots at his withdrawal. A chill crept over her skin that made her fingers clumsy, fumbling with the buttons of her spencer. She missed his warmth, his touch. She longed to reach out for him and to hear that whispered endearment again. Something deep down told her that turning her back on this feeling would be the worst thing she could ever do.

In that strange, bewildering instant, she understood that part of her had changed—the part that was certain she only wanted George. All at once, she knew she'd come too far to erect such a paltry barrier between Brandon and herself now. Much, *much* too far.

And it was terrifying.

"I should like to continue onward," she said quietly, her voice strained and unsure. He glanced at her, his gaze alert and searching as if, like always, he could read her thoughts. She lifted her shoulders in a feeble shrug. "Even so, I'm not certain that I know how to cross this bridge when we next approach it."

The furrows on his brow cleared and he exhaled a slow breath. His lips parted as if he intended to say something, but Meg spoke first and took her hand again.

"Fear not, Ellie. We'll help you. Won't we, Brandon?"

She saw him glance down to her and his sister's joined hands and his expression turned thoughtful, considering.

Looking at Meg, he offered a nod. "Of course, we will."

Chapter 23

⌒

"Surviving a harrowing event may open a
debutante's eyes to new possibilities. But these
are temptations she ought to resist . . . if she can."

—A NOTE FOR *The Marriage Habits*
of the Native Aristocrat

The Thorleys' two-story brick house was situated inside a
perfect square of manicured lawn and bordered by the same
white stone that framed the slender, symmetrical rows of
windows. Everything seemed to have its place. A pair of
mature elm trees stood on either side at equal distances, and
they were flanked by juniper topiaries, shaped and pruned
to identical precision.

To Ellie, it all seemed rather too perfect, like a dollhouse
in the attic, kept far from the nursery where a child might
wish to play with it.

From Prue's letters, she knew that the Thorleys were an
exacting pair, demanding perfection in all things. But somehow, seeing the house for herself gave Ellie an unsettled
feeling. If the owners were so determined to present the
facade of perfection on the outside, what manner of perfection was demanded of those living within it?

By the time they approached the gateposts, George was
already at the mouth of the narrow drive, his glossy black
mount turning in a high-stepping pace. The carriage was
forced to stop since he didn't direct his horse to the side.

"There you are. I've been waiting an age, don't you

know," George scolded. "And this Arabian doesn't like to stand still."

A muscle ticked in Brandon's jaw. "We decided on a more scenic tour."

It was kind of him to say nothing of her episode. The ordeal had been embarrassing enough on its own, but she certainly wasn't in the mood to endure George's usual teasing when it came to her fears.

"You might have told me beforehand," George said, affronted.

Brandon took a patient breath. "You needn't have lingered out of doors on our account. After all, you seem to know the way here well enough."

The more Ellie listened to the exchange, the more she began to feel rather cross with George for the way he'd recklessly charged past them on the bridge. And, for that matter, for the way he'd gone off without them, never turning back.

"Yes, that is peculiar," Ellie said, directing her comment to George. "How did you know where Mr. and Mrs. Thorley live?"

The horse shifted beneath him and he glanced down to tug the reins, correcting his mount. "I told you my steward has been looking at properties. Because of that, I'm familiar with all the houses."

"But I don't recall ever mentioning them by name."

"Well, you must have done. There's no other way," he said resolutely, then took off down the drive, leading the way. Again.

Staring after him as the carriage spurred into motion, she supposed she must have told him. Or, perhaps, he'd glimpsed the address on one of the letters she'd sent to Prue. It didn't matter, really. In the end, all that she cared about was seeing her friend at last.

The minute the carriage stopped at the edge of the manicured lawn, the oaken door opened and Prue appeared. At least, Ellie thought it was her friend. In truth, however, so wan and frail that she briefly hoped she was mistaken.

The woman in the doorway wore sprigged muslin that had seen too many washings. She was thinner, too, her flesh taut over high cheekbones and the slender column of her throat. The strain of separation and ostracism was clearly etched upon her knitted brow and within the haunted blue of her eyes.

Yet, even with all those changes . . .

Brandon handed her down. Both she and Prue rushed in quick strides down the pristine white stone path. Had it truly been only a year since they'd last seen each other? It felt more like a decade.

"Prue," Ellie said with fondness, trying to smile through the sting of impending tears. She reached out with both hands to clasp her friend's, but instead found herself quickly pulled into a surprisingly strong embrace.

The instant she felt Prue's tremor and heard her stifled sob, her own blubbering began.

"I had convinced myself that you weren't going to come," Prue said on a broken breath, muffled against the fabric of Ellie's spencer.

"Of course, I came," she said on a sniff, wishing she had been able to visit sooner. Clearly, the letters had done little to serve as a balm for this isolation, and she couldn't help but wonder what other pains Prue had endured from her exacting aunt and uncle in these months. "No matter what has occurred, I will always be your friend."

Another choked sob gripped her. "Oh, Ellie, I cannot tell you how glad I am to hear that. And I am so very sorry for all that has occurred."

"You have no need to apologize. I'm fully capable of understanding how these things can happen when we are not quite ourselves." She never faulted Prue for whatever occurred in the gardens at Sutherfield Terrace. And now that she'd experienced her own moments of unexpected and overwhelming passions, she could easily commiserate with her.

Lifting her face, Prue swiped the tracks of tears from her cheeks and nodded. "Yes, that is it precisely. I wasn't myself. Though, that is not to excuse my own actions. To tell you the truth, I thought you would hate me."

"Nonsense. I certainly won't hold a grudge over a handful of letters. It doesn't matter that you sent Jane twice as many as you sent me. I wasn't counting."

Prue frowned, the flesh above the bridge of her nose corrugated. "Letters?"

"And it wasn't as if I spent hours of every day wondering if you saw me as the less interesting friend or any silliness like that."

At Prue's bewildered glance over Ellie's shoulder, she turned to see George standing there.

He doffed his hat and sketched a bow. "Miss Thorogood. What a complete pleasure it is to see you after such a lengthy absence. You are even lovelier than I remember."

Ellie smiled at him in approval. If nothing else, she could always rely on George's charming nature to lift her friend's spirits and put a blush in her cheeks. However, when she turned to face Prue again, she saw that her complexion had gone even whiter.

At once, Ellie realized that a woman who'd been shunned by society might see the usual flirtations as mockery . . . or even, she thought with a shudder, a threat. After all, it wasn't uncommon for men to prey upon a woman that society deemed as *fallen*.

Looking at Prue's stark expression, Ellie couldn't help but wonder, once more, what all she'd endured.

She came to her friend's side and took her hand. "George is such a flirt, but you needn't worry that he means anything by it."

"No. Of course not," Prue said on a swallow and slipped her hand free to chafe it roughly down her arm as if she were chilled on this warm sunny day. She glanced toward Brandon and Meg, who were still waiting at a discreet distance.

Ellie waved her hand, bidding them forth and introducing them.

Ever the gentleman, Brandon was amiable and engaging, remarking on what a perfectly situated house her aunt and uncle had. And Meg was so affable and effervescent that it was impossible not to like her.

And yet, after the introduction, Prue seemed withdrawn and tired, like a person who'd arisen from a sickbed all too soon.

"I wish I could I invite each of you inside," Prue began, her feet shifting on the stones, "but my aunt and uncle are at the vicar's cottage on their usual morning visit and they don't approve of callers when they are not at home."

"Of course," Ellie said immediately, though with some surprise. She wondered why Prue's missive had suggested they come at this time if she expected her aunt and uncle to be out. "I can call later, or even tomorrow if you prefer."

Prue nodded. "I'll send a card to you and we'll decide from there. It's just that"—she paused, hesitating, and lowered her voice—"I'm not entirely myself at the moment."

Ellie nodded in quick understanding. It stood to reason that Prue might very well feel uncomfortable in the presence of too many people who weren't well acquainted with her. Or she might have been overwhelmed and needed time to acclimate herself to society, small though it was.

Worried about her friend, Ellie offered a supportive

smile. "I will be here whenever you wish, for as long as you wish. My aunts and I have no fixed engagements for the coming weeks, and Lord Hullworth has been more than generous to offer us lodging."

"Any friend of Miss Parrish is welcome to Crossmoor Abbey, as well," Brandon offered gallantly as he came to stand by Ellie's side.

George stepped forward again. "And I'm planning to take a house in the area soon. I'll undoubtedly have a party to celebrate. Until then, Miss Thorogood, I am ever your servant."

He reached out and grasped Prue's fingertips, but she frowned and snatched back her hand. Cheeks aflame, she looked at Ellie one more time.

"You must forgive me, but I . . ." Her words trailed off as she shook her head. Then she rushed back inside.

When the door closed, Ellie swatted his arm. "George, I would thank you not to terrify my shy friend in the future."

"What did I do but pay her a compliment?"

She heaved out an exasperated breath. How to explain George to himself?

As they headed down the path toward the waiting carriage, she said, "Prue is reserved and quiet. Someone with your nature is likely to send her into hiding. So please, as a favor to me, try to be on your best behavior."

"Well, that's the thing of it, Ellie. I'm always on my very best behavior when I'm with you." He winked before he sauntered off toward the horse. Calling over his shoulder, he said, "And now, I'm off to take a scenic tour myself. You don't mind if I keep this Arabian a bit longer, do you, Hullworth? Good."

George never really gave Brandon a chance to answer. He simply untied the horse, stepped into the stirrup and swung his leg over. Then he spurred his mount and set off.

Chagrined, she turned to face Brandon. "I apologize for George. He means well, but occasionally takes things for granted. I'll have a talk with him later."

"It's clear that he takes a good deal for granted"—he frowned, watching the rider disappear down the lane, then he looked down at her—"including you."

She bristled but only mildly because she happened to notice the same thing. "That isn't fair."

"Perhaps not. But neither is it your place to apologize for a grown man. He's accountable for his own actions and, if I have an issue, I will speak with him myself."

She nodded in agreement and walked beside him to the carriage. "As for my friend, I mistakenly believed that she would be eager for society. Had I known the truth, I'd never have pulled you away from estate duties you doubtlessly need to attend to after being in town for months."

"Your only fault, Miss Parrish—at least as far as I can tell—is that you mistakenly imagine that I would rather be holed up in my study, poring over estate ledgers, instead of enjoying this beautiful day with you and my sister."

His frank statement caused a rush of ebullience to leaven her mood, making her feel lighter and brighter. She tried not to let it show as she slipped her hand into his waiting grasp. "But surely you have other obligations."

"Come to think of it, I do," he said, assisting her into the carriage. "I have it under good authority that there are plums ready for picking in the grove. I would be shirking my responsibility, indeed, if I did not see for myself. But I would require assistance, of course. Meg is never any help. The indolent plum-eater merely picks one and sits beneath a tree to devour it."

Meg scoffed. "Pay no attention to him, Ellie. He'll have you believe that he doesn't eat as many as he picks. He hardly leaves enough from the first harvest for our cook to make the most divine plum and rosemary sauce. It's a secret family recipe. I can already hear Maeve and Myrtle trying to wheedle it out of my aunt Sylvia."

"You know them so well," Ellie said with a laugh. Then she looked to Brandon and, without any fear of bee stings or falling branches or whatever nonsense her mind could conjure, she said, "I should like nothing better."

It wasn't until much later that she thought about George at all.

Chapter 24

"Patience is a gentleman's greatest asset . . . even if
it should kill him."

—A NOTE FOR *The Marriage Habits*
of the Native Aristocrat

Brandon wondered if anyone, other than Ellie, would truly mind if he just happened to murder *George* by accident.

He'd been having a glorious afternoon with Ellie in the grove. Meg had conveniently abandoned them, once she'd declared she had picked the perfect plum, then sat beneath a tree to appreciate it. During that time, Brandon had assisted Ellie. Since she was afraid of ladders, he was obliged to lift her by the waist on occasion to reach her intended fruit, and stole a kiss or two as he lowered his blushing armful to the ground.

It was a superb day until . . . he walked into the stables as Nethersole returned his Arabian with a slight limp. The man-child merely shrugged and suggested that the horse had taken a rock. Which ended up being true. Nevertheless, his insouciant manner of delivery poked at Brandon's ire.

Then during dinner, Brandon again endured Nethersole's countless tales of life with *his Ellie*. And now, in the music room, he had to listen to Nethersole sing and entertain everyone while Ellie accompanied him on the piano. The worst part of it was, they were actually good together. Her fingers were light and quick on the ivories and he had a baritone rich enough to earn him a place on any stage.

But if Nethersole rested his hand on her shoulder or winked at her one more time then . . .

Well, that brought Brandon back to his quandary. How to murder Nethersole and make it look like an accident?

"I've seen that look before, nephew," Sylvia said as she strolled over to where he was standing near the open balcony.

Hoping that his lethal thoughts weren't obvious, he attempted a harmless smile. "And what look is that?"

"Thoroughly besotted," she said and he expelled a breath of relief.

His gaze naturally settled on the lovely pianist across the room. "I am, indeed."

"I'm glad for you, truly." She patted the hand he had resting on the balustrade. "It is also clear that you are ready to begin the rest of your life. And, if you are anything like your uncle, you don't want to wait a single day."

The mention brought a smile to his lips. "I never knew Uncle Phillip was impatient."

"Oh, yes. He was the most persistent and stubborn man I ever knew," she said fondly, her eyes soft and wistful. "Back when he was courting me, he had the same look that you're wearing now. I don't know if he ever told you our story, but I was once in Ellie's shoes. At the time I met Phillip, I was thoroughly besotted with someone else." At her nephew's surprise, she nodded. "That gentleman had been courting me with the intention of marriage and I couldn't wait to be his wife."

Brandon frowned. This was nothing like the fated story his uncle had told, the one that he and his cousin would roll their eyes over whenever they heard it.

"But then, one day, Phillip knocked on my door by mistake," she continued. "He was actually paying a call on my neighbor, the beautiful Miss Trentham, who was like a siren to the men of the *ton*. In fact, he wasn't even the first to mistake my address for hers. And yet, I took one look at him and all at once I knew—"

"That he was the one you were going to marry," Brandon interrupted with dogged certainty and relief, until his aunt shook her head.

"—that I wanted to avoid him at all cost," she admitted candidly. "There was something too magnetic, too potent, about him. It frightened me. And, more than that, it made me question my feelings for the other man. Your uncle, stubborn as he was, had already made up his mind about our marrying, no matter what I told him to the contrary. So he decided that I needed prodding. He kept pushing and pushing, and the harder he pushed the more I wanted to give my heart and soul to the other gentleman. What I felt for that man hadn't frightened me at all. It was simple and pure and we could have had a fine life together."

Again Brandon frowned, feeling the sting of betrayal on his uncle's behalf. "I thought you always said that you regretted waiting a single day to marry Uncle Phillip."

"It's true. I do regret it. But I never would have waited if Phillip had just given me a moment to breathe and to realize how much I'd loved him from the very start."

The news did not improve Brandon's mood. If he recalled correctly, at the start of his acquaintance with Ellie, she called him *King Goose*. Not exactly an auspicious beginning. "But what if Uncle Phillip had given you *room to breathe* as you'd asked? You might not have realized he was sincere and determined. You might have chosen to marry the wrong man."

She shook her head. A silver tendril escaped the tight coil at her nape and drifted against her cheek. She absently brushed it back, her gaze straying to the gold band she still wore on her finger. "There was never any chance of that. There was no passion between the other man and myself.

I didn't blush whenever I looked into his eyes. But when I looked at Phillip"—she breathed in and out with a wan smile on her lips—"I could see midnight stars and sunrises enough to fill my entire life." Then she looked at Brandon. "I want that for you."

"But what if," he hesitated as he glanced across the music room to see Ellie smiling up at Nethersole as they reached the crescendo, "she still doesn't choose me?"

Lifting her hand, Sylvia touched his cheek with a fond pat. "Then you deserve someone who does. It's as simple as that. And as difficult as that."

As she left the room, he stared after her and pensively watched the vacant doorway, thinking of his next steps. Every part of him yearned to haul Ellie up from the piano bench, kiss her soundly and leave no question in her mind or in anyone else's how right they were for each other.

But that wasn't the answer. Just because he was certain, didn't mean she was. And the last thing he wanted was to push his skittish Ellie into Nethersole's arms.

If he'd learned anything from his experience with Phoebe, it was that he wanted to be his wife's first choice. Her only choice. And if that meant he had to give Ellie room to decide, then he would do that, even if it killed him.

Therefore, at the end of the evening, he did not ask about her plans for the morrow or speak of his own hope to watch the sunrise again with her. He merely bid her a good night in the same manner that he did her aunts, his sister and . . . *George.*

❦❦❦

EARLY THE following morning, Brandon walked to the loggia without any expectation.

Lamp in hand, he entered the long gallery. Then he smiled when he saw the silhouette framed by the pale lavender of fading night and a single candle flame.

"Good morning, Ellie."

The way she tucked her chin to her chest told him that she was blushing. "Good morning, Brandon."

He wanted to pull her into his arms so badly that resisting the urge was like trying to stop a boulder from careening down a mountain. Somehow he managed, but found himself flirting quite close to temptation by leaning against the other side of the door frame. Close enough that the hem of her dress brushed the toes of his top boots. Close enough that her sweet fragrance filled every breath. And close enough to see that her gaze slipped to the open neck of his shirt.

"Are we watching the sunrise together?" he asked, deciding to cross his arms so he didn't accidentally reach out, grab her and kiss her a thousand times. And he noticed that she started to fuss with the end of the sash tied at her waist as if she were struggling with some inner temptation too.

"I thought we might. However," she said, hesitating as she drew in a breath and he suspected he knew what she was about to say, "I also wanted to speak to you about yesterday."

"And would this be in regard to the carriage or the grove?"

"Both, actually." Her gaze dipped again to his chest, her fingernail beginning to fray the edge. "You shouldn't have called me sweetheart in front of your sister. Nor should you have kissed me in the full light of day where anyone might have happened upon us beneath that tree."

"Don't forget the other tree."

"I could hardly forget that one . . ."

"Neither could I," he murmured, listing closer. But then, remembering what his aunt had said, he stopped, telling himself to be strong. "Nevertheless, I'll have you know that I gave myself a stern lecture for my behavior."

"Did you?" she asked with a small grin.

He issued a scholarly nod, his lips pursed. "Then, of

course, *myself* countered with the argument that he regretted none of his actions and that, if given the chance to
live those stolen moments in the grove all over again, he
wouldn't change a single thing."

"I see," she said and swallowed. "Well, I had a similar
conversation with myself but she wasn't nearly as strong-
minded."

"The bashful sort, hmm?"

She nodded. "It stands to reason that she would be, considering that she has always imagined spending her life
with a man who was not with her at the grove or at the . . .
um . . . inn."

"And now?" Brandon asked, his gaze drifting to the
pulse fluttering at her throat, beneath the surface of the delicate skin where his lips had been not a full day ago. Damn
but he wanted to return to that spot.

"She is torn and confused by her burgeoning feelings
toward someone new, and by an overwhelming passion that
she's never had before."

"He finds great promise in the words *torn* and *confused*."

"*She* doesn't," Ellie said with a disconcerted glare. "And
your smug grin is showing."

"Would it help if I told her that he has honorable intentions?"

"No. It only adds to the confusion. Which is precisely
the reason I think we shouldn't let what happened—in the
grove, at the inn, at Sutherfield Terrace, *and* the Zoological
Society Gardens—happen again."

"It's shameful that our alter-selves cannot be trusted in
gardens. And now, here we are at Crossmoor Abbey, surrounded by them on every side."

"This isn't amusing in the least."

Brandon wasn't laughing. He was simply elated. "What
would put your mind at ease?"

"Well, to begin with, no more calling me sweetheart and no more mentions of inevitability."

He nodded, but in the back of his mind he was already planning an *I told you so* on their tenth anniversary.

"After all, we must think about Meg," she said sternly. "I am supposed to be her friend. All the time that she's been in London, she's never had one who wasn't conspiring to gain your attention. I cannot betray her trust. But I'm still . . ."

"*Torn* and *confused*?"

"Mmmhmm," she murmured with a nod and continued picking at the angled end of her sash. "In London, it was easier to convince myself that my attraction to you was nothing more than a consequence of our growing friendship. But that is no longer the case. Something has altered inside me, leaving me with the perplexing dichotomous impulses to either run as far away from you as possible or simply . . . to fall into your arms."

He didn't trust himself to say anything for fear of sending her in the wrong direction. And so, when she fell silent and turned her face to the sunrise, he did the same.

Chapter 25

⌒

"A debutante must face her fears with each new dawn."

—A note for *The Marriage Habits of the Native Aristocrat*

Ellie met Brandon for sunrise every morning after that. They stood in the doorway, leaning on opposite sides to face each other without touching. He didn't attempt to pull her into his arms or distract her while taking her, step by step, out onto the terrace.

Instead, they simply talked. They shared quiet stories and observations, getting better acquainted each day and finding more and more reasons to enjoy the other's company.

In fact, she'd begun to prefer *his* company to all others.

She found herself looking for him on the estate throughout the day. Sometimes it was simply to wave at him from across the courtyard while he was standing at the stables and speaking with a groomsman or farrier. During the few occasions when he wasn't meeting with various gentlemen and landholders who sought his counsel, she would tiptoe past his study door to find him in quiet contemplation. She'd catch a glimpse of him at his desk, scratching ink into his ledgers or absently reaching for the cup of tea resting on the edge of the blotter. And in those moments, her breath would always catch at the sight of his long-fingered hand closing around the delicate cup and the way he settled the porcelain rim against the firm flesh of his bottom lip.

He had such a sensual mouth. A strong, angular jaw. And when he swallowed, the cording of his neck contracted in the most appealing way that made her want to press her lips there, to feel the movement.

It was quite different from the way George drank. He had a tendency to clack his teeth together when he swallowed, as if he were chewing every beverage. The habit always made Ellie cringe, but she had accepted it as part of the man she loved. One must make concessions, after all.

She knew that she wasn't perfect, either, especially given all her phobias. And yet, Brandon never teased her or seemed exasperated about those flaws the way George did. Then again, Brandon was a different man altogether.

She could never imagine him over imbibing or telling bawdy jokes in mixed company at dinner. But neither could she picture him singing for a roomful of guests to encourage others to exhibit their talents.

George was bright and enthusiastic like a blazing hearth fire. Whereas, Brandon was the single candle in a dark room. He did not seek attention by showy measures. And yet, the eye could not help but be drawn to him.

By her fifth morning at Crossmoor Abbey, Ellie had come to a realization as she stood in the doorway with Brandon, waiting for the sun to rise. Or rather, it was several realizations at once.

The first was that she missed being in his embrace. No matter how much it complicated the already confused jumble of emotions inside her, she couldn't stand being near him without touching him. And, for that matter, she couldn't stand not being near him . . . which led to the second realization.

She was falling in love with him.

This wasn't a great surprise because she'd suspected that her feelings were stronger than mere friendship since they were in London. However, she was now able to admit it to herself.

She was falling in love with him and it wasn't as terrifying as she thought it would be. In fact, it was quite nice. She even liked the way her heart fluttered and stomach clenched. The way he could make her head spin and lungs contract with a single heated look.

All the ailments that she had feared were now the very things that filled her with a sense of anticipation and wonder at what new stirrings she might discover . . . which led her to the third realization.

She wanted to conquer all her fears. But this was still terrifying.

"You're quiet this morning," Brandon said, sliding his foot forward in the doorway to touch the toe of his boot to the toe of her slipper.

She had no idea why the gesture made her smile, but it did. "As are you. The coiled vibration emanating from your person tells me that you are thinking and wondering, just as I am."

She straightened from the door frame, her skirts crowding his trouser-clad legs in a soft shush of pink. Then she reached out to slip her bare hand in his. Such a simple gesture and yet . . .

She heard his breath catch. Felt his fingers close reflexively. The sensation jolted through her, the press of skin to skin causing tingling currents that sent her pulse skipping as her fingertips slid into his palm, warm and roughened from his outdoor pursuits.

Days of longing to be in his arms compelled her to move even closer. So she lifted his hand, turning their arms to intertwine like a loving cup and pressed her lips to the taut ridges of his knuckles. Then she heard him swallow. Her eyes drifted closed as she breathed in the scent of his skin, the lingering traces of shaving soap and smoke from when he'd extinguished his chamberstick with a pinch.

"I like this thoughtful contemplation of ours," he said

huskily, his lips grazing her temple, his fingertips tucking a loose curl behind her ear. Then he took her other hand and brought it to his mouth.

This only made her want more. She wanted to wrap her arms around his neck and pull his lips down to hers. To feel him pressed against her body, his arms holding her tight, his hands gripping her hips until they were flush and yearning and being consumed by the flames that always ignited when they kissed.

But there was something she wanted even more than that.

Without explaining her actions and before she lost her nerve, she looked up at him and said in as calm and steady a voice as she could summon, "Take me out to the terrace."

"To the . . ." He stopped, his brow suddenly furrowing in perplexity. "What do you mean? *All* the way out?"

"Not to the edge, of course. Good heavens! I haven't completely succumbed to madness." She glanced to the seven arched openings and swallowed. "I just want to sit on the bench with you and watch the sunrise and"—she drew in a breath and released it slowly—"overcome my fears one by one. With your help. If you are willing, that is."

He pressed another kiss to the back of her hand, his irises soft and warm like a velvet coverlet. "Always."

She liked that word. There was such promise in those six letters. But she didn't want to think about that now. Instead, she offered a somewhat shaky nod.

"This will provide inspiration for the book. I'll write a chapter about conquering fears and call it *Lion Taming*," she said in a nervous ramble.

Holding her gaze, he moved backward onto the terrace stones. "Excellent notion. I'm sure there are many gentlemen who require a chair and a whip to be dealt with properly. Not me, of course. Well, not unless I'm caught alone with a ravishing woman in a garden."

Ellie tried to smile at his quip, but the rasp of the threshold against the sole of her slipper sent a chill of dread up her spine.

She'd done this before, she told herself. Therefore, she could do it again. Of course, it had been much easier when his arms had been around her . . .

"It might help if you took a breath," he suggested smoothly.

"Oh, right." She licked her dry lips before she dragged in a lungful of air. "I nearly forgot."

The dark, hazy shadows enveloping her vision gradually cleared. From the corner of her eye, she could see the apricot glow of dawn approaching the horizon, the plum-colored sky. It was almost time.

"Are we there yet?" Her hands were locked in a death grip with his, her palms perspiring. Her lungs were burning, her corset tight. Was self-combustion something she should worry about?

He smiled reassuringly. "Almost. You made it the first step. Now take another. Good. You're doing splendidly. Remember to breathe."

She complied woodenly, her knees locked so they wouldn't give way even if the stones did, in one fatal avalanche. A mewl of distress escaped her at the thought.

"One more," he encouraged, and then she felt the edge of the stone bench brush the side of her leg. Drawing her a half step closer, he bent his head to press his forehead to hers. "That's it. I knew you could do it."

She smiled and closed her eyes, elated as she nuzzled his nose with her own. "I really did it. And I'm simply . . . exhausted all of a sudden," she said, panting. "You'd think I'd . . . just climbed a mountain. Could we sit down, do you think?"

"Of course." He chuckled and kissed her cheek. Then he eased her to the cool, smooth surface of the stone bench, tucking her securely beside him. "Are you going to open your eyes?"

"Mmmhmm," she murmured, snuggling closer with her head resting against his shoulder, fully intending to watch the sunrise with him. But then she yawned drowsily. "In just a minute . . ."

His scent and his warmth filled her lungs and a sense of pure contentment washed over her in lulling, slumberous waves. She could feel the glow of the sun on her skin and see it behind her eyelids, yet she had no desire to alter anything about this moment.

Her thoughts began to drift aimlessly, over the gardens and trees and beyond the riverbed. All the while, she felt the security of his embrace, the gentle passes along her arm, the calming caress of his hand interlaced with hers, his thumb tracing the tender curve of her palm.

Dimly, she worried that she might be falling asleep. After all he'd done, he deserved to have a conscious partner to watch the dawn with him.

But he eased her mind on that account when he pressed his lips into the twist at the top of her head and whispered, "There's no rush, sweetheart."

BRANDON TOOK to his mount later that morning, needing the exercise to clear his thoughts and take command of his willpower. Both were impossible feats after his sunrise with Ellie.

She'd slept through the whole of it and then some, her breaths steady and deep as if lost in a dream. Even though it had been the last thing he'd wanted to do, he had to rouse her when he heard the servants' footsteps in the hall along with the rattle of brushes and ash bins.

She'd been surprisingly difficult to awaken. But he'd

enjoyed the process of pressing kisses to her temple and into the fragrant dark curls that rested against her cheek. Each time he whispered her name, she'd sleepily said his own. She'd curled closer, too, turning toward him with her thigh sliding along his, her hand drifting over his shirtsleeves. And his body responded in thick, liquid pulses that tempted him to no end.

He'd wanted to lift her onto his lap so that they could fall into this dream together. But it was also that very desire which kept him from giving in to it. When she chose him, he needed her to be fully sentient and conscious.

Lifting her hand, he'd nibbled softly into her tender palm. And she had awoken on a breathy giggle that would fuel his fantasies for weeks. She'd blinked sleepily up at him with a smile on her lips and a tiny puddle of drool at the corner of her mouth.

"Good morning, again." He'd watched as color, brighter than the sky had been nearly an hour before, suffused her cheeks. She'd attempted to stammer out an apology but he stopped her with a finger to her lips, reassuring her that every moment was perfect in his eyes. Then he briefly kissed her, drawing the dewy dampness at the corner of her mouth into his own, taking only a sweet sampling before leading her off the terrace.

By the time he saw her at breakfast, only a tinge of embarrassment lingered, her eyes soft with their shared memory.

With that moment lingering in his mind, he headed back to the stables. Brushing down his horse, he contemplated ways to keep their momentum on a steady path. Thus far, they'd made excellent progress, not only for their future together but for her own. He wanted her to live a full life without fear or hindrance of any kind. Because when Ellie lost herself in a moment—like in the garden at the inn when she'd broken apart and shuddered in his arms—there was no sight more beautiful in the entire world.

Distracted by the recollection, he jolted when he turned and saw her standing in the stall's open gate.

"Did you hear what I said?" she asked with a light laugh when it was obvious that he hadn't. "I told you that Meg and I are here to spoil the horses. This is for you."

Like the original temptress, she smiled beguilingly and lifted the apple in her grasp.

His pulse pounded thickly in his veins. His mind swiftly conjured an image of her making the same offering while wearing only a fig leaf with her dark hair cascading down her shoulders and curling around the perfect shape of her breasts.

Poor Adam never stood a chance.

Brandon moved toward her with hungry intent. Her honeyed eyes widened, lips parting. Grasping her wrist, he brought the fruit to his mouth.

But she stopped him, slipping free and shielding the apple with both her hands. Her head tilted in bemusement. "That's not for you, silly. It's too green. You'll suffer a stomachache. I brought it for your horse."

Behind him Samson whickered impatiently, or perhaps the stallion was laughing at the fool who couldn't pull himself together long enough to think of anything other than lowering Ellie down onto the nearest bed of straw.

"Right. Well then . . ." He scrubbed the back of his neck. "Would you like to feed it to him?"

She pressed her lips together to hide her smile, but he could see mirth dancing in her gaze. "Are you blushing, Brandon?"

"You caught me off guard, is all. I was . . . preoccupied by other thoughts when you came in."

"I didn't think such a thing were possible. You're always

so levelheaded." She grinned, clearly pleased by this defect, and tossed the apple in the air, catching it readily in her palm. "I have to wonder what could keep the estimable Marquess of Hullworth—most elusive bachelor in London— so preoccupied?"

When she tossed the apple a second time, he reached out and snatched it. Then he caught her wrist and tugged her inside the stall.

"You," he said huskily, curling her arm behind her back to pull her flush against him. "I'm always thinking about you."

She gasped, pink-cheeked and hand splayed over his racing heart. But she didn't push him away. In fact, she molded deliciously against him as her lashes lowered and her gaze drifted to his mouth.

He struggled to remember why he was being patient. To hell with taking things slowly! He wanted her with a desperation he'd never felt before. Needed to taste her, to feel her bare skin against his own, her body clamped tightly around him as he plunged deep inside her slick heat.

Losing his battle against temptation, he lowered his head . . .

"Ellie," Meg called out, her voice near enough to make them spring apart. "Which stall did you disappear into? I must warn you that Brandon's horse can be quite wolfish when it comes to treats. Give him one taste and he always wants another."

As if his sister were speaking of Brandon instead, Ellie speared him with an accusatory look, her delectable breasts rising and falling on shallow, panting breaths.

Guilty as charged, he shrugged and gave Samson a solid pat as he fed him the apple. "What can I say? We like our treats."

Meg appeared in the doorway. "There you are! And I see you've found Brandon. Have you asked him yet?"

"Asked me what, exactly?"

"If you would send another invitation to Mr. and Mrs. Thorley and my friend for dinner this evening. I know you've done so each day thus far, in addition to taking time out of your schedule to pay calls, and I hate to be a bother but—"

"You could never be that," he interrupted with firm but fond regard.

"And I've already talked to Aunt Sylvia," Meg interjected, "who conferred with the cook and said it wouldn't be any bother at all to have three more. Between us, I think Monsieur Poive is trying to impress Aunt Maeve after the"—she looked over her shoulder and continued in a whisper as if it were a scandal not to be repeated—"broken Dutch sauce incident."

Ellie laughed. "Yes well, my aunts shouldn't have invited themselves into the kitchen in the first place. And Maeve is rather notorious for being particular when it comes to sauces."

"Your aunts are welcome to any part of Crossmoor Abbey, as are you," he said to her. "And I would be more than happy to have your friend and her family here with us, if you think she will come."

Ellie sighed and within the slow exhale was reminded of days of disappointments, of not receiving a call or a missive, and being told that Miss Thorogood was out when they'd made other attempts to visit.

Her reluctance to spend time with Ellie, who'd traveled all this way for that solitary purpose, was a mystery. He wished he had a better understanding of Miss Thorogood's nature in order to assist Ellie with this struggle. He hated to see her hurt.

"There is a good chance, I think," she said. "Sylvia informed us that the Thorleys have no fixed engagement this evening."

"And how would my aunt know this?" he asked.

Meg chimed in to answer. "Well, according to our scullery maid who went to the market this morning, the fishmonger's wife told her that the vicar's wife has gone to visit her mother in Bath and, therefore, had to cancel her standing dinner with the Thorleys for the next fortnight. And, of course, the vicar is beside himself with worry."

Brandon eyed his sister. She knew very well that he could hardly stand that toadeater. Mr. Gerbold had done nothing for his family in the dark days during *or* directly following the typhus fever that claimed three members. And yet, he didn't hesitate to call on Brandon at every opportunity—fawning all over him in unending praise—when he wished to have a copper spire added to the church's roof.

Gritting his teeth, he said, "I suppose this is where I offer to extend an invitation to the vicar, as well."

"It certainly would give the Thorleys food for thought when considering whether or not to accept our invitation."

His gaze veered to Ellie. It was bad enough he had to put up with Nethersole, let alone that crawler Gerbold. But there was only one thing he wouldn't do for her, and that was encourage her to marry George.

"Consider it done," he said. "You shall have your dinner."

"What's this about dinner? Are we having a party?" he heard, the voice coming from just outside the stall.

The man-child appeared in the open doorway, freshly shaven and pressed as if he'd just awoken and his only obligations were to play with horses and make the girls giggle at his jokes.

"We're to have guests this evening," Brandon supplied. "If the Thorleys accept, that is."

"The more the merrier, I say." Nethersole's thick brows inched toward his hairline and a mysterious gleam flashed in the depths of his dark eyes.

Brandon had seen this look before, when they'd been in

London planning the trip. Then, he'd assumed that it was merely Nethersole's childish excitement. Now, he wondered if there was more to it. The man was an incorrigible flirt, after all. Perhaps he was looking forward to having a greater audience to impress with his robust baritone.

"Thank you, my lord. I should like to send an invitation straightaway," Ellie said with a smile, and he inclined his head. But he hated the barrier that the formality put between them. He would much rather hear her call him by his given name, especially with *George* present.

"Yes, yes, run along now, Ellie," Nethersole teased with a shooing gesture, following her and Meg out of the stall. "Wouldn't want the horse to frighten you."

"As I've said before, I'm not afraid of horses," she returned with a curtness that pleased Brandon to no end. "That would be silly, like being afraid of a boat out of water."

"And you're only afraid of boats *in* the water. The rarity," he chuckled, dripping with sarcasm.

Though he loathed to leave Ellie in Nethersole's company, Brandon needed to finish brushing down Samson.

"But damn it all," he muttered under his breath, "I wish she was ready to forget about that horse's arse."

Samson protested with a snort.

"Sorry, old chap. Not you. As far as I'm concerned, you're the far superior animal."

Chapter 26

"A marriage-minded gentleman will not settle for second place."

—A NOTE FOR *The Marriage Habits of the Native Aristocrat*

At last, Prue came to Crossmoor Abbey.

Ellie was eager to finally have a moment to speak with her friend, but her aunt and uncle interrupted every attempt. The sour-faced Mr. and Mrs. Thorley expressed disapproval in nearly everything they saw, from throat-clearing criticisms on their niece's posture to the sniffed disdain regarding the superfluous number of servants employed at the abbey.

Frustrated, her gaze swept across the drawing room to Brandon. He stared back at her with commiseration, deep in a one-sided conversation with Mr. Gerbold. The mole-like vicar hardly took a breath in between complimenting his lordship's good taste then listing a number of items that the church needed, such as marble statues and silver collection plates.

Guilt plucked at her conscience, knowing that this disastrous evening was her own doing. But Brandon, ever-privy to her thoughts, shook his head at her in a manner that suggested he refused to let her take any blame. Then, he summarily persuaded his guests to take a tour of the house, inciting their interest with a mention of the chapel's history, and generously falling on the sword to give her the perfect opportunity to slip away with Prue.

Ellie would be sure to thank him later.

All week, she'd been trying to understand the reason there'd been so little contact between her and Prue since her arrival. Of course, her worrier's mind mulled over all sorts of dreadful things, from wondering if the Thorleys kept Prue locked in the attic to whether or not *Lord F* had returned and she felt the need to hide herself from him.

Tonight, Ellie hoped to find that answer.

"The gallery is my favorite," she said as they stepped into the long, paneled room. The comforting fragrances of leather upholstered chairs and furniture polished with beeswax and turpentine reminded her of mornings with Brandon. "It's so peaceful, don't you think? And the best part is, no one will bother us for a while. So we may talk in confidence, like we used to before everything changed."

"But what about dinner?" Prue gave a nervous glance to the longcase clock in the far corner. "My aunt is quite strict about punctuality."

"She doesn't . . . hurt you, does she?"

"No, of course not," she said quickly. Then, shaking her head, she expelled an exhausted breath. "My aunt is just greatly disappointed by tardiness. That is her favorite phrase throughout each day. She is often *greatly disappointed* in me."

To Ellie that didn't sound much better, but Prue seemed to take it in stride without so much as a blink. It was only for that reason that she was marginally subdued. For the moment.

"Well, you needn't fret on that account, for I briefly spoke with Brandon—or rather, Lord Hullworth," she corrected. "He said he would continue the tour, delaying the kitchen for as long as we needed. There will be no announcement from the butler until you and I have returned to the parlor."

Her friend nodded but still didn't seem at ease. "He must think a great deal of you then. I could not imagine the lord of the manor making such concessions for just any guest."

They paused at the portrait of the first Marquess of Hullworth—a handsome, bearded gentleman in a high, livery collar and blackwork embroidery on his frilled cuffs. Feeling Prue's scrutiny on her profile, Ellie responded with a flippant, "Oh, you'd be surprised. He allows my aunts to interfere in the kitchens without a word. Why, he even allows George his choice of mount at the stables."

"Ah, yes. George," Prue said, her tone drawing tight like the cords of a reticule, her arms crossed. "During the last Season that we were all together—you, Jane, Winnie and I—you seemed ready to give up the chase."

"Well, I wouldn't say I was ever *chasing* him, per se. I was just waiting like he asked me to do. As you know, we've always had something of an understanding, though without making any formal announcement."

Ellie felt her brow knit above the bridge of her nose as she heard the words from her own lips. Such an insubstantial promise, with all the concessions on her end.

If she'd overheard a young woman tell the story that her betrothed had proposed in such an offhanded manner, would it earn a place in her ledger? Likely not.

Zero sighs. Zero swoons.

"I'm sorry," Prue said softly. "I didn't mean for you to take offense. I suppose, I was just wondering if you were still waiting for him, or if you'd set your cap for Lord Hullworth."

Ellie had asked herself that same question often this past week. She wasn't completely sure how Brandon felt about her or how she fit into his life. But he'd become such an integral part of *her* life, and so quickly that she couldn't imagine spending a day without him. He was her shoulder to lean upon to conquer her fears, offering reassurance. He'd gone out of his way countless times for her benefit. And he was always ready, able and willing to help her through any task, never once making her feel like a burden or an inconvenience.

As she thought about this, in the back of her mind, she heard the memory of him giving advice for the primer.

A marriage-minded gentleman should always provide support and encouragement to the woman who holds his affections . . .

A marriage-minded gentleman will surmount any obstacle in his path in order to win the woman he wants. To make her his, and his alone . . .

Her breath caught. Though he hadn't unequivocally declared himself, the lessons seemed to be his way of telling her he wanted to marry her.

We're right for each other, Ellie. I think you know it, too.

She felt her head spin in a giddy whirl. And yet, her feelings for Brandon were complicated and interwoven with the ones she had for George.

With him, she felt comforted by a sense of familiarity and a fondness that had grown her whole life. And even though she loved George, he wasn't ready for marriage. He had oats to sow.

Brandon, on the other hand, made her feel as if there was no other woman he'd rather be with. No other flirtations. No oats. Just her. She rather liked that about him.

But could she see a life with him? A future with children? Growing old together?

At the thought of what came *after* growing old, a cold coffin-like chill swept over her and she wrapped her arms around herself to ward it off.

"The answer is, I have no idea," she said, a bit too brightly, and reached out to squeeze Prue's gloved hand. "And now that you know my dilemma, can you tell me about *Lord F* and what happened at Sutherfield Terrace?"

Prue slowly withdrew, clasping her hands in front of herself. "I'd prefer not to speak of it."

Then she walked on toward the next portrait—the lovely first marchioness, wearing a dramatic red gown with a low-cut, square bodice that laced in the front, and open sleeves embroidered in fine gold thread—and gazed vacantly at it for a long moment without speaking again. Ellie was left floundering for what to say to that, and so was rather surprised when her friend continued.

"But, I suppose, you have every right to know," she said with a solemn nod as if resolved to the inescapability of the subject. "It is difficult to explain and nothing I ever imagined happening. My father was deep in conversation about politics, which left me standing off to the side pretending to wait for my next dance partner. Though, in reality, there was no name on my card. So, I'd stepped out for a breath of air. Then, somehow I'd gotten turned around in the garden and suddenly *he* was there."

"Lord F?" Ellie asked, hoping her friend would finally offer his name. But it became clear in the next moment that she had no intention of revealing his identity.

Again, Prue nodded. "Teasingly, this gentleman promised to be my garden champion and see me to safety. At the time, I saw nothing wrong with accepting his escort since I was already somewhat acquainted with him."

Ellie's brows lifted in surprise. This was news, indeed. In all the letters they'd exchanged, her friend had never indicated a prior association with the mysterious *Lord F.* Unfortunately, before she could utter a casual inquiry, Prue continued without pause, her attention directed toward the floor as she walked the length of the gallery.

"As he led me through the lanes between hedgerows, he flirted shamelessly," she said. "I begged him not to, of course. But then he surprised me by confessing that he'd always admired me. Given the nature of our acquaintance, however, he'd never had the opportunity to divulge it. And in that moment, he'd seemed so vulnerable and bashful that I believed him. Even so, I wanted to hurry back. I could not indulge in a flirtation with this man. He accepted my answer but"—she paused on a breath—"at the same time, told me how much he would regret it if he let another instant pass without telling me how pretty I looked in the moonlight. Then he'd said that if he were to wish upon a star, his wish would be to kiss me."

"How romantic!" Ellie sighed, swept away in the story and blushing as she recalled her own time with Brandon in that same garden.

Prue smoothed her hands down her skirt, her voice pained when she said, "So I let him kiss me."

"Dearest, do not fret. It was just a kiss. I daresay there are few who would have been able to resist such a pretty declaration. I know I could not have done."

A wan smile briefly touched Prue's lips as she gazed distractedly toward the far corner of the room. "Thank you, Ellie. I'm glad you understand. But if I could have one wish, it would be that clocks would turn in reverse and we could go back and change the things we have done."

There was such a sense of hopelessness in her friend that it broke Ellie's heart. "I wish you had not been discovered by your father either, but there is hope yet. After all, if Jane was able to return from ruination, then you shall be able to as well."

"It is not that simple," she said flatly.

That much was true, Ellie admitted. Jane recovered because she married, and also because her husband's grandfather held a prominent place in society. Still, she didn't want to leave Prue with a sense that there was no hope for her future.

"In your letters," she said carefully, "you mentioned that *Lord F* has visited you while you've been living with your aunt and uncle. Is he still pursuing you?"

Prue hesitated, then nodded.

"Has he"—Ellie swallowed—"made an offer for you?"

Again, she nodded. "On several occasions. However, his promises are not as plainly spoken as I would prefer. He likes to talk of parties and amusements, of taking a house and holidays, but not of the future."

This man sounded a lot like George, Ellie thought grimly. But she didn't want to say it aloud and diminish her friend's hopes more than they already were.

So, instead, she offered, "I'm sure he'll come around and your doubts will be laid to rest once and for all."

"Perhaps," Prue said, but didn't appear convinced in the least.

Hearing a soft, melodious chime from the corner, Ellie glanced to the clock. *Oh, dear.* It was time they found their way to the parlor.

Sidling up to Prue, she linked their arms together and led the way back down the long gallery. "Nevertheless, it's a lovely feeling, being desired by a handsome gentleman. It causes an awakening of sorts, the rousing of an inner self that one may not have even realized existed before."

Prue looked at her with the twinkle of understanding in her eyes. And all at once, it was as if they were back to that last day of finishing school, sharing secrets and discussing their dreams while lying on the grass and staring up at the clouds. "Is that how Lord Hullworth makes you feel?"

Now it was Ellie's turn to hesitate. Then she nodded.

✦✦✦✦

AFTER DINNER that evening, Brandon's guests gathered for cards while he and Aunt Sylvia played backgammon at a small table near the window.

"I do hope Miss Parrish decides to stay on for a while," Sylvia said with a rattle of dice in her cup. "For then I'm sure to beat you handily each time we play."

He turned back to his aunt and glanced down to the inlaid board with chagrin. He'd been watching Ellie more than he was paying attention to his own game. "Best out of three?"

She shook her head. "As much as it pains me to admit,

I'm old, my dear nephew. Dinner parties and late evening's entertainments are for the young." She rose and patted his cheek with her soft vellum-skinned hand. "But I meant what I said. I hope she decides to stay. It would be nice for Cross-moor Abbey to become a home again."

His gaze trailed after his aunt as she bid adieu to the others, holding her shawl tighter over her gently sloped shoulders. He wished he could have given her a guarantee that, yes, Miss Parrish would stay. But he wasn't sure.

At times, especially when they were alone, he was filled with the famous Stredwick certainty. The problem, how-ever, was *George*.

Brandon had thought the man-child would shoot himself in the foot by now. But his behavior of late, especially this evening, had been altogether gentlemanly. Courtly, even. Nethersole was a bloody chameleon when he chose to be, subduing his boisterous nature to present himself in a re-spectable fashion. He did not overimbibe and hadn't even told a single bawdy joke.

And worse, he wasn't treating Ellie as a mere after-thought as he usually did. He was attentive instead, not just to her but to Miss Thorogood as well.

The transformation delighted Maeve and Myrtle, who tittered on and on about how proud they were of the lad they'd always considered a part of their family. The state-ment wouldn't have bothered Brandon so much if Myrtle hadn't chosen to lay her hands over Nethersole's and Ellie's as she spoke, smiling to both of them as if their union was a foregone conclusion.

Witnessing the spectacle, Brandon winced inwardly. He hated uncertainty. Hated the way the past hovered like a specter that, instead of jangling chains, laughed and told him that he was only a second-choice substitute.

Turning away to face the darkened window, he saw something that surprised him in the reflective glass.

Apparently, he wasn't the only one who cringed in that moment. Miss Thorogood didn't appear to like the idea of Nethersole and Ellie marrying either. But was her expression because of concern for her friend's ultimate happiness? Or was there another reason?

Chapter 27

"Acts of lunacy can be liberating."

—A NOTE FOR *The Marriage Habits*
of the Native Aristocrat

The following morning, Ellie stood by the door to the loggia, a single chamberstick in her grasp, thinking of her conversation with Prue.

She should be glad that her friend had come and they'd finally shared the conversation that Ellie had been needing to hear, confiding in each other as the friends they used to be. And yet, by the time they'd joined the others, Prue had slipped back into her distant self, hardly speaking a word.

Turning back to the sky lit by only a band of silver-frothed clouds along the horizon, Ellie tried to reason it out. It was understandable, she supposed, that Prue likely felt as if she were under the quizzing glass every time she stepped out into society since her expulsion from town. And, last night, George hadn't helped matters any.

He had been . . . well . . . different. For the most part, he'd behaved himself, which Ellie appreciated, of course. But there was just something peculiar about his sudden decision to play the gentleman.

At one point, when they'd gathered in the parlor after dinner, he'd insisted on holding Ellie's chair. Then as he'd nudged her forward, he'd bent low and whispered in her ear, "You look quite fetching, Ellie. If I wasn't already besotted with you, I would most assuredly be tonight."

Her breath had quickened, but more in surprise than pleasure, and her heart had not fluttered. Instead, it beat in a disorderly rhythm, her stomach twisting in guilty knots as her gaze swerved to Brandon, only to see him looking over at her with a glower.

Ellie felt as though she were standing in the center of a seesaw. Part of her wanted to cross the room to Brandon and place her hand over his, letting the statement speak to the entire party. But another part of her clung to the idea of marrying George, because that's what she had done her whole life and it didn't scare her as much as the unknown that a life with Brandon offered.

Confused, she had returned her attention to George as he assisted Prue with her chair. In that instant, she caught sight of his ungloved fingertips absently brush along the bare skin of her friend's shoulder, just above her clavicle. Prue had stiffened, casting an alarmed glance to Ellie, clearly uncomfortable. George's gaze alighted on Ellie, too. He'd begged forgiveness for the accidental touch, blaming it on clumsiness.

But Prue had not been the same for the rest of the evening. In fact, she'd appeared more than withdrawn, but stricken and lost. And Ellie's heart ached for her. She found herself also wishing to go back in time, back to before *Lord F*—whoever he was—had entered her friend's life.

Distracted by these thoughts from the previous evening, she only heard Brandon's approach when his footfalls were directly behind her. She turned to see him, eager to be drawn away from these musings.

"Good morning," she said, but frowned when she saw him coming toward her in a dark blue morning coat and cravat. "You're dressed."

He flashed a grin. "The disappointment in your tone does my ego tremendous good."

"Your ego requires no assistance, I'm sure," she said dryly

as he reached out to take her chamberstick. And just before he pinched the flame to immerse them into the surrounding shadows, she thought she noticed the dubious lift of his brow.

"The reason I am dressed," he offered as he took her hand, his voice low and intimate, "is because we are not watching the sunrise from here."

A pleasurable shiver chased through her, and her breath caught at the feel of his lips on her fingers. "We're not?"

"I have something else in store for you, Miss Parrish."

He left his statement to hang mysteriously in the darkness as he led her through the gallery and down the hall to the stairs. It surprised her even more when he took her outside.

They walked together, their steps guided by the silver light of a gibbous moon rising above the tree line and the pale sliver of gold on the horizon. He took them beyond the formal terraced gardens, and stepped down behind a wall of climbing roses.

A laugh escaped her, the instant she saw what he had *in store* for her.

There, resting atop the still, glassy surface of the rectangular reflecting pool, sat a rowboat.

Ellie was caught somewhere between amusement and adoration at the sight. Turning, she gazed up at him with a smile that felt as if dawn were breaking inside her, shining out like a beacon. "You are a madman."

"Obviously," he said drolly, leading her to the side of the pool. Standing there, he began to speak with all seriousness as if he were a sailing tutor, and she had to smile. "Now, the first things one does before setting sail, is to ensure the seaworthiness of the vessel and the weather conditions. Do you see a leak? Is the hull making any alarming groaning noises? Are the clouds threatening gale force winds or storms? Are the waves rising over the bow?"

"No. But . . . you do realize, do you not, that my fear of

boats is more about capsizing and being carried under the waves? If we were to capsize in your pool, the worst I would suffer is a wet hem and ruined slippers."

"Well, if you are fearful on that account, then I would not object to you removing any article of clothing you choose. I'll even assist, if you like."

"How gallant," she laughed.

With a roguish glint, he turned from her and swung a leg into the shallow vessel, gripping the sides. It rocked for a moment, shifting beneath him with a splash that lapped water up to the lip surrounding the pool, but he quickly found purchase and sat on the cross thwart near the stern.

"Steady on, Parrish. I've got you," he said, extending his hand toward her.

Without hesitation, she took it. However, her own efforts to navigate the side of the pool and up into the boat were far less impressive. Her knees and ankles gave her all the support of isinglass jellies and she ended up falling onto him with an unladylike grunt.

He chuckled and arranged her limbs so that she was sitting before him, his arm around her waist, her bottom perched intimately between his solid, widespread thighs. *Goodness!* Facing away as she was, he couldn't see her blush, and yet she had no doubt he knew her cheeks were aflame.

"See?" he said, his husky voice slipping inside the whorls of her ear to curl pleasantly inside her body. "It just took a moment to gain our sea legs."

"You make approaching my fears seem so simple. But if we were on the river—"

"Then we would go through our inspection, just as we did here," he said assuredly. "But we're not facing the river today. No amount of worry will make us suddenly appear on the river either. We are here in this ridiculously tiny boat on the reflecting pool awaiting the sunrise together.

And the most important question is, how do you feel in *this* moment?"

As jolting as it was to sit thusly, there was no denying how safe, warm and secure she felt. She was lulled by the steady cadence of his breathing at her back and the gentle rolling lap of water against the hull. As if it were the most natural thing, she eased fully against him, resting her head near the curve of his throat, her fingertips roaming lightly over his, exploring the knobs of his knuckles and sparse dusting of hair.

"I feel contentment. And the boat isn't ridiculously tiny, at all. It's cozy."

Against her temple, his lips curved in a grin. "As you say."

They said nothing after that, but only watched the sun rise on a new day until golden light shimmered over the pool and gilded the dewdrops on every petal, leaf, and blade of grass, turning the world around them into a tapestry of rich colors.

A while later, he helped her out of the boat as it tee-tered beneath her feet, escorting her over the edge to solid ground. Curling her hand into the crook of his arm, he led the way back. But instead of taking a direct path, he turned and began the longer walk around the side of the abbey.

She knew why in an instant. He was helping her avoid the arches of the lower loggia which led to the main hall at the rear of the house.

Ellie tugged on his hand, halting him. "There's no need to go around."

"Are you certain?" he asked, his warm hand lifting to cradle her jaw as he tilted up her chin, his eyes searching hers.

She nodded and they walked together toward the loggia. "Although, I am tempted to take the long way around, if only to keep this morning from ending."

"Then I'll endeavor to make tomorrow morning its equal. In fact, I might already have a plan."

She slid a sideways glance to him. "Should I be worried?"

"*Should* you be? No," he said with utter assuredness that gave her comfort. Then he smiled and brought her fingertips to his lips. "But I know you will be, regardless."

ભનભન

THE NEXT morning, Ellie felt perfectly justified for having nursed a small kernel of apprehension the previous day. "You must be joking!"

"Afraid not," he said gravely. "I fully intend to get you on the back of that horse."

Tethered to the post near the mounting block, Samson looked blandly over at her, then went back to eating the hay piled before him. But she wasn't deceived for a minute. He was enormous. At least seventeen hands high.

"What part of *fear of falling to my death* don't you understand?"

"That's why one always checks the saddle straps to ensure they are secure. Go on, give it a good tug." He took her numb-fingered hand and guided her through the process. "There. See? Now, you'll want to ascertain the temperament of your horse. Does he startle easily? Is he agitated and flicking his ears or shifting from side to side?"

She eyed the beast who merely stood there docilely, his big brown eyes blinking slowly. "I think he's almost asleep."

"Well then," he said and without warning, lifted her by the waist and set her feet on the mounting block.

She issued a tiny squeal of alarm. And the only reason she stayed there was because she was leg-locked from terror.

Gripping the stile behind her, she said, "I hope you know that I hate you right now."

Not bothered in the least by her declaration, he set his

own foot in the stirrup and easily swung his leg over. Situated in the saddle, he must have done something with his movements that caused the horse to shift sideways, drawing closer to her.

"Then come here and hate me as much as you like," he said, holding out his arm. "Or . . . we can just go back inside and I can stop being so overbearing—"

"*That* isn't likely," she groused.

"—and you can go back to doing only the things that make you feel perfectly comfortable, and worrying about the things you've never tried before," he concluded, but there was a knowing smirk lingering in the corner of his mouth, as if he already knew what she'd do.

She narrowed her eyes. "You are insufferable. If I die this morning, I'm going to haunt you for the rest of your life. You'll never have a moment's peace."

"Promise?"

She huffed. The man was far too pleased with himself. And if her hands turned any clammier, then she wouldn't be able to hold on to the stile.

"I won't let you fall, sweetheart," he crooned gently as if *she* were a skittish horse that needed calming. "Turn around and close your eyes. I think it will be better that way."

Too afraid she'd lose her nerve if she asked what he had planned, Ellie complied.

In the next instant, she felt the solid strength of his arm slide around her waist. Before she could even form a gasp, he plucked her off the mounting block and pulled her across his lap.

She scrambled over him, clinging and twisting to wrap her arms around his neck, behaving like one of the monkeys at the zoo. But it couldn't be helped. He issued a grunt of pain and then adjusted her hips so that her bottom was more securely between his thighs. All the while, she kept her eyes screwed shut. Then his hands trailed down her back, arms and hips in soothing passes, easing the panicked tension gathered in the frozen muscles.

With her face buried in his cravat, she breathed in the warm scent of him, taking in huge lungfuls. "Is it . . . over . . . yet?"

But then she felt the horse shift beneath them and she emitted another startled squeak.

"That was just Samson getting used to you, nothing more. You're safe, Ellie." His heated palm began working at the knots at the nape of her neck, his lips at her temple. "But I don't want you to take my word for it. I want you to trust your heart. How do you feel right now, in this moment?"

By the time his capable massage meandered to the small of her back, she felt as supple and relaxed as freshly kneaded dough. A soft sigh escaped as she wiggled closer. His other hand drifted down her leg, aimlessly charting a path around the cap of her knee, pausing to squeeze and soothe and massage. He did that with every pass, down to her stocking-clad ankles and back up again, even over her hip, kneading the plumpness of her flesh, heating her blood to a luscious simmer.

"I feel the strength of your arms around me and your legs beneath me. They're quite solid, like an arch," she added with a small grin. "An arch fitted over the saddle."

His muscles flexed beneath her. "Good. And what else?"

"The drumming of your heart is steady and strong and it makes me feel"—she angled toward him, her fingertips sifting through the wavy layers of his hair—"as if nothing terrible could happen. You wouldn't allow it."

"That's right. I wouldn't."

Bravely, she opened her eyes.

But her heart quickened in something just short of alarm. Not because she was afraid of being up so high on Samson's back, but rather because of the way Brandon was looking at her with such tender intensity that she finally understood exactly what it meant.

He loved her.

Perhaps she'd known it for a while. Though, for some strange reason, she'd wanted to pretend otherwise, as if hiding from the truth would keep her from realizing she loved him too. But it was no use. Somehow, she'd gone from falling slowly to slipping headlong into a love so deep and fathomless that she may never find her way to the surface again.

It frightened her because she'd never felt this way about George. This was new. This was the unknown. And yet, she refused to deny it to herself any longer.

"Just so you know," she said softly, her voice shaking, "I wouldn't let anything terrible happen to you either."

He tucked a lock of hair behind her ear, his fingertip exploring the sensitive shell. "I'm glad to hear it. But we don't have to think about that right now."

"All we need," she agreed with a nod, "is to enjoy this moment and not worry about what might happen in the future."

Chapter 28

"A debutante can always rely on a marriage-minded gentleman and his trusty steed."

—A NOTE FOR *The Marriage Habits of the Native Aristocrat*

They met even earlier the following morning. The dawn was still dreaming while a full moon hung over their heads, and a silver glow blanketed their path to the stables.

But Brandon noticed something different about Ellie. She was quiet and contemplative, and it caused an unwelcome sense of worry to spring to life.

He'd thought everything was grand between them. In fact, he was going to tell her that he loved her.

He knew that what he felt for her was different than what he had for Phoebe. It was deeper and more intense in a way that made him question if he'd ever actually loved before. Looking back, his feelings for Phoebe seemed more like a youthful infatuation. She'd dazzled him with her coy flirtations like a spider spinning a pretty web and he'd been naively ensnared.

With Ellie, he tried so hard to deny and resist his feelings that he refused to admit that he'd fallen in love with her. It was a love so intense that he feared he'd never recover from it. And perhaps that was the true reason behind his sense of worry.

Reflexively, he reached out and took her hand. He was instantly rewarded with the soft press of her palm, her fingertips weaving into his own. But she was still quiet, the sounds of her footsteps just a soft susurration over the small stones and hard-packed clay.

"Something on your mind?" he asked.

She nodded absently. "The book. I was just thinking that it has been a while since you've contributed any advice on the thoughts of marriage-minded gentlemen."

"Have I been shirking my duties as your fount of information?"

Her mouth twitched. "You have, indeed."

"Then allow me to remedy that this instant." Brandon lifted her hand to press a kiss to her fingers. "He will always endeavor to ensure she understands that she is his first thought every morning and his last thought each night."

She squeezed his hand and smiled in apparent approval of this lesson.

Inside the stall, he carefully went through the steps of saddling Samson. He was gladdened by her enthusiasm to be part of the process, and her growing confidence. It was even clear by the lamplight gleaming in her gaze that she was looking forward to it. And he was all too eager to have her in his arms again.

These sunrises were the only moments he allowed himself to be near her, to touch and embrace her, albeit far more chastely than he preferred. It had been an eon since he'd kissed her and felt the press of her sweet body flush with his own. And he wasn't sure he could endure another morning of agony like he had yesterday.

Having her on his lap and feeling how well she fit against him had been the most exquisite torture of his life. All he'd wanted to do was kiss her endlessly, caress her until she was shuddering in ecstasy beneath his hands, shift her pliant and willing body to straddle his hips, and sink inside her welcoming heat.

A tremor of longing rolled through Brandon. He tried to

push that out of his mind and focused, instead, on walking his horse to the mounting block. "Do you feel brave enough to take Samson out of the stable?"

An incredulous laugh escaped her as if she thought he was teasing. Yet, when her gaze met his, her eyes quickly widened. She swallowed, gripping his hand tighter. "Well, you certainly like to push, do you not? One morning on a horse and suddenly I'm a seasoned equestrian?"

Turning her toward him, he took both of her hands in his. "If you are afraid, then he'll remain tethered in the stall. We'll take this as slowly as you like."

"If we went at my pace, I'd likely never have made it across the bridge," she said ruefully. Expelling a slow breath, she offered a tentative nod. "Very well, then, we'll try a step or two."

Caught up in a moment of admiration for her remarkable bravery, he leaned down and stole a brief searing kiss.

Before she could change her mind, he lifted her to the mounting block and swung himself into the saddle. Reaching over, he pulled Ellie into his arms. She clung to him even tighter than before, like a yoke and collar, inhibiting the movement of his shoulders. That wouldn't do.

"You know," he began, considering. "When my sister was first learning to ride, she complained that she felt unsteady on the sidesaddle. So I allowed her to ride astride for a time until she grew comfortable with the movements of a horse, at least when she was not in public. You might feel more secure if you did the same."

Ellie pulled her head back to blink at him. "*Astride?* But I'm not wearing a riding habit . . . undoubtedly my skirts will . . ."

Color suffused her cheeks.

His gaze drifted down and every muscle in his body flexed, causing Samson to shift slightly. He knew at once that he wouldn't be able to withstand the temptation of looking down and seeing stocking-clad legs spread open on either side of the pommel, with her skirts bunched in between.

Darting a glance around, he saw a horse blanket hanging over the top of the stall. He eased Samson over, close enough for Brandon to reach it. The coarse wool unfolded as he drew it over her lap. "There. All settled."

However, it wasn't that simple.

The instant he turned her and carefully arranged her body, he realized his mistake. The plump curve of her bottom was nestled intimately against his groin and his body reacted in a low, unmistakable surge of lust. The blanket might be concealing her from his eyes, but did little else to erase the ideas his mind conjured.

Hearing her breath quicken, he secured an arm tightly around her waist, pulling her secure and flush with him. He held back a groan, knowing he would just have to endure the sweet agony of it all.

"Are you ready, sweetheart?" he asked, his voice hoarse. Feeling her head jerk in a small nod of acquiescence and her hand grip his arm, he assured her in a whisper, "Just a step or two. It might help if you closed your eyes."

"You mean keep them closed? I haven't dared open them since you turned me around."

He smiled at her scolding tone. And, with a press of his thighs and the click of his tongue, he prodded Samson away from the mounting block. Then, as he'd agreed, he pulled back on the reins and stopped.

Ellie heaved out a labored breath. "Strange, but I feel as if . . . I am carrying two people . . . on *my* back."

"And you survived it well," he said tenderly, pressing his lips to her temple. "We'll head back to the block now."

"Wait. I think I want"—she hesitated, the gulp in her throat audible—"to go farther."

A shock of surprise spurred through Brandon, but he

didn't reveal it. And he didn't question her either, fearing that would only make her doubt her decision.

"Ah. I see what's happened," he said in a teasing drawl as he gradually eased Samson out of the stables. "You've decided to torment me endlessly with the feel of your body in my arms and leave me with nothing to do about it."

She rested fully against him on a soft puff of laughter. "I probably shouldn't admit it, but I do like being in your arms. They're like mooring ropes, keeping me tethered and secure. And I like that I can feel the rise and fall of your chest against my back . . . the hot brush of your exhale against my cheek . . . the sure beats of your heart . . . the strength of your thighs as you flex and shift to direct the horse . . ."

Unendurable arousal coursed through his veins in thick pulses, not only at her words but the light, teasing caress of her hand over his. When had she stopped gripping him as if her life depended on it?

He didn't know. He'd lost the ability to think as she traced the lengths of his fingers and slipped beneath his sleeve to touch the furring at his wrist. Then those petal soft pads stole around to the other side to skate across his pulse. It quickened for her.

Unable to help himself, he bent his head to graze his lips against the shell of her ear, the exposed curve of her throat, seeking the fluttering place beneath the fragrant skin. "Do you like this, too, Ellie?"

"*Yes*," she rasped, her breaths shallow and panting.

Arm around her waist, he drew her back against the slow cantering of his hips, easing the ache of his lengthening erection. "And what do you feel now?"

"That your heart is thundering, like mine." She took his hand, easing him higher over buttery soft muslin to the warm valley between her breasts, sending a scorching jolt of pleasure through him. "Can you feel it?"

He groaned in response, and loved the way she wasn't shy or reserved with him, as if she needed their contact as much as he. Even so, he didn't know how much more of this he could take.

To gain a measure of control, he tightened his muscles. But, unthinkingly, he'd spurred Samson into a loping gallop.

Beneath his hand, Brandon felt her breath catch, and the harried rhythm of her heart. He cursed inwardly. Looking ahead at where they'd gone, he realized he'd let the horse lead the way for some time. And now they were farther from the house and stables than he imagined, headed toward the field of clover that surrounded the pond and the folly.

"It seems that Samson has a taste for clover," he said, trying to keep his tone light and reassuring as he eased the reins back to a canter.

She didn't answer.

Damn! What a distracted fool he was! He'd been so lost in having her in his arms that he wasn't thinking. At all.

He could head back to the stables, but the folly was closer. So he stayed the course, crooning reassurances to her. "It's almost over, sweetheart. We're nearly there."

At last, they reached the folly, the white marble gleaming like a beacon in the hazy moonlight. He directed the horse to the steps, needing a place to dismount safely with her in his arms. Then he turned her in his lap and she clung to him, tremors quaking through her.

Keeping her tucked in the cradle of his arms, he carefully dismounted. "Ellie, forgive me. I never meant to go so far. I—"

"Brandon," she cried, clutching him tightly. "I opened my eyes."

Standing on the flat stones, he pressed his lips fervently to her temple and damp cheek. He hated himself for what he did to her. "I know, and it was my fault. I'll make it up to you. Just please, don't be scared."

"I'm not," she said with a quiet bemused laugh. "I opened my eyes. And, yes, it was terrifying at first . . . but exhilarating too. With you at my back, I wasn't focused on falling to my death at all." She laughed again and slipped out of his stunned embrace to twirl on the flat stones, her face tilted up to the dome overhead. "It's such a liberating feeling to gallop, isn't it? Like we were flying under the moon, just the two of us." Samson issued a snort, lifting his head from his clover snack. "Pardon me, the *three* of us."

Brandon was confused. A moment ago, he'd been worried that he'd pushed her too far, that she'd never look at him with trust in her eyes again. But now, watching her, so carefree and elated, he didn't know quite what to make of this. "Then you are fine?"

"Fine?" she teased, then twirled again, her yellow skirts flaring like a bell. "I just rode a horse for the first time in my life! I feel so alive that I can hardly contain it. Is it possible to burst apart from happiness? Never mind. Don't answer that because it doesn't even matter. I'm not afraid. If I explode, then it will be on your head since you are the one who has filled me with this terrible, uncontainable joy. Oh, Brandon, I just love you so *mu*—"

His heart stopped. She stopped, too, her skirts tangling around her legs in a final swish before falling still. Her cheeks were flushed, her wide eyes blinking at him in patent startlement.

"What was that again?" he asked, his throat dry.

She swallowed. "The part about being happy, or my imminent explosion?"

"No. The last part."

"Oh, *that*. I must have . . . mentioned it before."

He shook his head.

She tried to shrug it off with a nonchalant air. "Well . . . I'm sure you've had . . . scores of women tell you."

"Tell me what?" He took one step, *two*, then stood toe-to-toe with her, his breaths shallow and quick.

"*Have* you had scores of women tell you they love you?"

"There's only one woman that matters."

She huffed. "That really isn't an answer."

"*Ellie,*" he warned, feeling as if he would go mad if he didn't hear those words again.

Reaching out, she placed her hand over the center of his chest and looked up at him shyly. "Shortly after we first met, I decided to hate you until the last dying breath left my body. After all, you were terribly overbearing. But even that didn't seem long enough. So I decided to hate you for all eternity." A soft smile brushed her lips. "What I didn't know then, was that it wasn't hate I felt. It was something much stronger. And I'm sure that, whatever amount of time falls beyond eternity, I will love you with all my heart until then. Perhaps even *lon—*"

He didn't let her finish. Her sweet words rushed in his ears and ripped open his heart, obliterating every obstacle, every reservation, and all he could think was *finally, finally.*

So he took her face in his hands and pressed his mouth to hers.

Chapter 29

"A debutante must always be prepared for sudden explosions of exhilaration."

—A NOTE FOR *The Marriage Habits of the Native Aristocrat*

The declaration had slipped out before Ellie realized what she was saying, or how much it would change everything between them. Then, all at once, the words were caught in a scorching kiss as he took her mouth, fusing them into permanence.

There would be no taking them back, even if she wanted to. But she didn't. She wanted to live in this moment for an eternity.

Her body rejoiced in the hard crush of his arms around her. The deep, searching pulls of his mouth. This was where she belonged. She felt it with marrow-deep certainty that was stronger than any fear that had ever plagued her.

So she kissed him back with every ounce of love and unfettered passion inside her. And when he groaned in response, she knew he couldn't fight it either.

He angled her head and delved deeper, nudging her lips apart for the welcomed intrusion of his breath and tongue. He licked into her mouth, tasting her, his hands fisting into the fabric of her dress while her fingers splayed greedily over the firm wall of his chest, palms coasting over broad shoulders to the silken threads of the hair at his nape, tugging his flesh deeper inside. She wanted to taste him, too.

Wanted to draw the flavor, the essence, the *very soul* of this man inside her body in a way that she couldn't explain.

She had a sense that she wouldn't survive if they ever stopped kissing.

Clutching him, she wriggled closer against his solid strength, needing to find the perfect alignment that would fit them together and assuage the desperation teeming through her veins. But the harder she tried, the more it seemed just out of reach.

A frustrated mewl tore from her throat and he responded by hitching her higher against the hard, insistent ridge. He pressed against the liquid throb—*there. Yes, there*—and she went weak in his arms on a pleasure-singed sigh.

He gripped her bottom, his large hands molding over the plump flesh. And then he lifted her until the toes of her slippers dragged backward in a hiss against the temple floor, all the way to the center cella, embedded with arched niches for urns and statuettes.

This niche was empty. She felt the cool marble at her back, the ledge beneath her. Heard the rasp of his breath echo inside the carved space as he stepped between her parted thighs.

A week ago, an alcove such as this might have caused a rise in fear, a shiver of dread. But not any longer. She was free from that, and far too alive to think about death at a time like this. Not while his lips coasted over her throat and his hips canted forward, pinioning her into the shallow alcove in focused rhythmic slides.

Gasping and wanton, she clutched his broadcloth-encased shoulders, frustrated by the impediment. She needed to feel the heat of his flesh beneath her hands. Tugging at the crisp layers of his cravat, she huffed, "I much prefer you in just your shirtsleeves and trousers."

His mouth caught at hers and she drank down his gruff growl. He jerked out of his coat, always keeping one arm around her and she was glad that a lifetime of sewing had gifted her with a deftness for untying knots.

A second later, his cravat fell to the folly floor, then his waistcoat, and her hands stole over the fine linen shirt, warmed to a sueded softness by the heat of his body. She clung to him, fitting herself against him as her mouth drifted over his throat, tasting the damp, salty essence on his skin. She tugged at his shirtsleeves, gripping fistfuls from the waist of his trousers.

"Wait, Ellie, wait." Brandon stilled her hands, his voice strained, his breaths rushing against her temple. And his heart thumped like a galloping horse against her own. "Let me catch my breath."

It was in that moment, she realized something truly terrifying—he'd come to his senses.

Of course, he would, she thought miserably. He wouldn't simply abandon years of chivalrous behavior and succumb to passion. But she needed him to.

"You don't need to catch your breath," she said, tilting upward to kiss along the edge of his jaw. "There's no reason to overthink this. Trust me, I've wasted too much time being cautious and fearful. That's no way to live."

He smiled against her lips. "It isn't?"

"Just give yourself over to this moment. Embrace how you feel right now."

"Hmm . . ." he murmured in a soft caress against the fluttering pulse at her throat. "So if I need to see your bare skin beneath the moon before the silver slight fades, then I ought to surrender to the desire?"

Her pulse quickened as she felt the gentle tugging at the back of her dress. "Yes."

"And if I want to see you in the glow of the sunrise and taste your blush on my tongue as I fill your shuddering body, over and over again?" He left no room for misunderstanding as he rolled the hard ridge that strained against the fall of his trousers into the cradle of her thighs.

Spears of pleasure spiraled deep inside where her body felt liquid and empty. It was exactly what she wanted. And yet . . .

As of this moment, her intimate experiences could be summed up with a few vague pages from novels, fully clothed kisses and a rather passionate encounter at an inn. Because of this, she felt an unanticipated rise of virginal trepidation.

She swallowed. "You . . . you plan to be quite thorough . . . it seems."

"Quite," he said succinctly, his lips lightly grazing across hers with just enough pressure to leave a path of tingles in their wake.

She inched closer. There simply was no controlling the need, the gnawing ache inside her. Then he did the same again, another graze, not enough to fully satisfy the desire he kindled for another kiss. On the next pass, she found herself gripping him to keep him close, straining to fuse her lips to his.

Then he took her mouth and . . . *oh* his kiss. He devoured her in slow, tender sips as he held her securely against him, kissing and teasing and caressing until her body bloomed with liquid, pulsing heat that left no room for trepidation.

His ardent attention fell hotly on the curve of her throat, his parted lips searing along the vulnerable skin. With the flat of his tongue, he tasted her, drawing gently on her flesh until she was panting and breathless. Her corset was too tight, her lungs straining against laces and whalebone. But then she felt the skillfully soothing passes of his hands down her back, the breeze through the parted fabric, the persistent tugs that loosened her corset.

At once she could breathe easier. The weight of her dress

shifted, slipping from her shoulders, down her arms to pool at her waist. Her corset followed. And there, she stood before him in the cool night air with her flesh drawn taut over her simmering insides, and the rosy tips of her breasts pebbling beneath the thin layer of cambric.

His gaze devoured her. Those velvet irises turned dark and hungry, his bronze lashes lowering against the rise of burnished color on his cheeks as a breath shuddered out of him.

"Damn, Ellie. Just look at you," he murmured as his hands skimmed up to trace the undersides of her breasts. "You're a confection of white dusting sugar and pink icing. And the only thing to keep me from devouring every single luscious inch of you, is that little red bow. I'm afraid it doesn't stand a chance."

At the graveness in his tone, she felt a smile curve her lips. Boldly, she reached up and untied the ribbon.

The gathered fabric caught for an instant on the moon-white swells, just long enough for her to hear him swallow. Then he shucked the gauzy fabric away and cupped the rounded fullness in his bare palms. His thumbs swept over the ruched flesh and she closed her eyes against a gasping shock of pleasure that quickened and clenched, deep in the core of her body.

His lips brushed hers, trailing a scorching path of open-mouthed kisses down her throat. He plumped her flesh in his hand, the heat of his mouth enveloping the first aching peak. A strangled sound tore from her throat to blend in with the evensong of crickets and the haunting call of cur-lews. She clutched his head, fingers weaving in silken locks as his tongue spurred the tightly budded flesh, drawing the tip deeper. With each tender suckling kiss, connecting pulses throbbed between her thighs. And as he trailed a siz-zling path to her other breast, licking and laving in erotic tugs on her flesh, she wondered dazedly if it was possible to die of pleasure.

"*Le petite mort*, but nothing altogether fatal," he answered huskily.

Until that moment, she didn't even realize she'd spoken aloud. *"A little death?"*

"Ummhmm . . ." he murmured, rising up to take her mouth. He teased her lips apart, the fine linen of his shirt abrading the tender peaks of her nipples. As he spoke, his hand skated beneath the bunched layers of her skirts, the heat of his palm warming the fine cambric over the top of her thigh. "At the inn, you referred to it as *falling apart at the seams,* right before you shuddered in my arms with my name on your lips. Did you like that *little death*, Ellie?"

She nodded wordlessly, lost under a siege of erotic sensation. And when his exploration reached the apex of her thighs, a wordless plea left at the first teasing pass against the opening of her drawers.

"Yes, sweetheart, just let me touch you here," he whispered brokenly as his fingertips delved through the lace to the dark thatch of private curls. Her breath stuttered as he brushed the hidden seam, back and forth with tortuous slowness, until her shameless body was trembling with eagerness and tilting toward him. Then he slipped between the swollen folds, opening her slowly to his gentle prodding, expertly navigating the damply furled flesh. A tremor rolled through him and he expelled an oath on a strained breath. "So soft. So wet. So snug. And here"—his breath caught as the tip of his finger nudged inside—"is where I'll fill you."

His tender strokes eased into the velvety constriction, stretching her untried sheath until she welcomed the slick slide, her hips cambering toward the deep flex of his knuckles. *Oh, oh,* the torment was sweet and sublime. Her body arched, supplicant and aching. She wanted that cataclysm. Craved it.

But then he withdrew, and the night air swept over her dewy, throbbing sex.

"Wait, wait . . ." she panted, clinging to him, knees shaking with unspent desire. She gripped him, her hands coasting over his shirtsleeves and shoulders, needy and demanding.

He fastened his mouth to hers as if to soothe her, but it only intensified her desire. Unlatching her hands from around his neck, he slid them down the hard planes and ridges of his torso over the thick bulge straining against the fall front of his trousers. "Is this what you want, Ellie?"

There was no mistaking his meaning. If they continued on this path, there wouldn't be any going back.

"Very much so," she said without an ounce of trepidation.

Of course, that was *before* she began to trace the length of that hard column beneath the fine wool. In her mind's eye, she was trying to imagine the museum statues that she, Winnie, Jane and Prue had once taken turns observing in depth while the others stood guard. However, this wasn't the same at all.

She worried her bottom lip as she continued her exploration. Smoothing her hand down from the top fastenings to the taut mound below, she heard his breath stall as she cupped that part of him. Darting a glance to his face, she saw his eyes were heavy-lidded, hungry and dark, and slashes of color burnished the crests of his cheeks. He liked this, she realized, and a shiver of excitement clenched sweetly inside her as she nimbly worked the fastenings free.

The fall front draped open and his turgid flesh bounded free, proud and heavy. And intimidating. She couldn't look away.

"But are *you* sure?" she asked. "You are, after all—and I don't mean to criticize—rather *considerable*."

A strained chuckle rumbled in his throat as she tentatively grasped the rearing flesh, hard and smooth like granite, hot like molten iron. "There's nothing I can do about that, I'm afraid. But we'll manage quite well. I'll make sure of it."

He covered her hand with his own, guiding her up and down the weighted shaft. Then he stopped, his breathing turned rough and labored. Lifting her hand to his shoulder, he stepped closer between her thighs and she felt the firm mushroomed head nudge her entrance.

A tremor rolled through her. But he kissed and caressed her again until her blood started to simmer in her veins, bringing her body to the very brink of ecstasy just before he edged inside the snug slickness. Just far enough to feel the stretch and burn of the intrusion. She heard his breath catch. She was holding hers. Then his hips jerked, pushing farther inside her shrinking body. Her fingernails bit into his skin. He withdrew and thrust again, and again until, finally, the seams of her maidenhead were torn.

He swallowed down her soft cry, kissing her tenderly as her virginal flesh clamped tightly around the stiff invasion.

"Breathe, love," he said, his voice hoarse as if *he* were the one in agony.

How was she supposed to breathe? She felt surrounded with the marble niche at her back, and the man she loved impaling her from the front.

"*Please, Ellie, please.* Try not to wriggle just yet," he groaned, his words stilted and strained and she went still. "That's better. It will be easier now, I should think. Just kiss me again. Oh, how I crave these bee-stung lips, so soft and plump. Yes, love, yes. Give me your tongue. Mmm . . ."

She loved the way he kissed her, so tenderly, endlessly, while his hands massaged the stiffness from her nape, all the way down to the base of her spine, over her hips and thighs and fingertips. He touched and caressed her as if they had all the time in the world. As if the midnight sky wasn't turning from black to violet to indigo and the moon's descent wasn't marked by the pale peach glow of the approaching dawn. Then he began to move within her in slow, gliding thrusts.

Ellie wasn't certain when the pain shifted to a lovely ache, or when the ache turned into an awakening need, or even when she began to grip the taut muscles of his back. All she knew was that something altered. And it felt like the most natural thing to twine her arms and legs around him, giving herself over to the moment.

Somehow, she was moving with him, welcoming his driving body, clinging. Washes of sensation rippled through her. Their rasping breaths blended together. Perspiration bloomed on her skin, her fingers tangling in the damp locks at his nape. He gripped her hips, tilting her as he slanted in, deeper still, and stroked the pleasure-slick walls.

Her breath caught. Quickened. She saw the gleam in his velvet gaze as if he knew what was happening to her. A mewl left her, helpless and needy. He was relentless, drawing out stuttered pleas from her lips. The friction was exquisite and unbearable. Each thrust sparked spirals of heat, coiling tighter and tighter inside her until she wasn't certain she could survive it . . . until she was sure death was imminent . . . *until* . . .

She shattered in a torrent of cries and unending spasms, her nails rending the seams of his shirt. Brandon drove faster, throat taut, staying with her until every last quake and tremor was spent. Then he gripped her hard against him and plunged to the hilt on a guttural groan, shuddering his own release in thick, molten surges.

For the long moments that followed, they remained joined, unmoving aside from the bellow-work of their burning lungs. Heads bowed to each other, their breaths converged, hearts racing in defiance of the *little death* they'd both suffered.

Then he kissed her again, fiercely, wordlessly, and then tenderly as he smoothed her hair away from her face.

She stared at him in wonderment as the pale light of dawn caught the burnished copper of his lashes. It was hard to believe this moment was real. She felt as though she'd awakened for the first time in a new world. And the way his gaze bore into hers with such intensity, she knew he felt it too. Seeing that look caused a rush of warmth to rise beneath her skin, climbing to her cheeks. He smiled as he pressed a kiss to the pinkened crests, then lingered at her lips. And lingered some more.

Playful sips, nibbles and nuzzles, deepened into slow licks and deep tumbling kisses taking them headlong into another heady swell of passion. Her body clenched on a brief, sweet aftershock, gripping his flesh. He hissed, eyes squeezed shut, his hips pushing reflexively. And even though she could feel that he was not as hard as before, his girth and prodigious length still filled her and drew out her gasp.

She realized with a start that she wanted him again.

"You've turned me into a veritable beast," he accused on a growl, seating himself firmly between her thighs. "Yet, as much as I would like to remain as we are for all eternity, if we tarry too long, I will end up taking you again. And that would be insupportable."

Ellie was about to argue but he withdrew. A whimper of distress left her, not only due to her smarting sex but to the warm, viscous wetness that followed.

She was not so naive as to be ignorant of how babes came from coupling. But she'd never truly thought about it like this. In the past, she'd simply imagined herself surrounded by children—George's children, to be exact. The sharing of breaths and heartbeats, the clinging desperation and soul-piercing intimacy of the act had never occurred to her.

It seemed foolish to her now, childish even, to not under-stand how much it would change everything.

Dazedly, she felt him gather her in the cradle of his arms, heard the echo of his boots strike the stones as he carried her across the folly floor and down the steps. "Where are you taking me?"

"Well, had I known you were going to declare yourself," he said with a teasing grin tucked into the corner of his mouth, "I'd have come better prepared to see to your comfort. As it stands, however, it looks like the pond is to be your bath. Nevertheless, the cool water should soothe the tender flesh I ravaged."

Embarrassment flooded her as reality rushed in. They had made love in the folly. *Out of doors* where anyone could have seen them! But she had been so swept away by an all-consuming passion that she hadn't cared. Once that ebbed, however, she was only too aware of the repercussions of her actions. Of the proposal of marriage that would surely fall from Brandon's lips. He was too much of a gentleman to leave it unspoken.

As he set her feet on the soft cushion of the clover bed by the pond and his hands coasted lightly over her body, she wondered how he would broach the topic. She was so distracted by the thought that she startled when he went down on bended knee. Then she blinked with another jolt to see that she was naked aside from her stockings and shoes, her dress and undergarments all pooled around her ankles.

Surely, he wouldn't propose . . . not here . . . like this . . .

Shyly, she placed her hands in front of her sex and heard his low chuckle in response as if he'd read her thoughts. But he said nothing as he untied her garter ribbons and pressed a quick kiss to the bare skin just above her stockings. Then he lifted her foot, which forced her to move her hands to his shoulders, leaving her fully exposed before him.

He removed one slipper and then the other, before he eased the silken stockings down her calves. Slowly, he stripped them away and dragged the tip of his thumb along the bared arch, sending darts of tingles up along her inner thigh.

It stole her breath, the way he gazed up at her as if the universe formed in her eyes, the beginning and end of all creation. George had never looked at her that way.

A rush of guilt filled her as the thought entered her mind. She shouldn't be thinking about George at a time like this. And yet, how could she not when she'd planned her whole life to be with him? Her love for Brandon was so new by comparison. But she did love him, and so much that she was still reeling from it.

Brandon shucked out of his trousers and kicked his top boots off to the side. He stood in front of her in his shirtsleeves for only an instant before he lifted his arms, elbows high, and reached back to his shoulders. Then, in one fluid motion, stripped out of his shirt and dropped it on the ground.

Any thought of George—or really any intelligible thought at all—left her.

Her gaze skimmed greedily over broad shoulders, tightly loomed arms and a firm chest lightly furred with bronze curls that shadowed the flat brown nipples. His rib cage looked solid and strong, completely impervious to harm.

Unconsciously, she stepped closer and her fingertips took the same path, feeling the exciting flex of warm muscles, the smooth texture of his skin, the crisp hair, the velvet discs that pebbled beneath her touch.

Her unabashed exploration continued down the taut horizontal ridges of his abdomen, seeing a slight ripple as she descended to the shadow of his navel where a thin line of hair trailed down to a darker thatch and the imposing jut of his erection. Fascinated, she stroked a fingertip along the hard length, the flesh bobbing toward her palm as he hissed in a breath, his hands fisted at his sides.

She gripped the heated girth that was like forged iron enrobed in silk, the dusky flesh slightly damp and glistening from their coupling. "Are you always thus?"

A choked sound left him, his voice frayed and ragged like old rope. "Only when I see you, or hear your voice. Catch your scent in the air. Touch you. Taste your sweet kiss"—he hissed as she glided toward the tip—"or think of you. In other words, Ellie, yes. Always." Panting, he covered her hand and drew it away, his eyes dark and hungry. "I fear, I will never get enough of you."

Her pulse quickened, as did other, more tender, parts of her anatomy. She thought that admitting and expressing her love would give her some relief. And it had. But it was short-lived. The need, that gnawing ache, seemed even greater now.

So, she stepped into his embrace. Twining her arms around his neck, she lifted her face for his kiss and she was rewarded when his strong arms cinched tightly around her, the heat of him throbbing against her midriff.

"Then take more," she whispered. "Take all you need."

In a flash, he unlocked her arms and withdrew as if scalded, his gaze almost accusatory. "You're too new to this to understand what temptation you're offering."

An irrepressible giggle escaped her and he admonished her on a low growl, clasping her hand firmly then marching her to the water's edge without further delay.

As if sensing the dark mood of a large aroused beast in their midst, even the frog-song quieted at their approach, a small splash following. She heard a distant drip and plop, felt the startlingly cool rush of water over her ankles and calves, and was surprised to realize that she wasn't worried about what lingered under the surface. She was too caught up in watching the way he moved, the shifting of the muscles along his back, the firm flex of buttocks and thighs with each step past the lily pads.

He stopped abruptly beneath an arch of bending willow branches that dipped into the dark rippling water. Then he turned to face her and caught her looking.

She blushed and he cursed under his breath. The next thing she knew, he was pulling her against him. With a hand at her nape, he kissed her hard, roughly searching as if he'd lost all control. And she welcomed it, her own desperation building.

She loved the feel of him, the abrasion of his chest hair against her nipples, and she undulated against him until they were taut and achy. He kneaded her breasts to heavy fullness, spurring each tender tip as her womb fluttered and clenched. Then he cupped her sex, bathing her with the cool water, navigating every furrow, drawing out each sensation with deft strokes until she was gasping and writhing, then breaking in unending shudders.

She sagged against him, her knees seemingly made of bowing willow branches, too weak to support the sated, suddenly sleepy weight of her body.

Lifting her in his arms, he carried her up the bank and pulled his discarded shirt over her head. The scent of him filled her lungs as the linen settled in a soft embrace against her skin. She yawned and blinked at him, passion-drugged and drowsy.

"It looks as though you're in need of a nap," he said, a hint of male pride in the curve of his lips. He tucked a lock of hair behind her ear, his thumb leaving a trail of tingles as it skated over the shell. "We'll rest here for a short while."

After donning his trousers, he left her for the barest moment only to return with all their clothes, and then spread the saddle blanket over the grass and clover. Lowering her to their makeshift bed, he arranged her body to face away from him until they were like spoons in a drawer. And with her head resting on his arm, he lulled her into a quick slumber with gentle passes down her arm to her hand, twining their fingers.

She'd never felt so sheltered or cherished.

❧❧❧❧

UNFORTUNATELY, THAT did not stop the nightmare from coming.

She could smell the worms, the odor like mildew, rotting fish and death. Death was all around her. She could hear it in the strike of the hammer to the coffin nail. And when her dream-self opened her eyes, there was only suffocating darkness and the hollow patter of wet dirt falling on her coffin.

Gasping, she clawed at the wood, a scream lodged in her throat.

But something was different this time.

Brandon was there. She felt his arms around her in a comforting band, shielding her from Death's grip. And she heard his voice whisper in her ear, "Shh . . . I'm here, Ellie. You're safe. I won't let anything hurt you."

His hands wandered in a slow massage that worked away all the stiffness from her muscles. Caressing her endlessly, he knew precisely where to touch and soothe, until she was like pulled taffy beneath those skilled fingers. She melted against him, back to front, and felt his heat and hardness press against her bottom. But as much as she enjoyed this, it wasn't giving her what she needed.

She wanted him inside her. Needed him to fill the wounded emptiness. To make the nightmare disappear completely.

She didn't care if it hurt or if she was too raw from before. Time was slipping away from them. Time was the enemy of every person because it brought everything—even bright new beginnings—to an ultimate end. It hovered like a dark specter. She could feel it like the approach of a heavy rain.

"Love me again," she whispered, pushing back against him.

A low sound of pleasure vibrated in his throat as he rocked forward reflexively. "Later, when you've had a chance to—"

"*Please*, Brandon," she implored, feeling the sting of tears gather in her eyes. "I need you. I don't want this sunrise to end."

He didn't respond at first. But she could feel his thoughts turning, along with the chaotic clamoring of his heart at her back. Then he kissed the curve of her neck and the exposed crest of her shoulder where the shirt draped open.

Frustrated tears slipped out in a hot rush from beneath her eyelids. She thought that was his answer.

But then his warm hand swept under the soft linen, massaging and stroking her gently over her back and bottom. His careful attention moved to the front of her body, around to her middle, to her breasts and between her legs. He lingered there, pressing hot kisses to her nape as the length of his finger coasted circles around the pulsing bud. Then he edged inside the slippery sheath and his breath shuddered across her damp skin. The sound excited her. Her hips pushed eagerly back against him at his slow, searching rhythm, her inner muscles gripping tightly, propelling her closer toward another climax.

Just before it overtook her, she felt him shift, his leg sliding between hers, the broad head of his sex at her entrance, the careful nudge inside, the tender burning sting. And then he filled her in slow, liquid thrusts, in and in, until they were both lost and falling endlessly over the precipice into molten pools of rapture that chased away the nightmares.

At least, for now.

Chapter 30

⁓

"Being overcome by passion isn't as terrible as
society matrons would have you believe."

—A NOTE FOR *The Marriage Habits
of the Native Aristocrat*

Brandon took Ellie back to the house, navigating the halls
to return her to her bedchamber without being seen. She was
sluggish and sleepy and he had to keep her tucked against
his side the whole way, but he didn't mind. In fact, he felt a
smug grin on his lips as he thought about the cause.

Thankfully, he knew all the passageways and the schedule
of the servants, so he'd managed it. And yet . . . if it had been
impossible not to touch her before, now it was a physical ache
not to have her skin against his.

Once they finally reached her chamber, he locked the
door and kissed her again, holding her as close as he could
without being inside her. "Damn, but I don't want to leave
you."

She smiled against the corner of his mouth, her lips
parting as if she were about to say something. But then she
yawned. Curling against him, she rested her head on his
shoulder, her arms wrapped around his waist beneath his
coat. "Can we stop the world and crawl into bed together?"

"We could," he said, temptation whispering in his ear as
his hands wandered over the placket of buttons down her
back. "But stopping the world comes at a price."

If they were caught together, she would have no choice

but to marry him. And he wanted her to choose him without reservation, instead of being forced by circumstance.

She gazed up at him thoughtfully, the light of understanding in those amber pools. After a moment, she laid her hand over his heart and said, "Perhaps not today, then."

He nodded, willing to delay their inevitable conversation. Brandon wasn't about to propose when her eyes were skittish and wary.

Besides, he'd already planned out the whole thing days ago. First, he would persuade her back into the boat, but on the river this time. Of course, that would take a while. However, once he managed that feat, he would row beneath the arch of the marriage bridge. They would stop for a picnic along the bank. Then, with her lying beside him on the blanket, he would kiss her tenderly, confess the contents of his soul and ask her to be his wife. Afterward, they would row upstream through the second arch as Stredwick tradition dictated and announce their happy news to one and all. And he would try not to gloat too much in Nethersole's face.

With the morning sun shining through her open windows, he undressed her again, marveling at her beauty and the overwhelming joy inside him. A blush still tinged her cheeks and lingered in pink patches over the upper portion of her chest, having bloomed during her climax. He loved knowing all the alterations in her skin's hue when she was either shy or aroused.

Unable to help himself, he kissed the crests of her cheeks and nuzzled softly into her plump mouth. But before he forgot himself, he pulled back the coverlet and eased her down onto the bed, carefully removing the pins from her hair. All the while, she gazed up at him, her dark lashes drowsily dipping lower.

"I'll order a bath sent to your room as soon as I leave," he said and pressed a kiss to her forehead as he tucked her in.

She shook her head. "Please don't. The servants . . ."

He understood. The servants, no matter how excellent or pure their intentions, would likely talk. They were too eager for Crossmoor Abbey to be a home again and filled with children and life. So was he.

She reached out and took his hand. "Thank you for giving me the chance to settle things. I'm glad you understand that it wouldn't be right to make plans just yet. At least, not until I've talked to George. After all, we've been planning an entirely different future for most of our lives."

Hearing the "we" and the "our" told him that she was still having trouble imagining the rest of her life *without* George. She didn't say it aloud. Then again, she didn't have to.

A dark shadow threatened his bright mood, but Brandon shrugged it off, refusing to allow the ghost of his past to rear up again.

Leaning down, he tucked Ellie in. "Rest for now. We'll talk about this later."

He'd been patient this long. What was another day or two in the grand scheme of their lives?

❧❦❧❦❧

IT WAS nearly noon when Ellie left her bedchamber.

For the first time in her life, she hadn't wanted to wake up. She'd been lulled by wonderful, clover-filled dreams of moonsets and sunrises with soft velvety eyes staring down into hers. She hadn't wanted them to end.

The young mob-capped maid, who was so used to her mistress being dressed and ready to head down to breakfast, was doubtless startled to find her still asleep and with hardly a stitch on underneath the bedclothes.

Ellie blinked open her eyes in time to see the maid lift the yellow dress from the foot of her bed and frown at the damp hem. "I . . . um . . . went for a walk early this morning . . . much, *much* too early . . . then decided to come back to bed."

"Oh, Miss Elodie!" Henrietta fretted, her pale brows

knitting above a freckled nose. "You ought not wander around on your own before there's anyone about. You never know what trouble might befall you. Why, in a few more days, the village festival will be in full swing. Last year, we had a visiting troupe of *carnival people*." She mentioned the last in the barest whisper, her eyes wide, as if she feared they were lurking behind the drapes, ready to spring out and begin juggling apples and knives.

"Thank you for your concern. I will be more careful in the future."

"I should hope you are, miss. His lordship would not wish you to come to harm."

At the mere mention of Brandon, Ellie's heart raced and the heat of a blush climbed to her cheeks. She averted her gaze and decided it was best to sit up and get on with her day as quickly as possible. Unfortunately, the sudden movement brought her attention to the bruised soreness she felt in places that she'd never been much aware of before.

Not only that, but her stomach rumbled. Loudly.

Henrietta giggled. "I'm sure his lordship would insist on having the kitchens send up a tray for you, since you slept through breakfast."

"That would be most welcome," she said, placing a hand over her middle to quiet another thunderous growl. "And, if it wouldn't be too much trouble, I'd also like a bath."

The maid tilted her head in inquiry and glanced down to the damp hem once more. But before Ellie could determine whether or not a hint of suspicion crossed her gaze, Henrietta bobbed a curtsy and said, "I'll order it straightaway," then left the bedchamber.

A short while later, Ellie eased into the steaming slipper tub, forgetting all about her conversation with Henrietta. Lying back, she rested her nape against the curved lip and closed her eyes, the hot water soothing the tender aches of her intimate flesh.

She was surprised to discover her mind wandering to the future—a future at Crossmoor Abbey. More sunrises with Brandon. Walking hand in hand, amidst endless gardens and meadows. For just a moment, she even imagined the tinkling laughter of children with bronze curls and mossy green eyes. And it was such a lovely daydream that her heart ached.

But her inner worrier chimed in, wondering if this feeling was longing or uncertainty?

Strangely, the first person Ellie wanted to speak to about her confusion was Brandon. Perhaps that was an answer, in and of itself.

Leaving her bedchamber in a fresh rose muslin, she walked the corridors toward Brandon's study. Her thoughts were preoccupied and in a jumble of hope, love and guilt. She wondered how to tell George that everything had changed, and that the life she'd always thought they'd have together was now—

"There you are!" Meg said, appearing suddenly around the corner.

A choked yelp lodged in Ellie's throat. "Meg! You startled the life out of me."

In the same instant, Meg said, "I have been looking everywhere for you."

Before Ellie could ask the reason, Meg quickly drew her into a nearby parlor and peered both ways down the corridor before she closed the door.

"Where have you been?" she asked, her tone scolding.

Ellie's cheeks instantly flushed with the vivid recollection of every moment she'd spent with Brandon. Another rush of guilt followed, this time for having kept so many secrets from her friend. "I was . . . a slugabed this morning. Couldn't seem to rouse myself."

Taking her hand, Meg stared at her with concern, her voice dropping to a whisper. "Is that all?"

Ellie swallowed. "Of course. Why do you ask?"

"I heard talk from the servants just now. Apparently, there's speculation over a damp hem and you walking the grounds in the early hours . . ." Meg worried her bottom lip and looked askance as if it pained her to finish. "Just please tell me you weren't with Lord Nethersole."

"*With Lord*—What? No! Of course not." Her own alarm must have eased her friend's fears for Meg expelled a sigh.

"Good. That is such a relief, I cannot say. I overheard talk that he, too, was out early this morning, which is quite unlike him according to the servants at the lodge who say he rarely rises before noon. And, not only that, but Hamlet is gone from the stables."

Ellie's pulse started to race. On their return, Brandon had ridden Samson, keeping her curled on his lap. Instead of going to the stables, however, he stopped at the house to secret her inside, leaving the stallion tethered. So she had no idea if George had been awake that early, when he'd borrowed the horse . . . *or* if he happened to see Ellie and Brandon together.

"I regret that you were worried. You needn't have been on my account, and I'm sure that George will return Hamlet to the stables in no time at all. I cannot imagine what he could be up to at such an hour."

"I heard something else, as well," Meg added. "One of the scullery maids said that she's seen Lord Nethersole in the village on a number of occasions in the past year. And not only that but . . . he was seen talking to Miss Thorogood."

Ellie frowned. The *past year*? That was impossible. He would have mentioned something to her, surely. "The maid must have been mistaken. Lord Nethersole has only been searching for properties here for a few weeks. Though, it stands to reason that, when he encountered an acquaintance he knew through me, he felt obliged to greet her. I'm sure there's nothing more to it."

And yet, he'd never mentioned meeting Prue. Neither had her friend for that matter.

"It seems perfectly innocent when you say it. I suppose, when one hears rumors through the serving staff, everything seems rather sordid." Meg issued a rueful laugh then smiled. "I should have known better. I mean, after all, you've been spending far more time with Brandon than with Nethersole."

Again, Ellie tried to swallow down a rise of guilt but it seemed to be lodged in her throat. "Your brother has been gracious enough to help me overcome my fears."

"Then, you must trust him a great deal. Perhaps, even *like* him?"

Ellie's shoulders deflated like empty bagpipes. It was no use. "Oh, Meg. I'm so sorry. I do like your brother. In fact . . . I've grown quite fond of him."

"There's no reason to apologize, you goose," Meg said with a roll of her eyes. "Besides, I knew there was something between you from the beginning. My brother had never been so rude as he was to you that first day, and yet, the way he looked at you . . . Well, let's just say, I've never seen him look at any other woman that way. And as for you, there's always a blush on your cheeks when he's near or even when we're talking about him. Just like now. So tell me"—Meg's hold on her hand turned to a playful swinging motion from side to side—"do you love him?"

She drew in a deep breath and nodded. "Unbearably, I'm afraid."

"And are you going to marry him?"

"Meg!"

"Well, are you?" She grinned unrepentantly. "After all, the least a true friend could do to make amends for falling in love with my brother is to become my sister."

"Then you are not angry or disappointed with me?"

"Of course not. The only reason I could ever be cross

with you is if you broke his heart." Meg squeezed her fingers with affection, her blue eyes bright and happy. "And that is something you would never do."

oooooo

AFTER HER conversation with Meg, Ellie decided to walk the grounds instead of seeking out Brandon. She needed to think about the future without any distractions.

He'd come into her life so unexpectedly that she still wasn't quite sure how it had all happened. How could crashing into him in a garden have led to all this?

It boggled the mind and it didn't particularly look believable on the pages of her ledger. Her original plan of discovering the mysteries of the marriage-minded gentleman and using those tools to marry George would have turned out much better for the book's success, she was sure. After all, how could she profess a knowledge on a subject she still didn't understand?

It was all Brandon's fault. He made everything seem simple, from courtship to conquering her fears. Too simple, in fact.

Her inner worrier wondered if, perhaps, she'd fallen in love too quickly. Could she trust this overwhelming feeling?

By comparison, her love for George had always reassured her. It was steady, enduring, and built on the solid foundation of years spent together. A lifetime. He was her first love. She'd always thought he would be her only. Her last. They had made plans, of a sort. And he was depending on her to be there for him when he was ready.

So how was she going to tell him that a lifetime of plans and the security they'd found in each other was gone?

Lost in these musings, she found herself walking amidst clover with the folly in the distance. And that was when she saw George cutting across the field.

She blanched, feeling the sting of betrayal on his behalf.

Catching sight of her, he waved a hand and slowed the horse, coming up beside her. "Fancy seeing you here. I was just thinking about you."

Her lips curved in a reflexive smile at his greeting, but her stomach churned with guilt.

Then, recalling the news Meg had shared, she suddenly wondered if George had been thinking about her because he'd seen her with Brandon this morning . . . in the folly . . . in the pond . . . on the blanket . . .

Not knowing what he may have witnessed, she decided to pretend complete innocence. "Oh?"

"Indeed. I was just wondering why it seems an age since I've seen you," he said, swinging down from his mount, oblivious to the relief he'd just given her. "I mean, here we are, practically living beneath the same roof, and yet we've hardly spent any time together. If I were the jealous sort, I might think you're spending time with Hullworth instead."

At once, her breath stalled in her throat. "I . . . well . . . actually—"

"But that's preposterous." He laughed, interrupting her before she could begin explaining. "I mean, you're my Ellie and everyone knows it."

Hmm, she thought, *perhaps not everyone*. "So . . . What had you up and about so early today? Settling business with your steward about the house you plan to rent?"

"How did you know I was out early?"

"The servants talk," she said with a shrug to soothe the defensiveness in his tone. They turned away from the folly and began walking in the direction of the stables. "There was also mention of one of the scullery maids having seen you in the village before. It was even suggested that you might have chanced to see my friend, Prue, on occasion."

He looked off in the distance with a frown. "I might have done but I hardly remember."

Then it was as she expected. The encounters couldn't have been of any consequence if neither he nor Prue thought to mention it. "Doubtless, if you had seen her, you would have felt obligated to extend a greeting. And there was nothing more to it."

"Just so," he agreed and his grin returned.

With that settled, she decided to plod forward with her own purpose. "Of course, there are times in a person's life when he or she chances to meet someone purely by accident, and suddenly—"

"That's just how I met with my old mate Lord Bewley the other day—by accident," George interrupted. "We went hunting this morning. I, of course, bagged more than my share of birds. Did I tell you that his was the property I'd decided to rent? But that's neither here nor there. What I want to say is that I'm going to keep that house as a hunting lodge. After all, every man needs his own domain, a place to engage in his own pursuits, unleash his robust passions. As for you, my Ellie, you will simply have to hold sewing circles and ladies' teas at the other two houses."

"Actually," she persisted, albeit carefully. "Since last we spoke, my thoughts regarding the future have changed."

He reached over and tweaked her bonnet ribbon. "Not possible. I know you too well. And if there's one certainty in life it's that people never change who they really are."

Ellie was about to try again, but her words stalled on her tongue. For the first time in her life, she heard George. Had she ever truly listened to what he was saying? No. She did not think so. Instead, she'd spent too much time searching between his words to find some hidden meaning, some secret key that might have unlocked their long awaited happily-ever-after.

It was a peculiar realization. And yet, not entirely startling. His primary interests had always been his own pleasures and pursuits. His favorite topic of conversation was himself. And she could never imagine him dropping on bended knee at a garden party and pledging his heart and soul to her.

Oh, he liked her well enough. He might even love her in his own way. And she would always love him in *her* own way. But not like she loved Brandon.

"And there's some news I have that'll interest you," he continued, oblivious to the complete and utter rearrangement of Ellie's views on the past and the future and everything in between. "There are preparations for a festival underway. I happened to hear that a man with a Montgolfier balloon is lodging at the inn. What do you think—shall I have Hullworth invite him over to dinner and compel him to take us up in his basket?"

She paled, her previous thoughts temporarily suspended in a pool of icy dread. "Absolutely not. I wouldn't want anyone I care about to step inside one of those death traps."

"Just as I thought." He chucked her gently on the chin. "But, you know, one of these days you're going to have to get over these silly fears of yours."

"Some fears, like falling from a basket hovering over the earth, are perfectly sensible," she groused, disliking how much he teased her about these things. He'd never once tried to help her. "And by the by, you shouldn't have taken Meg's horse without asking permission."

He merely grinned back at her. "Are you finished scolding me yet? If this is what I have to look forward to for the rest of my life, then maybe I won't marry you after all." Again, he laughed. "Oh, Ellie! That look upon your face is utterly comical. It's as though I've condemned you to a life of spinsterhood." Then he reached out to steal her hand and brought it to his lips for a quick kiss. "Fear not, my girl. When the time comes, you'll be the first to know."

"The first to know *what*, exactly?"

Hearing Brandon's voice behind her, Ellie turned with a

start. Her wide-eyed gaze collided with his thunderous one as he darted a quick glance down to where her hand still lingered.

Abruptly, she snatched it from George's grasp and awkwardly crossed her arms. "My . . . my lord, whatever brings you out here?"

"Indeed, Hullworth. I'm surprised to see you away from your study in the middle of the day. Run out of ledgers and ink?" George interjected with a sardonic chuckle before Brandon could answer. "Spend any more time at your desk and you'll be a hunchback by the time you're forty. Take a lesson from me, old man, and learn to enjoy yourself a bit more. You'll soon discover that any estate will eventually run itself."

Brandon looked at him with an unreadable expression. Then, without a word to George, he turned back to Ellie.

"What brings me here is my sister," he said. "She came into my study a short while ago to find me quite distracted, scribbling whatnot in the margins. In fact, she accused me of woolgathering."

George issued a disbelieving scoff at this.

But Ellie's heart fluttered at the idea of catching Brandon daydreaming, his eyes unfocused. Charmed by the vision in her mind she felt her lips tilt up at the corners. "And what did you say to that?"

"I told her I was doing nothing of the sort and that my mind was most definitely engaged in a proposal of the utmost importance." His choice of words was not lost on her. He was skirting the line between giving her time to settle matters with George and hurrying her along. She squinted at him in warning and he flashed an unrepentant grin before adding, "After all, I have it on good authority that certain speeches require the proper phrasing, for the sake of posterity and guidebooks for future generations."

Not only was he arrogant and overbearing, he was also

incorrigible. In the best possible way. She should be mad at him, but instead she wanted to laugh at his audacity.

"And this authority," she said, doing her best to sound disapproving, "would likely tell you that proper timing is also of the utmost importance."

He arched a brow at this and his gaze veered pointedly toward the folly. "So then, this *authority* would never think of making a spontaneous declaration herself, hmm?"

Well, he had a point, she thought. But surely, he wasn't intending to propose to her, here and now. Was he?

George uttered a grunt of boredom, his head dropping back toward the sky. "Whatever it is, it sounds like it requires far too much effort. And anything that takes that much forethought is never worth it."

Brandon stiffened, all good humor vanishing from his countenance as he slid a glance to George. "If you're finished riding for the day, Nethersole, I'm sure the stablemaster will be relieved by the return of *my sister's* horse. Though, in the future, Mr. Warton and I would appreciate knowing in advance before you plan to borrow any mount in the early hours."

George smirked as if the matter were of little importance and Ellie cringed in apprehension when he opened his mouth to speak.

So, before he could, she interjected, "That sounds like a splendid idea. George, why don't you take Hamlet back to the stables and then you and I can finish our chat."

"Not possible, Ellie. I'm simply too tired from hunting. And I've been invited to dine with Gerbold later. So, how about I take you on a drive tomorrow, hmm? We'll have a jaunt through the village. What say you?"

"Well . . ." She looked with uncertainty to Brandon and to the muscle ticking at his jaw. "I suppose one more day wouldn't hurt."

"Good," George agreed and, before she could prepare

herself, he leaned in and kissed her cheek. "Until then, my Ellie. Good day to you, Hullworth. Try not to be too industrious or else you'll be *London's most elusive hunchback* before long."

And with that, he swung back onto his mount and rode toward the stables.

When she turned back to Brandon, he was offering her a handkerchief, his expression hard and unbending. She took the linen and dutifully wiped her cheek, fighting the urge to roll her eyes.

"You needn't be jealous. After all, you know very well that George and I have never . . . well . . . you know." She blushed. "What did you expect me to do?"

He snatched back the folded square and crammed it into his pocket. "I'll burn it for you."

"Not about that, about George," she said on a sigh. "After all, I am going to speak with him tomorrow."

"*And* you'll take a chaperone."

"Brandon, you're—" She broke off, gritting her teeth. "What is your middle name?"

"Christopher," he enunciated crisply.

"Brandon Christopher Stredwick, you are being ridiculous," she fumed. "I've known George all my life. We can certainly have a simple conversation without the need for a chaperone."

"And you should be glad I don't demand an armed guard instead. Not to mention the fact that it is taking every ounce of my willpower not to throw you over my shoulder, carry you inside the abbey and lock us in my bedchamber for the next fifty or sixty years," he growled, crowding closer, nostrils flared.

But it wasn't anger or even irritation she saw in his gaze. He was looking at her as if he wanted to devour her, right then and there.

Strangely, his primitive male display caused a thrill to

rise inside her, inciting an unexpected swell of feminine power. Reaching out, she slipped her hand in his and heard the catch in his breath as his fingers curled around hers.

Holding his gaze, she bargained, "Your carriage. Your driver. No chaperone. And tomorrow, I'll talk to George. *Then*, I'll talk to you."

After a lengthy moment, he nodded. Taking her hand, he laid it against the center of his chest, the heavy thud of his heart rising up to meet her palm. "One more day."

His words were spoken with such resolve that it left her wondering if he was making a concession . . . or making a plan to wait twenty-four hours before locking her away in his bedchamber.

Chapter 31

"When writing a letter to a gentleman, a debutante should choose her words wisely."

—A NOTE FOR *The Marriage Habits of the Native Aristocrat*

That afternoon, Brandon took his usual ride with his steward to inspect the property. Their conversation gradually turned to the daily report of the comings and goings of the guest at Stredwick Lodge.

Early on, he'd asked Mr. Weymouth to make a few casual inquiries around the village about Nethersole. He just couldn't shake the sensation that the man-child was up to something. But the report only revealed that Nethersole engaged in a few flirtations with the local laundress as well as a few of the widows. Nothing altogether scandalous or corrupt. By all accounts, he was merely a man unencumbered by obligation, who enjoyed his life to the fullest. And yet, he seemed a bit too discreet for a man who enjoyed the limelight so much. Far different from the Nethersole who bragged to his sycophants in London.

Besides that, what man would simply decide to travel to a small village in Wiltshire and then return often throughout a year's time, without sharing an acquaintance with one of the inhabitants?

As far as Brandon knew, the only newcomer to the village who had any connection to Nethersole whatsoever was Ellie's friend.

When the dark suspicion had first entered his mind, Brandon had asked Mr. Weymouth to make a few unobtrusive inquiries into Miss Thorogood's habits.

What he discovered did not set his mind at ease.

She was regarded by many of the villagers as a fine young lady, quiet and very kind, who enjoyed long walks. However, there was one account from an old gardener on a nearby estate, who'd said that he'd seen her with a young gentleman in fancy togs on occasion, and that he would be relieved to hear happy news that they were to marry.

The information was not definitive. However, if Brandon took into account what he'd witnessed between Nethersole and Miss Thorogood himself, then it was highly suspect.

The report from Mr. Weymouth troubled him and, all night, Brandon wondered how he would talk to Ellie about it. Or even if he should mention it at all without proof.

But he knew one thing for certain, there was no way in hell he was going to leave her alone with Nether—

Brandon's dark thoughts stalled at the rustling sound outside his bedchamber door.

From his chair by the fire, his gaze shot to the ormolu clock on the mantel. It was a quarter of two in the morning. He stood to investigate, watching as a folded scrap of paper slipped beneath his door.

He crossed the room in two strides, opening the door with such haste that it caused the chamberstick in his visitor's grasp to sputter out, but not before he saw her amber eyes widen with surprise.

"And just what have we here, an interloper in the lord of the manor's wing?"

She gasped as he took hold of her wrist and tugged her inside. "Brandon, you startled me. I thought you'd be sleeping."

Closing the door, he bent to pick up the missive. "And what's this?"

"Just a note." Her cheeks colored as she reached for the letter. "I could tell you about it later, tomorrow, after you've had a chance to . . ."

He stilled her hand, keeping it in his as he shook the page open.

> *My Dearest Brandon,*
>
> *I do not need to wait a moment longer. If you have a question for me. The answer will be yes.*
>
> > *Ever yours,*
> > *E*

Brandon's heart galloped as he read it twice more to be absolutely certain of the contents. Then, as nonchalant as he could manage, he laid the missive on the marble console table by the door, followed by her chamberstick.

"I see," he said. "Though I have to wonder, Miss Parrish, if that *yes* applies to any question. You weren't very specific, after all."

Her head tilted quizzically and she blinked. "I presumed it was obvious . . . after this morning."

Seeing her cheeks flood with new color, Brandon could hardly resist the temptation to kiss her. But he had much more than kissing on his mind. Something that would take hours and hours and complete privacy.

Shifting to the door, he turned the key in the lock. "To be precise, that was actually yesterday morning. Nearly a full day ago. That gives a man a good deal of time to think of more questions. In fact, I have a few in mind right now, such as—do you want me to undress you? Do you want me to taste every luscious inch of your body? Shall I begin right here?"

"Brandon," she rasped as he pressed his mouth to her throat. "You know very well what I meant."

Hands braced on the wall on either side of her, he shook his head and clucked his tongue. "No, sweetheart, that isn't the answer you promised me. I think it's time for another lesson for your ledger. I'm going to teach you all the ways a marriage-minded man likes to hear the word *yes.*"

Chapter 32

> "Fear not, debutantes, there will come a time when happiness will settle in the palm of your hand. All you must do is take hold of it."
>
> —A note for *The Marriage Habits of the Native Aristocrat*

Ellie never expected to awaken to a nightmare that night. Not when Brandon had left her thoroughly exhausted and pleasured and sleeping contentedly in his bed.

But before dawn's approach, her dream-self stumbled to an open grave, a clod of dirt in her hand. And when she gazed down into the yawning hole, she saw Brandon's pale, lifeless body arranged on black silk inside a coffin.

She was sobbing quietly, curled on her side, when she felt Brandon's arms slide around her, pulling her back into his comforting embrace. He didn't ask her about her dream, but simply held and soothed her, distracting her with gentle caresses and wicked kisses that left her gasping and shattering until she drifted into dreamless slumber.

That afternoon, the nightmare was forgotten.

She smiled up to Brandon's profile as they walked down the lane, side by side.

He turned to grin back at her. "You're still blushing."

"And you're awfully smug."

"But you like me this way." He glanced over his shoulder toward the abbey in the distance, then reached out, hauled her to him, kissed her breathless, and then set her apart again. And she staggered a step until he secured her hand in his.

He made it impossible for her to think. In fact, her thoughts had been so distracted by him that, when George popped by to speak with her earlier to postpone their outing for another day, she'd completely forgotten to broach the topic foremost on her mind. However, considering how he still wasn't ready for marriage, and perhaps never would be, she imagined that he'd accept the news without any qualms. At least, she hoped he wouldn't be hurt.

"Not much farther now," Brandon said, drawing her out of her musings.

She squeezed his hand for reassurance. "Aren't you going to tell me where we're going?"

"Like I said before, you'll just have to be patient."

"I don't like surprises, you know."

"You'll like this one." He hesitated. "Mostly."

She didn't like the sound of that either. And when she looked ahead and saw where the path was leading them, she was certain she wouldn't like this particular surprise.

Her feet became sluggish. "Brandon, is there a reason we're heading toward the bridge?"

"Yes."

She waited for him to elaborate, but instead he turned down a narrow side path, guiding her down the slope with him. And then she saw it.

Her heart sputtered to a stop. She dug her heels into the hard-packed earth underfoot. "You are not thinking of putting me in that boat *on* the river, are you?"

"Only when you're ready," he said tenderly, coming back to her to brush his knuckles over her chilled cheeks. "I thought we might run through the checklist together. I have a mooring line tied to the trunk of that dogwood. And there's a picnic waiting on the other side."

Her wary gaze drifted from the boat to the water to the bridge.

My father called this the marriage bridge, because of the two arches and how they support one another, Meg had once told her.

Ellie recalled the story about the Stredwick family tradition of navigating the two arches beneath the marriage bridge. The betrothed couple were to float down the river through one, then paddle up the other together.

Together, the word lingered in her mind. A single arch would only have been half as strong. That bridge, as well as any future she might hope to have with Brandon, required the strength of two.

He put his arms around her and pressed his lips to her forehead. "Another day, perhaps. To tell you the truth, I'm already tired of waiting to ask you my question. It's been burning a hole through my heart and I just cannot contain it any longer. And so . . ."

He started to kneel.

"No," she said abruptly, her own heart rabbiting as she gripped his shoulders in an effort to make him rise again.

And he did, albeit stiffly, his brow furrowed and his mouth drawn taut. *"No?"*

"What I mean is," she began, flustered and breathless, "not yet. Take me to our picnic first?"

His breath rushed against her cheek and his arms enfolded her once more. "Are you sure?"

She swallowed but held tightly to him. It was knowing that she didn't have to brave this—or anything—alone, that gave her the ability to say, "I am."

Two hours later and with his pink-cheeked fiancée on his arm, Brandon walked up the lane toward Crossmoor Abbey. Toward *home.*

For the first time since he'd succeeded the title, he could look at this place and think about the future, instead of all those he'd lost. He and Ellie had navigated the arches, enjoyed their picnic, along with a few other delights, and she'd said *yes* to his proposal without any hesitation.

"That had to be a record number of sighs and swoons," he said smugly. "How many was it exactly?"

She looked up at him with her heart in her eyes and then rolled them skyward. "So arrogant. What makes you think I'd put your proposal in my book? You said you'd love me every day for the rest of your life . . . even when I'm being impossible. Hardly romantic."

"Your eyes were filling with tears and I'd needed to make you laugh. It puts me through hell to see you cry," he admitted quietly. "Now, see? You're doing it again."

Turning to her, he brushed away the wetness from her sooty lashes with his thumbs and then with his lips.

"It's your own fault. I'm just too happy," she chided with a soft smile and lifted her hand to smooth back the curls from his forehead. Then her expression turned somber and serious. "I want to marry you now. This very day."

"As much as I would like to—even if that means Gerbold would marry us—I don't have a special license."

"Then lock us inside your bedchamber before anything or anyone interferes."

Only then did he see a brief glimpse of panic dart across her gaze. He held her close and soothed her fears. "You don't have to worry about being too happy, Ellie. It happens to people all the time and they survive it. So will we."

She wobbled her head in a nod and issued a self-deprecating laugh. "You must think I'm completely mad— a woman afraid of being happy."

"I would never think that."

"Good," she said and hugged him tighter, her cheek

pressed to his chest. "It's just that I've never felt this way before."

He tenderly kissed the top of her head. "Tell me the symptoms of this new ailment."

"The need to be near you, always. Finding random excuses to touch you. Watching you in your study through the crack in the door. Yes, I confess I have done that quite often. I've even become jealous of your teacup when you put it to your lips."

"I shall have it banished forthwith."

"Good," she said with a smile in her voice. "And the worst ailment by far is an absolutely ridiculous notion that you are perfect in every way. It's almost unbearable how much I love you. Is there a cure, do you think?"

His heart soared as he held her. "I hope not."

"And you know, there's a very good chance that my aunts—" She broke off and drew in a breath. "Do you smell something burning?"

Lifting his head, he scented the air and, sure enough, there was.

This wasn't a hearth fire from a chimney, but something different. Perhaps Mr. Weymouth was burning brush. Whatever it was, Brandon wasn't inordinately alarmed. At least not until he turned and saw the curls of black smoke rising behind the abbey.

Chapter 33

"But sometimes, happiness is as elusive as smoke."
—A NOTE FOR *The Marriage Habits
of the Native Aristocrat*

Meg was the first to greet them as Brandon and Ellie rushed to the back of the house. But he noticed no alarm in her expression. In fact, she was grinning from ear to ear.

"You are so full of surprises," she said, tugging on his hand to pull him around the corner. "Why did you not tell me you invited a balloonist here? How thrilling!"

"What?" His gaze swerved to the field of clover and there it was. Billows of smoke pouring from the fire to fill the giant red-and-gold balloon.

Beside him, Ellie gasped. "That wasn't your brother who extended the invitation. It was—"

"There's my Ellie," Nethersole said, swaggering through the terrace doors. "I've been looking for you everywhere. And now Hullworth has spoiled my surprise. Well, no matter. What do you think? Are you ready to finally be rid of that pesky fear of heights? Once you're up in that basket, you'll never think my phaeton's too high."

"George, you have overstepped. It isn't your place to invite people to Brandon's house."

Nethersole's brows lifted in quick speculation over the informal address, his gaze shifting between the two of them as if he knew nothing of their involvement. But no sooner than Brandon could even look to Ellie in question, Nethersole affected a smile and bowed in a false show of deference.

"Forgive me, Hullworth. This is only my meager attempt at enlivening the party. It never occurred to me that you would take offense at something so trifling. Perhaps, you and I can explain the misunderstanding to the balloonist together?"

Seething, Brandon inclined his head and set off, intending to handle the matter straightaway. Nethersole, on the other hand, proffered his arm to Ellie and brought her along as well, keeping a step behind.

As Brandon left the back garden, he saw Sylvia, Maeve and Myrtle step through the terrace doors and address Meg, who likely had no idea what was going on. Well, they were all about to find out when he gave Nethersole the boot and told him that he was no longer welcome at the abbey.

"Mr. Sinclair is a right solid chap," Nethersole continued in his usual garrulous manner. "Told me everything there is to know about ballooning. Just wait till you see it up close, Ellie. The basket is shaped to have a hole in the center to make room for the fire. Then, the smoke wafts up and fills the balloon until it expands. And the thing would rise on its own and drift off for a couple of miles if it wasn't tethered by those ropes. What do you think of that, eh?"

"I think it sounds dreadful."

At the tremor in her voice, Brandon stopped and turned around. He ignored the irritation he felt at the sight of her arm curled around Nethersole's. "Ellie, if you'd rather go back, I'm sure that your aunts and my sister would like to know what's happening."

"If she had any qualms or complaints, Hullworth, she would voice them. I should know, for she's been scolding me for decades," Nethersole said charmingly and gazed down into her upturned face. "No need to treat her as though she's made of glass."

"I know very well how strong and capable she is. What I doubt is your ability to heed any wishes other than your own."

Nethersole chuckled. "Do you hear that, Ellie? If we were already married, I can imagine you giving him an earful."

Already married? Brandon was now fuming. Obviously, during the conversation Ellie had had with Nethersole earlier that day, she'd neglected to mention that she was in love with another man.

Had it been too difficult for her to speak the words? To make a choice? It hadn't seemed that way last night. Or this afternoon, for that matter. However, it was becoming all too clear that, when in Nethersole's company, her affections were still divided.

Even so, he knew that Ellie was incapable of being deceitful in any way. So, this was simply a matter to be sorted out later, between the two of them.

Before he did or said something he would regret, he turned to address the mustachioed Mr. Sinclair, who was wiping smears of soot from his forehead with a red handkerchief that matched the giant balloon.

"Sir," Brandon began, "I believe there has been a misunderstanding . . ."

For the next few minutes, he spoke amiably with the balloonist and offered to compensate him for his time. The man was apologetic, having not realized that Nethersole wasn't the lord of the manor. When the smoke from the fire drifted in their direction, they stepped off to the side to conclude their conversation.

But from a short distance away, he heard Ellie's voice, strained and frustrated. "George, I really don't want to see it."

"Don't tell me you're so afraid of the balloon that you cannot even stand next to it while it's inflated?" He tsked. "Come now, it isn't going to hurt you."

Out of the corner of his eye, Brandon glimpsed Nethersole's attempt to lift Ellie into the basket. Rage suddenly filled his veins.

She struggled and thrashed to be free. "George, put me down this instant! It isn't amusing in the least."

"You just need to give it a go."

"Nethersole, take your bloody hands off her!"

❧❧❧❧

ELLIE HAD known something terrible was going to happen. But she never imagined this. Every moment that followed blurred together into one horrific nightmare.

She pushed away from George at the same time that he let go of her and she tripped over one of the ropes. She fell, hard, landing on her hands and knees.

Brandon rushed to her side. But when he saw the smear of blood on her palm, he cursed in an animalistic growl and then launched himself at George.

They punched and grappled. The sounds of pained grunts and the sickening smack of flesh hitting flesh filled the air. She'd witnessed a bout of pugilism before and never imagined that she would look back on it and find it civilized. Today she felt differently.

These men were feral. Their coats were stripped, sleeves rent, cravats tangled and discarded on the ground. One moment they were both standing, the next they were on the ground, unleashing their inner beasts as they wrestled for domination. And it only grew worse from there.

Shoving George out of the way, Brandon tried to come back to her, chest heaving for every breath. Then George came at him from behind, jumping onto his back and cinching an arm around his throat. Brandon staggered, falling against one of the tethers. The balloon shifted, bobbling in the air as the basket groaned and crackled from being too close to the fire.

Hearing a shout from Mr. Sinclair, she turned for just an

instant. But by the time she looked back, she saw that Brandon and George had fallen into the basket, still fighting and oblivious to the sudden jerk of the last tether rope as it was wrenched from the earth.

Ellie knew that she would wake up at any moment. This couldn't be happening. Not really.

But then she heard Aunt Maeve and Aunt Myrtle cry out behind her and saw Meg and Sylvia grip each other tightly as the balloon lifted off.

Ellie wanted to rush forward, to grab the rope and hold on for dear life. But she was frozen, trapped in a nightmare and unable to move.

And then, to her utter horror, Brandon tumbled over the edge. No! No!

Ellie wished she would faint. Wished she would collapse and then, later, someone would tell her the dreadful news.

But she didn't faint as Brandon fell through the air. She watched, helpless, for the entire agonizing drop. For the boneless thud that followed. Her gaze fixed on the still form lying on the ground.

Her legs moved on their own, rushing to his side. But it took forever to reach him, as if she were running through worm-clotted mud. And all the while, she saw flashes of him lying in a coffin, heard the dirt being emptied by the shovelful onto his grave.

His chest was so still and tight beneath her hands, his face contorted in a rictus of agony, and she wanted to scream but no sound would come. Only blinding tears.

This must be what it felt like to have her soul ripped from her body.

Shudders and wrenching sobs tore through her. Her nightmare had come true. She could feel the dirt in her hands. The rawness inside her. And the cold emptiness that surrounded her like a shroud.

She knew then that this was what she'd been afraid of

all along—to love him so much, to imagine a life with him, only to have it ripped from her grasp. How could she bear to live without him?

She didn't know how long she lay, collapsed over his supine form. Yet, gradually she felt hands on her back. She imagined they belonged to one of her aunts in an attempt to comfort her.

But they weren't her aunts' hands.

She heard the strained wheeze beneath her ear. The strangled spasm of air into arrested lungs. A cough. And then she felt arms cinching around her. Strong arms, just like Brandon's.

She thought she was dreaming. Or that she'd lost her mind and couldn't accept the fact that he was never coming back to her. Either way, she would rather stay in this dream, and so she remained perfectly still.

"Ellie," he rasped, his voice like gravel. "Don't cry, sweetheart. I didn't mean to scare you."

"Come on now, my dear," Sylvia said softly. "You need to stand up so that we can see if my nephew has anything broken."

"I'm fine, Aunt. Just a bit of wind knocked out of me."

But he wasn't fine. Nothing was fine. It never would be again.

Yet, as the minutes ticked by, Ellie came to her senses enough to realize that Brandon *was* holding her and soothing her. He truly was alive . . .

But she couldn't allow herself to rejoice. Not now. Not when she'd had a sample of the agony she would suffer from losing him. And she'd only just begun to love him. How much worse would it be to lose him later, after they'd started their lives together?

He thought she was capable and strong. But to her, this only proved that she wasn't. And she wasn't ready to face a life without him either.

So she let Sylvia draw her away, helping her to stand off to the side. A crowd quickly formed around him—his aunt, Meg, Mr. Sinclair, the gardener, even the butler and his valet had rushed from the house.

Ellie slipped away, walking numbly toward the sound of her aunts' voices.

She'd nearly forgotten about George.

The balloon, it seemed, had gotten caught in a nearby tree. He likely would have survived the ordeal completely unscathed, if he hadn't leapt from the basket, only to get his arm tangled in one of the ropes. The aunts were quick to fashion a sling out of one of their shawls.

Even though he was injured, he still had a smile for her. "There's my favorite nursemaid."

"Are you in pain?" she asked as if by rote. The truth was, she didn't care about anything at the moment, or feel anything. She was numb inside and tired. So very tired.

"A little," he admitted. "But more than anything, I think I just want to go home. What do you say, Ellie? Would you like to go home?"

She nodded and looked to her aunts who stared back at her with concerned furrows along their brows. "I would. Today, if we can manage it."

"Very well, dear," Aunt Maeve said, coming to her side.

Aunt Myrtle kissed her damp cheek. "If you're sure."

"I am."

Chapter 34

"A marriage-minded gentleman will not have patience forever."

—A NOTE FOR *The Marriage Habits*
of the Native Aristocrat

Damn it all to hell.

Brandon felt like he was still falling from the balloon. His life was coming apart and he couldn't figure out a way to make it stop.

In his study, he stared with incredulity at Ellie, who simply stood there, gripping the handles of her valise, her face pale and void of expression, as if she were empty inside.

"So you're just leaving? With him?"

Her head jerked in a nod. "I have to go. George doesn't have anyone. I've always looked after him. And besides"—she swallowed—"this entire ordeal was partly my fault. It wouldn't be right for me to stay."

"None of it was your fault."

"Not true. George mentioned the balloonist and I didn't take him seriously. I should have mentioned it to you. If I had then . . ."

This wouldn't have happened, he thought, finishing her unspoken sentence. They were supposed to be celebrating. Planning the rest of their lives. Instead, she was leaving, choosing George over him.

How could this have gone from the happiest day in his life to the worst?

He stepped around his desk and stood in front of her. Taking the valise from her hands, he set it down then he cupped her shoulders in a tender massage, trying to warm the chill emanating from her.

"Sweetheart, listen, this was all a mistake," he said. "I know it was hard for you to witness the fall, but we have to move beyond this. You cannot let fear control you. There's nothing we can do about what's already happened. It was an idiotic stunt that Nethersole pulled by bringing the balloon here, and he went much too far when he tried to force you inside. So I've ordered him to leave, but you needn't go with him. This is your home."

And I need you far more than he does, he thought, but didn't say it aloud because the words were too raw and too true. He knew that Crossmoor Abbey would never be a home to him unless she were here, filling the halls with laughter, sharing her thoughts in a single look across a room. He loved her. Their connection was stronger than any he'd ever experienced before, as if they'd been formed from the same clay.

But, right now, he hated how vulnerable that bond made him feel.

Ellie took a step back, just out of his reach. "You're wrong about George. He didn't mean any harm."

Brandon's empty hands closed into fists and his frustration came out in a growl. "Unbelievable. When are you going to stop making excuses for him? He's a grown man, Ellie! He knows perfectly well what he's doing. And he's got you wrapped around his little finger."

"This isn't about him," she said, her eyes flashing.

"Isn't it? Then why didn't you tell him about us? About *our* plans?"

"It wasn't the right time. And besides, I knew he was never going to be ready for marriage. Not really."

Ah. Now he understood perfectly. Nethersole wasn't

ready, but Brandon was and she decided to accept the proposal of her second choice.

Bitterness flooded him as he walked back to the other side of the desk. "I think it's fairly clear that if he'd ever gotten down on bended knee you wouldn't have hesitated to accept his proposal."

She didn't answer, but he knew the truth. It had been staring at him all the while and he'd been a blind fool. Again.

"Friendly word of warning, Miss Parrish. There are no checklists for someone like Nethersole. He's reckless and thinks nothing about the consequences of his actions. And one of these days he's going to do something that cannot be undone. In fact," he said tightly, "I have the sinking suspicion that he already has."

Her gaze darted to his, her brows knitted. "What do you mean?"

"I believe that is a question you should ask him directly. Or perhaps ask your friend, Miss Thorogood, if you'd rather have the truth."

"What are you saying? That he was the one who—" She shook her head, adamant. "No. No, I refuse to believe it."

"That doesn't surprise me," he muttered under his breath, every syllable uttered with anger and hurt. Picking up a quill, he stabbed it into the open bottle of ink and scribbled a note to send with the driver. In the very least, Brandon would ensure that she and her aunts were well provided for on their journey.

Out of the corner of his eye, he saw her pick up her valise and move toward the door. A flood of cold finality seeped into his veins.

This was it. She was simply going to walk out of his life. Perhaps it hadn't been certainty he'd felt when they met. Likely, it had been a more ominous feeling, a sense of a storm approaching. A squall that would decimate everything in her path, leaving nothing but a barren landscape behind.

But maybe not completely barren, he thought, recalling all the times they'd made love in the past couple of days and how he hadn't been careful. Because he'd been certain they would marry.

"You'll send word on how you're faring and if"—he paused—"there's to be a child?"

She hesitated, her hand on the doorknob and she nodded.

"You do realize that you would have to marry me then."

Again, she nodded. As he stared at her profile, he saw a tear fall from the tips of her lashes. And he moved before he was even aware of it.

His hand braced against the door to keep it shut, and she surprised him by turning to him, throwing her arms around him with her face buried against his coat.

"I love you," she whispered brokenly, trembling. "But you deserve someone strong, someone who isn't so afraid."

He cinched her closer, his voice taut, pleading, "Then stop being afraid, Ellie."

"I wish I could."

He tried to hold on to her, but she slipped away and out the door.

Chapter 35

"A debutante must awaken her inner lion-tamer."

—A NOTE FOR *The Marriage Habits*
of the Native Aristocrat

"Elodie, dear," Aunt Maeve said as she entered the parlor, slipping into her gloves, "Myrtle and I are going to the park so she can flirt with the nut seller."

"When I told Etienne that filberts were your favorite, he promised to have some today," Aunt Myrtle added with an overbright smile as she situated her bonnet on her silver-floss hair. "Do you feel up to joining us this time?"

At the mention of filberts, the needle slipped and Ellie stabbed the tip of her finger. She instantly drew it to her lips, thinking of sharing burnt filbert ice cream with Brandon. And she hated that everything and every place reminded her of him.

The only reason they'd returned to London instead of the country was because of George. He wanted to be near the excitement. In recent years, more members of the *ton* were staying in town during the summer, having let their country houses out of financial need. But to her, these months tended to be stifling, the air humid and fetid. It made her long for Crossmoor Abbey . . . and the lord of the manor who was still there.

However, since she would never return to that particular patch of heaven on earth, she wished she were least at her own country house instead of in London where memories of Brandon were too vivid. And she might have been, if not for George.

Though, as it turned out, she needn't have bothered putting his ever-inconstant wishes above her own. Because just as Ellie and her aunts had opened the town house on Upper Wimpole Street and settled in, George had come by to tell them that he was leaving for a week or more on estate business. She didn't know what that might entail. After all, he surely wasn't thinking of renting that property in Wiltshire any longer. Not that it mattered to her. His using "estate business" as an excuse was likely a polite pretext for engaging in his manly pursuits and oat sowing. She did not care either way.

Ellie pulled her finger from her lips and absently examined the hole the pinprick left. There was no more blood. No death by slow exsanguination, then. Not today.

"I'll just stay in," she said to her aunts. "I like to be alone."

Once the words left her lips, she felt a small jolt of surprise at how well she'd just lied. She didn't stammer or blush at all. Then again, she didn't do any blushing these days.

Aunt Maeve stepped farther into the room, her handsome features drawn with worry. Then she came over and sat beside her. "You remind me of someone I knew, long ago. She had a falling-out with the man that she loved over an obstacle that was insurmountable, or seemed to be back then." She drew in a breath and exhaled slowly as she smoothed the loose threads from underneath the tambour. "They went their separate ways. He married another, while she . . . preferred to be alone. She felt that it was safer than risking her heart. After all, if you don't trust someone with it—if you never give it to them—they cannot break it."

Ellie felt tears sting her eyes and she blinked them away. "I understand what you're trying to do, but it isn't that simple. Not when the heart is already broken beyond repair."

"I never said it was simple." She patted her on the knee and rose, crossing to the door again. "And as much as I love you, Elodie, you know nothing of a broken heart until you watch the man you love live a full life with a woman you have tea with every Tuesday."

Aunt Myrtle sniffled and squeezed her sister's shoulder. "Adelaide Millington never deserved him."

"Lady Millington?" Ellie said with a start, having never suspected during all the years of their acquaintance. And when her aunt nodded, she suddenly remembered that Lord Millington had passed away last summer.

Last summer, when Aunt Maeve had taken ill and they couldn't find a physician to heal her.

Those stinging tears returned with a vengeance, welling in her eyes until she was unable to blink them away. "Oh, Aunt Maeve, I'm so sorry."

"So am I. Every day," she said quietly and left the room on the arm of her sister.

Ellie wiped her tears with the corner of her sampler and listened to her self-pitying sobs echo in the empty room. "Actually, I hate being alone. It's so . . . lonely."

But she'd done it to herself. She'd left the man she loved more than life itself because she was afraid. Afraid that he would die and leave her alone to suffer in agony without him.

Meanwhile, she was suffering in agony without him anyway.

She'd thought about crawling back to him a dozen times a minute since she'd walked out his door. But she was certain, by now, he'd realized that he deserved someone better. Someone stronger to stand by his side fearlessly. Miss Carmichael, perhaps. Someone who wasn't afraid of everything, including happiness. What kind of idiot was scared of being happy?

She'd thought it was safer than risking her heart. Ellie heard Aunt Maeve's voice in her head.

The words made her think about George.

As a girl, Ellie had always thought of him as her romantic hero, her armored knight, her stalwart neighbor who would be by her side no matter what. As she grew older, however, she saw that he was often unreliable and easily distracted. Still, she'd held on to her idealistic notion of him, ignoring how many times he'd proved her wrong.

Though now, she wondered if she'd clung to the dream of marrying George simply because he was her connection to the past, to her youth, to the days when the inevitable end of life and an eternity alone inside a coffin seemed too far away.

But when little Elodie Parrish grew up, she'd become so focused on not dying that, somewhere along the way, she forgot to live.

At least, until she met Brandon.

Suddenly, a thousand candles sparked to life inside her. "Risking your heart isn't supposed to feel safe, is it? That's why we *fall* in love. And it's terrifying," she said to the parlor walls. "Especially if there's no one there to catch you."

She stood up so quickly that her head spun. Normally, she'd have been worried over potentially dying of a stroke if that happened, but she was too lost in a new plan.

Racing to the open window, she looked to see if the carriage was still out front.

It was! She cupped her hands over her mouth and called down, "Aunt Maeve? Aunt Myrtle?"

In response, she heard a chorused, "Yes, dearest?"

"I think I'll join you after all." And perhaps, she could persuade them to go to the Zoological Society Gardens once more.

Ellie decided that it was time to learn to stand on her own, to face her fears. And it was time to feed a bear.

A FEW days later, Ellie was locked in a death grip with the ladder in the library when the butler announced she had a caller waiting in the parlor.

"Very good . . . Mr. Rivers," she said panting, her eyes squeezed shut. She'd made it to the second rung from the bottom when a wave of dizziness overcame her and icy perspiration bloomed along her scalp and forehead. "I'll be there presently."

"Would you like"—he paused to clear his throat and there was a distinct curl of amusement in his voice—"assistance, ma'am?"

"That would defeat the purpose. I'm conquering my fear of ladders."

"And doing splendidly. Shall I send to the kitchen for a tea tray for your guest?"

She managed a shaky nod. "Thank you."

Ellie wasn't certain how long it took her to descend to the floor. However, it seemed like an age. She even wondered if she looked as old and exhausted as she felt.

As she blotted her face with a handkerchief and tucked it up her sleeve, she realized that she hadn't inquired on the name of her caller. And a sudden flurry of vulture wing-beats flapped inside her stomach and her footsteps halted just outside the parlor door.

Could it be Brandon?

But no. She knew he was still in Wiltshire because she'd called at his town house yesterday to see if he might have decided to return to London.

He hadn't. Apparently, their time apart had only driven an insurmountable wedge between them.

Hearing a soft, melodious humming sound, Ellie knew at once who it was.

Stepping into the parlor, she saw Prue standing near the window to study one of the samplers in the light. Ellie was about to rush to her, to embrace her. But she stopped on the verge between the doorway and the rug, remembering awkwardness between them when they last saw each other. And it didn't help that Brandon's accusations regarding George and his possible connection to *Lord F* were lingering in her mind, no matter how hard she'd tried to dispel them.

Prue's gaze met hers. She went still, watchful in the way that a squirrel in the park stopped and stared, waiting for the parasol-wielding pedestrian to pass by. Then she was the first to move, gesturing with the tambour. "You were always better at needlework. Even your knots are tidy."

"And you were always the better songstress. You could charm a bird from his nest, to live on your windowsill."

She smiled wanly. "How are you, Ellie?"

"I'm only embroidering in shades of black, gray and the darkest violet if that tells you anything."

Prue laid the ring down on the table. "So then it's true. You're not returning to Crossmoor Abbey. On my walks there seemed to be a dark cloud always hovering over the grounds."

"A good deal has happened since I last saw you there."

"Because of"—she hesitated—"Lord Nethersole?"

Ellie shook her head. But the question that had been on her mind for the past week pricked sharply on the tip of her tongue, like a splinter that needed to be pulled out no matter how painful. "Is George *Lord F*?"

Prue startled. Then her wide eyes collected with swift tears that must have been waiting just beneath the rim, ready to break. And when they did, she slumped onto the high-backed chair as if exhausted and put her face in her hands, her shoulders shaking on silent sobs.

"I apologize for my blunt delivery," Ellie said, crossing the room to soothe her friend with gentle passes down her back until the tears subsided. Pulling out another chair, she sat beside Prue and offered her handkerchief.

Taking it, Prue blew her nose. "You have every right.

You should be railing at me. I deserve it. But I swear to you that I never meant for anything to happen."

"Of course you didn't. I know too well how charming George can be, and I remember all that you said when we were standing in the gallery. So I do not blame you. But why did you refer to him as *Lord F*?"

"Because I wanted the reminder that he was forbidden to me."

"Lord Forbidden." Ellie's brows lifted in wry humor. "Oh, how he likely relishes such a moniker."

"He doesn't know. But after reading your letter, he made mention of *Lord F* so he knows that I was attempting to keep his identity a secret from you." She looked down at her hands on the table, fiddling with the scalloped lace edges of the handkerchief. "I knew that it was absolutely unforgivable to engage in even the smallest flirtation with the man my dearest friend had her heart set on marrying. So I accepted my father's banishment out of remorse. I never imagined that George would follow me to Wiltshire. It only increased my guilt."

"You must have been angry at him for what he'd done, to damage your reputation like that," Ellie said, feeling plenty of her own anger toward him. The unthinking man! Did he care about anyone other than himself?

"I was, at first. I resisted every attempt of his to see me," she admitted. "But as time drew on and the isolation from my friends took hold, he became the only connection to the life I once had and I started to crave the times when he would come. I even felt mystified that he would drive all that way just to see me. After all, in the eyes of society, I was ruined. But the way he talked, always making plans for a house of our own and parties, it made me feel like I might have a respectable future. He even had me convinced that you and he were like brother and sister."

Ellie frowned, a sour taste at the back of her throat. This

wasn't the George that she thought she knew. Yes, he was a flirt and undeniably charming. But this reeked of manipulation, especially when he was also promising to marry Ellie "one day."

"And he said such wonderful things," Prue continued. "That he'd never loved anyone the way he loved me. That ours was the only future in his dreams. Then he laughed and looked almost bashful when he said that he'd never been overcome by such romantic drivel but that I brought out the best in him. And I"—her breath stuttered—"believed him."

Ellie would have believed him, too.

In the past, she'd always thought that George was simply boyish and impulsive. A man with a youthful spirit and a zest for life. But after really listening to him that day they'd walked through the village, she'd realized he was a man who had never truly matured. Like a child, he only thought about himself, and was driven to satisfy his own desires without considering consequence.

As she looked at her friend's stark gaze beneath the shadow of downcast cornsilk lashes, a fresh new fear came over Ellie. She wondered if George was truly capable of what she now suspected in the back of her mind.

A kiss in the garden was one thing. But would he have truly *ruined* her friend beyond repair?

Even though part of her was afraid to know, she *had* to know. "And so, when my letters contained nothing of George but a good deal of Lord Hullworth, I imagine it was difficult to keep your heart from taking a leap of faith and allowing yourself to believe what he was telling you."

Again, Prue's eyes flooded with tears. She swallowed them down and nodded.

"Did he," Ellie hemmed, "make an offer for you?"

"Of sorts. After we . . ." Her voice shook and it took her a moment to stifle her sob. "He offered to put me up in a house. To keep me content. To *keep* me. But not to marry me."

Absorbing all this, albeit numbly, Ellie covered her friend's hand with her own. *George, what have you done!* It was unforgivable.

"Did he bring you to London?"

"No. I left a note for my aunt and uncle, not that they'll shed a tear. And then I brought myself. Well . . . mostly. I took the mail coach until it became all too apparent that it was not prudent to travel in such a manner when you are the only woman aboard and you have neither a ring on your finger nor a chaperone."

"Prue!" Ellie cried. "Tell me you were not harmed."

"Fear not. The worst I received were leering glances. But they were enough to put me of a mind to find another way when the coach was jarred to a halt after hitting a rut. When the drivers stopped to repair the wheel, I took my satchel and began to walk."

"All the way to London? Alone?"

Prue shook her head. "I would have done, for I was in such a temper and angry at every male who ever roamed the earth."

"And you had every right to be."

"Thankfully, soon after I began, a fine coach and four stopped. Lady Chastaine, a woman who had called upon my stepmother on several occasions, opened the door. Since I was acquainted with her, I felt confident enough to accept her invitation to travel with her and her companion—the gentleman who happened to own the carriage. Or rather, I should say that she was *his* companion, or had been until their arrangement recently ended."

Ellie almost felt as if she were listening to one of Aunt Myrtle's novels. "And who was the gentleman?"

"Lord Savage. And yes, I can see by your wide eyes that you know his reputation for being a man who . . . well . . . *keeps* women." She issued a self-deprecating puff of air. "I seem to be a magnet for them, don't I?"

"And yet you are handling it quite well, indeed." Ellie

blinked, utterly gobsmacked. "You are not the shy and reserved Prudence Thorogood I always knew. Where in heaven did you find all this bravery?"

Her friend stared back thoughtfully. "I think I found it at the bottom. It's like the stain that lingers inside a teapot. It will still be there when everything else has been wiped away."

This time, the tears gathered in Ellie's eyes and she clutched her friend's hand in her own. "Well, you'll be staying with us now and I won't hear a word of argument about it. And besides, we have a book to finish, which could use your perspective."

She wanted to say so much more. But, just then, she heard a familiar booming voice speaking to Mr. Rivers, the sound rising up from the foyer.

Both Prue and Ellie shared a look and said simultaneously, *"George."*

They both stood, Prue looking like a startled doe, her gaze darting to the hallway. "I don't want him to find me."

"Quick! Into the cupboard," Ellie said, dashing to the corner to open the narrow door.

In the same moment, a headless dressmaker's dummy toppled forward and into Prue's arms. Behind it the shelves were stocked full of fabrics, appliques, ribbons and hats. "Why is all this in the parlor?"

"We're three women living together. We don't have room in *any* closet." They bobbled the dummy between them and the entire scene was so absurd that they both started to laugh. But Ellie heard the heavy footsteps on the stairs and whispered, "Hurry."

She was just shutting Prue inside when George swaggered in.

"Who's your friend, Ellie?" he chuckled.

Startled, it took her a moment to realize that he was making a jest about the dummy. She just stared back at him like she was seeing him for the first time.

Honestly, she still didn't want to believe that the *original scoundrel* had been right in front of her eyes all this time and she'd been blind to it. How could she not have known?

Brandon had known. He'd even tried to warn her. But she had been a fool.

"I thought you were out of town," she said curtly.

He gave her a wink. "Aren't you glad to see me? I know you are. You cannot fool me with that false glower of yours."

"Actually, I'm not—"

"Come now, is that any way to greet me when I came to ask you a very important question?"

Ellie huffed. She was in no mood for games. In fact, she was irritated at herself, worried that Prue might suffocate in the cupboard, and feeling an overwhelming urge to murder George by beating him with the dressmaker's dummy. But then she heard the voices of her aunts chattering as they returned home and she knew she wouldn't have time to hide the body.

With her thoughts so distracted, it came as a complete and utter surprise when George sank on bended knee and took hold of her hand.

"Ellie, my dear, I've never loved anyone the way that I love you. In fact, ours is the only future in my dreams." He laughed, affecting a bashful expression. "Of course, I'm not usually given to all this romantic drivel but you must bring out the best in me. So what do you say, hmm? Are you ready to be *my Ellie* until death?"

Until death? What a morbid way to propose! Had she truly waited all her life to hear *until death*?

She was so stunned and seething and utterly disappointed that she didn't react at all. Not until she heard her aunts' collective gasps from the doorway.

Not until her own gaze swerved over and she saw Brandon standing there, too.

Chapter 36

"Never underestimate a debutante when marriage
is on the line."

—A NOTE FOR *The Marriage Habits
of the Native Aristocrat*

"*Brandon!*" Ellie called out, but it was too late. He turned on his heel and walked away. She tried to pull free, to run after him, but George held fast to her hand. "Let go of me, you oaf!"

He frowned up at her. "I don't think I like you referring to other men by their given names."

"Is that so? Well, I don't like you proposing to me with the same words that you did to proposition my dearest friend, with the hope of trying to make her your mistress."

Aunt Myrtle gasped. "George! Is this true?"

"I knew you didn't deserve our Elodie," Aunt Maeve said, stalking forward to swat him with her reticule.

Ellie wrenched her hand free and he fell back on his haunches. "You are a bounder, a cad and a spoiled child! And I hate that I've wasted so much of my life on you. Because of you, the best man I've ever known just walked out of my life." In her tirade, she swung her arms widely and the dressmaker's dummy fell on him, sending him sprawling to the floor.

Aunt Myrtle rushed forward to pick it up but *accidentally* dropped it on him again . . . with a bit of force. "Go on, dearest. Lord Hullworth couldn't have gotten far."

"It's true," Aunt Maeve said, pausing her reticule swatting to brush a tear from Ellie's cheek. "The fact that he came to see you means that it isn't too late."

Then Prue sprang from the cupboard. George went pale, lifting his hands in defense. "I can explain everything, my dove."

"I'm sure you can." Prue set her hands on her hips, then she looked to Ellie. "Well, what are you waiting for? This is *your* chance to be brave."

Ellie smiled and rushed to the door.

BLOODY HELL. What had Brandon been thinking?

He'd known better than to seek out Ellie. After all, she'd made her choice the day she'd left.

There must have been a twisted masochist living inside his brain that decided to come to London and try one more time to make her his. And yet, when he'd learned that she'd been stopping by his town house to see if he'd returned, that same part of him was optimistic.

Arriving at Upper Wimpole Street, his anticipation intensified as the elder Miss Parrishes greeted him on the pavement in front of their steps. They'd both smiled eagerly, claiming that their niece would be overjoyed to see him. And as they'd walked inside, the ladies told him of the perplexing behavior of their niece—the need to linger beneath every archway they encountered; a visit to the zoo to feed the bear, the elephant and the giraffes; and tomorrow, they were scheduled to take a boat onto the Thames. They couldn't fathom what had gotten into her.

But Brandon could.

He knew that Ellie was trying to conquer her fears. That she was tired of being afraid. And for each stair he'd mounted, a tremendous glut of hope filled him.

Until he saw Nethersole kneeling and Ellie's hand in his.

There'd been no need to linger. No need to drive the nail in the coffin.

Obviously, the only reason she'd come to see Brandon was merely to tell him that it was over for her. Well and truly over.

So he'd turned on his heel and left.

His open landau waited out front and he stepped inside, calling up to his driver. "To the town house, Diggs. But I'll only be staying for a moment to settle some business, and then we'll head back to Crossmoor Abbey."

The old driver screwed up his face in perplexity. Regrettably, Diggs was as deaf as a turnip. So Brandon repeated himself, adding a wave of his hand to encourage him to spur the horses.

"Very good, milord," he said with a smile and a nod.

Just as Diggs began turning the carriage around to head toward Regent's Park, Brandon heard his own name. He turned reflexively to the familiar voice that had been embroidered into his soul. Even though he had no desire to see her again, his gaze could not stray from Ellie as she flew out of the house and down the stairs in a cascade of skirts, dyed in a color that only brought an aching reminder of her blush.

"Wait! Wait!" she called, her arm outstretched as she rushed into the street.

Brandon looked away as if he didn't see her. They had bid their farewells. And besides, he knew she would turn back.

But, as the coach wheels rumbled slowly over the cobblestones, he realized he was wrong. There she was, jogging beside him, out of breath and flushed.

"Miss Parrish, don't be a fool," he said tightly. "Give up this nonsense and go back to Nethersole."

She shook her head, her curls in disarray. "Lord Nethersole is currently being pelted with pillows and reticules by my aunts and Miss Thorogood. You were right about him. And I daresay, he will not trespass on our doorstep again."

"Ah. I see that I've arrived just in time to remind you of your second choice." Believing she would end this farce if he pretended to ignore her, he jerked his attention forward as the carriage straightened on the road, the horses spurred to a slow trot.

But she kept pace beside them, lifting her skirts higher. "I realized something recently. I wasn't afraid of dying—well, no more than the average person—but I was terrified of living. I thought that I was keeping myself safe from the heartbreak of loss. That's why I'd set my cap for George."

"And you made a splendid choice," he said gruffly, kicking himself for coming here at all. "Now, stop this nonsense."

The horses sped up marginally.

So did she, her amber gaze darting to the road and back to Brandon. "I cannot. I have to tell you that I'd set my cap for George because I knew I'd never love him completely. I held on to the idea of him like a shield that would protect me. But with you, I was vulnerable."

"And now you're putting yourself in needless danger," he growled on a rise of alarm as they neared the intersection, his pulse galloping. So he did his best to scare her away. "Are you not afraid of falling beneath the carriage, of being crushed by the wheels?"

She nodded vigorously, her eyes wide. "It would be a garish way to die, I'm sure. But I wouldn't mind, if it meant that yours was the last face I saw."

"Don't be foolish. Diggs! Stop the carriage," he called out, but the driver had started to sing as was his habit and he couldn't hear a thing.

"I left you, Brandon," she continued, running in earnest now, panting for breath, "not because I feared that . . . if I lost you . . . I wouldn't be able to survive it. But because

I was afraid I would . . . and that I'd have to go on living without you. I just couldn't bear it."

"Death is part of life, Miss Parrish," he barked, preparing to make his way to the perch to get the driver's attention or to grab the reins himself. But then the carriage hit a rut and slammed Brandon back to the bench.

"So is living," she called out, loud enough to be heard over the clamor of traffic as they neared the teeming Marylebone Road. "That's what I didn't truly understand until I met you. And now I know that I want to live my life to the fullest. That I want to spend every minute with you, even if we only have one minute together."

She put a hand on the black lacquered half door, the other gripping her skirts as she lengthened her stride to keep up.

He shouted to his driver again and again, but the man didn't slow.

Brandon's heart thudded in a panic, his lungs tight. Taking hold of her fingers, he leaned over the side of the carriage to put her away from the reach of the wheels. "Stop this. Let go, Ellie. I mean it! You'll get hurt."

She gripped him tightly with both hands, her voice strangled, her eyes frantic and glistening with unshed tears. "You won't believe me because I wasn't certain at first. But be warned, I plan to be relentless. I'll carry a dozen handkerchiefs and drop them at your feet. I'll attend garden parties and soirees that I know you've been invited to. I'll bribe any hostess for the chance to sit beside you at dinners. I'll pretend a wounded ankle to gain a ride in your carriage. I'm prepared to make a spectacle of myself over you. I'll even—"

He cursed. Bracing himself, he lifted her off her feet, hauled her into the carriage and into his arms. They fell together, slipping down the edge of the bench until his back hit the floor, hard.

Holding her tightly, he inhaled her scent like an opium eater. He pressed his lips greedily to her hair, her temple, her damp eyelashes and cheeks until he was sure he was lost. Hopelessly lost. "Damn it, Ellie. Will you never give me a moment's peace?"

"Never." Tearful and smiling, she shook her head and wrapped her arms around him in this confined space, threading her fingers in his hair and raining kisses over his face and jaw. "Because if you still resist my diabolical machinations, then I plan to love you, quite thoroughly and as often as possible. Even if I must climb up to your bedchamber and tap on your window."

He couldn't seem to hold her close enough, kiss her long enough. "Far too dangerous and we cannot have that."

"Perhaps you can give me a key to your door instead?" she asked as he nuzzled the underside of her earlobe.

"But how do I know if you'll use that key to lock us both inside for the next fifty or sixty years?"

"I must confess, the thought did occur to me. Do you think it too bold?"

"Well . . . People will talk."

She nodded sagely and rose up to look down at him with sudden severity, and he tucked a wayward curl behind her ear. "Then you leave me no choice. You'll simply have to marry me."

His lungs and heart stalled on a sudden rush of elation. He tried to keep it inside, but the corner of his mouth quirked in a revealing grin. "Is that your proposal, then?"

"Hardly worth any sighs or swoons, I know. But, to tell you the truth, I'm suffering some terrible ailments at the moment and it's difficult to concentrate. It's my heart, you see."

"Hmm . . . That sounds serious. Shall I summon Dr. Lockwood?"

"Why? Do you think *he'll* marry me?" She blinked, all innocence.

Brandon growled as he slid a hand to her nape and took her mouth in a claiming kiss that left them both gasping for breath. "The only man you'll be marrying is me."

She grinned. "As you say."

Epilogue

Ellie had wanted to marry Brandon by special license or race off to Gretna Green to say their vows over a blacksmith's anvil, but the aunts wouldn't allow it.

"We haven't been stealing recipes for years simply for our own amusement," Aunt Maeve had said.

"Well, not entirely. Although, I did start to enjoy our escapades," Aunt Myrtle had added with a sheepish grin. "But that is neither here nor there. The truth of the matter is, we did it for you, dearest. You are going to have the grandest wedding breakfast that society has ever seen."

And it was. In fact, her wedding breakfast had even earned a mention in the newspaper.

"They are calling it a *vulgar display of sublime dishes*," Jane said as she lowered the page, her brow knitted in perplexity. "The statement is quite a contradiction. What do you think it means—did the author like it or loathe it?"

Beside her on the settee in the parlor on Upper Wimpole Street, Winn laughed brightly. "It means they loved it, but hate themselves for eating too much."

Ellie grinned, overjoyed to have all her friends with her. Winn had just returned that week, after a lengthy sojourn in the south of France with her husband, Asher, his aunt Lolly and former pirate, Sir Roderick Divine, along with their newborn son. The young Marcus Holt was currently in the study, holding court as his father, Uncle Raven, Uncle Brandon and the aunts fussed over him.

The delay in her nuptials also provided Ellie time to

mend her bond with Meg, who had been justifiably cross with her for breaking her brother's heart. But after an earnest talk and many tears, they were more like sisters than sisters-in-law. In fact, Meg had even charmed Jane, Winn, and Prue with her effervescence.

"I know I hated myself," Meg interjected with a groan as she slumped back into the upholstered chair. "After all, eating fourteen courses by anyone's standards is quite *vulgar*, indeed. Oh, but the gooseberry tarts at the end were worth it. I'm only glad that there will never be another wedding breakfast like it."

"I wouldn't be too certain," Ellie said. "I overheard the aunts talking about your next Season and how they had grand plans for your betrothal dinner."

"Well, they can plan all they like, but I'm not going to marry." Her determined gaze swept around the room and she pointed teasingly to each one of them in turn. "I see the calculated gleams from each of you happily married women, but nothing you say will persuade me. My brother may have found the love of his life; however, it will not be the same for me. The man I once gave my heart to, gave it right back to me, stating that I was too young and naive to know what I wanted. He then set sail and I have not seen or heard from him in the two years since."

"We could find him for you," Jane offered. "It's all a matter of research."

And Winn added, "Yes. We can even kidnap him, if you like."

"Then tie him to a chair and put a sack over his head," Ellie added, sharing a look with her friends.

Meg shook her head. "Thank you all, but no. I have decided that I should rather be content on my own than with a man who does not love me. Besides, there's a somewhat vengeful part of my personality, rather pleased by the notion that he will regret losing me. One day, in the future, we'll see each other again. I will be a stunning sight to behold, of course"—she shrugged, a small grin on her lips—"and he will be rendered speechless. Then I will pretend that I do not even know him and walk away." She dusted her hands together for good measure.

"Brava!" Winn cheered. "I absolutely adore your confidence."

Jane nodded in agreement. "I think that your voice is most decidedly needed to help us finish our primer."

"I completely concur," Ellie said as Meg already began to nod. "Good. With your additions and with Prue's, too, I truly believe that *The Marriage Habits of the Native Aristocrat* will be the best guidebook ever written."

But as she spoke, she felt a pang of regret, wishing her friend had not suffered so much at the hands of a man that Ellie had known and trusted for most of her life.

George had left London to lick his wounds. Yet, she knew, it would only be a matter of time before he returned for the pleasures of town. Shame would not be cast down upon his head. Men in society were given leave to pursue their own passions without consequence.

Prue, however, was not.

"Where is Prue now?" Jane asked quietly as if they were all sharing the same thoughts.

Ellie shook her head. "She said she had business to take care of and that she would likely not return until later this evening. In any event, she promised to return before Brandon and I embark on our honeymoon."

"And has my brother told you where he's taking you, yet?" Meg asked slyly.

She playfully squinted at her sister-in-law. "No, he is determined to surprise me."

Winn laughed. "And we all know how much you *love* surprises."

As the warm summer breeze blew in through the parlor

window and the clock in the corner tolled the hour, Ellie couldn't help but smile and think fondly of the accidental collision that brought her husband into her life. "I suppose that certain surprises are worth the ailments they cause."

⚜

LATER THAT evening, Prudence Thorogood drew the hood of her tattered mantle over her pale hair and reached for the lion's head door knocker. She drew in a breath and rapped soundly.

There was no turning back. Not for her.

After all, the marital prospects of a penniless, ruined debutante were grim. Such a woman may have the opportunity to wed the man who took her innocence, if he were forced into a proposal while being beaten about the head with a reticule. She may even find some widowed farmer or merchant who required a wife.

Of course, she could continue to accept the kindness of dear friends and live beneath their roofs, watching all the while as society slowly turned their backs on them.

Or, she could take matters into her own hands.

It was an undeniable truth that any future at all would require the selling of her very soul, in some form or another.

The lacquered door opened.

A stately manservant greeted her with a bland inquiry, as if it were commonplace to see a cloaked female on this doorstep in the dead of night. A shiver of trepidation skated down her spine, but she shrugged it off and simply said, "Lord Savage, if you please."

Author's Note

Dear Readers,

I stumbled upon some interesting research for this book that I'd like to share with you.

Joseph-Michel and Jacques-Étienne Montgolfier were brothers and pioneers in hot-air ballooning and aviation. The Montgolfier balloon made its first public appearance in June of 1783. At the time, the brothers did not realize that heat caused their balloon to rise. They credited their success to a surfeit of thick smoke filling the paper-lined sackcloth, creating a lighter-than-air gas that they called "Montgolfier gas."

The Zoological Society Gardens of London is the world's oldest scientific zoo and opened in April of 1828. At first, the *zoo* only admitted fellows of the society. So, I'm afraid that I took a bit of artistic license and opened the gates to the public early. Also, I confess that Ellie's *potentially carnivorous* giraffes (or camelopards, if you prefer) did not have an exhibit until 1836. But Toby the Bear was, indeed, real.

I've so enjoyed writing Ellie and Brandon's story, and I'm truly grateful that I could share it with you. Thank you for welcoming this book into your hearts and homes.

Warm wishes and happy reading,
Viv